My Hollywood

My Hollywood

A NOVEL

Mona Simpson

Alfred A. Knopf · New York · 2010

THIS IS A BORZOI BOOK
PUBLISHED BY ALFRED A. KNOPF

Copyright © 2010 by Mona Simpson
All rights reserved.
Published in the United States by Alfred A. Knopf,
a division of Random House, Inc., New York,
and in Canada by Random House of Canada Limited, Toronto.
www.aaknopf.com

Knopf, Borzoi Books, and the colophon are registered trademarks of Random House, Inc.

Grateful acknowledgment is made to HarperCollins Publishers for permission to reprint
"Ode to Ironing" from *Full Woman, Fleshly Apple, Hot Moon: Selected Poetry of Pablo
Neruda*, translated by Stephen Mitchell, translation copyright © 1997 by Stephen
Mitchell. Reprinted by permission of HarperCollins Publishers.

Portions of this work originally appeared in slightly different form in *The Atlantic,
Harper's Magazine*, and *The Best American Short Stories 2003*, edited by Walter Mosley
and Katrina Kenison (New York: Houghton Mifflin, 2003).

Library of Congress Cataloging-in-Publication Data
Simpson, Mona.
My Hollywood : a novel / by Mona Simpson.—1st ed.
p.   cm.
ISBN 978-0-307-27352-9
1. Motherhood—California—Los Angeles—Fiction.
2. Hollywood (Los Angeles, Calif.)—Fiction. I. Title.
PS3569.I5117M92 2010
813'.54—dc22   2010000726

Manufactured in the United States of America
First Edition

for Elma Dayrit

My Hollywood

50/50

Once, we sat with a small candle between us on the tablecloth, drinks for our hands. After the salad, he asked if I wanted children.

"I don't know." I fingered the glass votive. "I'd like to, but I don't know if I can."

That got his attention. His whole head stilled.

My hands fluttered to reassure. "No, it's not that. I mean, I don't know if I can *afford* them. I want to write music. And I've already started that."

He had a nice manner. He said he didn't know musicians that well, women or men, but he counted on his fingers female writers who'd had children. He actually couldn't think of any.

"Nope, died of lupus," I countered. "Young. Thirties, I think." Then, "Married but no kids."

"Happily married?"

"Probably would have preferred Henry James."

"Well, who wouldn't?"

I laughed. For years and years, he could make me laugh.

"Does Yo-Yo Ma have kids?"

"Two," I said. "But he also has a wife."

"Madame Ma, c'est moi." He had an odd brightness I'd heard all my life. *You can be both!* my mother had said. But my mother was mentally ill.

He was not. I believed him, a trumpet promise. Some Bach came into my fingers. Cello Suite No. 2 in D minor. The haunting Prelude. I had to sit on my hand.

That evening, our first date, we had a conversation about who would do what.

"With a woman who worked, it'd have to be fifty-fifty," he said. "Of course."

We didn't talk about that again until after William was born.

In Paul's gaze, it seemed I couldn't fail, as if the terrors I'd known, so looming they'd strapped me in bed a few days a month, had been products of an overly active imagination. So this is how it works, I thought. It turned out to be easier than I'd expected. When I talked about my childhood, his face took on an expression of pity, which also looked like reverence. Then he'd twirl in a dance step, with a confident air. I marveled at these shuffles and turns, as one would at the performance of a child not yours: watching happiness.

I became accustomed to myself in this new atmosphere. My opinions grew emphatic, my gestures expansive, my stumbling attempts at jokes more frequent. Who was to say this wasn't love?

I burrowed into his chest at night. He lost his hands in my hair and I could sleep.

Children were a star-wish.

Love had been a problem, already. Perhaps I wanted to curtail my range. In the custody of Paul, within the larger corporation of his family, things I'd feared all my life became impossible. No Berend lived in poverty, or even without a weekly cleaning woman. I loved their formality and cleanness. We would always be in rooms like this. Insanity occurred, but that, too, with the proper funds, rounded to eccentricity. He carried within him a solid floor. Like most women, I'd spent a great deal of time thinking about whom I would marry. Paul never felt like the end of all that yearning. Could anyone have been?

I hadn't really known, up close, a good love.

I promised myself to be grateful.

I'd always perplexed my mother. She attributed my temperament to my face and never ceased trying to fix me up. My wedding made the happiest day of her life. Balloons loose in a blue sky, forty-two of Paul's relatives stood in suits as we said our vows. On my side, only my mother. My friends felt exuberant with relief. Paul was beautiful—that word. A perfect profile, dark smooth skin, Grecian hair, the small wire glasses of a yeshiva boy you wanted to lift off. He had a mother-father Jewish family, who belonged to the Harmonie Club.

The student photographer followed a guest we hardly knew. A dozen pictures of this oboist appeared on the proof sheets and a half page of my mother, in her long white skirt and cranberry jacket, looking, as one of the ushers said, like something out of the Kennedy era, but not one shot of the mother of the groom. In the only picture that included both of us, we were greeting friends, looking in different directions, his hair blown wild, my arms still young. His face looks open and surprised.

God bless them. Wish them luck.

It's the picture my son keeps on the face of his cell phone.

Claire

THE SEARCH

That's how they get you. I'd heard that phrase all my childhood, though who *they* were was never clear. Ten in the morning, Will seventeen weeks old, I knocked over the bottle of milk I'd been pumping. It hurt to pump, but I'd already adjusted to the sucking bites and the odd porousness of my nipples after. I hiccuped sobs, moving around the black kitchen. We *needed* those ounces. I had a concert in New York in nine weeks.

Then he started crying too. I rocked him, his blanket loosening. No matter how many times I studied the folding diagram, my swaddlings opened. His small arms shook, his face blotchy. Everyone told me babies liked the bouncy chair. I slid Little Him in, and he screamed. Paul was gone. Will and I were both exhausted. I couldn't sleep because I believed our baby might die. I didn't know why he wouldn't sleep. This was a monumental responsibility, like nothing I'd ever known.

The black kitchen depressed me. I would never work again, I thought, as if these two problems were equal.

Just then Paul's mother paid me a visit, while her son was at work. She'd come to town for the weekend. I raised my eyebrows, *See! Look at my ruined life.* But she chatted on about the advisability of live-in help so Paul and I could dash out for a romantic evening. A romantic evening! I looked at her. Will cried. He seemed more furious than other babies, more bereft.

I had no talent for this. Paul could make funny sounds like the track of a cartoon, momentarily interrupting Will's misery. But Paul wasn't here. Will and I both felt astonished that he was stuck with me.

"Do you ever just put him in the crib and go up to your office?" Paul's mother asked. We'd chosen this particular rental house because it had an upstairs room with windows on all four walls. Easterners, we'd wanted light. Unfortunately, the windows didn't open and by ten o'clock, the room hit seventy, by noon ninety. I led her up, to show.

We'd needed four men to move the piano here. They had to take the legs off to get it upstairs.

"Can you order shades?" A reasonable question, but I'd wanted her to *see.* "I want to be a perfect mother-in-law," she'd once said. That weekend alone, she'd bought us a set of stainless cutlery and six antique dessert plates. I loved those dessert plates. She'd seen opposing sides in her daughter-in-law and picked the one she preferred.

"You'll have shades installed and then just give him to a babysitter and get to work."

"But he cries."

"Then let him cry."

He wasn't the only one who cried. Paul understood that I stumbled around the rental house broken and that this, too, might be something we'd have to endure. Still, I cried too much. That at least had to be fixed.

He knew a way. And we would use it.

On a Saturday in August, in Los Angeles, we interviewed thirteen women, all immigrants, on the quarter hour. Three toothless, more than half heavily made up, a few truly ragged, they resembled the hags of Grimm more than Juliet's nurse or any Disney nanny. From far away in this flat city, women had boarded buses to audition for our fifteen-dollar-an-hour job. Paul set up a waiting room in the black kitchen of our rental house. He knew how to do this. He put out a newspaper and a plate of store-bought cookies. That was like him, the nice formality. But the 10:45 woman scarfed the cookies.

Paul's mother had advised us to ask the women for their theories of discipline, but when he asked the first one, she just stared. "Like, say, if they don't behave," he said.

She shook her head.

After that *Where are you from?* became our opening question.

We were new too, Paul explained. We'd moved five weeks ago from New York for him to have his chance. At thirty, he felt like a recent graduate, with a ten-week offer on a show he admired. I held his tremendous hope like an egg found in a fallen nest, but I wanted something too—what I'd always had. When we'd left, I held the baby and Paul carried my precious instrument onto the plane. We'd had to buy the cello its own seat, but Will flew free. Now it hurt to look at the scuffed black case. Since childhood, I'd played every day. Even holidays, even sick. I remembered, with a loosening of sobs, which fell onto my baby's face.

"Could you *please* make it home for dinner?" I'd begged into the phone. "Can't you go earlier and come home earlier?" How had I become like this?

Once, we'd sat in a restaurant, with a candle flame between us.

"Claire, the other guys in the room have wives too."

"I don't know about the other guys' wives, but I work." I did know, though, and they didn't.

He'd sighed. "And you're lucky you don't have a boss."

Lucky.

"I have to work late," Paul said, to the 11:15 woman. "Most nights, I won't make it home for dinner. So we'd need you to help Claire get him to bed."

"Sure, okay," the woman said. "But what time I can go?"

Paul wrote down numbers and told her we would check her references.

"Would you be able to stay over some nights?" he asked the 11:45 woman. *With live-in,* his mother had said, *there's never the problem of her calling in sick.*

Why not? I wondered, like an idiot. How do they not get sick?

The gums of the 11:45 woman puffed over her teeth. She looked sick already. Paul's own nanny had been a black woman from the South. When she died, after living with his family fourteen years, only Paul flew to Mississippi for the funeral. Every year at Christmas, he sent a card and eighty dollars to her living daughter.

I liked the noon woman, from Bangladesh, who wore a purple head scarf and looked fifteen.

"How old are you?"

"Nine*teen*," she said, cascading giggles. "I am eldest. I have many younger. All brother."

I never had a nanny. I had a mom, like everyone else I knew, and occasionally, a babysitter: a caustic high school girl who was not above mentioning that she was only tending me for the money (a quarter an hour, in those days). Because my mother had to work, after school I walked three blocks to a religious bookstore, where I was allowed to sit on the floor and page through monographs about saints and listen to the incorrigible girls the owner took in. I loved to watch them crouch over their toenails, stroking on polish with terrible concentration. Once I met a priest there who'd walked the length of Italy barefoot. Then, in third grade, my mother gave me a key. But I lost it. We lived on a street with neighbors whose houses I knew the insides of; if I'd knocked at any one of those doors, I'd have been offered a glass of milk. But I waited outside on the stoop. When my mother finally lurched up the drive, she screamed, "I'm going to have to string it around your neck." It enraged her, seeing her mittenless kid in the cold.

I couldn't choose my life over Paul's for Little Him.

The twelfth woman sat silent and nodding, her hair cut like Herman Munster's.

"Are you able to work live-in?" Paul asked.

"I want live-in, yes," she said. "Is cheaper."

"Do you have children?" Six of the women before, three of whom said they could stay overnight, had young children.

"No children. No husband. Single," she added, with a lilt.

Paul said, "May I ask you to step out a moment, while we call your references?"

"Go where?"

He led her back to the black kitchen.

"I liked the one with the purple scarf," I said.

"She looked fifteen. And she only has one reference." Her reference sounded like a Bangladeshi man who set the phone down for a very long time, before another Bangladeshi man came on the line to say "Meskie? Yah, I know Meskie. She's good."

Paul stood nodding as he talked to the twelfth woman's references. "Couldn't be better," he said, hanging up. "Let's try her for a week."

"When could you start?" he asked, when he called her back in.

She nodded.

"Would tomorrow be possible?"

She nodded again.

Until recently, I'd thought a nanny was something English, from long ago. But now I would have one, just because I wanted to work. Needed to or wanted to? A question I'd never asked before. In college, where everything felt equal already, I assumed I'd have children *and* work. He, the putative he, would work a little less and I'd work a little less and the kid would have long hair, paint-spattered overalls, and be, in general, a barrel of monkeys.

William was hairless and the other *he* left for the Lot every morning and never came home.

The doorbell rang. The last woman. William lurched up crying.

"You get him and I'll tell her the job's taken," Paul said.

"Remember sunblock," I instructed the twelfth woman, "but not the face, okay?"

She nodded. Every day in California started the same: hot, plain, and bright, mocking. Paul left, his jaw a way I'd never seen. For the first time since me he wanted something badly.

I was becoming a woman who sighed. Now I had my baby and I saw. Why women got so little done. How much my own mother had given. Why so many people feel mad at their mothers; because whatever childhood was or wasn't, they're the ones who made it. Fathers loomed above it all, high trees.

"How was the park?" I asked, when the twelfth woman bumped in the stroller, an hour later. (Only an hour!) She nodded again. This may have had something to do with English comprehension. Will's tiny arms reached for me, his scream high and steady.

But her mere presence relieved Paul.

"Go to work," he said, on speakerphone. "Go to your office and shut the door."

I obeyed. I went up to my office, shut the door, and slept.

I had no confidence as a mother. From babysitting, I remembered sweet concoctions I'd made with milk and strawberry powder in other people's kitchens, but I couldn't recall the children. I met one family in my twenties. Both parents cooked and every meal was a slow production; they were particular about wine and cheese. They had two calm, pudgy, intelligent children whom they were raising, they said, "by hand." She worked in the mornings. The father's dissertation, which he wrote afternoons, was about the privatization of time. Time had once been public, in a clock tower on the town square; everyone saw the same hour and minutes. When watches were invented, he said, people could carry around their own time. That interested me, because musicians can always tell time. Even when I slept I knew what time it was. Except composing. That's when I lost it. Of the five-year-old, the father had said, "I consider him already done."

They must have had family money.

I'd also read a study in which scientists allowed children to choose their own food. Over a month, the kids picked nutritionally balanced meals. If these two ideas—the laissez-faire smorgasbord and the raising of children "by hand"—contradicted each other, they nonetheless constituted my entire philosophy about parenting. And neither seemed to apply.

To make matters worse, birth had taken me apart and put me back together again, with one piece missing. I'd had a series of appointments with a gastroenterologist. "You'll probably get better," the doctor said, recommending Kegels.

When I came downstairs, I found Will in the stroller again, sunblock smeared on his little face. The tube had a printed warning. NOT FOR USE ON INFANTS' FACES. I pointed this out to her.

She nodded.

An hour later, I walked in on her playing with his tiny penis, swinging it between her palms. This didn't qualify as molestation, exactly, but I didn't want her to give him baths. I stayed up late that night to tell all this to Paul.

The next morning he barged in while she was changing the diaper. She pointed to the penis. "His *et-et!*" She laughed.

"She actually flicked it with her finger," he said. "Obviously a cultural difference. I didn't love it either."

But Paul had to go. His first ten weeks were up, and they decided to give him another ten-week trial.

I began trolling parks. I set up interviews in coffee shops. My generation's adultery, I thought, scanning the tables for the one dark head among blondes.

I found Lola sitting on a bench and hired her, without references. I liked the way she looked. She was small, dark, well joined.

The next morning in bed, I told Paul.

"Whoa, slow down."

"I already did it."

He stilled his head, blinking. "A person likes a little stability in his life."

"Then you work at home and worry all day."

"So what do you want to tell this one?"

I fired the twelfth woman. It turned out to be remarkably easy. I gave her money; she nodded and left.

I'd always wanted to do no harm. That was my banister. In my twenties, leaving my temp job, which I faithfully attended, I walked in the pedestrian stream. Like all those others (black tights, slitted coat-tails), I made a living. If I tried to do more and failed, at least I would leave the world as I'd found it. But now I had a fresh boy, who took every imprint, however faint. I feared that my invisible soul could harm him.

I knew my deficiencies and so I selected a supplement. I hired a happy nanny.

"I prefer a mother who works," Lola told me. "Because then I can have the friends of Williamo to the house."

"You're hired," I said.

"When will you be needing me?"

"Today."

When Paul first told me he wanted to write television comedy, I'd been surprised. That's your *dream?* I thought. It didn't seem big enough for a dream.

"Yup. I really think I coulda done it."

"I bet you still can." He knew guys from college who made four hundred thousand dollars a year. Those little cartoon people? I used my thumb and forefinger. I hadn't known such a thing even required writers. But I could see in his face, this was an ardent wish. Before, even with his sharp features, there'd been something undefined. Work still meant the true great thing to me; I wasn't old enough yet to know people whose dreams had wrecked them. I only gleaned the wistfulness of those who'd quit.

My tenderness for his hope must have been what Paul saw in me. His dream might have set other young women's jaws, at a time they wished to furnish a nursery. When Paul got the offer in California, I'd said, *Let's go.*

"That show about the hunchback who lives with his father?" my producer asked.

"Yes." I nodded solemnly, trying to be a wife.

The group I'd written most of my music for recorded in New York City. Only my mother was in LA. Doctors had called me in the past. Hospitals. *Is this the daughter of . . .*

My life or hers, I'd thought. Each time.

I'd chosen mine.

But now we took slow strolls with her friend Tom, an ex-Jesuit who led garden tours for white-haired ladies and the occasional still-extant husband. My doorbell rang midafternoon, and there the two of them stood, seeming surprised I didn't expect them. At seventy, my mother maintained a policy of wearing only one color at a time. She had a strict philosophy about jewelry too. I saw Tom several times a week those first years back in California, and from what I could tell, he always wore the same clean khakis, the same shoes, and the same striped shirt. I asked my mother about this once and she made a face. "Oh, he buys five of everything," she said.

"I hate to shop," he mumbled.

As we walked, Tom pointed out plants, saying their Latin names. *Platanus rasemosa. Miscanthus Gracillimus. Lavandula Goodwin Creek.*

My mother tripped. She wore three-inch heels, matching her pantsuit.

Willie, in the stroller, fell asleep.

"I just don't think they're going to renew me."

"Why not?" I didn't stop to think—maybe that would be better, for us.

"I pitched ten, twelve jokes and they used one yesterday. *One.* Claire, I know I'm funny, but I'm just not funny in there."

"But you are funny. You really are." Every time we went out to dinner with our friends in New York, he'd set the table laughing. But we didn't go out to dinner here.

When Will woke screaming, I brought him back to the bed to breast-feed. He fell asleep between us. It was too late for sex even to be an issue. But it was, anyway, sort of, a wave above us in the air.

"You know," Paul said, one morning, "I really can't take having him in the bed. I don't sleep."

"I'm tired too." It had been more than a hundred nights since I'd slept.

I wanted Will with us. He could turn over and nurse without fully waking. But Paul worried about rolling over Will in his sleep.

"We should use some of that pumped milk and let her take him in her room. You need some rest too," he said.

"He eats three times. We can't ask her to do that."

Paul promised to feed Will at 5:00 a.m.

That night we gave him to Lola and we slept.

Lola

I WAS DISCOVERED

Lana Turner they discovered at the Schraft counter, me on a bench for the Wilshire bus. Claire hired me for nanny, live-in, without even asking a reference. When I first came the house, I was surprised, because it is small small. Normal touches a mother would do, I did not see here. Pictures, they left just leaning against the walls. The livingroom looked like a school, books everywhere and a telescope by the front window. Good, I thought, Lola will learn.

But the first day, I found my employer crying by the heating grate. She was trying to breast-feed and she had very little. Maybe she is too old, I thought. My uncle in Visayas keeps cows and after four, five years, they will not anymore milk. My employer married late. Accomplished does not matter so much for a woman. Unless you are a movie star. I told her, *It is okay, you cry. But when your tears dry, you will see, your baby he is very healthy.*

In the Philippines, what we do is make a soup of bones and then you will have plenty milk. That first day I took the baby in the Snugli and walked to the market to get a chicken, but really it should be the bones of a goat. The nipples of Claire had cracks that oozed, already infected. I applied hot compress. Still, she wanted to keep going. That night, she sprang up every time Williamo cried and let him suck. Then, even after she fed him, he drank a full bottle. One of five in the freezer.

"I'm trying to save up," she told me, in the morning.

After she fed him, she stood at a pump. This was the first time I ever saw that and in twenty, twenty-five minutes, all that came out was two ounces. I called Ruth, my teacher of America. At the time the daughter of Ruth, Natalie, had her baby, she stapled up signs to sell vegetarian breast milk. I asked if I could buy anywhere, but Ruth said Natalie did not know. With my youngest, I did not have enough either. I was working too hard. Issa complains that is why she is short. Only the height of me.

I asked Claire. "Do you want that I buy formula?"

She looked at me a way I could tell I had done the first thing wrong.

"No formula, Lola. He can't have anything but breast milk. Not even water."

Formula, it is like poison to them here. For us, it was only too expensive. "Me, I did not use either."

"That's probably why your kids are healthy."

But this baby, he cry a lot. Maybe he is hungry; but I am not allowed to give anything. I stayed up thinking this riddle.

Paul, when he came home at midnight, dropped keys. Through the wedge open to his bedroom, his wife slept, her face a small cameo above the cover. He looked at the closed door to Williamo. "Do you need anything?" he asked. At this time, I liked the father of Williamo: it was easy to see the coiled terror inside.

"I will be the one. Save your energy. Later on, a boy will need his *tatay*."

They paid me two hundred and fifty a week.

I was sending home money. She was saving milk. We measured ourselves by ounces in the freezer. She wanted enough to feed him while she went away. She pumped at seven in the morning, again after lunch, then before bed, but at that time she did not milk even one full ounce. And what we gained in the day, we spent at night. In the early hours, his cries shrieked wild; she and I walked him in the hallway, the bedroom closed so Paul could sleep. At that time they would have paid anything for this baby to be quiet.

A week before her trip I calculated: we would never have enough.

"I've been meaning to talk to you," she said. "Can you come? Of course, I'd pay you extra."

I was working then weekends for my old lady, but Ruth gave me one from Iloilo to fill in.

I packed the pump in my suitcase. We brought two frozen bottles. All. But even nursing, Williamo cried on the plane.

"My nipples hurt," she whispered. I had something for pain, made from monkey gland, but it was back in my place.

Halfway across the country, I had to ask the stewardess for hot water, to warm one bottle.

New York, it is more cold than the Philippines ever. My jacket it is too thin. My employer unzips her suitcase to give me one of hers. I put Williamo in the Snugli underneath. A line of wind comes from the crack where the door fits into the taxi; we bump; the car is old, like cars in the Philippines. The New York sky is a way I never saw before. Still, forever-looking, as if the clouds had frozen.

And the hotel, it is not so good. I do not want Williamo on the carpet. All of a sudden, I am missing the guy. Paul would not let this be half clean. The baby cries.

"I've been feeding you the last five hours!"

"But there is no." I touch her breast, an empty flap. I run water in the sink to warm the last bottle.

Then, the husband calls. I am the one to answer. Williamo cries and cries.

"Lola, what's wrong?"

"I do not know. Maybe he is hungry. And outside it is very cold."

"Put Claire on," he says.

Her leg bounces as she talks. Williamo screams, so she lifts her shirt and reaches for him, but he yanks the head away. I hear the voice yelling out the small holes. "You have to feed him! Send her out to buy a box of formula. You can't let our baby starve, Claire."

I check the bottle bobbing in the sink. Just right. I give to him and he quiets, dream eyed, sucking steady as a bobbin. Then he falls asleep and I set him on the bed. "Do you want that I will go the store?"

She tells me her friend Lil, who lives here, sent us five bottles.

"Through the U.S. mail?"

"Messengered," she says.

"When it will arrive?"

"Before I go." She nods at him. "I feel like a nap too." My employer undresses in front of me. I pretend to be busy with our suitcase. Then I set up the travel crib.

She sleeps through the phone ringing. "A messenger here," the voice says. "Would you like the bottles in your room, for the minibar?" Or, he says they can send up one and keep the rest. They will bring when we need. Day or night.

A knock at the door; a man carries a tray over his shoulder with a doily, a vase with one small pink rose, and the bottle of milk.

I set the room straight. A pout of steam comes from the radiator and my two sleepers breathe. I make a changing place on the dresser, stack the diapers. I hang the dress of my employer, line her creams on the counter. I unpack our suitcase, put together the parts of the pump. Then I sit by the window, the right temperature at last. Outside, I see rooftops. At the corner, yellow flowers in buckets look like a picture of somewhere old. Then Paul calls again.

I tell him they are both asleep and ask if I should wake Claire.

"Nah, let her rest. But Lola, listen, if you're at all worried, you go buy a can of formula."

"But-ah, the mother told me not to give."

"She's a new mother. The doctor said to breast-feed and she wants to do everything right. Just don't tell her."

"But Lil, the friend of Claire, she sent. We have now five bottle."

"Okay, good then. No problem."

At four o'clock, I wake my employer. She takes her shower, dries the hair.

"Should I pump or should we wake him?" she calls from the bathroom, where I have the pump plugged in, clean tubes fitted on.

"It is okay. We have a bottle here, more downstairs."

I zip her back, then Williamo wakes, so she steps out the dress again to nurse, a blanket over her. Now when we have in the minibar, Claire milks too.

When she is walking out the door, he reaches for her, the face crumples. "Lola, why don't you just come," she says. "But bring the bottle. Bring two."

So we stand in the freezing air that cuts. Before, she said I could order food that would come to the room on a tray, with a doily and a rose. I could have watched the TV. Now, what will I eat?

Cookies. That is all they have in the Before Room. The other ladies, like Claire, they wear long dresses. I am just in my jeans. Williamo, too, I did not have time to change. Claire stands by the stage curtain and he starts fussing. I tell her, "Do not worry." I have warming in the sink one full bottle, with a layer of cream. More than eight ounces. I doubt the breasts of Claire ever made that much.

Then I sit to feed. I hold the bottle the way we do, at a slant, test a drop on my wrist. A little hot. I wait a minute, shake. He opens the mouth, closes his eyes, sucks, then he stops, yanks the head. I test the temperature again, push the nipple toward him. He twists the head, the back arches and he starts to cry. He knows: this is not the milk of his mother. I try one more time but he will not take.

"I am impressed," I say. He screams. I push him around the back the auditorium. From here, he can still see his mother on the stage.

The audience almost all has gray hair. Silver. Women majority. Many in blue jeans. Like me.

I hear the musicians tuning. I attended a concert once before. My father took us to hear the Philippine Philharmonic Orchestra. The audience there wore hats and gloves. On top the stage, three words: KATOTOHANAN, KAGANDAHAN, KABUTIHAN. I see Claire, in the distance, standing with her back to us. Williamo still screams and I walk back and forth, back and forth, between the open doors, patting him. Usually, when they arch like this, it is gas, but I cannot get the burp. The screams go up and down. "So you are singing along."

I am thinking what Paul said, if I should buy formula. But I do not know where. If I go out the auditorium, maybe there will be gangs. Still, at the intermission, people push through the doors. We step too into frozen air. At the corner store, with fruits outside, I ask if they have formula and buy with my own money, but as I am getting the change, I think, He has never had formula. If he can tell the milk of another mother, maybe he will not take. But I already paid.

When the music starts again, we go to the Ladies. I empty a bottle, rinse, put in the formula, and stand running it under the hot water. He is watching me.

I sit on the floor just outside the auditorium. At first he sniffs, turns the head. Instruments, they are tuning again. Maybe he is tired. Claire told me after the intermission, they will play the music she made up. Far away, on the stage, she leans over the stand, her arms begging.

"This is your mother's song," I whisper.

I push the nipple between closed lips, squeeze a drop onto the gums. He lets it in, then sips. A little more he drinks, fusses, squirmy. Turns away, then comes back. A little more again he drinks. I stand now walking with him.

There is a melody I think I have heard before, a scrap, very pretty and sad. I lose the thread when he fusses, I pat-pat, and there, now I get the burp, a big one, loud; and after, the bottle settles, loose in his mouth. He looks like a little drunk.

After a while, it comes again, that small melody. This time it makes me think of my grandmother sitting, her hands on a velvet lap. Before I came here, my family visited Antipolo, the church of the Black Madonna. In the Philippines, we go there, before we travel overseas. For good voyage. Emigrants, foreign workers, you see many families, because usually it is the mother who will go. That is where I heard sounds like this before. Music that floats from somewhere you cannot see.

Then there is a thunder. Applause. At first it sounds like rain on the roof. But people rustle, gathering bags, and they are coming outside.

Williamo, now he is finally asleep. In the cab, Claire touches his cheek. All of a sudden, I remember: the formula.

Do I have to tell? I cannot. She might fire me.

The next morning, Claire has to teach at a symposium, but we stay in the room. I hold him at the window to watch her go. A car comes and a woman helps her put in the cello; but the car it is very old. There is a piece of the fender tied on with a rope.

Alone, I can give him formula. He drinks one and a half, almost two bottles. Good: he will be full for the plane.

I pack everything to bring downstairs. As I fit the clean clothes in the bag of Claire, I see a check, typed, from the concert hall. The envelope, it is ripped open already, but the amount is wrong: one thousand U.S. dollars. Another check from Yale University. This one for two hundred.

That does not make sense. I know what she is paying me. She told me one hundred extra each day for three days. I get out my airline ticket. On the bottom, the price says six hundred eighty-five and forty cents. What I earn from this trip will be more than she gets.

I put Williamo in the stroller still adding. I unpack her bag again to see if there is another check. Only clothes. A mystery. She is doing this for something else. It does not pay.

Me, I work for money. I haul the suitcase, thinking, I will call home tomorrow. My husband tells me Issa, she is complaining. But what does she have to complain? We pay her tuition; all she has to do is study. She is saying too she does not want to work for money only.

If I were very good I would say to Claire, *It is okay. You do not have to pay the extra if you make so little profit.*

I have one bottle formula hidden in the bottom of the carry-on. But it is a different color than breast milk. She will see.

All the way home, she lets him nurse. Then he falls asleep on her breast. I think, Later, I will say about the money, that she does not have to pay all. Even when we arrive home and Paul hands me an envelope with cash, I think, maybe tomorrow. But all I say is thank you. I am still remembering that small melody.

That night, I unpack all the things. The formula, I empty in my bathroom. That is the last; I will not tell. I run the water, set the clean bottle to dry. She could have fired me for that. I walk through the house, close the lights.

In the hall I hear: "*Pretty* big crowd, I don't know."

Big crowd but not much money. What do they charge admission? They should up the ticket price. That little melody still runs in my head.

"He has a voice, all right. Clear strong instrument. I don't know why she had to walk him there."

When I hear that, something opened: I can keep my money.

I wanted him to see his mother.

21

For months, I worried what I could feed Williamo and not get fired. I thought it would end when we began solid food. But then, they wanted only vegetables I mashed and Williamo did not like. One day, a long time later, I thought of that formula I never told. By then, I had our playclub.

Vicky, a new Filipina, said, "Lola, my employer wants a weekend babysitter."

"What about you?"

"Me, no! I want my weekends off!" Vicky had plenty because she never spent.

"How much?" I worked for my old lady weekends who paid me sixty, and she really could not pay more. But I worked for her a long time already. I did not like to quit.

"Maybe you can ask them a lot."

I brought Williamo along to the job interview, and he hung, a vine on my leg. Later, they told me he was why I got the job. "And what will be the salary?"

"We were thinking eighty," the father said.

I was going to ask seventy-five, but I said, "How about ninety?"

"Eighty-five."

The parents, they were the age of my eldest and like the ones I warned her from: too good-looking. They had the baby in a basket on a chair. The husband swung up his arms. "Isn't it just the greatest thing!"

I had to ask Ruth to give me someone for my old lady. I took the elder from Iloilo again, because she can cook. I gave her my notebook with recipes the old lady liked.

That first Saturday, my new employer made coffee and milk heated so it tasted together like caramel. We sat at her round table. Before she had Bing, she told me, she worked lawyer. Like my second youngest. Then my weekend employer finished her coffee and rinsed her own mug. You hear about jobs like this. Like the house on the corner of Twelfth that we call the Castle, where they say the wife is Filipina.

That first night, I bathe the baby, wrap him in white flannel, and hand to them to kiss-kiss.

"Like a cigar," I said.

They told me he woke up three times in the night, and then she opened the freezer. Rows of pumped milk, yellow with a skin, each with the date marked in black. At the house of my employer, we had had so little; Claire pumped and we kept track of ounces of the bluish liquid.

The next morning, I heard sounds, birds one at a time. I bolted. But the little guy, he still snored next to me. I carried him to the kitchen.

"The milk is still in the refrigerator," she said. The guy stood up. They looked that they might call police.

"Last night, we slept, the two of us."

They looked at me, almost afraid. There is such a thing as luck, at the beginning. Even for magicians.

"He never slept through the night before," the wife whispered.

Vicky and me—both Filipinas, they were thinking. They like me better.

All those bottles in the freezer, and this baby, he did not even need.

Claire

THE WEEKEND PEOPLE

But I was not right.

Paul took Will on his shoulders, to *give Mommy some time by herself.* I'd had one of what Paul called my Clairenados. Now, Sunday morning, I wandered to the Farmers Market and touched hard fruit, grateful to be in the world again, able to appreciate. The footsteps around me and pigeons made a melody. I took out my notepad. Woodwinds, I scrawled. After more than a year, California fruit still amazed me. White nectarines, tiny seedless watermelons, enormous figs. I picked up a small yellow globe with barky skin and smelled it. It cast a whiff of something faintly like sex.

"Take it," the young man said.

"How much?" I fingered a soft worn bill.

"Just take it. Tell me how you like it. White inside."

The man was giving me a melon. I started to cry. He put the fruit, the size of Will's head, in a flimsy bag. Why me? Did I look good (my hand shot up to my hair) or did I appear to be someone who needed a melon? I glanced over my shoulder, but he stood weighing two cantaloupes, one in each hand.

Walking, I swung the bag so the melon tapped my thigh. But when I got home, it was after ten: I'd blown half my time. I made coffee, spilling grounds—no matter; I'd clean it later—and climbed the rickety steps to the small hot room upstairs.

Marriage hadn't changed me. Having a child did. I was a dandelion blown. But I had no right to be tired. Paul got up when Will did, at five. He let me sleep until seven. I woke up and listened to them making sounds to approximate the whoosh of wheels.

I was thinking of rain, that rhythm, chaotic yet patterned. Then the door rang, like a high school bell, excusing. I ran down, two steps at a time.

A couple stood there, too hip to be door-to-door religious. She filled her T-shirt, her hair touching her elbows, and at various points she sparkled.

"Helen and Jeff." He stuck out a freckled arm. "Lola's weekend people."

Last spring Lola had said something about her new weekend employers, I didn't remember what, but there was lace at the edges. *He was somebody*, my mother would've said.

An hour ago, I'd deemed the foray to the market idiotic, even destructive, but now, I invited them in. I needed friends. In the kitchen I sniffed the melon, then decided to save it and brought out a plate of figs, almonds, and Israeli feta.

The possible Somebody began a rambling talk about Lola, which his wife interrupted. "We hired her because we saw how close she was to William."

My Will! This stranger knew my child, in his hours away from me.

"It'd be nice for the boys to play together."

"Who's your son?"

"Bing." She waited. But I'd never heard of him. What kind of name was Bing? They must have named him for Bing Crosby. It couldn't have been the cherry.

"And I'm starting a mothers' group with the moms of kids in Lola's playclub."

Typical of me, I said, "Oh, sure, great," when I knew I couldn't do it.

Then the door yawned open. Will ran to me. I said, "These are the people Lola lives with on the weekend."

"Jeff Grant."

"Helen."

Paul's face tightened when the Somebody said his name. Paul knew who he was. I asked him to help me with coffee in the kitchen.

"He's an indie director, he made that movie *The Dayton Widow*."

I thought, He could help you maybe. Paul was in his second year working for a showrunner who didn't think he was funny. Just this week, though, he'd had a triumph. At the table read of his script, people laughed. The head of comedy clapped. But Paul still felt precarious. "The room punched it up," he said. "The biggest laughs were Jack's lines." Since we'd moved here we'd been on a treadmill. I'd been holding down the fort waiting for things to settle. It would still be years before I'd realize—we had settled. I was the only one waiting.

"So Jeff Grant uses our nanny? Man. What are the chances of that?"

At first it felt weird having Lola in our small house, but now I was used to her. It was too easy to have someone pick up after you to mind much. Will hung on to my knee.

"She wants to start a mothers' group and I said yes."

"You can get out of it."

We went back in, carrying a tray with coffee. Paul said he'd loved *The Dayton Widow*.

"And we love *her* work," the Somebody said, pointing at me, but I didn't believe him. My music tended to pull in nuns, librarians, and middle school teachers (not surprising, I suppose, since these were the people I'd grown up with). I'd had my picture in the paper a few times; that was probably how these two knew me. The Eroica Trio named themselves after Beethoven's Third and the first month they performed, people said, *Oh yeah, I've heard of you.*

We ended up taking a walk with them, sliding Will into his stroller. Outside, the pavement sparkled and the palms looked still and old. Even though we'd been here two years, we didn't have friends. Paul was always working, and I stayed with Will. Weekends, Paul crashed on the bed, flipping channels, exhausted from the pressure to be funny. For two years, he'd felt about to be fired. *They could let me go tomorrow,* he'd told me. *Contractually, I have nothing.*

We needed fun.

The men walked ahead. I always liked the way Paul walked. There was ease to him, a gracefulness. Years later, Will would own that same gait. Paul's arm conducted Jeff Grant's laughter, which exploded in bursts. They lived close, two streets over. We found Lola sitting inside a city of blocks. She looked odd in this other house. Their boy ignored Will.

But meeting this couple, with a boy Will's age, by the chance of our goofy nanny, felt promising. Though I didn't know what to say to Helen. She was not really my type—beautiful.

We ducked into a coffee shop. The boys sat in their strollers snubbing each other. When we stopped at the park they ran, pushing to be first to the top of the slide.

Looking at Will, Jeff said, "Where'd you get the . . . the outfit?"

Will swooshed headfirst down the slide in the blue jumpsuit that looked like a gas station attendant's uniform. I loved that one. When I'd bought it, Paul had gone ballistic.

He groaned. "Those tiny things cost seventy dollars. And she brought home two."

"Size eighteen months and size three." I'd skipped size 2. That was prudent. The Guggenheim I'd stashed away had paid for our move here, but Paul made it his job to preserve that fortification against my raids. It gave me pleasure, though, to write the check at the sweet children's store. I disliked having to find the right moment to confess to Paul, whose mother was an outlet shopper. So I didn't always. Confess.

"Got that?" Jeff asked Helen, when I said the name of the store: Imagine.

"I'll remember," she said, rummaging in her purse.

"Or I'll tell you again." I liked it that I'd picked something Jeff Grant wanted. His approval seemed hard to get.

Jeff handed her a pencil. "Let's write that down."

"I buy Bing's stuff at Ross Dress for Less," Helen said. "You two could never be married. You're too much alike."

Are we? I thought, the sun burning my arms. Jeff probably was impossible.

Helen laughed. "But his craziness comes with his genius."

The putative genius nodded along.

I was already talking myself out of him. I'd once thought I'd end up with a guy like Jeff. But I was thirty-three by the time I got married, old enough to know I wanted to make music. The difference was huge, a deformity that had its cost. Once, music had been enough for my whole happiness. (I named my tap concerto *Rapture.*) But then I'd begun to want a life. Mistake. Now I had one and was no good at it. So I won't get that, I thought, watching Jeff, thinking of bells, their linger.

The four of us stood at the swings, our boys pumping, a take-out latte in each mother's hand. A middle-aged form of dating. It felt as if this new friendship could change us the way that, in my twenties, I used to think a guy would. Maybe, I thought, as wind dragged flecks of eucalyptus against my face, this would give us a thread of excitement. I didn't imagine whispering under the sheets at night the way we once had or turning each other's bodies in the gray dawn. But even dressing up to go out, talking with the bathroom door open, was something we hadn't had for a long time.

Helen and I sat on a seesaw, behind our boys. I didn't know how hard to bump. Bing looked delicate, his teeth small and even, like corn. Helen's hands absently reached up to her hair and made a deft braid. A girl stopped in front of her, belly out, the hem of her dress torn. "Could you do that to me?"

"What do you say?"

"Please." She turned around and stood still. "Can you make a French one?"

"Come *on*," Will demanded, stranded on the up slant.

Willie jumped down then, jolting Bing, and ran off to the monkey bars. Helen gave him a look, her hand still working on the careful immobile head. "I should have a girl," she mumbled. I understood that they planned to have more. That was true of them in general.

That day Will looked his best, wind riling his curls, a gift from Paul's mother, who blow-dried her own straight. He climbed a play structure, manning a wheel. I jumped up to tell him *five more minutes,* a way I'd copied from an offhand mother. Another kid crawled near my shoes and I tripped. Will pushed onto the kid, almost horizontal, swimming in air. It happened so fast. I sat on the metal floor—the kid had tied his shoelaces with mine. By the time I staggered up, Jeff had pulled the boys apart. He handed the shrieking kid to a big-faced woman, who moved forward, the girl with Helen's braid holding her leg. The woman clamped Will's shoulder. "Say you're sorry."

"Say you're sorry, Will," I warned. Lola would've known what to do. She prided herself on her instincts. I didn't seem to have any.

The woman looked at me with a beam of accusation. "Lookedit. Knocked his tooth loose." Her fingers pried open his mouth, wiggled the tooth. "That's bone!"

"Was defending his mom," Jeff said.

Paul dusted Will off, then lifted him onto his shoulders. Good.

"You okay, bud?" Jeff said to the other kid. Jeff stared at the mom, whose face fell trapezoidal. "Our guy shouldn't have hit, but your guy shouldn't have tied her shoelaces."

Helen murmured agreement. Still, it would've been different if Bing had been beneath our boy's windmilling arms. The fight had been almost beautiful to watch. Paul had his arm out; like me, inclined to apologize.

"Hey, I worry Bing's too timid," Jeff said. "I fought when I was a kid."

Back at their house, Lola jumped up from where she'd been watching TV, looking caught. Their fireplace poofed on with the turn of a knob, giving real, lifting flames. In no time Jeff put a glass of wine into my hand.

"I will go now," Lola called, from the door.

Helen stepped over things, handing us plates of warm take-out food, with big napkins. "Look," she whispered. Our boys were finally playing together. It was as if that was something we'd made. I didn't know it then, but this was our happiness, kids on the floor, intent on a tower of blocks. After a while Helen lifted Bing to his crib and I put Will in his stroller, wrapped in a borrowed blanket. He closed his eyes and started sucking. Behind us on chairs, the guys were laughing.

"Walking down the aisle, she's thinking, The last blow job I ever have to give."

Paul would never say that. But he shook his head. "Think about it every day."

"Try every hour," Jeff said.

Helen sighed. We all laughed. That somehow made it better.

William slept in his stroller, his hand on his delicate ear, as we walked home. Behind branches, our windows glowed. Lola had turned on lights. I had that full-day feeling as I undressed Will and slipped him into bed. But the weekend ended with a sighing quality.

Tomorrow, it would all start again—Paul gone until next Saturday.

Lola

COINS

"Come on comeon comeon comeon comeon. Come to Lola. I have something for you." Because he is very angry.

Today it is the mother he was hitting. She has her hand over her eye and I dab ice, the way I do his boo-boos. She lets her face in my hands. Then I take him away. But Williamo, he is strong. I cannot so easily hold. And Lola told a lie. I do not have anything. So I make promises. "Some-a-day," I whisper, "I will bring you home with me. And there we will make the ice candy."

He lies still, not any longer fighting. His bones fall in a pattern, like the veins of a leaf.

"I will put you in my pocket and feed you one candy every day. You will be happy. Because the ocean at our place it is very blue. The sky higher than here. And the fruits that grow on trees, very sweet." Jack-fruit, durian, lanzones. Attis. Santol.

"In my pocket I will give you one lychee. You can bounce for a ball."

"If you were a kangaroo you would have a pouch," he grumbles, better now, slower the heart.

Through the window I see my employer. She looks like she has too much assigned to her; she cannot complete it all before she dies. She holds the ice and paces, talking long-distance to a woman who reads books about the raising of children. When my employer becomes upset she calls this friend. My employer has the American problem of guilt. But you should not be guilty to your children. It is for them that you are working! Then I remember that check for a thousand, long ago. I do not like to think that; it still opens a taste of confusion.

31

But Williamo, he is better now. Only the mouth smears. I promise him candy, not the ice candy, just candy we can buy here. "But-ah do not tell your mother."

I call to her, "Excuse, we are going now."

"Okay. Thanks, Lole." My employer believes she cannot live without me. She is telling her friend who reads the books that he is better with me than with her. Lil will tell her that this is perfectly normal. My employer, she needs to be left alone. But that is not a quality for a mother. Children, they are dependent for their life. "Playdate," my employer says. "I can't even stand the word."

"Do you have poo-poo?" I pull out the diaper. I am paid to smell that. But what she said to her friend is true. With me, Williamo is no problem.

My employer, she says when a baby comes home from the hospital, a Filipina should arrive with him. That, for her, would make a perfect world. "It's the Asian thing," I heard her say once. "They're more gentle with kids than Hispanics." She thinks it is all Filipinos. Maybe every single human being from Asia. I could introduce her to a few.

Claire walks out carrying keys. With a child small small, it is like a ball and chain. You are never free. Not even sleeping. "Bye." She slams her car door. An escape. She will stroll in the conservatory, thinking about old songs. Americans, for them the highest time is college: books in a bent arm, on the way to learning. Us, we go to school to get the degree.

I push Williamo in the stroller and he sits. That is the good of fighting; it makes them very tired. The sun is solid, like many small weights on our arms. This neighborhood is ours during the daytime. You do not observe mothers, only in and out of cars, carrying shopping bags. In my place, I was, at one time, one of these married ladies. Now when I watch from afar, it looks like a lot of work.

I put coconut oil and zinc powder on the nose because Williamo he is very white. My albino grandson. All the while, I talk to him. Ruth told me, *You have always to talk, even a baby, it is important.* And I talk to him, more than my own, because my kids I had one after the other, five in nine years. In the class of two thousand and ten, at Harvard University there will be two Santa Monica boys saying to cooks in the cafeteria, *Excuse, where is my adobo?* Lola by then will be swaying in a hammock, back in the Philippines.

"What for?" He is young. He does not yet understand the importance of rest.

When we pass the play store, I turn in and ask, "Where is Lola from?"

He points on the globe.

"Very good."

Outside again, in the distance we see children, past tall trees, old in the glittering air. But Williamo says he does not want to play, not now, so we roll under the eucalyptus once upon a time from Australia until the eyes close. I knew from Ruth to work for a working mother. The women who stay home want their babies tucked in cribs for naps, so they can tiptoe in and peek. But Williamo, he can sleep on grass. Today he will nap in his stroller.

I told my employer already: When they go to Europe to celebrate their tenth anniversary, I will take Williamo to the Philippines. We are saving for the tickets. I cannot save much because every month I send home eighteen hundred. My kids, they are a little jealous, especially Dante and Lisa, because they have their own. And it is true. I am closer to Williamo than I am to my grandchildren. Because I see Williamo every day.

Tomorrow for the playclub, I will make tapioca. Williamo likes the big kind we have to soak overnight, so I walk to the grocery. For a long time, I worried this job. Then one day I was not trying anymore.

Someone touches my arm in the aisle. *"Hola!"* she says. *"Cómo estás?"*

Here, they think I speak Spanish. "Hi," I say.

"I know you. You're the babysitter of the boy who says *To be or not to be.*"

I point to the stroller. Thumb in his mouth, eyes closed. "Not to be," I say. My employer made an orchestra from a play by William Shakespeare. That is why Williamo. At the end of his speech, after *'tis a consummation / Devoutly to be wish'd,* I told him, *Then you bow.* And he will bow.

"I'm Beth, Brookie and Kate's mom," she says. "You're Lola, right?"

"I know Esperanza," I say. Esperanza, she is the only one in the playclub not Filipina.

The woman stands writing on a small card. She puts the name and address and she scribbles *Call me! We need help Saturday nights!*

But I am not tempted. Esperanza says her employer leaves her exercise clothes, underwear and all, in damp lumps on the floor. The next time Beth Martin wants to see those things they will be clean and folded in her drawer.

I am a little popular. With my new weekend salary, I send home an extra hundred every week. In America, I am on the way up.

I push the stroller to the place of Mai-ling, where babysitters sit at a picnic table eating her fresh lumpia, light and porous, and savory adobo, with bay leaves planted by the landscaper. Mai-ling stands ironing, using an extension. Here, the man and the boy go out every day; it is only babysitters and children small small and sometimes a half-dressed woman upstairs, cataloging the possessions. Afternoons, they are not like this in Manila, even in the gated residential districts of Makati where outside you see only workers in uniform. In tea shops mothers gather with their children in an after-school world. Williamo still sleeps, so I park him facing the wall.

"My employers, they change when they move to the big house," Lita says. "They really change."

"For your salary, let them change!" Her employer is Alice, the doctor. The husband, he wakes up in the middle of the night when the stock market opens in New York. And Lita gets one hundred dollars a day. They live in a Beverly Hills mansion.

We compare jobs, the way women compare husbands. The house of my employer it is the smallest. But one day I will bring the disc with her music and play that little melody I heard. This is the mother of Williamo, I will tell them. Usually, you would trade a part of what you have, but not all. When I think of my husband Bong Bong, I see him bent over his table, drawing the lines of a white chrysanthemum, a tropical Christmas flower. I close a fist in my pocket. "But-ah, your employers, they are good." I am always the one telling babysitters to stay. Because too much change, it is bad for children. And the two of Lita are well behaved, because they are Asian. Chinese, adopted.

"They don't think I will leave but lot of people, they are looking Filipinas."

"Rich people," Vicky says.

"We are status symbols. Like a BMW." I can usually make babysitters laugh.

"No, you know know what Alice told me?" Lita whispers. "In the hospital they have a joke, what does 'yes' mean in Tagalog? 'Yes' it means, 'fuck you.' "

"Yes," Vicky repeats, loud. "Fuck you."

"Shhh," I say. Williamo is a myna bird. Sure enough, the head pops up.

"What?" He is very advanced. "What?" He tugs my sleeve.

Vicky, she does not think! The employer here is usually in the house, even when we cannot see her. Some unmarried women, you wonder why. But not Vicky. It is a face I have seen before on retardeds, the profile a crescent, the jaw and forehead more out. Vicky thinks only about her meals and money. In our place, we would not know each other. Mai-ling I would never meet either, unless she worked in my house. A peasant, ethnic Chinese, she has no education. Only Lita lived in my social class, in the suburb next to mine.

"Alice will be very surprise." One or two times a year Lita says she is leaving.

Lita wears the clothes of a wife, the fingernails filed oval, polished pink like the inside of a shell. Twelve years ago, she came here to work and married an American. Not in the church but in a courthouse, her real husband still alive in the Philippines. We call that Ca-Ching. But later on she got her kids here. All three.

She lifts a teddy bear from her bag and clicks a button in the fur, and a panel opens. "Look, it is a video. They are spying me. I should have known, the toys all wood. They would not keep a bear so ugly."

One Chinese Adopted stands pouring a stream of glittering sand from a teapot. Her dress strains at the belly. I am always telling Lita, Do not feed so much. The mother a doctor. Why would you let your child be like that?

"A long time, that bear is in their room. They probably watch what I am teaching. They see their daughters learn to wipe."

"Let I!" China says. We have Chinese Adopteds named Emma and Larkin and a blond, blue-eyed girl named China. "Let I do it!" She grabs the teapot from Emma.

"We will buy a film," I say. "The parents will be the movie stars."

"Alice, I really do not like." Most babysitters, they do not like their employers.

"Ling-ing!" we hear from above. See. All along Sue, the employer, was here. In my house, I did not hide from my helpers. Mai-ling runs up and then comes back with another basket of laundry. I tap her belly, *Slow down.* Living here, with husbands across the ocean, we touch each other more.

Esperanza says last night in her place, the guy took everything out of the refrigerator, looking for a piece of meat leftover. Her hand slaps the mouth. "But I ate."

A lot of what they talk about is food, what they can eat in the houses where they live-in. Many keep food under the bed. When the Sapersteins have chicken, Ruth will not accept a leg or a breast, even though she is the one preparing. "I take the neck," she says. "I eat bones." And she is working there, taking care Ginger nine years. I am lucky; my employer every night she puts too much on my plate. Lettie, the new babysitter, says her people are nice, but the food, it has a different smell. "I miss my baby," she whispers.

Mai-ling hangs the blouses she finished ironing on a branch. Esperanza lifts one melon color to her cheek; it would look more on her than on Sue. Mai-ling has told us the closet of Sue fills tight with clothes. She is always buying. Two blouses here for Mai-ling to iron still have tags. Between the hangers in the closet of my employer, you could fit an orange. Her formal hangs on the end, inside dry-cleaner plastic.

"Ooh la la," Esperanza says, holding up a black sleeveless.

The young babysitters, they are not married. They would like pretty blouses. I would rather wear my T-shirt I can wash. When I came here I had already turned fifty. Romance is a belonging of my children, an obstacle I worry for, like drugs. But the young babysitters, they do not stand in the evening, looking back across the Pacific. They face the big dry continent here. Thinking of cowboys.

The laundry machines of my employer stand in the garage, on the other side of my wall. At night, I wash my clothes, put them in the dryer, and my wall purrs. I go to sleep like that. Wrinkles web my shirts, but I cannot sleep anymore without that purr.

"Black is good on you!" Lita says. "Like a Spanish Lea Salonga." Esperanza, she is Latin, too dark, but the skin looks good. A good dark. She is what they call here sexy.

The young babysitters, they are not like my daughters or the friends they bring home from University Santo Tomas. For my kids, I do not allow sport dating.

"Remember me for that one," Esperanza says to Mai-ling. Because our employers, they give us their old clothes.

But a price tag flaps on that blouse with no sleeves. One hundred seventy. Two of those blouses, that is one week Mai-ling, and they are two months behind on her pay. The life of Mai-ling is for her son; the husband is dead already. Her health is not strong. All she can do is work and send money to her son who was taking drugs before. Maybe the granddaughter can get in a good school, a Catholic. That is her wish. Some nights before sleep, I think Mai-ling will work here until she dies. We will be the ones to give the funeral and send the body home. She is another reason I need savings.

All of a sudden, I turn to check—the kids, they have been too quiet—and I see them fall in fighting. I have to separate the two. Some nannies favor their own and some the other, just like mothers. As a mother, I was stricter with mine. But with Williamo, I am more fair. "Two-minute rule," I say. "I am timing. You take turns on the truck."

Before the end of two minutes, Williamo throws the bear. The thing drops near my feet with a jangle.

"Craft time." I clap. Last week, we made newspaper boats. Then Sue had the idea to go to the lumber store. Mothers here find a way to make more work. We painted the wooden boats and put in small hooks she bought, and today I will tear a sheet for sails. I think of our kids holding strings to the colors of her blouses, cut and rigged for use. Then I take the sheet in my teeth and start the rip and show Lettie how to hem a sail. Lita is feeding Emma again. Emma eats too much! Mai-ling still stands ironing. The piles of bras, underwear, and T-shirts make different-shaped blocks in the laundry basket.

"Bing," Esperanza calls. "Look your boat." The boat floats, but the water stays still in this pool. Maybe if we turn on the jets for the Jacuzzi. Esperanza steps out her shorts, shaking her body into the bikini. All her parts fit the way they are supposed to. "Brooke, when you are big and rich, what will you do with all your money? Maybe you will live on a yacht!" Babysitters, even if they are in America one week from a swamp in the jungle, they know what is a yacht. The employers do not like us to tell these words to their children. But why not? That is the fun of here.

"I will buy you a house," Brooke says.

"Oh," Esperanza murmurs, happy in her cheeks. But this is a girl promising a babysitter; she will grow up and forget. The Latins, they are always watching telenovelas. It makes them too romantic.

Bingo! The jets start waves.

"What about me?" I call.

"I will buy you a house too."

No one asks Esperanza why she thinks Brooke will become rich. She is rich now, already. But in the Philippines, we seemed a fortunate family when I was the age of Brooke. Williamo, he stands with his arms stretching, then he loses his balance and falls into the water. I hook him out, under the arm. My happiest times are when we are laughing at our life. For that you have to be the same. To be above other people, you will say goodbye to laughter. "How about me?" I hear Vicky ask Bing. "When you are rich, what will you buy me?"

He puffs his cheeks, blowing, trying to whistle, but nothing comes out.

Esperanza holds a sail to her cheek. "No?" But all colors look good on her.

"You know the house on the corner of Twelfth?" Lita says. "A lady, she told me the wife was first the baby nurse. The mother, she die in childbirth."

"Yesterday," Esperanza says, "we are walking and I see him—the guy. Oh, he is tall. *Guapo*."

"Hand-sum," Lita says.

The young babysitters they want handsome husbands. My employer, she would like a new stove. I wish only for money. To buy schooling. So my kids, they will have their chance. Degrees cannot make them happy. Not guaranteed. But what else can you give?

Today is Friday, the last of the month. Lita is selling the lottery tickets she gets from her bad son. She has two kids hardworking but the middle one, he just plays. Lettie Elizande buys a ticket. She wants to go home. She does not like anything here. I buy also. This week I can send home fifty more. I have thirteen hundred savings, my little mound. If I win, poof, no more Lola. That was all I wanted, when I flew over, my hands useless on my lap. But that was when all I loved was there. Now I have Williamo.

And something else. These weekend people. I think of them and have to work to stop my smile. Another man never courted me. Bong Bong was the only one who wanted Lola. I am not a beauty who had a hundred proposals. But, I tell my daughters, all it takes is one. Now I have my empire of children. Six with Williamo.

We sail our wooden boats from the sides of the pool, our kids not yet old enough to swim. Heat shimmers. Palm leaf shadows dark the light.

I have in one fist the bunched T-shirt of China while Mai-ling runs to get the camera and in the other the collar of Bing while Vicky goes to the bathroom. Vicky, she takes care a boy who still naps twice a day, and the moment she is needed, she uses the restroom. Every weekend, our mutual employers talk about her. Last Sunday, Helen made me her coffee; Jeff stood one foot on the other knee. "She won't talk to us, Lola."

"She is not like you," Helen whispered. With them, there is so much not said. I am not used to hidden meanings. From a helper, people usually want what you do for them. That is all.

"But-ah, Vicky is nice," I said. "I will tell her to talk more. Me, I am *dal-dal*."

The last time I talked like this, it was the beginning with Bong Bong.

"How do you like being a big brother," Lita asks Simon. "You love your sister, yes!"

"I will never love that lump," he says.

Mai-ling has returned with the Polaroid the employers gave her for Christmas. We have our children sit cross-legged, holding the strings of boats. I put my arms around Bing and Williamo. Aileen, the granddaughter of Ruth, sits by Lita, who will watch her today. The colored boats bob on water. I am squatting behind to make sure nobody falls in, when the star of light sputters and blinks.

When I see that picture, I am surprised. I know the work we did, gluing one wood on top the other, each sail hemmed and rigged with string. But the kids look a way I remember being myself long ago: stiff, facing a camera, asked to smile, children put together, used to each other, not friends, in time to be gotten through, the middle of the day, the feeling that later causes people in jobs to look at clocks, but these kids do not even have those handlebars for boredom. They cannot yet tell time.

The babysitters stand, brush off their laps. "Tomorrow at the house of Lita," Vicky calls, hitting me too hard.

"I want to go there now," Bing says. "To Litahouse."

In their voices, that is the only place it is our house.

Back home, I have ready a project. We put into cardboard all the coins. Claire told us we could have the pennies for the choo-choo bank, where we are saving for the Philippines. We also find nickels, dimes, and quarters and I have brown tubes for those too. There is always money in this house. "It is a hunt," I tell Williamo, and we discover nests in the carpet, piles on counters, little dishes filled. If someone came to the door with a pizza and I needed ten dollars, I could find it, in pockets and cups, mixed with slips of paper. My house in the Philippines is like this too. That way if I become very low I can dig. My secret garden.

We pile the rolls of coins; build with them an American log cabin, using his Play-Doh for the mortar. Williamo is a very good worker. If we can keep the dimes, we will have a lot already. But I have to ask. The pennies, they are already ours.

"Hey," Claire answers her phone. She is only upstairs, but I am supposed to call. It is hard for her to hear sounds she is making if we go there. The neighbor gardeners cause problems, also, with the machine that blows leaves.

"We are asking, can we have also the silver coins?"

"Sure, Lola." There are certain people; you know they will always say to you yes.

At the bank, we fall in line. When we go to the front, the lady acts all business, making a total of the dimes. I say, "This little man filled the nickels by himself."

While she finishes the silver coins, I lift a bag of pennies from his wagon. It is heavy. We have many pennies. From the log cabin, we counted forty dollars nickels, twenty-seven dimes, and one hundred and three pennies. I lift Williamo up to see.

But the lady pushes our tubes out. "We cannot take pennies."

Williamo picks one roll, to hand it back to her. I remember this moment, again and again: it is like the giving of a flower. He does not yet understand.

"We don't *take* these," she says.

For a second, then, his face changes, what his mother calls berry-with-a-frown. Cartoon looks; they are really true on children. An upside-down smile, then bawling. He throws the roll of pennies at her face.

"I can't help you," the lady says with closed teeth. Her hand goes above her eye. She has already given us paper money for the silver. She looks at me with hate. I have seen real hate only a few times in my life. The shape of diamonds, it is shocking.

But she is hurt above the eye and I am not a white.

"Come, Williamo." I fight him down into the wagon. I will have to pull the pennies and him. "We will make our getaway."

But he runs, dragging pennies to a garbage can, and dumps the tubes in. Still crying he is mad now, also mad. I have to stop him. This is not right. All our effort. With him what I do is almost tackle. I get on the floor and hold him until the fight is out.

"Once upon a time," I say, "I work in Beverly Hills. A house very fancy. Three layers. Floors like a checkerboard. Marble.

"When I first came, the lady she open the door and right away she said, *You are hired.* She told me, she knew like *that*—she snap her fingers—you will never guess from why. Because the way I tie my sneakers. She thought Lola was tidy. But Lola is not so tidy, not really. I can be if I have to. And for her I clean every thing. But that is not the way I live. It is too much time, always straightening. I would rather taste some part of life. The husband, he had an office, and she hired me extra to go on the Saturday. He sat working at his desk. And he had one jar like this, up to my waist, full with pennies. I asked him, did he want me to get tubes from the bank? He said, *You can take the pennies.*

"But I could not lift. So I came back Sunday, my off, and I sat on the floor and put pennies into tubes. He stepped around me when he went down the hall to use the lavatory. He ask me how much money as he went by.

"*Thirty-six dollars,* I said.

"*Good job, Lola.*

"The next time it was ninety-four. By the last time he passed, I was at three hundred six. His face looked strange, like two lines crossing. He went down the hall and I heard Xeroxing. On his way back, he stopped and said, *'Maybe you better leave the pennies.*

"*Whatever you say. It is up to you.*

"When he returned to his desk, I stood and left it all there, the rolled pennies, the pile on the floor, the jar turned over. I took the bus to the place of Ruth and never went back. That was the end of my career for a Beverly Hills housekeeper."

"Is that when you came here?"

"You were not yet born. I had to wait for you. But-ah, when the husband took the pennies to the bank, you know what they are telling him? They are telling him what they are telling us. *We cannot help you.* And you know what he will do?"

"He shouldn't have taken your pennies, Lola. He is a bad man."

"Only a little bad. Listen, you know what he will do? He will throw the pennies in the garbage and go away in a hurry, he is always in a hurry. He is too busy, see?"

Now I fish with my arm in the garbage, feeling around wet things for our tubes. "But we will do something else. Come. You watch." I pull him in the wagon out into the bright air. We go to the five-and-dime. And then the candy shop. Then the Discovery Store, where we spin the globe. Each place, I count out money. I put the rolls on the counter, so it is easy for the register clerk. My father told me, *Spend your small money first.* He remembered when money became light and the lower denominations would not anymore buy. And still at that time, there was wealth.

In the wagon Williamo eats long orange candy worms.

"See, in the bank it is nothing, but out here it is still money. Not for the Philippines, but we can buy. Every day a little. It is our trust fund. I trust you and you trust me. You have your candy. Now, we will use pennies to buy Lola coffee."

That is what my kids, they will remember. That Lola loved her coffee.

When we return home, the hallway rounds to a cave and I hear chopping.

"I will be the one," I say. My employer, she did not grow up with a helper. She cannot easily ask. So I take the tomatoes. All the while with a smile. It is not hard. Not when you have a purpose. And I have five purposes, the youngest twenty-three studying medicine.

Always the parents first, Ruth said. A kid cannot fire you. Even here.

Anyway, my employer is a very good cook. I am happy to chop chop.

Williamo sits under the table, folding a newspaper to a hat the way I showed him. "Who taught *you*, Lola? Your nanny?"

"We did not call the ladies nannies."

"What did you call them?"

"I really do not know. She was just the One in the House." I shrug to Claire. "In our place, you know, everyone has somebody to help."

Tonight her eye where Williamo hit shines black and blue, yellow also. Over it, she has painted makeup. "I don't know what I'm doing wrong."

"It is the age too." But my children, they were not like this, not even Dante. Here in America, they are different. Also taller.

"Maybe I should find a psychologist for him," my employer whispers. "Do you think this is all still normal?"

Really, I do not know. "You are talking to the wrong person," I say. "Because-ah I like naughty boys."

She sighs, better now. We will not tell her the lady at the bank.

She gives me my plate, covered with a napkin, to carry back to my place.

"You won't eat with us, Lole?"

Ruth advised me, *Americans do not know what they want. They invite you, and then after, they will pine for their privacy. Americans need privacy. Because it is a big big land.* Also, if I am eating with them, when Williamo needs more milk, I will be the one to jump up. I like to watch the TV. Tonight I have a project. It is important to have hours you are comfortable.

Later on, he can come to my place. We will study the map. The lavender Philippines, orange California. We are saving for the globe. Each day, we will give the man two rolls. It can help teach counting.

They leave the dishes for the morning. They are a little spoiled, like my own kids, but I do not mind. They work hard. My money is earned. I can sit. That is my day.

Some people across the Pacific, they had better be studying.

I take my project with me in a bag and walk past the house they are building on Twelfth, where they say the wife is Filipina. Esperanza heard housekeeper. Lita today said baby nurse. Whatever she was first, they are now building towers.

It is different for the babysitters not yet married. They come here every day. For them it is a shrine: boards and empty rectangles of air. Each wants a husband to carry her over the threshold of a Castle. Their dreams take place here.

Me, I have my house already.

I always keep in the corner of my room a box for my next shipment home. For a large box, only sixty-five dollars. I make a map for my daughters where to put my treasures. My employer became upset when she saw I had her present wrapped in T-shirts to send. "I want your life *here* to be a little nicer." But I have a china cabinet in the dining room at home. I think of that room empty in the afternoon, a clean lung. I am not here to settle. America may be the future of the world but it is not the future of Lola.

Smells from gardens wind in the air, lights come on inside houses. Automatic sprinklers siss on.

Every home has a place that makes the center. In my house, it is the cabinet, where I keep our remembrance and the diplomas of our children. In the downstairs of my employer, it is the stove where Claire cooks every night. For Claire, it is her cello, upstairs in the room she works. In the place of Ruth, the center is a book, left open on a stand like the Oxford dictionary in the studio trailer of my handsome weekend employer. *The Book of Ruth* tells the story of our careers in America.

The teacher of Ruth was a picture bride, and then she worked domestic. On the first page, she typed HOW TO WORK FOR THE WHITE.

They do not like their own smell. Their waste. Their own used things.

Americans, they are very dirty. They used to be clean. The grandparents are clean. And the habits they lost are what they crave from us.

I have with me tonight this old book. Ruth gave it so I will make repairs. I walk to Palisades Park, sit on a bench, and lift out the frail book from T-shirts I have wrapped around. The spine is tearing from so many times being opened, and some of the pages glued in, the paste has dried and they are coming loose.

There is a carbon copy of a letter the teacher wrote to Mrs. Roosevelt and the reply, which came, eleven months later, from someone called Mary Anderson. The carbon paper is smudged from so many handling.

The teacher of Ruth trained Filipinas. *Because we know English,* Ruth said. *And Japanese did not work anymore domestic.*

A fellow student of Ruth learned English with the children of the family she lived-in. She left to Ruth that Visayan dictionary, with English words penciled in the margins. Into *The Book of Ruth,* women pasted copies of letters to Marcos and the unfamous presidents of Latin America. One housekeeper wrote a poem in Spanish for her granddaughter.

Underneath the torn leather of the spine, it looks like machine stitching.

The teacher of Ruth had a friend from the bus stop who wrote to the president.

```
Dear President,
I am a married woman and my Husband has been out
of work for nearly eighteen month. I have been
doing house work to keep my home together. I have
one boy four and one half years old and it is very
hard for me to leave my home and work at house
work by the week. I get $12.00 per week. I work
from seven in the morning till eight at night and
if they have dinner parties I work much later and
all I have off is from three o'clock one afternoon
during the week and on Sunday afternoon. I wish
you could do something to shorten the hours. I do
not mind working to support my family but I sure
do hate to be made a slave of. I hope Dear Presi-
dent you will not over look us poor things that
has to work for the Wealthy. I sure hope my Hus-
band will get work and I sure think if things keep
up the way you have been doing every thing will
come back wonderful. Dear President, we poor
```

```
things want to thank you so much for all you have
done.
                              Sincerely yours,
                                Grace Wicker
                            17 Mercer Avenue
                            Altadena, Calif.
PS I sure hope you can do something so I can be
home with my little boy for I feel he needs me.
```

That smudged carbon copy the teacher put on the second page. Grace Wicker worked next door to where she worked. *And she is a white,* the teacher told Ruth. *That is how they even treat their own.*

I take out a needle and three spools of thread. I try to match the faded spine and thread the needle. I sew cross-stitches very tight. After I sew, I will seal the holes with Crazy Glue.

Everyone who stayed at the place of Ruth signed her name. It is also a how-to book. How to set a table, with four forks and four spoons, tricks about pie crust, how to fan a napkin so it stands.

Always Do Extra, someone named Dora wrote in 1966. *Anything a little nice without spending their money. Here where I am they have orange trees. So I make an orange and lime salad.* She drew a picture of the way Valencia trees hold new oranges, along with some from the year before and white blossoms, at the same time. *Always pick the old,* she advised. *Sweeter.*

If someone made a dessert—floating island or a layer cake—she recorded the compliments.

I need one praise every day, Analise Deoferio wrote. *I work Professor Williamson, of UCLA, for twenty-nine years. When my husband die, she pay the funeral.*

The book includes tips. *Two baths a day, teeth cleaning at four-hour intervals, no curry, onion, or garlic, even on days off.* That is a page someone cut out and taped in: IF THE DOG LIKES YOU, YOU'RE HIRED.

—*Don't let yourself become the queen. You're not the queen. The mother is the queen. Especially, it will happen sometimes before the kids are in school. Because the mothers become so dependent. The mother, any fun she can have with her friends, any minute to go shopping, any for herself—she needs you, so at that time they will do everything to keep you happy. But the babysitter made her price so high that later on they decided they do not want. And instead of just changing the pay, they fire her.*

I know because this was me.

—*The babysitter who was La Reina*

The edges of the page lift up; the tape, it is too dry. I will glue this in. I wonder if I can use the old typewriter of my employer to retype the carbon letters. They make a mess on the hands every time you open.

The penmanship of Ruth is small. *If your employer offers you something, old clothes she will not wear anymore, even a food you like to take home, always say no. If she really wants you to have, let her insist.*

Avoid families that do not use paper towels. Cloth diapers even worse. Always put a plastic inside every garbage.

In the place of Ruth, there is a shelf with a row of black volumes. How many years to fill a book?

"Average four," Ruth said.

"What will be your series title?"

"*A Wealthy Woman's Guide to Being a Maid.* No, seriously, Lola, the real problem in our profession is age. Like Mai-ling. She is too old to chase kids. And the mother knows it. But the father likes the way she irons his shirts."

In *The Book of Ruth* this year, Lita wrote the address of Patricks Road House, where she and Esperanza sat an hour and still the waiter did not take their order.

Are you not a business? Babysitters work hard for their money; sometimes we want to spend too.

I still have not yet added anything in the *Book.* I only fix the old, where it is tearing.

I think what I can write. I have some advice about silence. If you are smart, when something happens, if the baby takes his first step or says the first word, the first of Williamo was "light," second "French," third "fries," you keep in your private journal so you will have the true

48

date but do not tell. You wait and that evening or the next they will call you shrieking, *Lola, Lola come here!* But the hitting; that I really do not know. Claire, she is nervous. And the guy, he is not strong. When he is there, he is only playing. I am the one to explain: *Williamo, that you cannot do.*

When I am finished my stitching, I wrap the book again in two T-shirts.

I stand at the fence and watch the Pacific. Fog blows in. Magic carpets.

Ruth likes to have a picture of every babysitter.

The book is also for memorial. Since we are working, we cannot always attend ceremonies. The weddings and baptisms, even the funeral. But we will send a letter of remembrance. And that will go alone on a page in *The Book of Ruth*. I have not known anyone yet who died here.

I stand at the fence looking down at the ocean, then I turn back. Coming the other way, a woman runs lopsided. My weekend employer. Jogging. "Lola! What are you doing here?"

"I am waving goodnight to the Philippines."

She asks me how long I will stay, meaning Los Angeles, but she is also meaning something else.

"As long as I am needed," I say. "It is not up to us." Williamo, he is an only child. Often, when they start school, the parents they do not want to pay. Or they ask the babysitter to clean the whole house, for no extra. Here kids start school already at three years. You boil all the bottles and nipples with tongs, and then one day, you stop. Raising children, it is all the same story—they grow above you. And you are no longer needed. They have a name for that here—obsolete. Things outlive their use, even people. And that is actually success. "My employer, she always says they will need me until the day Williamo goes to college. I will be the one to plan the graduation party."

Maybe this is what I will write in *The Book of Ruth*. If you can stay until they are five years old, then they will never forget you.

I wash my dish in the bathroom sink. On the bed, I glue in the pages that have loosened, put stones on top for the paste to dry overnight.

There at home, across the ocean, I have a house.

Here, one room, attached to the garage: a bed, bathroom in the corner. Television.

There I lived with other people. Bong Bong, our kids, friends and relatives arriving, sitting for a bite of gelatin squares on a plate.

This room is my place here. It is still light in the sky but already dark on the ground. Before, I did not like to be alone. My sister became the doctor, so I became the clown. Bong Bong, he is the serious one. The cheese stands alone. Not the clown. Because when I am alone I cry. It is a strange thing: here, it feels good, untangling strings. After a few minutes, when I finish, the lines of the day laid out straight, I begin to hope Williamo will come crashing to the screen, yelling *Lo-la.*

And when I begin to hope, he comes galumphing.

Claire

MY OLD CHAOS

The phone rang after midnight—my mother. "Come over right away, I was broken into."

I made out our dresser, Paul not there, everything the same. The clock blinked 12:18. "Did you call the police?"

"Just come over. This once you really have to. It's all I have!" Her voice peeled a shred off me.

I pulled on sweats, tucked in my nightgown, and walked out back, the wet grass sharp on my ankles, to Lola's room off the garage, where I heard the faint noise of TV—good, she was still up. But when I knocked, she didn't answer. I pushed the door open. She'd fallen asleep, the remote in her hand.

I ran back to the house and called Paul. "Can you come home?"

"Not yet. Oh, thanks. Diet Coke. Sorry, they're just passing out the pizza. You'll have to wake her and give her the monitor. Call me from your mother's."

I felt terrible touching Lola's shoulder in the dark. She bolted up, as if she'd done something wrong. "I have to go to my mom's, I think her apartment was broken into." I handed her the small plastic baby monitor.

But she said, "I will just stay in the house."

I felt grateful I could drive back to my old chaos and leave Will sleeping. Paul's mother's edict against live-out nannies finally made sense, for a reason she wouldn't have imagined. I coasted empty streets. Without traffic, my mother lived nine minutes away, which would swell into an hour when the sun rose. Had she really been broken into? Growing up, I'd become the man of the house because there wasn't one. I'd learned the power companies' addresses and how to pay their bills. But I'd failed to protect her.

51

All her lights were on. She met me at the door, her hair sticking out at wild angles and her eyes sketching back and forth. "It's gone," she said. "I had a money order for one hundred thousand."

I didn't believe her. She didn't have a hundred thousand dollars. But I asked questions with the distant patience of a police officer, one not particularly kind.

"No windows broken?"

"Huh-uh."

"And nobody else has your keys?"

"The landlord does. And I've been wondering about him. Last week, he came to repair that leak, you know, I told you in the back of the—"

"It's not the landlord, Mom." The landlords, two men who'd upgraded their forties building, got a kick out of my mother and hadn't raised her rent in seven years. A complaint could trigger a correction, I thought, or worse.

"Maybe one of his men. You know, fixing something." As she talked, describing small repairs, she picked up things off her kitchen counters and opened drawers. I'd completely lost track of her story, when all at once, she gasped "Oh." She'd lifted up a small cutting board behind a statue of Joseph and the Doves and under it she had her money order, Bank of America, for one hundred thousand dollars.

"Mom, what is this? Where did you get it?"

"That's my retirement. Everything."

"Why do you have this here? It should be in a bank! Where it can't be stolen."

"I know." She held it to her chest.

"Why don't you call Tom tomorrow and he'll take you to the bank?"

"Well, not Tom maybe."

I gave her a warning look. "Why not Tom?"

"I don't know if I trust him always."

"You can trust him," I said, remembering Paul calling Tom the most boring man in the world.

"Don't bother with it."

"Why are you crying now? You still have everything."

"I know," she whispered, as I went to leave. "I know."

When I got home, Paul stood eating a cold chicken leg. When I came to the part about her pulling out the money order, he started laughing. "Your mother. You should go with her tomorrow, make sure she gets that into a bank." My mother was an old story.

I woke up to the sound of Paul and Will growling engine noise. I heard the windup mouse scuttle across the floor, then the clomp of Will's feet.

Do it again, he said.

Paul left scribbed notes on the backs of envelopes by the door of our bedroom. I stepped over:

> PITCH TO BRADY
> CALL JENNY MEACHER'S SON
> CLAIRE'S MOM—BANK

Later that morning, I asked my mother if she'd called Tom. She said she had.

"He's coming to get me."

"To go to the bank?"

"Mm-hmm," she said. I didn't believe her, and we never talked about it again.

For a long time, I thought I'd gotten away with something. I wasn't behind the upper-middle-class kids who, from college on, moved everywhere around me, wearing their advantages lightly, like expensive clothes, only a tiny bit different from what the rest of us had. The trouble their parents had taken: lessons, tutors, AYSO. It seemed incredible that it hardly made a difference at all. Still, I'd understood that when I had children, they would resemble those kids more than me. I'd wondered if I could love them.

Now I had my answer.

Lola

HOW I CAME TO HOLLYWOOD

"So how did you find your way to Hollywood?"

That is the story people tell at the house of Ruth.

I came to America because of a flyer. I had heard already about the money from relatives of Lita. The daughter went to university with my eldest. Then I saw the flyer. JOBS IN AMERICA! MOTHERS, NURSES, COOKS! SEND MONEY HOME. RETIRE RICH IN FIVE YEARS! I folded the flyer and put it in my purse. At that time, Issa was writing her examinations for medicine.

My port of entry was San Francisco, because Bong Bong had a cousin in Petaluma. When Luz arrived at the lobby of my Chinatown hotel that was a little rancid, she smelled like a mint. All in white, in her red car, she looked like the American Red Cross. I sank into the seat and she drove. They live far outside. You cannot see other houses from that place—they are really alone. The movies we saw in Tagaytay—the Westerns! It is really like that.

Luz and the husband, they have monkeys, parrots, all different birds and snakes. Monkeys I really do not like, very dirty animals, and they made noise all night. There was a taste at the top of my mouth like an infection that did not go away. The guy bumped over the ground in a wheelchair; everything was built for him with wooden ramps. He was very good to the animals. One bird just sat on his shoulder.

I asked our relative, "Was he the same since you know him?"

She nodded.

"That is hard for you."

"No," she said. "He is so kind. More than a Filipino guy. Lot of Filipino guys, they are a little mean. He really cares what I am thinking. In my mind."

But Bong Bong, her cousin, he is not mean.

The next morning, she folded into her red Toyota. She drives one hour and a half every day to be dental hygienist.

I cleaned, first the bathroom, then the kitchen, then I washed myself. By the time the guy woke up, I was raking gray dust that was their front lawn. The ones working there were Spanish, but with their hands they showed me how to work the cages. There was old dirt, because the animals.

"Sit down," the husband said. "Let's see if you'll eat a Denver omelet."

Now, I can make that. With the heat there, a smell rises—baked dirt, bird poo, and eucalyptus. But in the evening, your arms feel good. We sat on chairs made of aluminum tubes and woven plastic. Made in the Philippines.

So many stars, it seems you are inside that sky.

The guy brought out the magazine where he first saw Luz. Each page showed rows of pictures. Our relative wore a school uniform with a small gold cross.

Then the guy carried out a square box of ice cream; he served it ruffled in bowls. Luz opened a tied folder of his letters. In the first one, he had written *I'm not any girl's idea of a prince.* He provided a typed sheet of his stocks and bonds and a copy of the deed for the property. He wrote in small, neat numbers what whoever became his wife could afford.

Did he include a picture, I wondered. Who ever sent any but the best picture? Still, our relative is thirty-seven now and prettier than she was in the catalog. Her face became thin. And her clothes look nice, because she is a professional woman.

But I had to find a job. I told them, just a few more days and then I will go south.

The guy had to deliver snakes to the San Jose Zoo, so he drove me to the train station. I called the number on the flyer before but when I arrive, there is nobody. I shouted into the pay telephone. "I am here! Yes! In Bakersfield!" They told me to take a taxi. It is an agency, I thought. The crippled guy had given me a bag of oranges, almonds, dates, and bills of American money that now I used.

The address from the flyer belongs to a pink one-story hotel with a chain-link fence all around. The taxi driver set my suitcase on the pavement. Another taxi waited, with a *tatay* and two daughters from Iloilo, trying to pay their driver in pesos. I gave him the rest my bills. They came to find work too, they said, and the people running this place were distant relatives that they had never met.

Inside, the ones who made the flyer looked at us, then at each other and giggled. The old lady said, since we are all here, they will go out to the movies! We can stay and give the patients their food! And we do not know anything! We have only been there fifteen minutes. The *tatay* does not understand English or Tagalog.

None of the retardeds has a mouth that is right. When the ones who made the flyer left, the retardeds cried. They pulled at us, whimpering.

"What? What is it you want?" The young from Iloilo shouted, every time louder.

Eight retardeds and only four of us. The ones who made the flyer left out cans of soup and packages of frozen hot dogs. And the way the retardeds ate! No one is teaching them. They are each different, one a mongoloid. Only all abnormal. Finally, I discovered by accident what will work. I snapped the TV and they all sat, weak as if it had power on them. We could clean up then; there was food over everything. When we finished they were still watching, tigers in a net, with their hands on their privates. The young from Iloilo went and placed the hands in the pockets. The elder shrieked. "I should do that! She is not yet married."

"They are asleep," the young said. "Anyway, I finished medicine already."

"So you are doctor?"

"Yes, Lola." Like my Issa will be, I thought. That is how I met Lucy.

The retardeds have dreams. They cry out, wanting their parents. And no family visited, all the time we lived there. The youngest of the ones who made the flyer, he told me the government pays them. But they are not really teaching! And the retardeds can learn. They are docile; before maybe, the ones who made the flyer, they were hitting. I taught the retardeds to dress themselves. Little by little. We spent many days on tying the shoe; the bow Tommy made, it was wobbly, but still a bow. We stayed forty days. The hotel is a pen. The ones who made the flyer, they just keep the money.

"I observe that I am losing weights," Lucy said.

They were not paying us, just our food. I had headaches trying to think. All around was chain-link fence. The two from Iloilo said they had to go to the Veterans Administration. "None near here," the old lady snapped. But the *tatay*, he receives a benefit check!

"We will go with you," the old lady said the next time. Her conclusion.

At night, the distant relatives watched TV, the *tatay* went to sleep, and I talked to Lucy. They took a boat from their place, then a bus, then a jeepney to the airport in Manila.

"Where is your mother?" I asked, because usually it is the mother who will come.

She is still there, running the store. I hug her goodbye, my arms do not go all the way around, she is so fat! She smells like water and sugar.

Their point of entry was LAX. The bus driver looked in the mirror and said to them, "Chinatown?" In the Philippines, it is better to be Spanish. Here, better Chinese. They found the Veterans Administration Building and brought in their papers, with the decoration of honor from the Second World War. Their family had that frilled ribbon on the wall before these two were born and now, here, they were spending it.

The ones who made the flyer learned right away that Cheska can cook and now every meal, she was the one preparing. I washed the dishes, and I saw the purse of the old lady open. I observed that the payments came in a certain kind of envelope.

"How about if you share that with us too?" I said, over my shoulder, like throwing a thin ball into the air, the one we use with the retardeds in the swimming pool.

The room behind me changed shape; it now had points. I scrubbed. Every chink and ring widened. Then I wiped my hands, turned around, and they were staring. "Because we are working hard. We are new here, we need money." We did all their work and they partied around, the *tatay* they asked him to bring them pineapple and coconut milk drinks by the pool. That is what they are doing!

The room made a funnel; the old lady the opening. "Not even legal here. We take you in. We could call police, they'd send you out on a jail boat."

A ring of my head lifted off the top.

"Not legal?" Lucy whispered. "But we registered already." She kept papers in the purse for novenas hung around her neck.

"You are lucky you have relatives," the old lady said, the jaw closing.

I had made things worse.

Good we know it is a happy ending, Ruth said, when I first told the story.

The hotel is the shape of a saw; the big end a lobby they changed into a kitchen, the smallest room number 9. The pool makes a saw the opposite way. On the other side of the fence there is another building the same except pale blue, where old people live in bathrobes. I observed, the people who took care—Sri Lankans—they are good. But the olds came right up to the fence and stared. They liked to watch the abnormals.

Then it was a heat wave and the retardeds were all the time in the pool. Every day the ones who made the flyer sat by the side and let the retardeds bob, in life jackets. Like human corks. They get no exercise! That is why they stay fat! I showed Tommy and the twins to hold the side and kick. The ones who made the flyer became wet, where they sat with their drinks. They watched me. They could not hate Cheska; she was making their foods. There was a cake they craved, with almonds and oranges. They let her out to buy ingredients. I told her to get sunblock, too, and we put white zinc on the noses of the retardeds.

"Lola! They are liking my cooking," Cheska said. She was proud!

The olds next door hung with their fingers in the fence and they got wet from the kicking. The ones who made the flyer did not want that I would teach the retardeds to swim. But if they cannot swim, they should anyway know to float.

"If anything happened," the younger one told me, the best relative, "the parents could sue. With life jackets, they're safe."

"But what if they fall in with no jacket?" Tommy sleepwalked. Three or four times we found him at night rattling the fence.

The best relative shrugged. The old lady controlled all.

The first time I saw Ruth outside the fence, I knew she could save us. A heavy middle-age woman wearing a T-shirt, the hair chop short. She looks like a hundred mothers, back home in the Philippines. She came Sunday morning when we were alone there. The ones who made the flyer locked us in when they left for church; Ruth rattled the gate and said she had heard about us here. Now I know Ruth goes to that place every month. She knows about their flyer. That day, she told us she had jobs, good jobs, one weekends, in a mansion taking care two children and the other an old lady.

"We can do that." I told Cheska to bring the pineapple-and-coconut-milk tea drink. "We are looking for a place to live." I went fast because church would be over soon.

The tall glass would not fit underneath the fence so Lucy held it, and Ruth leaned close to drink through a straw. She closed her eyes. "I have room," she said.

I wanted to leave. I could climb the fence and the sisters too, but not Tatay. A sprinkle of water hit my back. I remembered then, the retardeds. We cannot leave! But if we put them in their rooms, I thought, with the windows open on the top, they will not suffocate. Less than one hour. We will give water.

"One load in the wash, one in the dryer," Lucy said.

We will leave the wet, I said. I was hauling their huge suitcase when I saw the brown car slide in. It felt I am shot. I dragged my body, a bag of sand.

The ones who made the flyer unlocked the gate.

"So I have given a job to your friends," Ruth said. "Weekends."

"And Ruth has been so nice." I looked down. "She has a place in LA we can rent."

"But here you don't have to pay," the old lady said.

"It is okay," Lucy said. "We do not like to be charity case, like that."

The old lady made a sound that is her laugh. "Can pay us, then."

"Well, we better get going," Ruth said. "The bus comes at noon."

I picked up their suitcase and nodded to Cheska. Poor Cheska, she was very confused. The *tatay* was saying, in Cebuano, his wet clothes over there, and Lucy said, "It is okay." We were almost out the gate; Cheska turned and said, "Thank you, goodbye."

Then there was a noise. Like an animal, big, but human. It was Tommy running at me, I heard all at once he is shouting "No!" and the word stretched oval. That was his face, what he means. I cannot go and leave him. He spread over his side of the fence, still bellowing as we walk away. We follow Ruth and I heard a splash. Tommy ran and jumped in the pool, wetting the ones who made the flyer and the olds. On the other side of the fence, Sri Lankans stood clapping.

Right away, the first night, Ruth asked, Baby or elderly?

"Wherever I am needed," I said.

"You wait," she told me. "We will find for you a full-time."

Lucy hugged Ruth. She told me she expected her to smell like sugar, like her mother. But Ruth, she really has no smell.

Claire

THE COUPLES' DATE

Paul and I hadn't eaten together on a weeknight for more than a year.

"Wanna go out?" he asked on the phone. Usually he left in the morning and came back after it was all done. But apparently Jeff Grant had asked if we were free.

"I told Mooney my grandparents were in town," Paul said. "But it's probably okay, don't you think? I only asked to get out early once before."

The once before his grandparents really *were* in town. Paul never did this for us—Little Him and me—which was how I thought of myself now. As an "us." But I liked the idea of the other couple.

I picked clothes in a flurry while Lola fought Will into the bath. "*You* to do it!" he screamed, reaching for me as I tried to blast the blow-dryer onto my bad hair, all three of us in the room, William naked, me shirtless, and Lola dressed. I'd hardly spent any time with him today. I'd driven for an hour to the Colburn School to talk about teaching, and then it was him or a shower. I gave up on blow-drying and stepped into his bath. Lola understood my problems. She did our laundry, but I buried the ruined underwear, in garbage cans in the alley. When I stepped out, she handed me a new package of briefs. "From Chinatown. All cotton. Ten pieces for twenty dollar."

On our front step, William reached from her arms, screaming as I tripped in my heels, which sank, muddying in the sprinkled lawn, fog winding around my bare legs. You need tights here at night, I guess. And you have to stay on pavement. I walked into the loud, warm restaurant in a jacket with wet hair. My hand went to my head. Did I look okay? That was a question I'd been asking myself for at least a decade. The one thing more intimidating than growing up average with a beautiful mother is growing up average with a beautiful mother in LA.

Piped-in music made a score for my movements. Elton John. I liked it but it was loud. I wouldn't feel lonely tonight, I thought, sliding into the booth, but I was disappointing Will.

Jeff signaled the waiter to get me a drink. He was good at drinks.

"How's the mothers' group?" As a child, I'd been taught to remember something a person said and bring it up the next time.

"Oh, I've got to do that. But we're looking for a nanny. How'd you find Lola?"

"She did it," Paul said. "She saw her and hired her."

"At a bus stop," I said, crossing my arms.

"Wow," Helen said. "Lucky."

Then Paul asked Jeff a question about the new head of comedy at Disney and they were off. I was left with her. We sat quiet a minute—two women with hands folded on the table.

"It's weird isn't it, having this substitute for you every day?" I said. "I'm not even gay and William has two mommies."

"Wait a minute," Paul said, turning, "you're *not* gay?"

"Well, I would be if it weren't for . . ."

"Oh, come on, Claire, we could do it," Helen said.

Both men looked at us. I felt flattered.

"We should hire *male* nannies," I said. "See how they'd like being duplicated."

"Oh, these little boys would love—"

Suddenly, Jeff turned. "Before we do that, you'll stay home and take care of him."

"Yes, yes," she shushed. Their deal was tight. "We're just joking."

I looked at Paul. We'd talk about this later. But what was our deal? I wouldn't have signed the one we lived by, which was that I worried about everything. But I supposed you couldn't make someone worry fifty-fifty.

"What're you working at?" Paul asked Helen. She worked! To say I was surprised was an understatement: looking the way she looked was a full-time job.

"She wants to write," her husband said. "And she's talented."

"What're you writing?"

"Poems, mostly. There's a contest. A poet I really love is judging this year. Sharon Olds."

So many women here said they were artists. A surgeon didn't have to contend with other mothers at dinner saying that they were actually surgeons too.

I was out of practice. Paul asked Jeff how he'd come out here. The waiter came to take our orders.

"Guess I called back some Hollywood guy who'd left a message," Jeff said. "I think her getting pregnant did it. My dad was a pharmacist who'd always wanted to be a chemist. 'A real scientist,' he used to say. But he never went back to school because he had the two kids and the house and the wife and . . ." His hand finished the sentence.

"The life," I said.

"Yeah. Exactly. The life." He nodded. "A quiet guy. Bald by the time he was thirty. My mom gave the color."

"A beauty," Helen said.

"She says that 'cause they look alike," Jeff told us.

"You know, in *The Dayton Widow,* I thought Aleph Sargent reminded me of you," Paul said. "Is that why you had her dye her hair?"

"Does your father still have his pharmacy?" I asked.

"He killed himself when I was sixteen. A bad investment."

"Oh, I'm sorry." Paul's head turned down. What could you say?

"Jeff was the last person to talk to him," Helen said. "That's what his next movie's about. A comedy."

"Well, that's backstory. My father killed himself in April, and we were supposed to go on a safari that August. A nonrefundable safari. So my mother decides, here's where the comedy comes in, we're going anyway. And because we had an extra ticket now, she invites my aunt Bette, who's an agent at the county airport but who's never left the state of Ohio. She weighs a hundred and ninety pounds."

"You're kidding," Paul said. "This is really your movie? Does your mother know?"

"She'll be okay with it."

"His success matters more to her than privacy," Helen said.

"That wouldn't be true of your mother," I said to Paul.

"My mother's *completely* open to hagiography," he said.

"I wonder what they'll think of us, when they're grown up," I said. "Sometimes I wish I could be a different mother."

Helen shook her head. "But no one would trade their mother. Think. Would you?"

I didn't answer. I would have, of course I would have, but not for me, for her. We'd once driven to a place far from everything I knew. The vast grounds bordered in lilac; inside, the polished halls seemed peaceful and forbidding. Nuns put my mother in a wheelchair, fitted a blanket on her lap. She seemed different, grateful for her release. From responsibility for me? From walking? From all of it, I thought. "You'll miss me at first. But then," she'd said, looking up at the high windows, "you'll get used to it."

"I will not," I blubbered.

"You'll go to school still, you'll live with Gramma."

I could see relief seep into her. When the nun pushed the two horns at the back of her chair, she clasped the metal armrests and closed her eyes.

My mother's best friend, Julie, whom all of a sudden I didn't know that well, tried to hold my hand. That failing, she got me by the wrist.

"Aleph says she'll do Aunt Bette, but she has to gain fifty pounds and she's balking on that. We're negotiating. She'll put on twenty. I'm toying with the idea that she ends up staying in Africa, and when the guy goes back, grown up, with his kid, she's still there. Incorporated in a tribe. I want the kid to be blind or deaf or something."

"This is a comedy?" Paul said.

"Autistic. We were thinking autistic," Helen said.

"Seriously, I think it could be funny. Do you see it?" Was Jeff Grant asking Paul to work with him? I wanted to make Paul sit up straight. I kicked him under the table.

He looked at me with alarm. "I can see it."

"Oh, and if you get off the Jeep? On the Serengeti Plain, the animals'll eat you. So there's a suspense element."

The waiter refilled our glasses. When Helen excused herself to the ladies' room, I followed. "We have real love," she said, at the sinks, "a passion."

Maybe you do, I thought, but I couldn't imagine *him* saying that. "That's good," I mumbled, rinsing my hands.

"Great dress," Paul said to her when we returned.

If I'd brought it home, he'd have checked the price. And should he be commenting on the other wife's *dress*? But we hadn't been out for a long time. I was out of practice.

"Target," Helen said, with a smile of accomplishment.

The shoes, the bag—*they* weren't from Target. She didn't *shop* at Target. She shopped at Barneys and dipped into Target for an offbeat trophy.

Helen appreciated Paul's attention, but she wouldn't have traded.

I might, I thought. Then I reminded myself to be grateful.

She started talking about pregnancy. She said she'd religiously practiced Kegels. "Lot of good they did me." Most of what she talked about meant sex. She had an easy laugh.

I said that I'd thrown up. She said she tried to eat only sheer proteins and fruit. She didn't really worry about the baby. They were on the same side, the baby and her. The Keeping Him side, I thought. The conversation was breaking down, as couples' conversations did. I wanted to be in the other one.

Pregnant, I'd felt like a child bundled in a stiff coat, sitting in the backseat of a car being driven somewhere, wheels underneath spinning, the world outside reeling by, the sky so big, and me just along.

"Even though we did this thing together, all of a sudden I was the one changed."

"I hated that! What about fifty-fifty!" This was a conversation I could manage. I went days without talking to an English-speaking adult. Now I wished I'd ordered the salad the waiter was placing before Helen.

"My feet got fat. I had to buy all new shoes," she said.

"My grandmother owned a bakery," I said, "and she was heavy, so she concentrated her beauty efforts on her feet. She had crocodile pumps, velvets, satins. But she had tiny feet. Size five. We had to throw those out when she died, each shoe in its own felt bag. Lola found out after and said, *But I have small feet also!* She lifted her foot up. She still thinks about those shoes." I told that story to wrench us all back into one conversation. I thought I could do the Filipina accent. I heard Lola's voice all day long.

"I wanted a 1964 birth," Helen said, "including the trip to the beauty shop. But this one insisted on watching."

It had never occurred to me that Paul shouldn't see.

"And hers was a doozy," Jeff said.

"I expected to be a natural at it," she said. "Well, I wasn't." She'd probably been a girl whose ideas about growing up concerned dresses, a girl who loved pink. But birth was ugly: blood, shit, and noises. "I wasn't good at it."

"Good at it?" I interjected. "Just doing it was enough for me." Pain smeared everywhere, brown handprints on the walls. Not for one minute did I doubt that they could get the baby out, if they really tried. This was a hospital in America. In 1991.

"And then when he was born, I looked down at him and thought, Who are you?" She said, "I was waiting for that rush of love. For me that didn't come till later."

"She woke up and asked, *Did I have an episiotomy?*" Jeff said.

We laughed. Just then the waiter brought our dinners, setting down warm plates. Couples discussed birth, I thought, watching Jeff tear into his trout, as if it weren't our bodies. Paul waited, politely, as his mother had taught him to, until the hostess took her first bite. But who was the hostess in a restaurant?

The time just after William's birth, I was a scarecrow, stitched together. I knew my body was broken. I turned to the window and understood landscapes. They were seen from the dead. I recognized the world without me, still beautiful, more. I understood resignation that day and wanted to make some structure of pain, natural but fantastic, like the palaces of bees. "He's a redhead," someone remarked in the distance, in what sounded like an office party ending. Little Squib. I thought, He's funny looking, red and chinless, not cute, his hair pilly. But I loved him, oh, I loved him.

"How was it for you?" Jeff reached an arm across the table and touched my elbow, that small tunnel between bones. "How is it being a mother and one of the real composers of our generation?"

"Most of the time I don't feel like either." I shrugged. "My office here is hot. I fall asleep."

"Do you have any concerts coming up? We want to go."

I mumbled that I had something in Detroit next year.

"She has a symphony in New York the year after," Paul said.

"You ever think of film scoring?" Jeff asked.

"She's got her hands full."

"I'd do it. Sure. It was good enough for Aaron Copland. And I'm one of the people who likes *Koyaanisqatsi*." I shrugged. "No one's asked."

We'd come in four cars, and I stood, waiting for the valet. I used to eat like this all the time, I thought, holding my stomach the way I had pregnant. It felt like my intenstines might fall out. I'd thought, ordering, Why not! This was a rare night. I wanted to feel young. I guess I couldn't do that, anymore. I felt a trickle down my leg, tickling my knee. I tried to tell Paul later. He listened, nodding solemnly.

"Now that we have Lola, you should see that doctor again."

I had. Nerve damage, he'd said. That was it. Done. Gone. Thirty-eight years old. The odd thing about bad news is the humiliation. You feel ashamed to be less. They sent me off with a box of Citrucel, a package of adult diapers, and the rest of my life.

My headlights swung into our drive and I rushed from my car into Will's room. He lay sleeping, hands on his stomach. I watched him, listening to his breath.

He was little. He didn't know yet that I leaked.

Lola

THE AMERICAN SEX KIND OF LOVE

I take Williamo to the post office, seal the envelope, and send my money home. Four hundred fifty this week. A ticker tape of dollars runs now all the time in my head. Last year, I totaled more than twenty thousand—in pesos, three times what Bong Bong earns, and he is executive Hallmark. This year it will be more because my weekend job. Besides what I send, I give myself allowance of five dollars for daily spending. Twenty five go to my private savings, so when I return home there will be some they did not know. Also, I need my account here for shoes or treats for Williamo or if one of the babysitters gets married. When you are working seven days, you need some your own money. And I tell Williamo, Every day, Lola requires her coffee. Is twenty-five thousand ninety dollars enough to support a coffee habit on Montana Avenue? Lola is not a yuppie. I am here to pay tuitions and medicine, in our country that goes ten years.

When we enter the house, the mother of Claire and her friend Tom are there. Tom says, "Two years ago, no one paid more than fifty cents for a cup of coffee! Now they're all spending five dollars a day! That's a five hundred percent increase." The mother of Claire goes every day to the coffee shop. But Tom, he will not attend.

"But-ah, I get the plain. Only one fifty. Plus they give the sugar we use to make the cinnamon toast." I lift a handful of natural-sugar packs from my pocket.

"Coffee costs them cents, Lola! *Cents!*"

Does he think I am spending the money of Claire and Paul? Compared with other parents here my employers they are not rich, but they are still rich to me. You have to pay what it costs where you live to join the club of life. Anyway, my weekend employer makes my coffee for me.

I leave on the counter the receipt for tapioca and the change.

Walking to my weekend house, I hear my heart. Tops of planted grains tick my hands. Sprinklers spray a chain on my wrist. From a long time ago, I remember the strangeness that comes with hope. Love, the way I have known it—it is also dread. I move slower when I see the house. My happiest moments are before. When I first married Bong Bong, I felt afraid he would die. Then, after my children, I worried they would die. I still had long hair, like my daughters now. And every night, Bong Bong worked on my neck. "Time to work on your neck," he said. He made it a project, not a favor from him to me. He likes to turn his gifts invisible. Credit, the way children want, it would embarrass him. I lay down on the hard bed. He held my head on his knees. All those years, he never missed one night. He would start by extracting the sticks that kept up my hair. I felt the tug and loosening.

What my weekend employers want that they do not have is me. I try to keep this light in the air. When I sit on the floor playing with Bing, Helen brings me a pale green mug, steaming, the taste of something sweet and burnt.

"Drink it now, Lola. Tonight, when Jeff gets home, we're taking you out."

The doorbell rings. Estelle, the mother of Helen, arrives to babysit. Why?

"But I am the babysitter," I say. "I will be the one to stay home."

"We want to take you."

"Three is a crowd," I say.

Helen tries to push me into the front, but I climb next to the car seat.

The restaurant it is all couples. Small candles on the tables and no children; I am not comfortable wearing my secondhand T-shirt that says HARD ROCK CAFE. Here, I never attend restaurants in the night. It is all going very slow.

I am looking around that no one will see us.

"Her sea bass is very good," Helen says. "And people say she does a great steak."

Employers and employees do not sit together at restaurants. I never once took my helper out to eat. She would have been embarrassed in a Manila restaurant. With the other babysitters I am the one to talk. But here, it moves too slow.

"How are your children?" Helen asks, while Jeff finally orders his food.

I say all I want is soup. I am sounding like Vicky, but he tells me he is going to order me a steak, because I never get meat at their house.

"Fine," I say. "My kids they are good."

They tell me stories about Vicky. It is true, Vicky is not a good babysitter. I would never hire her for my kids. Maybe at this one thing, I am best.

"She still doesn't talk to us," Helen says. "I don't think she ever really liked us."

"At the playclub Vicky is *dal-dal.*" Actually, she is tomboy, what here they call lesbian. She likes the mother of Bing. It is the dad she complains. "No, Vicky likes you," I say.

At last, our food arrives and I keep my hands on my lap. The steak it is many pounds. Enough for the whole family of Lola.

Then we eat, quiet. The guy, he is serious, deboning his fish. He finally puts down his knife. "Lola," he says. "We're going to fire Vicky."

This is so fast, skidding, too soon something will be over. "But-ah, Vicky is nice" is all I can think to say. I have heard about proposals like this: professional parents go to the park to find a nanny and offer her double her salary. Maybe it is true for love also, what you see in the movies. I never believed those things before because they did not happen to me. My grandmother once saw the Virgin. The Virgin sat down, moving her robe to smooth it out, when my grandmother took her lunch at the school. The robe was blue cotton, not velvet, a brighter blue than she had always pictured it, my grandmother said.

I tell my daughters, *Do not trust roses; they will stink one week in the jar.* Maybe I have been wrong!

But Vicky was good for me, I never minded Vicky. They like me better and that will never change. With someone new, who knows?

"Helen tells me they're paying you fifty-five dollars." He pauses, napkining his mouth.

They do not know my raise. I am now sixty-two fifty.

"I just signed contracts for two projects. We could start you at one hundred."

One hundred dollars a day! Like Lita. Maybe the things I heard before—even the man in the Castle marrying the baby nurse—maybe they all come true. It feels like The End. Darkness eats in from the edges. I think of the carmelly coffee, fine silt at the bottom.

"But I will have to think," I say.

They look at each other. It seems they were expecting me to jump.

"Tell us, Lola, if there's anything we can do. Because we really want to have you."

He leans over. "Would a hundred and ten make a difference?"

I say no to dessert. Outside the restaurant the sky is dark blue. They tell me I can take the night off.

"You could catch a movie." He looks at his watch. "It's only eight-thirty."

Helen touches my wrist. "Either way, still friends?"

I am carrying a small heavy bag—my steak. "More than friends. You are my weekend employers."

They laugh. For them that is a joke. For me it is not funny. If I say no, what if the person they get wants seven days? One hundred ten dollars a day! The last few minutes in the restaurant, they upped me fifty a week! More than my year raise from Claire and him. After six months, Claire raised me five dollars a day and again when he turned two, seven-fifty. I walk around the dark neighborhood, past houses where I know children, entering a room of jasmine and a smell of pepper. After one more year, Williamo he will start in the school.

I always work for free the day of his birthday and the one before. For their wedding anniversary, I give a weekend. I throw in the Friday night. And they celebrate the anniversary of my coming by raising me. So when Williamo turned two, that is when I became sixty-two fifty. Some of my friends get more, but their employers, they are rich. Also, if Claire asks me to work late, she will pay extra. Many here pay one price for live-in. No matter what you have to do. I always say to them, "As long as I am needed."

But $110 every day! Five days or seven. Up to me. That is $770 a week instead of $482.50. Per year, an extra $14,950. My God. I think I have to take that. Plus in that house, I will have my coffee made every day. That is $416 saved. Helen is young. They will want more kids. Maybe two more. This is a good job for a long time.

I walk all the way to the ocean to say good morning to the Philippines.

I live Sunday in this life. There is a light wind, teasing. The sky you can see through to ships far away at sea. We sit in Starbucks, Bing asleep in his stroller, and I write my letter home. *This one a toddler, very easy. I do not have to clean. My career in America it is up.* For the first time, I keep my numbers private. They will guess a raise, but not this big.

I need another international stamp. Tomorrow morning I will walk Williamo to the post office. Those machines take pennies. I will have to find things to stack so he can reach the slot. On the stamps are pictures. I know from Bong Bong, that is the job of someone to draw. But a needle starts in my heel; sand scratches my mouth, opening a bad taste. I pray for a hint. I never asked for too much, from Bong Bong, from the teachers of my children, even from God. If you ask for only a little, maybe then the answer it will be yes.

As I come into the weekday house, Claire shouts, "Lola, we're in here." Her arms cross. Williamo looks the way he looks when he gets bad, his face the shape of a box. This is my sign. My heart slopes.

"Do not worry," I whisper. "Your Lola will not leave you."

Monday morning at six, I hand my weekend employer his newspaper. "I cannot leave Williamo yet. Maybe I will be the one to raise your next baby."

"Oh, okay," he says, scratching the back of his head.

"Williamo is almost the age he will no longer need. One or two years more only. I will bring to you Inday to fill in until I come."

"Okay, great, anybody you know, I'm sure Helen'd be glad to meet."

Helen stands here now, too, holding a sweater over her nightie. "But you'll still come weekends?"

"As long as I am needed."

Forty-seven dollars and fifty cents poorer, I want coffee. I fix Williamo his breakfast and take him to church. He is now old enough, I will teach him to pray. Pain shoots up my knees the shape of star fruit; this is a feeling I have known all my life, lowering myself in a high place. I understood after I married Bong Bong I would never have a love affair. This is the closest I came and see, I did not. I never wish for a different husband. In America, people make second marriages. Many women on our street, they are second wives. For me, a second marriage would be, I had a broken life. It is not that I think Bong Bong is the only guy in the world I could get along with. But he is the one, we had our children. Does that mean a Catholic can make herself happy with anyone? A good Catholic would say yes. An American would ask, But what about chemistry?

"Williamo, you light a candle." I count out fifty pennies for him to put in the offertory.

He knows to whisper in the church. "Can I make a wish?"

"It is not that kind of candle. Watch." I hold my letter to the flame and burn my written present home. A wafer of ash floats up and then lands, the last of it.

"I want to blow it out."

"Here you ask your prayer and let the candle burn." You already have your wish. I almost left. No more Lola. Now I can never tell Bong Bong. They will not understand. They would say, *Take the hundred ten dollars.* I have cried already from this house too many times Wolf.

"What is *Pax Deus?*"

"You read that?" Not yet three years old. Another sign.

There is no longer a letter, but I bring Williamo to the post office. We stay for a long time choosing stamps. In the bottom of the stroller I keep our rolled pennies. I am in the mood to spend. We go to the Discovery Store and pay the whole rest to get the globe. The counting takes us almost twenty minutes.

Every Monday, some babysitters meet at the Brentwood Country Mart. Today I play a trick. "I am getting coffee. Does anyone want?"

"Mmm, yes, please, a latte. Large." Lita looks down. Esperanza says, "*Sí,* cappuccino, *gracias.*" Mai-ling asks for a tea. But Vicky says she has already eaten, like I knew she would. Every week Vicky drinks only water from the fountain and says she has already eaten. Well, if you know you will meet friends, why you eat before? Vicky sends only to her mother. I have five kids. But Bong Bong understands, I have to live too where I am.

But the joke is on Vicky. When Lita hands to me her dollars, Mai-ling her coins, and Esperanza stands to pull a bill out of her tight jeans pocket, I say, "No, our treat. Come, Williamo. We will count the pennies." The price of coffee, it is a tax. The restaurants here, they cost too much, and the dress shops, but we can still afford coffee or a fries. Some-a-day at the end, when my kids work in offices with their diplomas and I sit in my house, with my cabinet full of glass, I will talk about my life in Hollywood, and the locations for my stories they will be Starbucks, McDonalds, and the Brentwood Country Mart, where we talked, holding children on our laps. I can say I drank the hot hot coffee I liked every day and never once spilled on my boy. You need to have every day in your life a small treat.

"They want us," Lita whispers, "because they are having problems their kids."

American children are different because their parents work far away at things they cannot understand. We were always working too. But even children understand money.

"You can never hit them," Mai-ling says. "If you hit them, they will call police!"

"Our kids, they are good." But I am not sure we can make these kids the same. Williamo sits, stacking pennies, attracted to everything he should not hear. "The boy of my brother was giving them trouble. So they hang him in a jute bag from a banyan tree and when it become night, they cut him down. They are not having problem with him anymore."

"What is jute?" Williamo asks.

"It is what they wrap on roots of plants. What you here call burlap."

I write down for Esperanza six words and Williamo draws the pictures. Every week we trade: six napkins English for six napkins Spanish. *La Mariposa.* She marks a butterfly. *La Estrella. La Flor.* Words of the day. We chant for the kids too, but after a few words they run. I learned English in grade 1, but my real voice it is Tagalog. Here, people shout at me in Spanish, louder each time I do not answer. I have memorized sentences, present tense and also simple past. I have learned by heart two poems. But while I work to learn Spanish, my English grows tall without anything. I tell Esperanza, I will make her honorary Filipina. Now we hear the faint music of the ice-cream truck and follow the kids, searching our pockets for dimes. They bend into the cool cavern coming up with cones and Popsicles, bunnies and ducks in colors that stain the face.

Then while we dab their mouths with flimsy napkins, all of a sudden Mai-ling says, *Where is China?* Mai-ling chases the truck parked down the street still singing. There in back in a small room we find China, her pants down, a Drumstick in each fist. We push the man away. Lita yanks up the pants. I take away both ice creams, throw them on the dirty floor, the others yell in three languages. When we get out, he drives off, no music, as fast as an ordinary car.

"What happened?" Williamo asks.

"Nothing happened." But we have to be more careful. With my own it was different. I made them, I thought, I can risk their life. But these they are not ours. We cannot break them.

"If anything happen to her," Mai-ling says, "I will sit in the electric chair."

"What happened?" Williamo says again.

"Nothing happened," I repeat. "But do not mention to your mother."

I think of the money I gave up. Now I am left with my old life and the afternoon slows. At the Castle, Williamo climbs on boards, his arms out the sides for balance. "Come down," I yell, but he keeps stepping the high plank I told him not to and he falls, so I am kneeling on the grass, hands against his, half dance, half fight. He wants to go back up and I say no. "You are not listening me."

Then he hits. He has hit before but never Lola. When he hit Bing and Bing cried, I said, *Really, you are going to be fine.* But now warm tears run paths down my face. Never once did a child of mine hit me. They hit each other, maybe, but only around corners, where I could not see. Of course it is different here; with nannies, one per customer, there are no corners. But he should not hit me. He should never hit me.

Just then they come, Jeff and Helen. My heart drags; I feel its short route, up-down. The curls of my employer fall on his collar, folded like an envelope. Her stare pastes us in a book—just as we are, Williamo in his old clothes, dirt on the top lip. I hope they did not see him hit me.

Helen looks at me with a question. I put my arms around Williamo.

"I want to talk to the woman you know," she says.

I need something, so we go for a second coffee, and I use pennies.

"*Lo siento,*" I tell Williamo, "means you are sorry. *Ikinalulungkot ko.*"

"They really hanged him from a tree?"

"Scuze, you the nanny?" a stranger says. "*Estás la doméstica?*"

"In a sack?"

"That's one beautiful boy."

"Williamo, what do you say? The lady said you are handsome."

"Doo-doo head."

"Mischievous, huh? I like that." What does she want with us? "Anyway, his mug could be worth money. I'm a talent representative, and if you think his parents would be interested, I'll give you my card."

"You are a Hollywood agent?"

"I handle kids. Through teens."

"You want to make Williamo movie star?"

She laughs, silver, between a fish and a robot. Her earrings, silver also, tinkle. "Everyone asks that. I can't promise the big screen. That's one out of a thousand, don't you know? But we place a lot of commercials and print. What do the parents do?"

Even though I am proud of the profession of my employer, I do not say. This lady, it is hard to tell if she is good. "I will give to them your card."

When we walk in, I see Claire at her old stove. While Claire examines the card, we tell the story. "We were discovered by a Hollywood agent! So, Tom he will have to change his opinion about coffee shops. Because of Starbuck, you will now become rich."

"Hey, you two, I've got some change." She puts pennies, nickels, and a quarter on the table.

Williamo begins to tell how we are spending. I interrupt. "Go get the globe." I would rather not dwell on candy.

"When I was little," Claire says, "I saved pennies to buy pagan babies."

"Maybe we were your pagans."

"You're Catholic, Lole. That's the opposite of pagan." The phone rings. "Esperanza," Claire whispers. "More love trouble probably."

I am the one they call for romance advice! And I do not even believe in it. My weekend employer, Jeff, he told me, the ones who make the dreams cannot live in them. *We know, Lola, just how flimsy dreams are.*

But Esperanza she is sobbing. "He will spend his birthday with his ex-wife." She is sorry, though, what she said to him. She did not mean it. She will deliver to him roses from the garden of Beth Martin and she wants me to compose the note, in English.

"Go ahead," I dictate. "Spend the birthday with her. Just save the rest of your life for me." I should be on the payroll of Hallmark too. Bong Bong, he has drawn over one hundred holiday cards. The *Christmas in the Philippines* series.

"All better?" Claire asks when I hang up.

"Never all better. Not until you are old like me. My son is the only one my children who gave me problems for romance and that is because I spoiled him. He wanted to study philosophy. For what you will do that? I asked. Then, taking his courses, he would tell his sisters the philosophies of love; I cannot remember them all anymore, the friendship kind, all different kinds. I told him, You do not need to pay a class. You see any American movie to learn that.

"He said, Mom, whether you know it or not, there are bigger kinds of love.

"Maybe so, I said, but forget those. They are only for the top one or two percent. And you are not good-looking enough. You have inherited my nose. For a while, he was spending for nothing—bowling parties, ballroom dancing. I told him, This better be courtship, because you are allowed only once. But he married an Ilocano, very good cook, and he is now working computers."

"What's your son's name?" Claire asks.

"Dante," Williamo says, from under the table.

I want to tell Claire my offer. Just so she will see me as a one-hundred-ten-dollar-a-day nanny. But instead I say, "Jeff bought Helen a new car. Station wagon Volvo. Silver. So you should be hinting to your husband."

She laughs. "You know I'm the one who does the money here."

That is true. Every week, she counts out my cash. "You are the family CEO."

Then the doorbell rings. It is Lil, the one Claire calls long-distance, visiting from far away. I take my plate to eat while I bath Williamo. After I tuck him, I return to the kitchen. Will the noises of cleaning bother their talk? But I want to be done, so I start the pans from the stove. I sweep around their feet. The friend Lil, she is beautiful but wearing a strange skirt and ugly sandals.

"I know, I know," my employer says. "I've got it on my list."

Maybe it is something she wants me to do. I see her list on yellow lined paper on the counter. Number 1 says, TONIGHT! PAUL!

"What I can't figure out is the dread."

They talk while I am wiping down the counters.

"There's that radio song, *All you gotta do is say yes.*"

" 'Yes I said yes I said yes.' " Claire's hands keep busy with invisible things, over the now clean table.

My hands, they are busy with the sponge.

"Remember John Adams? I probably should have slept with him."

It takes me a moment to really know what they are talking. But my employer, she is not this kind of person. She is showing off, maybe, for her friend.

"Well, you could've. He was raring to go."

"I was too worried about my career. Joke's on me. I didn't get so far anyway." She makes a bad laugh.

"Who knows? It might have helped."

"Might have helped *me* anyway. With my life."

They remember I am here and they forget. It is the way they would be in front of a pet. But her marriage, it is only average, for five years. Wood anniversary, in our country, that is practically newlywed. I am past silver. Almost pearl. *You have a good life,* I want to say. *Do not complain. God will hear.* If someone listened to our marriage, would it sound like this? Bong Bong still sends me a card every week.

"Paul's cute enough," Lil says.

"Oh, much better looking than I deserve. But I hug the pillow, and say *Night.*"

I empty the dustpan, seal the bag, and walk out to the alley. When I return, the house is dark. I will just check the stove and the locks. But Claire sits in the dark.

"You think your weekend employer is more in love?"

Why is she saying to me? Because I told her the new car? Claire, she is not one for romance. *I never wanted to be a romantic heroine,* she said once, *'cept for a few years in my twenties. Mistake. Silliness, waste.*

"You are not so different," I say. "They have a younger love."

"A stronger love, maybe."

"Younger loves are stronger. That is always the way."

"I wish we were more in love."

"For what?" I say. "You are fine." I start the dishwasher.

"Paul deserves it."

This I really do not know. "But he is not here. What good would it do?" His career really it should come to more, for all the time he works.

She holds a ripening tomato.

"Very few people get a big love. Maybe one in four hundred. Six hundred even. And even fewer than that like what they have to do every day." I am giving her a gift she can recognize: what she already owns. I was lucky. Virgin when I married Bong Bong, maybe two in a thousand bodies fit. *When they left the Garden of Eden,* my grandmother said, *God changed men and women, only a small bit.* Because it is really that, a trickle of water making its way down dry soil, involuntary, a digging that is right. So many times I was in the kitchen, thinking, No I do not want tonight, I am so tired, and then when we are in our bed together a restlessness began. The sole of my foot moved on his leg.

Now when I think of my husband, I see him carrying boxes. So many times he has packed for our daughters, wrapping every treasure in newspaper, waiting in line to send. Unwinding what I ship from here. So much care for our cherishables. He understands the importance of the things you cannot take with you. What you keep—the smoke of love—that trades in mementos, the way value trades in coin.

I hear keys dropping. Paul. I put a dinner for him in the micro.

"So you will call the Hollywood agent?"

But my employers decided not to become rich. "You don't drive freeways, Lole, it would take hours to get to Burbank on surface roads. I can't drive him all over LA for auditions or shoots or whatever they do."

"We have two careers," Paul says.

That is true, but maybe the career of Williamo it would be higher.

I use the calculator to add up the money. If I stay until Williamo is eight, it will have cost more than seventy thousand. That is counting a five-dollar raise once a year.

So Lola is romantic after all. I am the one who gave up the big bucks for love. But not the American sex kind of love.

Claire

THESE ARE THE JOKES
SO YOU BETTER START LAUGHING

I saw Paul one more weeknight that year.

A Thursday late in October he walked across our lawn while it was still light, *Surprise!* in his manner. I'd settled into my chair, reading, Gorecki's sad chants on the boom box. Lola had taken Will and the house had finally fallen quiet. When the door slammed, my eyes raced through the paragraph before I tented the book down. Paul entered with an air of faint disappointment, looking around the room.

"Would you like a drink?" I asked. Since when had Paul become a guest?

"Maybe I'll go pick him up," he said, eyeing the door.

But this was Will's first playdate with China Howard since he'd pushed her onto the gravel and she'd had to get three stitches. "They just went over at four-thirty. Lola planned this with China's nanny; she seemed to think it was important."

"Well, I think his father trumps China Howard."

He wouldn't have said that if Will had decked Bing Grant, I thought. But China Howard's parents owned a sporting-goods chain in the Valley.

"You didn't call me back." I shrugged. "I could've told you."

"Claire, I sit around a table in a room with eleven guys. What can I say? Their wives don't call as much." His hand was on the doorknob.

I turned back to my book.

"Well, I'm going to go get him." The door slammed.

Paul would gladly take Will to McDonald's. But I pushed myself up to get dinner. I'd had a good day. I'd written three measures and then I'd had a weird, opening moment with Lola. She'd been standing, putting Paul's clean underwear and socks in their drawers, when I walked in. She gave me a plastic bag.

"Claire, it is half off at Sav-On! Vons, it is too expensive!"

I'd never said anything to her, but she'd bought me two packages of diapers.

"Thank you." I crossed the room then, walking through a trapezoid of sun. It was an ordinary afternoon in the house, but warmer, my problems smoothed by a nurse's hand of routine. I went back and wrote eighteen measures.

I stood picking the last of our tomatoes when Paul's car yanked up the drive. "Not there," he shouted. "They left already!" He looked at me as if I'd done a terrible job. Of what? Keeping his son available to surprise during this rare and dwindling hour?

"They'll be back soon." Standing in an aisle of tomatoes, I felt rich in perishables, and shy. Almost November, and late heirlooms hung on the vines, giving off the smell of abandoned lots I'd passed, walking to school with my instrument. Tomatoes grow anywhere, like sun, the outside face of God in the world, given free. I'd planted four varieties, and the vines had outgrown Will in a little more than a month. Why didn't Paul come see? I picked off a yellow leaf, breaking the unmistakable scent into the air.

"I'm going to try and meet them. You don't have to make dinner. We'll go somewhere. Or get takeout. He's not the prince of England here," Paul said, climbing into the car. "And Yo-Yo Ma isn't Martha Stewart."

I did think dinner every night mattered. I doubted that Yo-Yo Ma subsisted on takeout. Paul worked twice as many hours as I did, yet I still believed I had a vein of talent. But wasn't *this* important too? I didn't know how to extricate care from time. Just then Lola came around the corner pushing the stroller.

Paul knelt down and opened his arms.

"Abba!" Came the scream, followed by pell-melling legs and a heavy leap.

Then they were up and twirling.

Will and I made quieter reunions. He sometimes sidled over and hung on to my leg. I went inside with fennel to chop for the salad.

We'd been hungry sometimes when I was growing up. It happened when my mother bought a dress. She was in the first generation of divorcées forced to work; she hoped to reverse her fate and fall back into the census norm. Clothes struck her as a necessary expense. Looked at from the vantage of failure, they seem a flimsy vanity. But if her plan had worked, it might be remembered as a middle-aged woman's pluck. "Clothes are an investment in *yourself*," she'd said. Her friend Julie took the opposite view and put her teacher's retirement money in Michigan lakefront property. I measured lemon juice and olive oil for dressing. I tried our soup; the squash had a deep aftertaste. I took pumpkin seeds from the oven to sprinkle on top, tossed the pasta with tomatoes, basil, and a little hidden mint. "Paul, Will, dinner!"

But they didn't come. The barley bread I'd just pulled out of the oven wouldn't be anything in ten minutes, but only Lola stood holding her plate. This was good food. I wanted them to eat. Paul would have been just as happy with a Happy Meal. Will would have been happier. *You don't have to make dinner.* But if I didn't, who would? And if nobody did, what kind of life would we have?

These were the riddles: if Paul was right, I was ridiculous.

Will skidded in; I spread the napkin on his lap and poured him a glass of milk. I asked as I asked every night, "Won't you sit with us, Lole?"

"I will just eat in my place."

Nights in the writers' room, they ordered takeout from expensive restaurants; the network paid. Paul didn't have to feel grateful for food. Maybe he'd never had to. But what was he *do*ing as our good meal got cold? I found him on the living room floor. He appeared to be clean-ing his briefcase. "We're sitting down," I said. "Come to dinner."

He sighed. "I never have the time to do these things." Then he fol-lowed, pulled out his chair, not a clue that I was displeased. Here he was, before dark, saying, "Great bread." He looked up. "Oh. There're two guys from the show I'd like to ask over to dinner with their wives."

I didn't answer.

"Just one of your pastas, like tonight."

Just. I wondered if any of my friends' husbands thrilled them. I was pretty sure not. Except Jeff. I didn't and did like thinking of him.

. . .

The sky grew dark blue with tiny stars. Paul kept William outside, playing tag. I read again, the chime of voices falling in through the open windows.

"Paul, remember, when he's overtired he can't sleep," I called out, charmlessly.

But, as if in collusion, Will slept instantly when Paul put him down.

"I did that brilliantly, if I may say so." Paul dropped keys on the dresser.

I had my book on the bed. Usually, I slept like a nun, my side so perfect in the morning that Lola didn't touch it.

Paul took off his jeans and crossed the room in his boxers. He looked over his shoulder, in a straight line.

I felt hunted.

He raised his eyebrows.

I looked down. Please no, just not now, I thought. Anything else.

He laughed. " 'S okay, you don't have to." He picked up a magazine, rolled it into a tube, and slapped his hand. He was attractive, a slim animal, with a jaunt to him. What was wrong with me?

I opened the casement window. Our rental house didn't have screens. You could smell the mineral ground and hear a steady trilling from crickets. I'd once asked a teacher what they were and he'd had to explain, you couldn't notate insect sounds or warbles.

"You're the most perceptive person I've ever known," Paul said, laughing that evening in October, flinging himself on our bed. "But we've had sex once in the last six weeks. It's just not enough for me."

"I know," I said, pulling the cover to my chin. "I'll do better. I'll try."

When had this dread started? I thought of them. Helen's open-mouthed laugh. Diamonds resting on indentations. I bet she didn't have dread. But I'd sleep with *him*, I thought, turning over and starting to cry. My lapses no longer surprised Paul.

"Oh, come on," he said, flipping through *Variety*, *Vanity Fair* stashed underneath. One hand reached over to scratch my back.

When William's scream surged at 1:45, Paul put a pillow over his head. My feet met the ground. I'd been constantly vigilant for more than two years. No wonder I didn't have the languor for sex. The damp, pajamaed body on me, I remembered the way Jeff had stared that night at dinner: a direct gaze, full of meaning, but meaning what? Will fell asleep in my arms, his head heavy. I transferred him to his crib, skidded back to bed, and remembered: we were in the middle of life. The outcomes had already been decided. Jeff had picked Helen. And as my manager once said about country music: *It's the kind of thing you like if you like that kind of thing.*

Paul had the covers pulled tightly around him. Tomorrow would be the same. The deprivations in the marriage seemed given, immutable as air. He proved able to live with my regular disappointment. I could, apparently, live with his working whenever the hell he wanted. Therein lay the security, too, the peace I felt in waking: small clanks as Paul fixed his tray of coffee, cereal, and the newspaper, with which he'd trudge to his den where at five he would call the 800 number and check the ratings of last night's shows, making four columns for the lineups on the three networks and Fox. He didn't have his own show yet. That was his hope and mine, too, for him.

When Lola arrived, she collected Paul's clothes from where he'd dropped them and followed his trail of coffee cups. But she left the various envelopes with the lists of ratings. They must have seemed important.

"Just do it," Lil said, long-distance. She made hanky-panky sound silly.

"Do I have to?"

"Yes." She laughed.

"Whatever happened to the froth?"

"That doesn't last anyway."

"But life doesn't last. That doesn't make it skippable." When I was thirteen, babysitting, I opened the mother's closet and looked at her clothes. She was an ordinary woman with a kind face, the wife of a rabbi, but she had gold sandals, the gold worn off in the place of each of her toes, like the paw print of some animal. I knew it had to do with sex. Her husband's body resembled a Bosc pear. Maybe it could last.

Lil had once built a box with sixty-two hooks that showed in a Fifty-seventh Street gallery. She hung keys, by their various chains, in the separate compartments. Behind a jailor's ring was a small photograph. In another nook, a chewed bottle nipple and a phone number scrawled in red lipstick.

Letters to a Young Mother, the piece was called.

The words chimed, to me who never was one.

Now her third child had pooping problems. A ribbon of lightness ran through her, a capacity for renewable hope.

At noon, my doorbell rang. A young guy already balding held an electric oscillating fan and a box. "Delivery from Jeff Grant," he said. "Do you want me to set it up?" It looked old-fashioned but it was brand-new.

The night Paul's episode aired, I wanted to invite people over but we still didn't have friends here. "Jeff and Helen?" I asked.

"I think he'd make me nervous."

I prepared our favorite pasta, linguine with small greenish cockles and Sweet 100 tomatoes, and we ate on trays on the bed. At the last minute, we invited Lola in, and she watched, her plate on her lap, sitting on the corner chair.

By Paul Berend appeared at the end, in the Worklings typeface.

Lola stood. "Paul, congratulations," she said, and left with her plate.

"I think it really did turn out well," Paul said. "Oh, now I wish I'd invited them."

"Call them," I said. "We have champagne." I'd made chocolate bread pudding. I slid in my socks to the kitchen to caramelize the top, but we never opened the champagne, because the phone kept ringing—Paul's mother, his sister, an aunt, and two cousins whom we'd hadn't heard from since the wedding. When Lola left for her walk, I gave her half the pudding to drop off at her other house.

The next day Jeff asked if Paul wanted to work with him. Paul's contract was picked up for two years. Everyone but the showrunner and the guy they called Jack the Genius said something. He wished Jack had. Jack should have. It was so much better than the other ones I'd seen.

"I'm lonely here," I said on the phone.

Paul sighed. "Can you call Lil?" This was how he got off now. We both took it for granted that he didn't have time.

And I couldn't find my way. I gave a cello talk to twenty-six children in the Brentwood living room of Paul's mother's college roommate. The kids sat cross-legged on the floor, eating catered lemon bars off china. A few of them wanted to hold the cello. A child on my lap, my hand over hers on the bow, I missed Will. *Mommy, I love the smell of my feet,* he'd whispered last night. I adjusted the girl's wrist so the bow dragged over two strings.

"Can you play something happy?" I did a riff of Philip Glass, thinking, Cello is not built for happy.

"Something sad?" Villa-Lobos.

"Something happy and sad at the same time?" That was the maid's kid. Beethoven.

Then I stood outside my front door, the arrival I'd craved for hours, but now that I was here, the rush drained. I put my ear to the wood and listened to the playclub, a reliable enchantment, one of the good beads on my daily chain.

"I did not dream of becoming a babysitter."

"What did you want to be, Lola?"

"Oh, a princess. Then the queen. Like every girl."

"I wanna be Batman!"

"No little girl dreams to be the helper. And a princess will need more helpers than the queen. The dresses, they have a longer tail."

I wished my mother could stand outside my life and listen, but she'd wonder, Why aren't you happy? I had what she'd always wanted. A home. A child.

A car lock oinked in the driveway: Helen, to pick up Bing. I rummaged for keys, caught on my porch inside a dream. She wore shorts. The tendon joining her calf to her knee appeared simplified, winglike. My knee, by comparison, had bulges.

"After queen, what did you want to be?"

"Who, me? Oh, Lola was probably born to be a mother."

I opened the door. And here they came! Boys stuck to our fronts, my chin on Will's head, I turned to Helen. "Want a drink?"

I opened wine and we made offhand, vaguely complaining mother-talk. I asked about her poetry, but Bing had taken one of Willie's trucks, my boy grabbed it back, and now Bing ran to his mother. A few other kids gathered around.

Crybaby, I thought. Where was Lola?

Helen knelt, *on their level.* "That's not okay," she said to Will, emphasizing the *k.*

I didn't love that. Bing shouldn't have taken the truck in the first place. But Helen looked taut and risen, scolding. She probably felt she earned authority by the hours spent talking to children, but I didn't buy it—she also scheduled pedicures. She doesn't like Will, I thought for the first time.

Once the boys settled down, she asked where we were applying for preschool.

"Nowhere yet," I said. "Should we be?"

Her face tried to contain alarm. "Well, the deadlines are right after Christmas."

I rushed to get paper. There was so much I didn't know. She told me there was a class I needed to take. "Help," I said.

Then the doorbell rang—another mother.

"I should go too," Helen said. "The group is at my house tomorrow. Come." As she collected Bing's things, she mentioned that she and Jeff had been invited to the White House. "He shot a TV spot for the Democrats." I found William by the door reciting his passage—*Ay there's the rub.*

"That's amazing," the other mother said. "I have to get Brookie to memorize. I see Claire, she's such a great mother, I get inspired."

"Claire, really?" Helen said, in a barely managed tone.

So I went to the playgroup. We arrived a little after eleven, and Will ran into the yard, Lola following, hands in her pockets. The moms sat inside. Two French doors, without screens, opened out, stopped by lavender bushes. A morning of no music, and I wouldn't even be with Will. Still, I felt a little relieved. I didn't really know how to play.

"Want coffee?" From her throney chair, Helen gestured to a pot on a table with Styrofoam cups and an open milk carton, next to a bowl of powdery Goldfish. That was the refreshment. No wonder she looked relaxed. A banner of wind riled the room, making everyone sink farther back in their chairs. "Mine taught Bing Rolls-Royce," Helen said. "How do you explain not to *do* that? You can't. So we're letting her go."

"Esperanza put nail polish on Brookie and Kate," said the mother who'd been impressed with Will reciting. "Bright red. And she's got a boyfriend. With a messy divorce."

Melissa had a reassuring voice. She wasn't as pretty as some of the moms, but she wore beautiful, tailored clothes. Melissa was the one I'd want to be if I'd had a more normal family, which is like saying if I'd had a totally different life. My mother used to say if she'd raised me married, I would have ended up a doctor. Melissa had been an ophthalmologist before she had the kids. Two years ago, she'd fought breast cancer. Her hair had grown back a darker color.

She toyed with this new-grown hair as she spoke. "I like Lettie, but Lettie's depressed. She told Simon he was sad because American parents aren't with their kids enough."

Helen laughed. "Bing came home and said Vicky'd taken him to see cheeses. I said, *Did you buy any?* And he said, *Chesus. You know, Chesus.*" She put her arms out and dropped her head. "I had to sit her down and say, *Vicky, please, I'm Jewish.*"

A tall Indian woman sat with her back extremely straight. "They need to be instructed, where to go and where not to go."

Outside, a tire swing hung from a fort. Will stood at the top, shouting, in with the rest. An accomplishment for us. While I watched, the conversation turned from nannies to Costco. How was I going to ask about the school?

"Shrimp for five ninety-nine a pound, but you have to get the jumbo."

"To buy food for kids' parties anywhere else is *mad*ness," Sue said.

These women owned houses. They drove dentless cars and wore diamonds. I had an old Jeep, but I didn't drive it to Costco. I'm not made for this, I thought.

"I *swear*, Pilates *changed* my body," Beth said.

My body could have used some change. "Weak cervix," Sue was saying, as I got up to find a bathroom. Paul was right. I didn't have to be here. They weren't talking about the kids anyway. Going through the bedroom, I noticed something I'd never seen outside a movie: *a vanity*. Kidney shaped, gray-blue with a transparent chair, it supported a three-sided mirror and an open laptop.

> From: hbgrant@earthlink.net
> To: jgrant@ix.netcom.com
> Subject: fat
> Is it pathetic or ridiculous to be thirty-two years old
> and still hate your ankles?

> From: jgrant@ix.netcom.com
> To: hbgrant@earthlink.net
> Subject: ankles
> I adore your ankles.

I felt socked. Whatever Paul and I had—and we had a lot! we had Will!—it wasn't this. It was never this. Could Paul have found it with someone else? From the shower curtain rod hung five panties, like different-colored strings. Had Lola neatly spaced them?

I really had to go.

I began to say my goodbyes. The women looked at me with faint and justified suspicion, as if I wanted something from them. I did: I wanted the secret of their ease, the way their houses felt. But I couldn't bear the life they had, to pay for it. In back, Willie hung upside down from monkey bars.

"Maybe I'll slip out the front," I said.

"Always say goodbye," the Indian mother ordered, as if I looked sneaky.

"No, Mommy, stay, Mommy, please, Mommy, stay!"

I couldn't. I didn't want to. Story of my life. Helen stepped out to see what was going on. Lola tried to help.

"Williamo. Come to Lola."

I pried him off me from the outside in, the way you'd lift a sticking crust from a board. "We'll have fun tonight. We'll do the glow-in-the-dark thing." I was always promising more later. At bedtime, with a flashlight and our fingers, we made a show on his room wall.

Helen looked away, cheeks hard, superior. "That parenting class starts right after Christmas. If you want, I'll try to get you a place."

"Yes, thank you."

I drove home, ran up to my room two steps at a time, unlatched my scuffed case, and the smell of rosin billowed on my face. There it lay, my old instrument. As fancy as the most elaborate dress. I held it with my knees while I rosined the bow. *Look, Ma, no hands.* I tuned my strings, the old known hope and bellow.

Did William need new shoes? I jerked back to the familiar room. I couldn't stay inside the music. I kept bursting up, as if from underwater.

I adore your ankles.

I set my cello down and bent over double, imagining Jeff Grant pushing me against a wall. Holding me between his knees. When had this started? I pressed the button that turned on his fan.

I tried to warm into a melody I'd written, when? Missing only a morning, I had to fight my way back in. Score paper on the desk, I told myself, no more outside things. Only that one workshop at the school for the blind. Composing had to be done alone, but did it have to be *this* alone?

My best friend from conservatory had come over every morning, even in rain or snow, because I fed him. He'd sit at the piano and work out a line while I heated muffins and made coffee. Harv was obsessed with Beethoven; he'd read every biography. He thought he was going deaf and heard humming and buzzing the way Beethoven did when he was finally rich and famous.

" 'Cept I'm not rich or famous," Harv said.

In Beethoven's time in Vienna, he told me, the king was an amateur cellist.

"Yeah, and musicians doubled as servants."

When he came to Vienna Beethoven tried horseback riding and took dancing lessons, but he never learned to dance in time to music. He quit performing, because of deafness, by the time he was forty.

After we ate, we took turns at the piano, trying out sequences. Sometimes, walking on the street with Harv, I'd whistle a phrase. I wondered if I could call him now, but it would be near dinnertime in the East, so I just used Finale to try flutes. Then I switched to oboe.

You should just quit. You'd love it, Sue had said, that mother of China, with the muscular legs. But what had she quit? I think she'd once been a tennis player. They owned sporting-goods stores.

My work was not exactly work. It formed something I'd had since I was a girl, a banister I touched to be calm.

The phone rang. Lola. "We are going to the pier. It is only five dollars, five-fifty. It is okay?"

"Sure." Five dollars was a cheap price for fun.

Lola had five children, and in her country she'd been Helen. A leader. Joker. Head mom. Once president of the Parents Association in Tagaytay, she now called herself the CEO of Filipinas in Santa Monica. I felt glad to give William what I couldn't be. I sharpened a pencil and set back to work. Tired. But from what?

Lola

THE BOOK OF RUTH

I will pick for my weekend employers their new Mary Poppins. They pay me to travel to our Mecca, in Eagle Rock. On the Westside of Los Angeles, where all the employers live, a good babysitter is hard to find, as hard even as a good husband. "I worry about Lola's birthday more than Paul's," I heard Claire say. But at the place of Ruth, in Eagle Rock, many Filipinas live and decent jobs seem scarce. Ruth knows a priest in Altadena who finds placements, but those are not high paying.

I take three buses and still, it is a walk. All for Williamo.

The building stands across from a water-bottling plant with big lights that stay on all night. Ruth bought this place twenty years ago and it has been her luck.

Once, Ruth was a wet nurse. *They were both doctors, modern people, Hong Kong Chinese, but they believed human milk had power. And the mother she had no milk. They made me promise to keep secret.* Then, when that boy turned seven, the mother felt he was too dependent on Ruth. *Too attach.* They gave her forty thousand to go away. Ruth bought this place with that money and now it is worth half a million. *They save me,* she says, of that first family. They found her, with her kids, at a YW shelter. Ruth is large and strong, but she was once like a slave in the house of her husband.

Inside the place of Ruth, it is a teeming pool. Like the string in chemistry, I will dip in to come out carrying the crystal. I think I will take the younger from Iloilo.

My first good bed in America was a low bunk in one of these rooms. A person needs a bed that is hers, even one night a week. Most here work live-in, so they use the beds in shifts. But Ruth gives each girl her own sheets and a dresser, hand-me-downs from an employer.

Ruth was my teacher of here. Before, I had never been the favorite of any teacher; I used to be the favorite of the class. I was the one who made the face that started laughter. But Ruth believed I had a talent for babysitting because of the schools my children attend. Even here, Filipinas know UP and UST. I was the only one Ruth ever asked her employer to find a job. "The others, they are not Beverly Hills," she said, quiet, because that is her way. Dr. Saperstein found for me the lady with the house three layers.

I dive in.

The *tatay* sits near a television, fiddling the remote.

Through the doorway of a far bedroom, I see a brown arm dangling from a top bunk.

Ruth stands, a dress bunched around her neck. "Lola, my success story!" she calls. "Her employer every night cooks for her!"

"Two hours a month free phone to the Philippines," I boast, for the newer ones. Faces poke out. "Remember, Ruth, I am still your valedictorian." I whisper into the confusion of lace. "I need one for to be my pupil."

"First, help get me out of this."

"Do you need a gown? For city hall?" Ruth will marry her roommate Danny, a gay. This fabric is tight, and I do not want to tear it, the tags still on. Maybe in her size they do not make wedding dresses. In our dialect we have a word that means bride-thin. Ruth is a person you do not think about her looks. I have seen nuns who have this quality. The teeth they are false, but she has a smile that means.

"Have to have a dress," Ruth says. "Have to have a cake. The INS, they ask to see the album. But Lola, I cannot shop." She usually wears shorts and a T-shirt. Every few months, one of the girls brings her a blouse or a pants, for thank-you.

Finally I get the zipper to move. On the skin, it made a dotted red line. She pulls on a big T-shirt and looks around. In the kitchen three with bowl-cut hair stand mincing vegetables. "They work already," she says. In the bedrooms: "Lettie lost her job—they told her she is depress and Melissa gave her three hundred to go for Prozac. But Lettie wants to put it toward her ticket home." Ruth shakes her head. "Cheska has interview there. At the place of Simon. I have Lucy again. We had for her a good job, a two-year-old in San Marino, but since she broke her ankle with the tennis she is just part-time. The babysitters babysitter."

The babysitters babysitter is a job for someone with no English or who limps. They only pay her a couple dollars. Ruth bends up an old blind. Outside now, the *tatay* holds a hose. He grows tomatoes, long beans, and squash on a patch of dirt. Talking, Lucy jumps up and down in flip-flops. She is clean. No makeup. I am already saving my employers the agency fee. "Maybe she can get good money." I feel bothered again, to have given away one hundred ten a day.

"You take her," Ruth says.

The *tatay* holds his T-shirt like a bowl, full of long beans. Lucy jumps to get the door. "Cheska will add to our dinner."

He sits with us for the meal. Ruth invites him every night, but most he likes to eat alone in his room. The ones cooking have made *pancit,* long transparent noodles, with flecks of meat, small squares of carrot, and shining dark eggplant. There is also a steamed fish with ginger and scallions. Rice. Chicken adobo.

The babysitters ask Ruth questions about the wedding. Natalie, the daughter I call Her American Trouble, talks about stores. The long noodles taste delicious but Ruth cannot enjoy while they are discussing the problem of her dress.

"At the park yesterday," Shirley says, in Tagalog, "I met a woman who is here a slave. Working Saudis."

"Filipina?" I ask, switching to English because two here know only Visayan.

"She is from Thailand, I think."

There are always some living TNT. We call that *tagong-tago,* always hiding. Employers hold their visas and dock their wages.

"More than a year they have not paid. She is still working off her plane ticket."

I look over at the child of Natalie. She should not hear this. But Aileen sits quiet, watching. Ruth must be glad we are talking about someone else. People who are heavy, they do not like to be seen eating. "I am from Asia," she says in English, because her daughter cannot understand Tagalog. "But I'll say it, rich Asians are the worst employers. Saudis also. Americans are much better, Jewish especially."

"Seven days! Cleaning the house and four kids," Shirley says. "The mommy when she changes the diaper just leaves the dirty on the floor."

"But we are full already," Ruth mumbles.

"Every afternoon, she has to rub the lady's feet. The lady says she has pains."

"Gross," Natalie says.

"Massage is also your profession." Ruth paid for Natalie to attend college, but she dropped out before the degree. Now she makes big money massaging.

"I'm a chiropractor, Mom. I treat people suffering from chronic pain." So the masseuse does not want to be masseuse. Nobody wants to be what she is to other people.

"Massaging the wife," I say. "Is that not the job of the husband?"

The noodles go around again. Ruth still has on her plate but she gets more. She understands living with other people: if you want something you take when the bowl comes around. It is a good feeling to be in with many when still there is enough.

"They give her only table scraps," Shirley says. "What they feed to the dogs."

I serve myself more *pancit* too, and pass it. The young babysitters talk, with rescue plans. Ruth and I have been here longer. We can eat. This slave, she is not Filipina.

"Can you help us, Ate?" Shirley looks up. She is young but she does not look young or old. She has the small always-gnawing face of a squirrel. If she had stayed home, she is a girl who would have entered the convent.

"What papers does she have?"

"That lady took her passport. Her bed is in the garage, on the floor. She sleeps with the dogs. One dog, the poodle, they let sleep in the house."

"How about getting a lawyer?" Natalie says. "This's gotta be illegal."

"A new passport." Ruth shakes her head. "Very expensive."

Natalie says, "That's why there's police."

"Does she have kids over there?" I ask.

"She has one daughter. She will tell you," Shirley says. "It is a sad story."

"But-ah, the world is full of sad stories. They are not all ours."

Outside, a truck backs into the water plant. Sapersteins have this water delivered. The city water we get from our faucet has to pass tests to graduate to our pipes, Tom says. My weekend employers buy bottled water too, but I drink just the tap. I do not want to get used to things I cannot myself afford. The refrigerator at the place of Ruth belonged to Sapersteins before. One of her pleasures is clean ice. Before bed, she makes herself a mug of ice water. Out back sits the old refrigerator. Still good.

I am the one to wash and Lucy dries. This is Filipino privacy: a two-person conversation in a house full of people. "I have for you an offer," I say. "But there is a catch. When I finish Williamo, I will take that job."

"It is okay for me," Lucy says. "Only one year, two years, like that. We will try to get our medical certifications here."

I do not know what to say. She will not go anywhere so fast. Los Angeles looks tropical, but underneath it is a desert. "I will show you everything. You will be my pupil."

"When?"

"Tonight. Get ready your things."

The evening is done. I have for Bing his Monday-to-Friday. While I wait for my pupil, I open *The Book of Ruth*. It is like lighting a candle in the church. Some of the older women wrote their advice so long ago, we cannot anymore use. Some did every week manicure and pedicure for their mistress, daily fix-ups with the buffer. My old lady, she wanted me to give her manicure. Because her hands, they had arthritis. I never told anyone, not even my husband. Bong Bong does not want me a servant. The teacher of Ruth once admitted that "Emily"—

the lady she worked for—"she has soft cuticles. Nobody but me touches. Because they easily tear." I once passed a sign in Quiapo that said:

NOSE TRIM
TATOO REMOVAL
VAGINAL REPAIR

Another woman wrote that when she went home to Argentina, the lady grew a huge clump, matted in the hair. Nobody else knew how to do the curlers and the combing out, not even the owner of the head. I have noticed, the ones from Latin America, they will not say "the mother of" or "my employer." They all say "my lady."

Some of these babysitters wait on their husbands, too, when they go home at night. I am the same with my husband and my employer. Not devoted.

Except to Williamo.

The groom arrives from his job parking cars as my pupil returns with an overshoulder. It has started to rain, silver in the big lights of the plant. "Thank you, Ate, I will be back the weekend," my pupil says, accenting the "end."

"How about you, Lola?" Ruth says. "Come to dinner Sunday?"

"Me? No. I have weekend job. I am only here tonight to get my pupil. In fact, right now I am actually working."

"You know," Ruth says, "not so long ago, our biggest fight was to get the girls weekends. For years, domestic was Thursday off and half day every other Sunday. The people went to church and they came home for their big meal. You served the luncheon and then you cleaned up after. You could leave when you put away the dessert plates. The girl didn't get out till three or four in the afternoon.

"My teacher tried to organize domestic with the YWCA. They sponsored a Queen Maid contest. The Queen Maid rode on a float in the Rose Bowl Parade. They thought they could unionize. Then, when that didn't work, my teacher was on the committee that wrote a pledge that the employer and the worker each had to sign. This covered hours, days off, overtime pay, uniforms, all such things. The right of the employee to a life outside the family. But the problem was always weekends. Working women wanted their weekends off. The married women needed time for their own families, the single girls for their social lives. My teacher thought she would never live to see the day. *The weekend is when the families want to relax,* she said. *And they cannot without us. They do not know how.* She died before the change. And it wasn't union or law. In the seventies, Americans stopped going to church. So then they didn't need their formal luncheons."

"And now that we work Monday to Friday, what do we do?" I say. "We go and find weekend jobs."

The place of Ruth begins to move. Natalie tucks in Aileen before she has to go to her night job. Ruth whispers to the groom, to drive us to the bus.

"I am taking your cleaning lady," I say, tapping her stomach. In the place of Ruth, the last unemployed, she is the one to clean.

Danny idles the car at the bus stop and we wait, hands out, for the blowing heat. We have a long way to go before our bed.

"I can just take you," he says, and I am getting used to this good car, sinking back, when the bus arrives, huge lights like a train about to run us over. We dash through the rain up into the unreal room of the machine, drop our coins, and then it sways out into the darkness. We sit next to each other, facing forward.

Light swings over us every few minutes, and then we are dark again. I am thinking of this one next to me. Here in America everyone wants that her daughter will be beautiful. In the Philippines, we hope for only average. We understand that beauty causes trouble. The road has a bump every so many rotations; it feels we are on a journey, every so often the swing of light and the bump.

We will transfer downtown, go into the cold again, and when we finally get off it is still five blocks walking. And I have only the one umbrella.

No matter how rich I ever become, I would not want to get like the ladies in *The Book of Ruth,* so weak, from doing too little, that they cannot even mind the hair on their heads. But my children, too, they are soft. My girls, all four, the hair grows long, down the backs of sweaters. I am glad they are tucked into warm beds in my house in Tagaytay, not out here in the rain. A mother tries to protect the young; that is natural. But it is also how kids in America get to be trouble. Even though these jobs have made me more, I do not want that my kids will work as hard as I do. Something else will have to make them grow. I am not sure what that else will be, schooling maybe. Schooling makes them smart. But what will make them kind? Maybe only I will.

I remind them, they have *utang na loob*—debt of the inside. That can never be repaid. Yesterday, I said, "I am here cleaning American toilets so you can study." Issa, my youngest answered, "You are trying to make us guilty. Do not worry. We are not using drugs." I have bought already for each daughter a fine gold chain with a cross. Here, I overheard a mother, when the husband did not arrive at a benefit she was chairman for, say, "Well. More diamonds." I decided then, better if the jewelries come from me.

This one from Iloilo, she is the age of my kids. She looks straight forward to a life she does not know. I guide her out at the Greyhound station, show her where we wait for the next bus. We sit in it empty while the driver goes to buy cigarettes.

The bus stop it is not far from the house of my weekend employers; it is a walk up, the road ending in mountains. I planned to say, *See, we are here.* An arm spread. But this is long slanted rain, the palms blow, and our shoes ruin in the trudge. We go under tall ragged eucalyptus and dripping pine, which smell more in the wet. Lucy looks down when she sees the house. It is not like some Danny and Ruth have driven her by.

"I see you were dreaming of a mansion."

"Ruth said he is movie director?"

"The homes here, they cost over a million. It is the television executives who live two layers. But do not worry, this family, they are good."

"Do you want this job for you, Lola?" She has something shy that I like.

"It is my gift to you."

I have obtained for my employers their new Mary Poppins, complete with the umbrella. We take our shoes off outside, and I use my own key. I expect everyone to be asleep, but the house tilts like a shipwreck boat, lit and sideways. The guy sits in the living room, a drink on the arm of the chair. Farther back I hear sounds that are not Bing.

"I'm in the doghouse." The guy looks up.

"I will introduce you to your new Monday-to-Friday. This is Lucy from Iloilo."

"Oh, hi, good, great. Helen know she's coming?"

"Helen knows."

"She'll be glad, but better wait till tomorrow. Like I said, it's been a rough night."

"I will show to Lucy the room. She can sleep in the bed with me." We change to pajamas and brush teeth. I am thinking if there is a problem in the house they may not take her. But Vicky is gone already two weeks. Five days without a babysitter and, usually, they hire. I told them already, they can pay less. Maybe seventy-five a day.

"In the morning I fix their bed," I instruct. "Americans enjoy to have done for them what a Filipina would do only for children small small." Making beds for my employers, I know too much of them. The bed of an active couple is like the crib of an infant, sheets twisted and strange stains. Spit up. Spit down. But the bed of my weekday house, it is the bed of a nun: neat, white, dry, what Williamo calls pretty princess perfect. The only stains I ever found were breast milk.

Tonight, it is the first time Bing is not in the room with me. I hear the thump of footsteps, the guy going around in a circle.

"Never could have happened a generation ago," he says into the telephone. "Never would have happened in our old apartment, for Christ's sake."

I put my robe over. I will offer my employer tea, by holding up the kettle. Some babysitters, they talk to the employer anyway, the ones who grew up in the jungle or some swamp without telephone service.

"Oh, I'm sorry, Lola, we keeping you awake? Paul, lemme call you back. She's sobbin' on the bed, wailing for the neighborhood to hear. The kid's shrieking. Now Lola's up. We don't live alone anymore, I pointed out to her."

When he hangs up, I ask, "And what did the mother of Bing answer?"

"Nothing." He rubs his eyes. "I don't think she's speaking to me."

"Would you like chocolate or tea?"

"I'll take some chocolate maybe. Lola, nothing even happened. She had Bing all day by herself and so she was tired. Who can blame her? She's been on her own all week. She ran a bath. But you know the way Bing goes around pushing buttons on the phones? Well, on the machine in our bedroom, he must've hit something. And so, I'm having a conversation with Paul. I mean, she probably talks to *ten* friends about our re*lat*ionship, her complaints about me, who knows what, and I don't mind, I really don't even mind—and we're just mouthing off, the way guys do, talking about how stuff isn't the same as when we were young. Oh, God, I said some things I probably shouldn't have, about, you know, *thoughts* during casting, and this guy I work with said he wondered if he'd ever fall in love again. I kind of agreed with him, just in camaraderie, oh and then I said something about her weight, when she had Bing she put on a little and the breast-feeding, something about breast-feeding. And now she says it'll never be the same. And I didn't even do anything. I haven't touched another woman, I haven't even *considered* touching another woman. I was just talking. Sheesh."

"Use your words," I say for a joke, because that is what we tell children to do instead of hit.

But he does not laugh. "Hey, you think you could get through to her?"

"You want that I will be the one to talk to Helen?"

"Maybe bring her a hot chocolate or a tea. Make it tea." He is the one watching her diet. Even now. She will want me to feel sorry for her, but she will believe I do not understand, because she is on a higher level, married to fame, married to glory.

"I will take Bing, so she can sleep." But I do not make tea. I prepare the white hot chocolate—her trademark; she serves with hollow cinnamon sticks the kids use to blow bubbles—on a tray with graham crackers. Going in, I feel wrong. But I cannot send back my first pupil. I do not want an agency replacement for Vicky. Someone from an agency, she will not owe me.

Helen sleeps facedown, one knee up the way of my youngest. Issa is the smallest of my children and the most expensive. Bing wiggles; he is not used to a bed without walls. Here people write books about the family bed. We had the family bed. The baby sleeps with the parents until the next one is born. Then out. That is all.

But this boy, he cannot sleep. And he is the cause of the trouble.

"Lola," Helen whimpers, mouth against the sheet. Then she sits up, her bare feet hanging, like a hospital patient.

"You are always making for me coffee. Tonight I have for you the white hot chocolate."

She is wearing pajamas with a light green edge, the hair tangled, nose red. I take Bing on my shoulder, begin the pat-pat. The finger goes to the mouth. It is best if they all sleep. I will sprinkle sugar in the eyes.

"Lola, he doesn't want me, he never did, not really."

I open one arm for her and she loosens to sob. "You have your cry."

"Paul asked him, was he in love with me when we got married, and he said he thought I was pretty enough, he was in love *enough*, I was a good person . . ."

"To be a good person, that is not something to cry for."

"I'm the consolation prize. He should love me." Her voice gutters, something animal you would hear in a birth or a death, not during the middle of life. "He said to Paul, he said, 'I wanted a bitch. I did the smart thing. I married a good woman and I expected the rest to follow. What can I say? Some did and some didn't.' Oh, and Paul said, 'Well, she's beautiful at least.' And *he* said, 'You think so? Really? On the outside maybe. Our insides don't fit.' Lola, you know, we're going to Hawaii; he said he was afraid to see me in a bathing suit! He's afraid my butt will jiggle."

The breath heaves. This is really the worst for her. "I know, I know." For a long time we just rock. Then she is ready to listen. I have seen this with children. You have to wait until they are still. That is when to tell the story. "My employer, he is grateful. For you, for the marriage, all of it. Without you, he would have—no life. He did not believe any of this would be possible." What I am saying, it is also true.

"He's said that, that he's grateful." She holds the cup now with both hands, drinking as if chocolate can cure her. "But Lola, he doesn't love me enough. And I've given up everything. I don't have anywhere to go."

"These are words of the night best forgotten in every marriage."

"Not Claire's, I bet."

"But-ah you would not have married Paul. You wanted someone higher. You married a man who will suffer, bang his head."

I have the Little Man on my shoulder; I present to her the sleeping face. "If you married someone else, you would not have this one." I look around the rich room. "You are better here."

"How about you, Lola? In your marriage." She begins to remember curiosity.

"Bong Bong, he is very quiet. It is late. Come. You sleep. When it becomes light, you will wake up and go in the shower. Put something, a cream on your eyes. After you are dressed, you will meet your new weekday nanny."

"How should I be with him, Lola? Maybe I should seem not to care." She is embarrassed, nothing at all like real shame. "I don't think I can sleep."

I take the boy to his crib and find the ragged bear he holds at night. I bring it to the mother, tuck her in. Finally, we can sleep.

When I wake, Lucy stands, dressed and ready.

In the kitchen, the guy looks up at me from slicing a persimmon. The last part to fix. Then the gears will move. It can be a morning like any other. The women in America want everything to be about love. And I do love their children. But I am working for money. I knew, a long time ago, for my family to move forward, I would have to be the one to pay it. What can a foreign man do here?

My employer looks at me. He needs to get to work. "So?" he says. "Tell me."

"If you are asking, I think, something of appreciation."

"Like flowers or something."

"Flowers *and* something. Maybe diamond." *More diamonds.* "Lucy will take Bing. You make a playdate with your wife. Have your fun. We will clean up later."

I hear the sounds of a shower, Lucy whacking pillows. It is almost time for my Monday-to-Friday. I send Jeff carrying in a tray of breakfast, coffee made the way she makes it. If the throw is correct, the hand can leave, and the top will keep on spinning.

Bing wakes up, so I introduce my buddy buddy to Lucy, explain that he is tired.

"In our place," she says, "I am the last. I stay between my mom and dad until I am fourteen years old."

Bing listens. Sleep for him is a problem.

"Later on," I say, "I will see you with Williamo in the park."

He tightens his lips and blows. A high, wavery sound comes—the first whistle. I will not tell the parents.

Claire

A COMEDY LIFE

"He'll be fine," Paul said. But I was beginning to think he always said that.

I'd signed the contract eighteen months ago. The money was decent, and we'd thought by the time Will turned two, I could get away. He was two and a half now but the Room was breaking the story for Paul's next script. So, if I went, for three days Will would see a parent for an hour in the morning, a period that would include Paul's shower, and then not again until the next day.

I called to cancel but programs had already been printed. "Bring him along," the director said. A jovial bassist, he told me when he performed his boys came too.

And so does your wife, I thought, noticing: *this is how you become mean.*

He said "Bring him along!" a second time. This wasn't one of those concerts where they invite the composer out a moment before the downbeat. They wanted me onstage for a preconcert talk. Where was Will supposed to be then?

"I'll stay with him. You're a new mother. Don't worry."

But I hadn't figured out yet how to take a shower without Lola watching him. *Black stockings,* I scribbled, picturing the drawer where they all tangled together.

I finally called back to say I was bringing Lola, but the word "babysitter" slipped out, evoking high school girl, ponytail, part-time.

Which the director clearly expected—not *this.* At the airport, he stared at Lola, who'd unlatched the stroller, strapped Will in, and clutched the handles as I tried to pry them away, one-handedly. I could manage the cello with my left. Shouldn't I, the mother, push?

Why was he staring? Lola was a middle-aged woman, wearing creased jeans and a clean T-shirt that said HARD ROCK CAFE.

"I'll push," I said.

She shrugged. *Then why am I here?* But she was here to take Will while I performed. Lola worked like a switch, on or off.

It was just after six, Central Standard Time, and dinner became our first problem. The orchestra administrators conferred in whispers, culminating in the delicate question, *Should* she *come along?*

Oh, nothing was working. Probably the women you read about who traveled with nannies stayed in hotels that offered room service. But the Holiday Inn had only a vending machine. Lola and Will needed to eat, so dinner featured me trying to prevent Will from throwing food that landed near the outreach director's magenta heels. The director's boys were conspicuously absent.

"Home with their mother. School night." Arab men have exceptionally wide smiles, I thought.

The next day, I gathered food for the room. Lola wanted to stay in; it was too cold. Still, I tripped over the cord of the Holiday Inn blow-dryer, the director arrived early, and my dress felt tight. Willie wailed when I left. Some strands of my hair I hadn't finished drying froze to icicles. Only a few years in California and I'd forgotten hair did that.

They brought the lights up, so I saw how few seats were taken for the talk. I told lies about how I worked, or were they lies? I described how I used to be. I'd started when I was a girl. Eight. Viola. "Viola's not second fiddle." My old joke lifted the hat off the small crowd. People rustled as they came in and took their seats. I didn't say that I'd recently started to chatter my teeth to show tunes. Or that my fingers moved on my other arm all day long.

"What are you doing with your hands?" Bing had asked, at playclub.

"She always does that," Will said.

I played the theme I'd started with. The modulation from the E-flat major to F still gave me a streak of excitement. Then I stopped thinking of the harmonic expression and played in a dream.

Later, when I unlocked the motel room door, I found Will inside walls of pillows, Lola on the edge. I stood looking at them, holding my cello. I had everything. Undressing in the gray dark, I listened to them breathe. My piece had sounded different played. The inside and the outside tied together with one chord and passed on to the next person in line. When I woke up, blinking, as the lights came on, I could hear the audience. It had felt good to be taken over, although what had been planned as a quick trip for money was ending up a wash. I'd have to pay Lola for three extra days plus a hundred. And her airfare. I'd become the fat lady, who had to be lifted to her perch by a crane. If I'd been a guy my age, my everything, I'd have gone home with a check in my pocket.

As it was, I decided no to Marlboro as I slid in on the other side of Will. Falling asleep, I pictured Jeff's arm. When had I stopped thinking of Paul? Could you ever think about someone that way when they were actually there?

Will loved Detroit's Arabic pastries. He carried a circular box up the tin steps of the plane and Lola lugged coffee with cardamom, a bag in each hand. "You'll come again!" the director called up from the tarmac. On the plane, William settled in my arms, fitted perfectly. In high school, the one girl I knew who'd had sex said that after, when the guy put his arm around you or you sat on his lap, everything just fit right, a way it hadn't before. I'd never really found that with another body, until now.

Sunday, Paul sat in a straight-back chair in my office, listening to what I had so far. I used Finale to play him both versions of instrumentation. He crossed his arms and listened. Then we took a walk and talked, in soft, adult voices, pushing the stroller. I'd have to call Decca Argo and tell them I'd be late with my songs; I'd ask to bump the recording date a year. Paul agreed; the collection would still get finished: it could still be great, only later. Strange that this caused no clamor. Where had I lost my rush? William was two and half, but I felt wetly joined.

We decided that I should take on a class at Colburn. They paid less than the Manhattan School, but they'd give me an office. Maybe I'd meet some friends.

We stopped at The Coffee Bean. A guy from work had introduced Paul to a coffee-based drink that tasted like a milk shake but wasn't supposed to be bad for you. Now Paul just loved them.

"Gramma Ceil called the other day and said, 'She's been in Carnegie Hall, why doesn't she quit while she's ahead?' " Paul told this as a joke. Retire like Grace Kelly. Look at Elizabeth Taylor, who stayed. She got fat. Men had to keep working. But for a woman an unblemished record is best, even if that record is brief.

There were too many virginities.

At the park, a female couple, one short and one tall, loped across the grass with a toddler wearing a white dress. Will and this girl rushed toward each other, slowing as they neared. The women smiled up at us. Then Will stuck out his arm and pushed the girl. She fell straight back. He looked up, as if he'd just conducted an experiment.

The women, on their knees over the victim, looked at me with horror.

Monday morning, I called. My producer was respectful and brisk. He wouldn't worry about me longer than the time of our phone call. I was a composer he'd thought would amount to more.

But Paul was encouraging. "You want them to be really good. It doesn't matter if they're done now or a year from now."

Once I'd pushed the deadline back, though, it was revealed as a flimsy stage set. No one was waiting for me. Only William.

I was lost.

I shopped fretfully for Lola's Christmas present. Lil and I talked about whether it should be jewelry or maybe a purse. And how much cash? If I asked Lola, she'd say she needed money, and then she'd send it home. I finally selected a Steuben bird. She'd told me she collected glass. I thought she could start a collection here. We could put up a shelf in her room. I held the bird in my hand. I'd tried like this once before; I'd found a nest with two paper-light, brown-speckled blue eggs and given it to my second-grade teacher. Now she lived with three other old nuns, in a bare apartment over a garage. I sent their commune a card with a check every Christmas. After a life of teaching elementary school children, they had insufficient grocery money.

I cashed my honorarium from the School for the Blind. We'd give Lola the wrapped crystal bird and a five-hundred-dollar bill in an envelope. Odd that this year, when I'd earned less than before, I considered that check mine to give. I still had money from a Copland prize, for work I'd done years ago. Coming out of the Beverly Hills store where I'd found the bird, I saw a sweater on a mannequin and bought it for Paul. Wasn't that what you were supposed to do—married?

He looked around the room when he opened the box. We'd opened all the presents by ten-thirty. Now what? I always wanted time together, the three of us. I suggested a hike, but Paul said he was tired.

"The beach?"

"Kind of cold. Sandy." He flicked on the TV. "Why don't we just relax?" He made stacks of duplicate photos to send to relatives while he explained football to Will. First downs. Field goals. I roamed through the rooms, picking up paper, distracted by the noise of the announcers and the bands. Lola had gone to Ruth's only the night before, but the house already felt unkempt. Finally, the phone rang.

"You guys free?" Jeff asked. "I found a church that has music."

"When?" Paul didn't like churches. We'd already declined an invitation to mass with my mother and Tom. But I wanted to get out of the house.

Jeff warned us that parking was terrible and we'd be better off walking, so we bundled up William for the dim afternoon. "And you can wear your sweater," I said.

"Can I just ask how much it cost? I like it, but I don't really wear sweaters."

I shook my head.

"Come on. I can look on the statement when it comes."

I'd paid the saleswoman half in cash. So I told him the amount that would show.

"I'm gonna take it back. I won't wear it. I really won't."

We made our way, pushing the stroller, to the Spanish Revival church. A taper burned at the end of each aisle. Paul spotted Helen in a coat with a fur collar; she held open the songbook and they were both singing. Bing stood on the pew. Paul glanced at me. To him, there was something faintly disgusting about Christianity. We did one-two-three swoosh with William, but he shrieked. "I want to leave here this minute," he said and kicked off his shoe. People turned. Paul had to crawl under a pew to retrieve it. Shoe in hand, Will on his shoulders, he walked down the aisle to tell Jeff.

"You free New Year's?" Jeff asked.

As we walked home, rags of fog blew past. Our street looked closed, but at the end, yellow light spilled onto the sidewalk. The Indian restaurant. We'd eaten there once with Will asleep next to us in his car seat. But everyone inside appeared to be Indian. A man with an inwardly amused face handed us plates and nodded toward the buffet. The staff Christmas dinner. Will ate dahl and rice, now perfectly behaved. When he finished, I untied the cloth napkin and he ducked under tables with Indian boys who wore small red bow ties. When Paul pulled out his wallet, they wouldn't let us pay.

This was where we belonged, among strangers. The Berends didn't celebrate Christmas. Anyway, Paul had off only twenty-four hours.

"Merry Christamas," the man called out into the street.

Just as I was putting Will down, Tom and my mother arrived, holding up a Mason jar. "It's this sauce I make from the soft persimmons. Heat it up a little and put it on vanilla ice cream. Where is he?"

"He's just going to sleep."

"Oh." She followed me in to look. "Oh," she whispered.

My mother was wearing a long red cashmere dress and red shoes. Tom had on his same striped shirt. We put the jar in the refrigerator and went to sleep; tomorrow would be a regular day. Lola would be back.

Paul brushed my arm on the way to the shower, giving my skin a shiver. Two couples going out New Year's Eve. An adult romantic form I'd never known. My mother hadn't been half of a couple. I'd grown up around women who needed saviors, every single one of them.

"So she never married?" I'd once asked my mother as Julie loped out to her Chevrolet. I knew she'd been proposed to but had called it off.

My mother sighed. "She would have if she could have."

Oh, why couldn't she just. "Go ahead, Julie!" I screamed out over the dark lawn at the long-skirted, balding, beloved middle school music teacher. "Marry him! You'll live!"

But that him was by then long gone.

I was married. I hummed, walking through our small house to find Lola to latch on my mother's costume pearls. Lola would babysit both boys. Helen and Jeff had a new young nanny, but she wanted an off. They weren't sure they liked her anyway.

Jeff arrived with a local newspaper that had a map for a midnight run to the beach. He followed me into the kitchen for a paper bag and wouldn't leave until he'd ransacked our bedroom, opening drawers and not closing them, to get our sweats and running shoes.

The restaurant turned out to be half full. The handwritten menu contained only food I couldn't eat without digestive disaster. Paul asked Helen a careful question; she answered, and asked him one, the conversation evenly distributed. Then she asked me if I still wanted to take the class.

I told her yes, definitely.

"Okay. Because I mentioned you to Mary and she thinks she can get you guys in."

"To the school?"

"Oh, no. To the class."

"Thanks." Left, right, diagonal. "You hear that? We're taking a parenting class."

"We?"

"They're taking private lessons." I pointed to Helen and Jeff.

"Thanks a lot, bud," Paul said to Jeff.

"Owe you one."

Our appetizers arrived. This wasn't fun. I felt too aware of my fork. But Helen asked Paul how his pilot was going, and he got started about the notes he'd received from the studio (*Not enough strong women!*) and then from the network (*Who are these tough broads? Give me a girl I can like!*). I laughed along to the stories I'd heard before, grateful that Paul kept up our side. It was relaxing not to have to talk.

He started telling a story about the one woman in the Room. Everyone hated her. They hated her almost as much as the guy who made excuses to get out at seven.

Jeff asked how my work was going. Diagonal.

"The fan helps," I said.

"Now we need you to kill the neighbor's gardener for her," Paul said. "Break his lawn mower."

"Leaf blower." I felt embarrassed by the attention. My head wilted over my plate. "This is delicious," I said, like an idiot.

Frank Sinatra was singing the saddest Christmas song ever written. *Let your heart be light.*

"So what'd you get for Christmas?" Paul asked Helen.

"She wants these earrings that cost thousands of dollars!" Jeff exploded.

"I didn't know they were so expensive," she said, matter-of-factly. "I just like them."

I knew the earrings she meant. Moms in the playclub had them. I'd never thought about diamonds before. Like nannies, they were something I'd only read about.

Someday soon, we all will be together.

"I'm not going to buy into this Westside life, it's just not me," Jeff said.

But she held her ground. "No one's asking you to get pierced."

"Maybe you should," Paul said. "One'd be cheaper than two."

Just then, a guy with tangled hair stopped at our table, pounding Jeff's shoulder. "Hey man, so I did the deed." He pulled over a chair and straddled it.

"Whoa!" Jeff said, slapping his back. "And?"

Paul interrupted to introduce us; the guy was Buck Price.

They'd been at the beach, he said, and he'd buried the ring in the sand. But when she got out of the water, she hiked up to the bathroom. "For like a mile. I kept my hand over the spot. And then, when she comes back, I say, 'Let's make a castle.' I thought that would start some digging. But she says, 'In a little while' and goes to sleep! My wrist got pins and needles." When she finally found it, she put it on and ran down to the water to rinse the sand off, but then she wanted to trudge up to the lifeguard station to see if they had a lost-and-found. " 'It's from me,' I had to tell her. 'I *put* it there.' "

Jeff turned to us. "*He's* the Paul in their relationship." That was the story about us, that I was adored. But what good did it do me? What did that even mean when he was never home?

The waiter brought our dinners.

"After we'd been going out a year," Helen said, "Jeff decided he only liked white plates. He wanted us to buy a set. I told him there's a time in life when one buys dishes."

"You want some?" Jeff offered a backward fork to the guy with tangled hair. He took the bite and gulped it. It was odd seeing a guy feed another guy.

"When he finally did propose," Helen went on, "he leaned against a store window, full of china. Actually, it turned out to be porcelain. 'So what do you say, let's buy it.' I asked, 'Which?' And he said, 'All of it.' "

Paul didn't mention my proposal. I didn't either. Paul hadn't accepted right away. He thought I'd gone from no interest to proposing. He thought I was a thirty-two-year-old woman who wanted to get married.

"I didn't care about the wedding," Helen said. "I just wanted to get it over with."

"I cared about our wedding," Jeff said.

The waiter approached. "Would you like another plate?"

"Nah, I'm getting up." Buck Price took his drink but left his turned-around chair.

"A girl in my office went from a daily discussion of *Is he good enough?* to anxiety about the silver. If *he* wasn't perfect, the silver was damn sure going to be." That wide-open laugh. Helen felt superior, more in love. But was that even good for her?

"You picked the china?" I asked Jeff.

"And he switched my bouquet from roses to lilies of the valley. Without asking."

"Much better flower."

"A carefully set dinner table seems valuable to me," I said. Permanence.

"And incidentally," Helen said. "That girl? She's still married."

Jeff turned to Paul. "You knew right away with her?"

"Yup. She was it."

"Did you have any serious relationships before?" Helen asked.

"Yes and no," I said.

"No and no, for me," Paul added.

"You had the Jewish Elizabeth Taylor. Paul's grandmother told me his college girlfriend looked like a Jewish Elizabeth Taylor. Petite." My hand went to my belly. This food! I'd be sorry later.

"But we're as good-looking for women as they are for men," Helen said.

"Hey, when's the White House?" Paul asked.

"God, I've got to get shoes."

"February," Jeff said.

"But what about your poetry deadline?"

"I'll just finish it early."

"So how 'bout it?" Jeff spread out the local newspaper he'd brought. "You guys in?"

Helen laughed, crossing her arms. "I was thinking about dessert."

Paul signaled the waiter.

"Do you really want that? Don't you think we'd feel better in the beach air?"

"I think I'd feel better eating warm persimmon pudding. Charles says my body fat ratio is eighteen percent, which is ideal for women of child bearing age."

I had my jogging clothes in a brown grocery bag under my chair. "I'll go."

"How 'bout you, man?" Jeff asked Paul.

"I'm in on the pudding."

I changed jerkily, half drunk in the restaurant bathroom, tripping over my leggings. Walking across the room, my dress in a Vons bag, I felt ridiculous. A persimmon pudding sat in the middle of our table. I took a bite. It was possibly the best thing I'd ever tasted.

"You really won't do a slow jog?" Jeff asked Paul.

"She's been trying to turn me into a runner for years."

Helen studied the map, using her spoon to dig around the bottom edges of the dish.

Floodlights changed the ordinary street so trees assumed fantastical shapes. Sawhorses blocked off traffic and people ran in clusters. A boy at a corner passed out cheap masks. The fine elastic cut into the back of my head and my mouth wetted the molded expression. In this buoyant herd, Jeff loped beside me. I worried that I wouldn't be able to keep up, but his arm kept bumping mine. What was that? Halfway through the Palisades on the stilled boulevard, he pulled up his mask and grinned.

"Am I slowing you down?" I shouted.

"Nah. It's good, isn't it?" He tapped my shoulder.

I'd waited so many years for this, whatever it was. Why now? Was I more attractive with a kid, inside a parenthesis of not meaning it? The clomp of running sounded on all sides of us. Around the next corner, I saw Helen—her face bagging, unguarded, next to Paul, whose arms moved, probably telling a joke.

"Wish I could get her running," Jeff said.

"I'll work on Helen. You convert Paul." Next year, I thought, I'd make a farro risotto, with smoky mushrooms and pecorino, before a midnight run. Paul would do it, if Jeff kept at him. A guy at the show had gotten him into that upside-down yoga position.

"Why, when *I* ask you to do yoga, you refuse?"

"Well, I didn't *like* it. You're my wife. With you I don't feel social embarrassment."

We turned down Chautauqua. I could see the finish line on the beach. Huge lights shone from truck beds, and people danced on the sand. We heard the boom and echo of waves. Paul and I had taken dancing lessons. Before our wedding, he'd booked us into a class, even though he already knew how. Harv had told me that Beethoven never learned to dance in time to music. He wasn't the only one. Musicians can't dance. I remembered conservatory parties, where one or two people would move around in awkward, jerky, extravagant angles. Dance had patterns of its own that had nothing to do with measures.

Jeff led me in a stumbling waltz on the sand. I counted, trying to recall the box step. Then he bent me backward, I felt his hand on my spine, and he leaned over and kissed the lips of my mask.

OhmyGod.

I had a good life. I didn't want to get swoony.

Home, Jeff lifted their sleeping boy to their car, the blanket dragging sparkles.

"They are no problem," Lola said. "They right away sleep."

Brushing my teeth, I poked my face toward the mirror. Helen had said I was as good-looking as Paul. Maybe I was getting better looking. "I'm beginning to like her," I called. "But I don't think she gets Will."

Paul lay on the bed, flipping channels. "Well, he's more intelligent than Bing, that's for sure."

I went to the crib. Our treasure.

Paul pulled down our shade.

"He sure sounded mad about those earrings," I said.

Paul laughed, opening the bedspread. "He just doesn't want to pay. And he told me his deal. I always heard TV paid more, but sheesh. He can afford to get her a pair of earrings." The way Paul started was happening. A hand on my shoulder, he aimed his mouth. It was after midnight. A new year. Tonight I'd touched a chain of stars. Light from a passing car danced over the walls and then was gone. What was good slept in the next room. I waited on my back. It was so hard to find the thread of starting. Paul tensed, alert to my movements.

I felt like an old lady, a triangled scarf tied under her chin. My stomach puffed. Running, I'd had a working body. But now, when I turned on my side it made a noise, like a rag being wrung out. It wasn't normal not to be able to digest one restaurant meal. "It's normal for you," a gastroenterologist had told me.

I felt invaded by his happy movements. I wanted to break in and talk. I was aware of his hand touching where it shouldn't, my body wrong. We needed a blanket of dark; some spell of enclosure. Our passionate life was not smooth, like what we sometimes watched, with a feeling of awe, at the movies, when people fell onto each other. (*I adore your ankles,* Jeff had typed, then plinked SEND.) Our physical life was slower, choppy, liable to stall. When it stopped it seemed my fault. His hip bone pressed into me.

"Do you think curtains in the living room?"

He looked at me with fury and turned over, yanking the covers.

It helped that night to think about Jeff in the last swoop before sleep.

But I woke to peace, the sound of Paul's shower. I loved so many parts of our days. "I really may not be able to do this anymore."

"Shush," he said, a towel wrapped around his waist. "We shouldn't be so hard on ourselves. We're still standing. We have a son." He opened drawers, happy, getting ready to leave.

"Where're you going?" I said. "It's New Year's Day."

"The rewrite's due end of the week. I thought I'd better work a few hours. Hey, you wouldn't want that kind of diamond studs, would you?"

I shrugged. "Sure."

"Oh. I'm surprised."

"Should I have an affair?" I asked Lil, an hour later.

"I will if you will," she'd once said, in that *let's go* mood, the ring on her finger, a dry pink champagne already selected. "No," she said now. "That would tear the masks off these marriages."

"You really think they're masks?"

She paused. "Yes," she said, and we both laughed with mirth and rue.

Paul called; two guys from the show had wandered in and offered to break his story. "They're doing me a favor, they don't get paid for this, so I've got to stay as long as they do." I had the phone cupped between my shoulder and chin like a viol; Will stood on the chair; we were whipping eggs, my hands over his on the electric beater.

"But you'll be home tonight?" We planned to put a bean in the yellow cake and fold a foil crown for whoever found it.

"That's the thing, I don't know."

"Paul, it's New Year's Day."

Don't all men work too much? Lil had asked that morning. *All the ones I see do.*

"I'd rather be there," he said. "Why don't you call Lola?"

"She charges double for holidays."

"Just get her," he said. "Because it could be late." Paul's nanny had lived with them, in a little room off his bedroom. I'd understood when I married Paul what we had. Enough, I'd thought. I'd chosen a family man. Paul was that, except he worked all the time. Maybe that was what family men did now.

My hands over Willie's small ones vibrated with the machine. Start of the year, before three o'clock, a fresh still day. We were baking a cake. Lola was on her way.

Later, I thought, I'd climb the steps to my office.

Willie pushed the beater to WHIP. Comets of batter flew into our hair. He took one dab in his mouth and grinned. The first day of a new year.

In the tiny upstairs room that was my work, I was composing an elegy.

But I had a comedy life.

Lola

A LITTLE BIT HERE

I am the first one up. Lola starts her day washing plates frosted with food. Low slurps and a sing of water in pipes; that is how Williamo will recall his thousand wakings, twenty years from now. I open blinds. At the end, I will be the one to close the lights.

But I am becoming old. I count white hairs in the mirror.

My pupil arrives with Bing. I look at her and think: You are lucky.

"Lola, I just want to ask you. He will not sleep! I am too tired!"

Sleep never was my problem. One night, they let Williamo cry. It was an accident. Claire was out running and he cried. I was on my way to the crib to pick him and the phone rang. Paul, the guy. *Williamo is crying*, I said, and he said, *Just let me give you a list for tomorrow*, and while I am writing the things down, dental floss, Tums, his shirts he needs from the place they iron, I listen. I noticed the cry went up and down. Then, the guy called back. He said, *Maybe let him cry*. When Claire came home, I told her, *Get in the shower*, so she will not hear. She washed the hair, she came out in the bathrobe, then she went in again. I was the one to sit with Claire through the shrieking hours, our backs stiff in chairs like pilgrims praying hard sad prayers. But it was only one night and then done. I did not like it either. Now, though, you cannot tell, I say to my pupil. "Children are like that. When they cry, you think they are breaking , but later on they are the same—no cracks."

"Inside, maybe."

"Cracks inside? Only God knows. Anyway, if your employers were the ones getting up, they would change their thinking. Maybe at night water down the milk."

On the weekend, Helen says, "With you, Lola, we knew right away."

"She's very bubbly," the guy says, knee bent, foot on the ref. "A giggler."

"Oh, that is my fault. I am the one telling her to smile."

On Monday at the P.A.R.K. Park I ask my pupil: "What else do you know how?"

"Tatay and the old guy he met," she says. "They are teaching me plants."

"Good. Do not forget, you are my insurance policy."

"Lola! The old guy he is telling me not to wear long pants. He says, 'You are not yet married. Your legs, they must stay fresh!' "

My pupil, she is giggling about her legs while the employers have doubt of her.

Bing runs over from the swings, his hair dark from sweat.

"You want a water?"

He lets Lucy hold the bottle while he sucks. Under his ribs, I feel the heart. A boy sandwich. Lucy squats in front, dabs sunblock on the nose.

"See, now with Bing. He listens you."

"Lola, I told him, 'Before, in our place I had a sweetheart, he was merchant sailor, with tattoos all over. He looked like, what you say? A pirate.' He says to me, 'But what about your boyfriend Tony?' "

"Tony? Who is Tony? Why are you telling your two-year-old employer before the teacher?" I have to instruct Lucy to keep her private life private. "Filipino?"

"Yes, Lola. But he is U.S. citizen. His mom was a nanny in Bel Air."

"Oh, Bel Air nanny." I pick up sand and let it run through my fingers. My weekend employer told me when they developed the beaches at Waikiki, they imported sand from our Santa Monica shore. But sand in sandboxes never feels as clean as sand on the beach. And our sand, it is much cleaner than here. "Where you meet?"

"The old guy, he said, 'I have someone for to partner you.' "

"What is the profession of Tony?"

"He is in the navy. He wants that he will become medical technician."

"Doctor and med tech. That is a marriage across classes."

"My up," China yells. Across the park, Mai-ling scuttles along the concrete wall, where China walks on top. Mai-ling reaches for the ankle.

"He did not finish his college?"

"Lola, he told me, he said, 'Mine is a very sad story. I did not live like you.' His mother was here while he grew up with *yayas* outside Maynila City."

"Sounds like the mother had a hard life. Not him."

"Lola, look at me," Williamo calls from the top of the slide, arms spread.

I cover my eyes, then open. Babysitters, we are used to conversation in pieces.

Lucy takes out an envelope from a small case, where she keeps her father's VA registration and her novenas. She unfolds a letter, postmarked *Municipality of Roxas, Zambo, Del Norte, Philippines.* "He gave to me."

> Dear Ate Nellie,
> We are hard here. It is so poor. We need everything. Please help our mother. She will try to be any you want. We saw the picture of you in the restaurant wearing a flower necklace. They say you are very successful in Glendale.
> Please help us from there in the Rich Country.
> Respectfully yours,
> Your nephew,
> Tony (first boy of Lita)

First boy of Lita. The bad son! I have heard about him. Gambling. Cockfights.

This kind of feeling I really do not understand; most of us just watch it at the movies. I would not have thought this one. "You are a good date." I give her back the brittle paper. "Less expensive than candy and flowers." That she does not like to hear. "Did you make their bed tight?" I am the one to worry her job while she is thinking of Popeye the Sailor Man.

"Yes, Lola. I wash the sheets. Tuesday and again Friday. Lola, I just want to ask, that first night I overhear, he is thinking of other women, like that?"

"Married couples, like children, you worry only when they are too quiet." I look across the field to the wall, where China is stamping down on the hand of Mai-ling. "The marriage really stopped, it is the employers of Mai-ling. The mother wants for China to be baptized. But the father, he is a Jewish. The parents of Bing, they are just young."

I see China, then, dangling on the monkey bars. She moves one arm, then the other, the whole body wriggling to balance. It is beautiful, this muscular will, her body swaying below the iron bars, white puff clouds above. Six months ago she could not do this. It will not last. But right now she has grace. Mai-ling scuttles below, the monster ready to catch.

Friday night, the time of our relay, Bing twirls on the lawn. Cheska sits on the porch with Lucy. She had her interview today with the parents of Simon, where Lettie Elizande used to live-in. She likes Melissa, she says, but she has never before taken care kids. And Melissa does all the cooking herself. She does so much, Cheska says. And she is still sick! She need to rest. Then Cheska bends over a movie magazine, tallying points with a pencil, for a quiz about the wardrobe of Aleph Sargent.

"Cheska," Bing shouts, "look at me!" That is the problem with only children.

The son of Aleph Sargent will join our playclub. I met the babysitter in the park.

Aleph Sargent was born on an orange farm. She worked babysitter through high school, then checkout clerk. But she is now forty-three and has the boy on her own.

"Lucy! You are a low score!" Cheska says. "You should spend sixty percent of your budget on the coat. You said *false*, but it is true. Because you will wear the coat all the time. Oh, yes, Lola, people always see. At the garage sales, we will look for coats." Weekends, Danny, the future groom, drives the babysitters to find yard sales. Cheska sticks up her leg at me with a thick shoe. "Michael Jordan! It is so cheap, Lola! Only two fifty! Just one size big."

Helen steps outside barefoot, plucks a pink flower from a bush. "I hate these."

I start picking off buds because she hates them. Cheska stands to help. My pupil, the one with a job to keep, stays on the porch step, holding her face in her hand. Where did she get this pout? She is from dirt, Panay.

Helen pulls a wad of money from the waist of her leggings to pay her.

"Helen," Lucy says. "It seems you are losing weights." She says that to her employer? Weight here is private, like money.

But Helen says, "Six pounds," and goes back in the house.

"I do not want that you will become serious with that guy!" Cheska says, still picking. "We are here to work."

"But you are married!"

"And I have kids already, Inday. You, you do not have."

One portion of the bush is already green. Lucy scratches her ankle while Cheska takes out two pictures from her wallet, with wavy edges. Typical Filipino children. Facing forward with their school uniform collars and clipped hair. Obedient. Sometimes, taking care kids here, I worry for our own.

"With Tony, I just go to Chinatown, like that. So I can relax my mind."

But that is not what she told me, walking to the post office. My pupil, she every week writes to her mother. She showed me. *Ma, do not worry anymore that I am suffering Armando. I met a man, he is in the US Navy and I think he will be the one.*

So you are a little more here, I said.

When the car of Danny pulls to a stop at the curb, Lucy springs up with her tennis racket. Where did that jump come from? They ride off while I pick blossoms from a tree-sized bush.

Armando must have been the pirate.

From pirate to sailor. I suppose that is improvement.

The next time I see my pupil at the playground, I can tell from the face something is wrong.

"I hear the guy saying, *Who knows what 'doctor' even means in the Philippines?* Maybe they think I am lying, to make myself big, like Ruth, telling about her jewelries."

My pupil believes the life of Tony is hard, but not the life of Ruth. But it is from Ruth she has her job.

"I observe, Helen says a lot of times that Lola is pretty." She looks at me, strange in the mouth. The young, their standards are too high. Even this young, who is only average. "You are the one they want, Lola."

I shrug. "But you are the one they have."

She takes a Kleenex from the waistband of her leggings. "Anyway, it is okay for me. Still dignified work."

Seventy-five dollars a day. It should be okay.

Bing runs over and smears her front. When Vicky was still babysitter, he ran to me. But I did not take the offer.

"Now what?" Williamo says, tugging.

A young Spanish, college graduate, went to an agency and got six offers. People bid against each other for her. Then, after the flurry she was stuck in a room with a baby that looked like a potato. "It drools," she said. You can never be too proud this kind of work. There is a rush to get you—but only to do what they would never do themselves.

Just when my pupil began to annoy me, God helped.

It takes a long time for mail to go from Santa Monica to their place. Ten days to fly over the Pacific to Manila Central. Then that folded paper, it will sail on a boat through the South China Sea. The mother of Lucy never received the letter that loosened her gait after she dropped it in the mailbox. Five days after we took it to the Santa Monica post office, my pupil learned her mother died.

All her clothes, they are from Gap, new: black leggings and a black shirt. "I told Cheska, we will just spend for that." The dad, he is on the plane already. Cheska and Lucy, they have only tourist visas. If they go, they can never return. So she will not say goodbye to her mother. For a Filipina, that is very hard.

"My sisters are there," she says. "Francesca and Lucila. Nelly."

"You have Lucy and Lucila? And Francesca. That is almost the same Cheska."

"Lola, my parents, they are Florencio and Florencia."

"Loo-see!" Bing got himself hanging upside down, and now he cannot get off.

"I tell him already," she says. "He knows."

"Tony?"

She nods to Bing. "He says to me, 'Lucy, did you miss her when she die?' "

So she is starting to love Bing. That is natural. Before I ask for our deal, I will have to find for her a grown man.

We are the last in the playground and it is getting dark. We pull our boys, warm from climbing, off the bars, their shirts bright in the fog. She told me once, her mother smelled of sugar. *Lola! She is so fat!*

Today, my pupil is not asking; still I have advice. "But-ah do not let the parents know. They think Bing is too young for death. Every time the goldfish floats, they flush and purchase a look-alike. He believes it is all the same fish."

I am thinking, They cannot fire her in black, with a mother dead.

"What is a slave, anyway?" Natalie says, on the May Company escalator. The legs of Natalie stand bare, with a bracelet made of threads. The daughter, Aileen, five years old, she wears a bracelet on the ankle too. But Aileen, she is chubby, a serious girl. She makes an odd fit with the mother.

Ruth turns to me. "See, my own daughter and she does not know."

I shrug. "She is American." I brought my pupil, to show her off. My protégée obtained the name of the American medical testing board. The next week, she had already purchased the review book. I felt the way I did when the brilliance of our youngest began to unfurl, big-headed, a coiled fern.

"The slave, there is no off for her," Ruth says. "No limit."

"Other people work live-in. Lola, are you really free at six?"

"But she cannot quit," I say. "They do not pay her."

"Still, it's not *that* different," Natalie says.

I am shocked. She is talking as if I am a blacked-out box.

"Of course it is," Ruth says. "Her shame. Her shame and fear."

"How about your friend Mai-ling? She's kind of like that."

"Even late, they pay her," I mumble, not to Natalie. "She can quit."

Ruth says, "We have to think, what to do about Mai-ling. They still did not pay."

Natalie shakes her hair and stamps the brown leg with the bracelet. "You know, there is such a thing as a lawyer."

My pupil avoids Natalie. Lucy is either a little afraid or a little bit a snob, I cannot tell which. Even now, the middle of February, she still wears her black. Natalie leads us to the top floor. She once worked Bullocks Wilshire, and so she understands stores. "My mother," she says to a saleswoman, "for her second marriage."

I never thought of this as a second marriage. But there will be a cake.

The saleslady returns holding a large cream-colored suit. Ruth slips the jacket on. She looks more herself in this than she does in her own clothes. We stare at the tall, three-sided mirror, where three arms of Ruth pick up three price tags from three sleeves, and then let them all drop. "Too much."

"Can we put it on hold?" Natalie asks. "See if we can cough up the moolah?"

"Do not say that," Ruth whispers.

"She understands. They make five twenty-five an hour." Natalie worked behind a lingerie counter; she punched a time clock too. My pupil chases the boys ahead.

"Are you going to show me your shoes?" Ruth says, on the way down. Then, on the second floor, Ruth marches her daughter to the shoes! They are little stilts, the ones Natalie likes. And she is already tall for an Asian. It is the milk they drink here. The dairy. When kids grow up in America, the mothers want them to look like the ones on television. But to what will that lead? *The wallflower has a better life,* I tell my daughters. *Unless you are so beautiful you can be movie star. And you cannot, because you inherit my nose.*

At the out door, Ruth looks back over the field of things in the store. I have never before seen Ruth wanting for herself. She wants for other people: finding the newest a job, now rescuing a slave. I like to keep her up at the front of the class.

She asks about my daughters, if they are dating.

"No," I say, "they cannot. Not until I get my diplomas." But my second youngest, she is almost the age of my pupil. She will be attorney already next year.

"I should not have stayed live-in while Natalie was in high school. That was my mistake." Ruth says that because the divorce, and now the boyfriend is a Korean.

"But she was beauty queen," I say. "That is very difficult."

"Just alternate princess," Natalie says.

"Still, look at me," Ruth says. "I was virgin. I married a good family. With a big dress. People who know me now would never believe my wedding. Like a royal almost."

I have seen the picture of Ruth as bride, very small, wrapped in fabric. Her mother-in-law gave the seamstress a bolt of silk gazar. But she was too young inside that cocoon. Everyone nodded at her, whispering, *Say thank you.*

I tell my daughters, *Not everything wrapped is a gift.*

Ruth and I joke about the INS interview. *What is the color of the shower curtain?* they will ask. His favorite vegetable. But Ruth knows these things. She and Danny, they live together. Bong Bong and I, we are really married, but we have lived apart now five years. He does not know anymore what I eat. Anyway, the government cannot question the bedroom.

"I had a high position," Ruth says. "Jewelries."

My pupil, she tries to catch my eye. But I will not. She knows Ruth goes to Las Vegas. Lucy told me when Ruth leaves at dawn she brushes her teeth with the hose outside that Tatay uses for his plants. I think of her on the bus riding into the desert. In America, there is a different loneliness. The loneliness in Asia, it is never sweet. She gets a room complimentary, free champagne and flowers. I suppose that makes her feel big. But Ruth has real achievements. She has helped many people. I wish I could buy that cream suit. It has put me in a bad mood. Sometimes, a stage curtain parts and you see: life could be better if you had more. Usually, I think, we can get just as good a different way. But tricks, they do not always work.

I stop to tie the shoe of Williamo while Ruth and Natalie bicker about the Garcia girl. Everyone knows the story of the Garcia girl. Home from Harvard College for summer, wearing cut-off jeans, she went with her mother to clean a house and married the son, graduate UCLA film. *House in Brentwood! North of Sunset! The husband works Fox Studio!* It seems Ruth saw the Garcia girl in the Brentwood Country Mart.

"She was reading a book thick like that," Ruth says. *"War and Peace."*

I nudge Williamo. "Some-a-day you will read that."

Natalie snorts. "I saw the movie. Thinks she's some Russian princess in the snow."

"She says she was skipping the war part," Ruth says. "Says she likes peace."

"But-ah she is too fat to be a princess." I would not want my daughter like Natalie, divorce, but Aileen skips ahead, spic-and-span. All day long while Natalie paints her pictures of beds, Aileen stays with her. My kids have good jobs and my grandsons wear the uniforms of the best school in Manila. Still, they are most of the day with the *yayas*. On the phone this morning, I fought with Issa. Because Lita came back and said my daughter was complaining of me.

My mother will not allow even a crush, she told Lita. Issa should not talk of me like that.

Claire

NO MORE TWELVE-TONE, PLEASE

My teaching started with no fanfare. Thursdays, I drove downtown, parked underneath a freeway overpass, and taught my workshop, then met with students in my bare office, going over their scores with a pencil. *No parallel fifths,* I wrote, *if you want harmonic language.* One used Mancini's theme for *The Pink Panther* as an instrumental obligato. *No more twelve-tone, please,* I scribbed on another's score. *I've suffered enough.* After, I hurried to my car. It wasn't at all like Julliard, where the practice rooms closed with ancient velvet curtains and I knew most of the teachers on the floor.

One afternoon, an older accompanist held the door open for me. He walked on the balls of his feet. Unusual, I thought, for a tall person.

He said he'd heard my oratorio, a piece I'd written a decade ago. "Oh, thank you," I said, as if he'd complimented me. Which he hadn't and hadn't meant to, apparently. Because he started shaking his head.

"I didn't think much of it. I actually reviewed it. I knew at the beginning just how far it was going to go." He grimaced. "I hear things in a Cagean way."

"Oh," I said, looking toward my car into which I desperately wanted to get.

A Cagean way? All I could think of was Cage's *4'3".* A player sitting in a chair, doing nothing, for four minutes and thirty-three seconds.

Then, incredibly, against the background of a dull Los Angeles sky, the freeway roaring over us, the accompanist bent over and tried to kiss me. I ducked away, patting his back. He was old and in need of dentistry; he'd insulted me at the same time he tried to seduce me. That was new.

I drove recklessly. Was this the romance available to me now?

As the 10 freeway flared west, I began to laugh.

$\mathscr{L}ola$

HALF-HALF

I tell the story of a car. Claire and I enjoy the extravagances of my weekend couple as we pare vegetables with small knives.

"Bet they liked Helen at the dealership," Claire says. "Pretty young mom."

"It is a nice story. The wife buying for the husband." The salesman and also the manager stood watching her pull out to test drive.

" 'Must be some hub,' the salesman said, even with Bing and me there.

" 'Wonder what he does?'

" 'Entertainment business,' I said, to remind them we had ears. Helen did not check the Blue Book but they like her, so maybe they will not cheat. She drove to the restaurant, with the convertible down. Lucy will pick her there. So tonight, they celebrate." Fog blows past the window, cold here, near the beach. "When they come out the valet will bring him the new car instead of the old. She will have to drive the old."

"Or go back for it tomorrow," Claire says.

Bong Bong and I, we would never leave our property outside overnight. When my weekend employer steps out from the restaurant, he will notice the car. "There's my car," he will say. She will stutter, "It is, it really is," without the confidence for a punch line. It will probably take a few minutes for him to understand. It was his money anyway, she will think. All I did was spend it. But the valet driver, the mâitre d', the waiters, they like her and they will feel disappointed in him. Because he will not be happy. Even with this car. He is a man taken with moths.

A week later, I receive a call from him. "Lola! I'm in New York!"

"So you are not driving your new car."

"I'm here for a focus group. But Bing's sick and Helen's alone. Could you go stay the night?"

"What about Lucy?"

"She's there. But Bing's really sick."

My weekend employers have never fired my pupil, but they have not yet given her the job either. "You have Lucy, you do not need Lola. One baby. One babysitter." I do not like going there with Lucy too. I stand outside that house at night. It is the place I end my walk now, after the Pacific.

"Lola, I'll pay you. I don't have time to talk to Helen. They have me booked every fifteen minutes. I can't even pee."

"I will have to ask my employer."

"Put Paul on. Tell him Bing has a fever."

I go in the back door. I have never before knocked the bedroom. Claire, she is already asleep under the covers, only the nose shows. He sits on top with the remote in his hand, wearing only the undershorts I know from washing.

"Excuse, but-ah, Bing has fever. It is okay for you, I will go there?"

He stands up, scratching the back of his head. "Sure, Lola. That Jeff?" He takes the phone. "You can have her as long as you want. Course."

You can have her. Walking through the dark, this permission pushes me down from the head. *You live-in too,* Natalie said. *What's the difference?*

Opening the door with my key, I call out, "Three women one baby. Usually, it is the other way around."

Lucy kneels by the bath, holding Bing from under the arms. When I get closer, I see Bing is limp and the pupils fall back to the outside corners. The eye is all white.

"He is hot, Lola! Convulsions. Febroid seizure. Oh my God." My pupil moves a way I have not seen her. She fills a plastic boat under the tap and pours cold water over his head. He blinks awake, shaking. Half the pupils return. This must be how she learned in the hospital. "His temperature, Lola. I am worried the brain!"

"Shhh." Helen stands one phone at each ear. "You give medicine?"

"They only have chewable. He spit it. So we cannot be sure."

"I brought Motrin. New." The new works better.

"A *high* fever," Helen says, the voice sharp with terror. This is her job, standing tight with two telephones. "Just the service again." She would rather let us touch him. On the cold bathroom floor, my pupil administers the medicine, forcing it in, while I hold him down. Red in the face, he kicks.

"All this work, he will be tired," I say.

"Really a seizure, Lola."

Finally, he quiets—the Motrin. Then, after he falls asleep, the doctor calls. Helen lunges. Of course. She is the mother.

"In the hospital, they will check for meningitis. Spinal tap," my pupil says.

"It is only fever," I say. "Children here do not so easily die."

"Yes. Yes! We did that! That's what Lucy said! Lucy, what's his temperature?"

"Down to one-oh-three, Helen."

"Are you sure I shouldn't bring him in?" Helen looks at my pupil now, after she put the phones down. "He said to do what we did already."

"Your nanny is graduate medicine," I say.

"Only names of drugs are different," she says. "And here you have psychiatry."

Bing sleeps on the bed of the mother, and she sits, watching a movie. "Hey, come here, you guys!" she calls. "Doesn't she look like Lola?" She points with the remote to a lady with short hair, in a black-and-white picture. Only the nose looks like me. She is blonde with more cheekbones. Of course, she is movie star. Helen goes to the kitchen to make her popcorn and returns with the tin-foil chef hat, opens it with a fork.

"You will become big again," Lucy says.

Helen points, with the remote, at the albino Lola. "She's the best comic actress who ever lived! She was married to a great director. Italian."

I dip the sponge in a bowl of ice water and touch the forehead of Bing, quick dabs, until the growl from his chest evens. Then we transfer him to the crib.

133

"That is why she thinks Lola is pretty," I say, getting in bed. "Because a movie star. For them to think a Filipina is pretty they have to see a white look-alike."

Fridays, before her off, Lucy changes the sheets for me and I change back for her Sunday. But tonight, we lie together listening to Bing breathe.

I tell her the story of our new neighbor, Jean, how she went shopping in Wild Oats and all of a sudden remembered she left the baby sleeping at home.

"In our place, we leave them, just in a hammock, Lola," my pupil says. We are quiet then. "Me, I will be going along fine, but then, I remember, my mother, she died. And the day is the same but mean. The birds, the kids—it seems they are laughing at me."

I do not know what to say. The birds, they are not laughing at her.

"I have two lives. When I forget it is good to go to playclub, like that. But when I remember, I want to be alone."

Bing is still the age when being with him is almost like being alone. The better parts of alone.

"On Good Friday, our mother does not want us to eat shredded coconut, because then our hair will turn white. She will not let us eat a cake or we will get freckles. On the New Year, she pulled my nose so it will become nice. I was a caesarian because I was face presentation, and so my nose was flat. See, now it is okay. We eat something long for long life. And something round for good luck. Before, Lola, I always daydream. The merchant marine, I thought of him long time after he marry that other girl. I only stopped when I could close my eyes and see Tony. But now, nothing. She was only fifty, Lola."

"That is bad luck," I say.

A roar surges; we freeze; maybe he will sleep back. Sure enough, the head drops.

"I try to get a little time every day alone. Even doing nothing, I feel I am doing something."

"That is the way I felt pregnant."

"Helen, she says she feels that way from dieting."

My pupil and I share a bed, two grown women. I love Helen, but I would rather sleep with my pupil. Both Filipinas, it is the right smell.

The day is warm and sticky. We move in stars of light. Bing has a morning-after dampness; I like the dirty smell. It is more than a decade since I slept so long. I feel good, loose in my limbs.

"I will talk to Helen about your permanence. But then I have to go my Monday-to-Friday."

Helen wanders into the kitchen, wearing pajamas. In fact, I am the only one dressed. "My protégée would like to know if her trial period is over."

"Oh, sure," Helen says. "Everything's fine."

So that is the end for my matchmaking. No "Thank you." Nothing but "See you Friday" and the walk back to work. Long ago, with my weekend employers, something warm started in my chest. What was that? The nose of Lola has always been her guide. I cannot start to use, at my age, a new guide. But things I did not believe before I cannot any longer deny. My grandmother felt this way about the Virgin.

I could not leave Williamo.

It would be different if I took care first Bing. The wish for another beginning, it is a problem for the middle-aged. Children are stones, keeping us down, in the world we already know. We cannot start again.

The next time I see my pupil she is pumping on the swings. "Lola," she says, a giggle in the voice, "in Washington, one of their friends show them a painting looks like me."

I thought before, There is no look-alike for my pupil. But it is the other way around: when they begin to notice us, they find a white. So Lola will not be favorite anymore.

Our kids run up the slide, but the sky begins to mix, until the tops of palms shake. Then a hard rain starts, slanted broken lines of water.

"*Iglesias!*" Esperanza says. "*Vamos!*"

Just across the street from the P.A.R.K. Park stands the church.

"Maybe there is a phone," my pupil says. "We can call the mom of Bing."

In the church, Mai-ling starts to fight a dress onto China. Mai-ling talks to the ground, "I will ask the priest to give her baptism."

"Baptize?" Esperanza says. "She is not baptize?" The Latins, they are more Catholic even than we are.

"Maybe she is a Jewish," Cheska says.

"Half-half. Only the dad." The church is empty, and beams in the ceiling and pews look like the ribs of a whale. Out windows, water runs, smearing colors. "You cannot baptize," I whisper hard. "The priest will tell that guy and he will fire you!"

Mai-ling is wide and the face flat. Something about her jaw, the way the top and bottom lip fit, with balls in the cheeks, it resembles the face of a lion.

"The parents baptize," I scold. "Not the babysitter."

Williamo pounds on my arm. "You stop this. Right now."

"What do you say?" I turn, opening a Ziploc bag of cheese cubes. The kids still have food left in their lunchboxes, the healthier parts.

"Please."

"The mother wants her baptize," Mai-ling says. But how much does Sue really want? Like another blouse she saw?

I have always been careful to want one thing only.

Far in front, a priest moves at the altar, just in slacks. In Manila, where it is hot, you see priests in robes that swish their shoes. Mai-ling keeps a hand on China, a leash. *If anything happen to her, they will court-martial me,* I have heard her say.

Here there are rights, Ate, I told her. *You have rights.*

Me? I no have the green card. But today she says, "I am afraid the soul."

"But China is healthy. Nothing will happen to her." Often, the parents go camping, in high mountains, with the older boy. Mai-ling stays with China. Before they leave, the mother pumps milk and when they return, they tell her how many feet in elevation they climbed. I have seen Mai-ling on all fours, China riding, holding her ears. It is hard luck; Mai-ling would like to sit and fix the hair. But the only time I have seen China still is nursing. Two years old, she still nurses. She is the last one to nurse. Right now, she lands on the back of Mai-ling, her arm around the neck, hanging. Mai-ling walks, carrying China, down the long empty windpipe of the whale. Bowlegged, one hundred percent Chinese, Mai-ling really is a peasant. Here they have homeless, but that is different.

My kids, I took each one to be baptized, but mostly I worry their diplomas. Mai-ling, she is a more true Catholic. I try to pray, but many times, I cannot. I know what God would say—*Why now, Lola?*

The priest walks behind the altar. When he returns, he hands Mai-ling a paper. He is tall, sharp featured, with neat hair. China breaks free and runs. I am the catcher.

Mai-ling continues her slow crab walk.

"I cannot read," she says, handing up the paper. "I stop at grade three."

I read out, "Father, mother, date of birth, parish. It is a form."

I remember once, China and her brother on the lap of Mai-ling in a big chair with a cardboard book. Mai-ling tried to wriggle up, but China kept pointing at the pages. With her ABC book, one word on a page for each letter, the kids were trying to teach Mai-ling. *Yaya, see, that is Cat. C-A-T.*

There is thunder again, so we look at the high windows. The colors blur, like the church windows the kids made once with the iron of Mai-ling; two pieces of wax paper and crayon shavings, melted to beauty.

I take up the collection for Lettie, to send her home. Some are just not strong enough for here. Each babysitter gives something; most give a ten or a twenty. My pupil and Cheska together, they count out one hundred dollars. I do too.

Helen picks us up at the church. We squeeze in the back, kids on our laps.

The mothers here drive in the front alone.

When we arrive at my weekend house, the phone is ringing, and Helen slides on her socks. She motions that the call, it is for Lucy.

"Who?" Lucy mouths.

Helen covers the receiver. *"Him."*

Lucy crosses her arms, shakes the head. I have daughters; I recognize this shake. But I have never said no that way to an employer.

"She's busy right now. Yes, I'll give her the message."

"Tony, he is in the doghouse?"

"That is not Tony."

"So, who?"

Lucy looks down.

"The dentist," Helen says. "He's been calling. *Frequently.*"

The second commandment of Lola: Do not involve your employer in your personal life. "A dentist!" is all I can think to say. "But a dentist is very good."

"I will just see with Tony."

Tony! I have known stubborn loves like this before. They do not end like the ones she has been watching in the movies. Then there is a honk outside. My protégée hooks her purse strap over her shoulder.

"Tony will drive you to your weekend place?"

"We will just go to Chinatown."

"You are not working tonight?"

"No more." So my pupil quit her Saturday job without asking me. Living in this house she is becoming confident. All because a painter we do not know the name. She probably wants that Tony will walk in and see her the way she can be here, not sit in the car and honk. She runs out, her bag bumping her side, and opens her own door. Everyone wants my pupil now. A dentist. My weekend employer. Everyone but Tony.

I am cleaning the kitchen when she comes back Sunday, carrying a can of chips. She takes from the waistband of her leggings a paper, folded to triangles, like a flag. "From *The Book of Ruth*, I found. The mom of Tony."

I never lived without a plan for going home. Every year I got one-week vacation. I told the Daniels eleven months in advance. But then, as the time approached a sadness overtook me. Those were the days when I was most here. So much money for that one ticket. Just for me. I was not strong enough. Max pulled on my clothes. If I did not know what to do, Max did. I did not expect much from my husband anymore, but I listened to my kids on the telephone. One cry from them and I would have gone because they were mine. But they let Max have me.

They needed shoes. They wanted games; they had to have tuition. My money could give them things I could not. And the problem of not following your whims for so long is you no longer know what it is you want. I felt an embarrassment, every time I postponed my trip, but

*also relief. Max became quiet and very good. We took a long walk in
the twilight. He stayed in his stroller and I pushed him past the band
pavilion in Griffith Park.*

I was frightened to see my children again.

It was easier to just go day to day.

Lita, Bel Air, 1975

My pupil looks to me; she has no mother. I will have to find her a
good Filipino husband. But I am still needed for Williamo. She can
play with her Tony for a while.

"Lola, I am gaining weights. In our province, a potato chip this
kind, it is expensive. Here it is so cheap! But Tony, he wants for my
stomach to be flat!"

Helen calls down. "Luce, you there?"

"Yes, Helen."

I will go to my place. Three is a crowd.

"Do we have milk?" Helen drinks white hot chocolate before
her bed.

"There is," Lucy says. The holy words of America: *There is.*

So I walk home from the affair I did not take, and Claire puts into my
hands a stain. "Chai," she says. Here, the clothes are older, like my
own. Williamo climbs up my knees; Paul gives me coupons for
SavOn, telling me I will also need to purchase Tums. He takes pills
now to sleep.

I help Claire to prepare the dinner. Here, they eat late.

"My weekend employers," I say, "they have returned from the
White House. He made a commercial for the Democrats. The president said thank you and shook the hand, but then he met Helen and
he is staring at her feet! He cannot get over her shoes! Jeff told me."

"Which shoes?"

"She show to me. They are very tall, many straps. Gold."

"So that's how they make it even." My employer laughs. "Good for
them."

I look at Claire. She could not wear those shoes. Still, there is that
melody, a tremble in the air. I am back.

Claire

A DAY IN DRAG

The kiss changed nothing.

Jeff called Paul. Helen called me. If I didn't *do* something, she said, William wouldn't get *in*. They took those private parenting lessons. How had I missed the school tours? Some essential mailing list had dropped my name. When I'd gone to the mothers' group, they talked about Costco and trainers and complained about their nannies. I thought I could skip it. But I had and now we'd missed deadlines.

I called Paul. "Did you know about any of this?"

"Nope," he said.

So I paid three hundred dollars to attend a class, taught by the woman who ran the school, and here I was, on a tiny chair, Friday at noon. I couldn't send Lola to this. We needed Lola so *I* could attend. All the mothers in the room must have had nannies. We, the prospective parents (there was one man), wore name tags. Mine said CLAIRE, MOM OF WILLIAM, 2.7. Our instructress kept referring to our work (what I still lived for, cried over) as "background"—for example, "Her background is in dance."

"I *was* a lawyer, but now I'm writing poetry," Helen said, when it was her turn.

"Composer," I said next.

"Poetry, music," the instructress repeated.

The ideal mother: great legs and a *background* in ophthalmology (MELISSA, MOM OF SIMON, 3). No wonder parties in our twenties felt giddy: a secretary interested in journalism could, in the span of a few years, tip over to a *background in journalism*. Background was just preparation for these small chairs.

With my instrument in its case, pitched against a fence, after my lesson we were months behind paying Julie for, I used to watch the successful girls leaping on the green field, twirling batons. They made beautiful shapes, blurry cartwheels against the sky. But for what?

These women were the well-rounded girls grown up, motherhood making the end of good-at-everything.

I had only an ear. No wonder I couldn't do it.

Each mother told a problem. Melissa talked about moving the baby in with her daughter. "I'd finally gotten the room just right. I'd been working with a decorator"—syntax to make Paul snicker: *working* with a decorator—"and now there's this crib . . ." But I liked Melissa. I could picture her daughter's room, beautiful and still.

The one father present shoved back his chair. "Meeting," he mumbled.

The instructress released him with a benedictive smile.

Paul would never be here. In fairness, he couldn't have cared less that I was. "You don't *have* to do that," he'd said, at breakfast. "My mother didn't go to any *class*. Just forget it." By now, noon, I was sure he had.

But this seemed to be the way that Santa Monica children got into school.

The next woman, dressed up and poorer looking, said, "I should probably be at my job too. We've been through a divorce. I had to go back working. And since then my three-year-old only wants to eat ice cream. Should I let her, just for now?"

The whole room turned, one notch. I could hear the thinking— *No to the ice cream, God no to the divorce, and especially that hairspray and the add-on nails.*

The instructress made a point about choosing your battles and spelled out the name of a healthy ice cream. That child should have gotten our kids' slots, but I doubted she would. The instructress sounded kind but overburdened, a teacher. And Helen and Jeff weren't the only applicants taking private parenting lessons.

Helen described Bing's sensitivity to noise.

I wasn't so earnest, but neither did I want Will preschool-less. I thought about what to say. Will had thrown a stick at Bing, but I didn't want to give the impression that he was a bully. Paul could have made these women laugh. I asked about going out of town for a concert. That seemed innocuous enough.

"I wouldn't go away at his age," the instructress said. "I just wouldn't do it."

I felt clobbered. Would she have said that to Jeff? Here, the female Jeffs were actresses. She would understand that a movie star had to leave. While the woman after me began to explain how her kids made too much noise in restaurants, I slipped outside to call Paul. "I'm a little wobbly," I said.

"How's your work going?"

"I'm at this school thing." I held still. "I worry about Will. He threw a stick at Bing."

"Oh, Claire, I've got to take that. It's NBC."

I stood for a moment listening to the dial tone. I knew what it was to rub your hands together, busy with your life's work. I'd been that way once, and I, too, had had someone tugging me back: my mom, sometimes in hospitals, always wanting. I could use a little romance, I thought, still holding the phone. That's what women got, to make them forget. How could you know that and still want it?

I wandered back in. The school looked sweet; I wouldn't have guessed three-year-olds needed letters of recommendation. Kids lay on the floor drawing, the way I had.

"They're making their autobiographies," the teacher said. "Using inventive spelling."

In 1960s-Catholic-school America, we didn't invent spelling or write autobiographies. The nuns tried to teach us the story of the world. We made time lines. I included the Pyramids, the invention of mathematics (by the Arab peoples), the Boston Tea Party (cups flying over a choppy Atlantic), D-day, V-J Day, and the election of Richard Nixon. (I'd worn a NIXON'S THE ONE dress, made of plastic campaign banners, stapled together at the shoulders by my mother's friend Julie.)

We hadn't considered that our lives might contain important events.

Being born, baptized.

First communion in a little bride dress. The nuns had passed out mimeographed forms for the communion package, and I longed for the three-inch missal edged with real gold. But in my class, no one could afford that one.

Prom.

Graduation.

Going to college.

Falling in love, getting married.

Then, it stopped. For a girl in 1965, that was *The End*.

Mo-om, I asked once, *what comes after?* She was driving our VW, with the window on my side that didn't go all the way up, so my right shoulder wetted.

Well, having children. Maybe buying a house, fixing it up. But my mother never owned a home. When she talked to me about life, she reverted to some ideal.

Even now, I wasn't sure what I could tell a daughter. I should have been raising Will to be different. But I felt a little of what the rich must feel: I didn't want to give away his advantages. When I picked up his clothes from the floor, I chanted iambic: *Your wife is going to hate me. But by then I will be very very old.*

I had a grandmother whose life was a stationary field. I thought *I* constituted her holidays. My grandmother truly did not care what marks I got on my report card. Once she was gone, I wondered, where could I ever go to rest?

Women crowded around the instructress like leaping dogs. Helen had the mom uniform: those thin pants that ended above your ankles and new athletic shoes. Most of them wore the earrings Helen wanted, with large screwbacks. The bigger the diamond, I'd noticed, the more tortuous the apparatus. The women asked passionate questions about toilet training, sleep, and separation. I cared about these things too, but I had to go. The mother of the ice-cream eater also hurried out.

A picture of a woman hung in the library of the preschool. With a cap of uniformly curly hair, the results of what we then called a permanent, she sat in an upholstered chair, her left hand lost in the fur of a collie, WIFE, MOTHER, LIBRARIAN engraved on the plaque.

Once the kids were born . . . women still said. (MOM OF SIMON, 3, BACKGROUND OPHTHALMOLOGIST.)

I'd once asked my grandmother when had been her happiest time. *When the kids were small.* Whole lives packed into five words.

Another plaque I'd stopped at was in the Natural History Museum, below huge, reconstructed dinosaur bones: PERSONALITIES IN PALEONTOLOGY: HILDEGARD HOWARD. A Los Angeles woman, she'd studied bird fossils, carried a notebook, a pencil, and calipers, and measured bird bones every day of her life, wearing a hat, a good dress, and pearls. "I have a hard time recognizing real birds," she said. She'd married another bird-bone paleontologist, a man seven years younger. They worked in the same museum for decades, but never had children.

Helen knocked on my Jeep window. "Want to go see them?"

The floor of our rental house made a dim shallow sea, strewn with toys. Lola sat, a queen amid the debris. There must have been nine nannies with again as many kids. William stood, a truck hanging from his hand. I felt my luck. I never once would have rather had a different child.

Foreign babysitters nodded too politely over their plates. Lola had spread a messy feast. I didn't envy anyone her nanny either. I knew Lola was the one.

"Where you go now?" she asked. "You will not work?"

"She wants to take a hike," I whispered.

"For what you do that?"

I shrugged. "Make friends, I guess."

Lola shrugged then.

I swooped up my boy. The room may have been a wreck, poor Paul working till midnight for a showrunner who still didn't get his jokes, but I thought it gave our boy something to have the party in our house.

"What do you say when I say *Joop joop?*"

He giggled in his way we should have recorded, because it would be gone forever soon. "Joop joop!" he said, full of mischief.

"Joop joop!" I said. "No, *I* say *Joop joop.* What do *you* say?"

When he was just learning to talk, I used to tell him if we were ever lost from each other, I'd call out *Joop joop* and he would answer me *Joop joom*. This was the private nonsense that knitted happiness.

William stood shaking his head, refusing to say it. "Joom," I whispered in his ear.

I locked the children back into the dimness, safe in the room of toys.

Then Helen and I stalled outside. Through the wood-and-stucco walls, we heard him sobbing. Helen shrugged. She left Bing all the time. For every errand, every Pilates class, she had to go. Will and I took it harder; usually I trudged upstairs only once a day.

But wasn't it better to touch love, even if that opened longing?

Halfway out on the lawn I heard:

> *To be or not to be; that is the question:*
> *Whether 'tis nobler in the mind to suffer*
> *The slings and arrows of outrageous fortune.*

Yes, then what?" Lola prompted.

"Joop joom," he said, for me not to hear.

Every time I left, I measured: *For what?* But today was mostly shot already. At three o'clock, when people at jobs had been working six hours, I followed Helen up a trail in the Santa Monica Mountains, her biscuit-colored calves moving like even scissors.

She lacked the bright patches of anger that brought my friends into relief. She was oddly blank.

"Marriage is hard," she said. What she told me then was pretty much what I'd expected, but it was the first time I'd known this kind of love up close. My friends had more or less the marriage I had. Someone kind. We'd married late and chosen with our eyes open. I was a realist; you didn't see guys like Jeff with women like me. I felt curious about their marriage, though. I wanted to prove once and for all that my wiring was faulty; I wanted to put my crush to rest. At night, it darted in the pool before sleep.

"I decided to marry him before we even met." She'd built it all out of his name. I thought of those extravagant miniature towers that grew in a water glass. Magic Rocks. The first summer, she'd walked inside a net. "Dates finally felt like dates were supposed to," the way she'd imagined them, sitting on the floor with her doll. Her attention honed with the focus of a miner's lamp: a thousand small efforts, meals cooked, punch lines remembered, she went on a diet—all for one judge. A hard one.

I'd watched it happen to a hundred girls, thinking, Stupid, stupid, stupid.

She'd made her whole life out of *love,* not daily love, but feelings that seemed to me as imaginary as angels.

Just then, three women tromped down the incline, exhaling like horses, carrying water bottles. There were posses of moms everywhere here. A lizard zigzagged across our path.

"One night, I was in the office staring at my computer, and a catalog opened on my lap," Helen said. "I thought, The world rests on the shoulders of a hundred righteous men. My father always said that, quoting someone. He expected me to be one of that hundred. My sister really is. But I wanted a cinnamon-colored mixer."

"Is that your zoo sister?"

"Yeah," she sighed. "All of a sudden I realized, I want out." I pictured her staring at that mixer in the catalog, then canting her ankle, thinking, Kitten heels.

But I wanted to be one of that hundred. A veterinarian at the San Diego Zoo, Helen's sister led a movement to breed extinct species in captivity and repatriate them. Eighteen bongo antelopes, hunted to extinction in Africa, were bred in San Diego and flown to Mount Kenya. If I'd had a father who expected me to do something, what could I be now? I'd have at least remembered whom he quoted.

"I wanted out and I got out." She laughed. "I got way out."

I wanted in. I still did. So what was I doing on a dry mountain in the middle of the day?

"I tried to stop myself from calling him." The urge to quit and order a cinnamon-colored mixer wouldn't have been, in the 1990s, a desirable feature. She'd known enough to hide it. Falling in love sounded like something she'd done alone. "You're not careful like that with Paul," she said.

"I guess not." I wasn't afraid to call him. That was for sure. He complained. *I got to my office and there were nine messages from you. Nine! That's just too many, Claire!*

"I wanted to marry him," she said.

That hit me like a fine arrow. Guilt. My crush dropped, crumpled gold paper, nothing on the ground. Okay. We could be friends, raise our kids together. I would try to be good. "But you're beautiful," I said.

"He was the catch. We both knew that. All of 1990, I waited for a proposal."

"I didn't wait," I said. "I did it myself."

She turned around, gave me high five. "But now that I'm home all day, I think he's bored with me," she mentioned, moving again, tall stalks blooming on both sides of us. In the clear air nothing mattered as much.

Paul watched TV when he came home. "I need to unwind," he said. "Been with people all day." He required an hour in the morning, too, with his paper and coffee. Thinking of Paul as someone I could have a crush on was as preposterous a notion as festooning a bear with ruffles. Still, it never occurred to me that I might bore him.

"Sex is becoming a problem," she said.

"Well, married sex isn't sex. It's something. But it's not sex." *I remember sex,* Lil had said and laughed. The lack of interest among my friends seemed less a matter of disillusionment with our husbands than with hopes, even knowing better, for married life.

"I'm pretty sure I've experienced climax, but never with him." She shook her head. "It's like tennis. I'm better at it when he's not watching."

But that open-mouth laugh! "Have you read that, what's the name of it? *Our Bodies, Ourselves*? It was big when I was at college." My dormitory had been a riot of jokes and devices. I could only assume times had changed in the five years between us, so that Helen had missed this crucial bit of collegial education. "Lil calls it the cliff of dread. The men want to have it. Women don't."

"I want to have it."

"I do too. Just not with him."

"I want to have it with him."

Who wouldn't want to have it with him? I thought, with a shiver, and I shouldn't know this. "Nobody's having great sex with the person they're married to. I don't know if we ever really kissed right."

"We don't kiss either." She looked as if she might cry.

I'd done something wrong, opening this.

Paul was Paul. But I didn't suffer over him, not that way. No more Jeff, I promised silently. From now on I'd be good.

But she picked up a stick from the ground. "This movie is going to be great, though. Paramount's giving it the A-list budget." This is how she rose again. Then she paused. "Do you even think of what Paul does as art?"

I wanted to hit her. More than anything *you* do, I thought. Paul was still dear to me. What if she was repeating Jeff's opinion? We'd been hoping Jeff would direct Paul's pilot. "Sure," I said. "Of course."

"How did you guys get together?"

What could I answer? Should I have waited longer? But wouldn't that have been the foolhardy romanticism of a spinster, like Julie, who'd stubbornly loved a movie star (in her case, a dead gay one) and refused to accept any local man? At the time, the last of my friends were enlisting. Giddiness in the air, the thrill of registering for china, mixed with an intoxicating relief that I wasn't being left behind after all. Paul and I met at restaurants; we strolled in shops. Wasn't this what people did?

The woman falls in love with her children, my landlord said, handing me the rent receipt. But what if I didn't? Children sniveled. Children dripped. I was thirty-three. There were omens: older women musicians, for whom no one expected *that* anymore. To me they looked uncannily alert, like owls.

"How did we get together? Oh, I don't know. I guess the usual way."

She bent over and poured a whole new bottle of water over her head. A rich girl, I thought. Another posse brushed past us, heading up.

She sighed, staring at one woman's ankles. "Jeans are going in again," she said.

When I got home, the house was still, clean vegetables on the cutting board, Willie and Lola out. Four o'clock. I almost started on supper, but instead climbed to my study and began to read my score. I went back fifteen measures, then ten more to get caught in it again. When the sound of their footsteps roused me, I thalomped downstairs and found Will under the table with two Power Rangers and Lola by the sink chopping fennel. Everything touched with light.

The phone rang: Paul calling to say it was going to be another late one, they were passing out the dinner menus now.

"Where're they ordering from?"

"That Thai place you like." I didn't mind. I'd talked enough today. One summer night in my twenties, I'd devoured a peach for supper, standing up, the juice running down my arm. Did dinner still feel like that for him? Tonight I hoped so.

I called Will outside to help me tie up peas. *Nine bean rows will I have there and a hive for the honeybee.* We stooped and picked mint for the soup, and I wondered what I'd remember of these years. Will sprawled under the table while I chopped, the scent rising. I hummed "I Fall to Pieces," "Is That All There Is?" What Paul called my good-to-cry music. We'd devolved to eating the way women eat: either the pasta or the soup. Lola kept a portion for Paul in Tupperware. He ate at midnight and left the container in his den, where she collected it in the morning.

"I didn't get married to have dinner every night with my kid and a maid," I'd railed on the phone yesterday to Lil, to whom the maid part didn't sound so bad.

"You leave him," she pointed out, "you're still going to be having dinner every night with your kid. And maybe not the maid."

Anyway, Lola wasn't a maid. And she didn't actually eat with us. She took her walk every night when we sat down. "I will go now," she said, lifting her soup, covered with a napkin. Tonight, Will and I ate from bowls on our laps in front of the heater grate, next to his LEGOs. A dinnertime house with a child.

I gave him his bath, warm water on the top of my hand. With the bubbles, we made his hair stand up like Marge Simpson's. Until shampooing, everything was laughs, surprising pokes, and gushes. Fingerbees, earbees, but then full-out sobs with the rinse. After the dry-dry, he got four books, then a one-minute, which is what we called the time I lay with him until his breath settled. When I slid out, dishes were put away, the jar of flowers restored to the table. Lola had our tea steeping in the red pot. We sat and talked about Will's day.

I made a second pot to take with me to bed with staff paper and a pencil, Little Him asleep, jasmine a warm sweet outside. Was this happiness in marriage? Within it, anyway. In bed, I read what I'd written. All of it so far. But Lola rapped on my door. "Excuse. Lucy is here, okay I make her a coffee?"

"Sure, of course," I said. "Lola, offer her some orange cake."

"You put one scoop per cup?"

"Two." At first I'd barely noticed Lucy. But she arranged branches in vases. I copied her, adding rosemary and Japanese maple to the roses I stuck in the jar.

I found the two nannies at the table, the cake between them.

"Thank you for the orange!" Lucy tapped her belly. "I am eating too much!"

I knew from Helen that Lucy brooded about her bad boyfriend. I asked, "How are things with Tony?"

"I say to him, *Other guys, they want to kiss their girlfriends. Hug, like that.*"

I'd assumed they were sleeping together. Maybe he just didn't touch her in public. But anonymous corners of life pressed in through the dark windows. Lola was already married; she had her children. I wasn't keeping her from life.

"My tummy, Claire, he thinks it is too big!"

"You are eating so much!" Lola said. "I am telling you. You are big now."

The last time we'd gone out with Helen and Jeff, they'd told a story about Tony's cockfights. Helen saved up scraps from her day to amuse her husband. That one worked; Jeff spluttered, requiring a second napkin. She said Lucy ended her bad reports, *But he is trying, Helen. He really want to change.*

"Not the worst thing that Tony's got his problems," Jeff had said. "Otherwise, they'd run off to Vegas."

I wrapped a square of orange cake in wax paper for Lucy to take home.

"But she does not need cake," Lola said.

For the first time, I thought about Lucy's life. "Maybe this really won't work out for her," I said. "And if it doesn't, it's no joke. Thirty-one already when they hired her." Helen talked about Lucy's tests, the way stay-at-home mothers imagined their daughters becoming doctors. "She has the doctor stuff," I said, "but Lucy might not want that enough."

"Well, she should want it," Lola said, putting things away. "Medicine, it is ten years in our country. She has three tests for doctor, two to be nurse."

"Maybe Tony seems a better bet than passing."

She took the sponge from my hand. "He is not a better bet than anything."

For us, sex was a problem too. But Lucy and Tony needed sex. Everything teetered on it. "It's him, clearly. She's in love, all right."

"The story will not end like the movies she is watching." Lola bent down with the dustpan.

Later, underneath Paul, on that rare night, I imagined being Lucy with Tony.

That was another way, those years, they served us.

"We should do that more often," I said to Paul. "I like it, I really do, and I feel good after. It's just starting that's hard."

January 31, 1994. A day that worked: out for hours, I didn't feel mad at Paul. We even had sex. But no music.

"That was the month my mother died," Lucy said, years later. We'd known that. The night she'd come to my kitchen and eaten orange cake, she'd worn black clothes already gray from so many washings. I'd never put together her quiet and her bereavement. I'd thought that was just her personality.

Lola

THE RAISE

I stand in a corner where once I made the center. Babysitters crowd around my pupil now; all of a sudden she is high status.

Wednesday starts out dark, with clouds. Under our tree, Mai-ling whispers that my pupil has a raise already. Not even her six-month anniversary. They let her drive their old car home weekends, Mai-ling says. It is almost hers now. My pupil, she did not even tell me.

So she will earn more than her teacher. I will have to quit that job if they do not give to me the same. All the babysitters know I work in that house first. Sunday, our mutual employer lifted his eyebrows and looked at a vase of flowers. *Lucy,* Helen mouthed. Maybe that bouquet decided them. Lucy makes the beds, like I told her. She puts on the pillow a waxy orange flower, washed under the tap and dried. That was her own idea. And today I planned to introduce her to Lita, the mother of Tony!

"My parents, neither had any education, but they wanted their kids to get, like that," my pupil says. "My oldest sister was supposed to be the doctor."

These same babysitters, three months ago, I had to convince, she really is a doctor; I saw the stethoscope. Only the babysitter of Aleph Sargent looks bored. Probably to her, one hundred a day is nothing special.

I lift foil off dishes; it is my playclub, but I wish it would end. That is the problem with people; it happened to God too: what you create, you cannot anymore stop. I feel like announcing on the toy mega-phone, *They offered me that job first.* But no one remembers the trip you did not take, the life you did not have. In our suburb of Manila, inside houses, our mothers talked about the things they would have done if our fathers had not come along and touched them with feathers, turning them into our mothers instead. According to them, the Philippines would have been chock-full of dancers and singers, glamorous professional women, if our fathers had not cajoled them with their temporary charms. We did not believe them. A cake has only so many ballerinas on the top.

"Lola, I think they are liking me a little because they raise me now." My pupil, she does not feel lucky enough. She thinks one hundred dollars a day is what she deserves.

"Then I will introduce the two one-hundred-dollar-a-day nannies," I say to my pupil and Lita.

They shake the hand of the other, polite and shy.

"Alice had me wrapping presents for Secretary Appreciation Day," Lita tells the babysitters. "Lola, you ask your husband to make a day for us. Her husband works high up in Hallmark. Manila branch. Nanny Day. For caregivers." Just for playclub, Lita is wearing a belted dress and leather flats. The rest of us all have on rubber shoes. She helps me carry foods, whispering, "If I can only get him to propose her." Then she looks up through the branches of our tree. "You know, it could rain today."

"Rain would not be the worst thing." Sometimes I am not in the mood to play. But the club, it is at our house.

"Because I am last," Lucy says, "my parents, they always expect me to be something big."

No one expected me to be anything big. And I am not. The parents here in the U.S., they are all expecting big.

The babysitter of Aleph Sargent takes a plate. Clarisse appreciates food. She is like the trunk of a tree. She grabs the arm of Brando and whispers hard. Brando is what, in the Philippines, we would call *salbahe*. But the small boys, they follow him.

"I never wanted to be doctor," Lucy says. "I like something with art, decorations, like that. But I am the last so I study and study, all the time I study."

If she did not want, then why use the spot? One of the high days of my life was when Issa received her letter of acceptance from Far Eastern. "So why you come here?" I say. "Doctors, they can find work in the Philippines."

"There is no money in the provinces, Lola, since Marcos already. If you are rich, sure, you come to America, and even if you are only attending seminars, when you return you get a good position. The only job I could get was in the army. I was given my ranking already. If you are a doctor, you become colonel. But then my father brought us here," she says, quiet, to me only. "So I could forget that guy."

The pirate. Anyway, she attended school in the provinces. Not FEU. Issa will find work. That is enough for me. Maybe Issa can come here to attend seminars. Later on, I will ask Alice, the employer of Lita, to help.

While the boys run in the driveway, the sky cracks. Los Angeles, it is not built for rain. The palms shake; the road turns black. Whole rooms of water tip over.

The rain has saved us from the life story of Lucy, unabridged. Kids crawl the walls in the room of Williamo; babysitters unclip fists from shelves. But Brando refuses to return to Will his Batmobile. The mouth is a slanted gash. Next will come fighting. It is not easy to share. That is the refrain of Claire. *What if our friends came over, put on jewelry, tried on our clothes, and wouldn't give them back?*

Good you do not have daughters, I say to her.

I clap. "Movie time!" The VCR sits on the dresser in the room of my employers. I whisk off the bedcover.

Brando still has the Batmobile, so I let Will pick the movie. He wants the video the plumber took inside our sewer. I say, *Not while we are eating.* Then he selects one that is gears, big machines moving slowly. Jeff made this at the site that will be the Getty Museum. But the girls fidget. I eject and slide in *Mary Poppins.*

The babysitters serve themselves. Our kids, they are small small; we still feed them from our plates. The telephone rings and it is Claire, at Colburn. "Power still on?"

I drag the cord so I can see *Mary Poppins* land. "Your bedroom it is a movie theater. But I took away the cover."

Babysitters sit on the floor, eating foods. Like the mothers we know, Mrs. Banks wears expensive clothes. But she does not look as much as her helper. My employer asks if it is okay she is late, and I say, *Do not worry.* In the Philippines, growing up, we wore dresses and gloves to the cinema, sat on plush seats, and entered a better world. The American streets looked pink, the lawns blue, and all the people's problems, they were about love. Husbands and wives threw pillows at each other; feathers filled the screens. And it is really true here; rarely is the trouble money.

Bad babysitters, old and bulging, not Filipinas, blow away.

I think of Lettie Elizande, home already.

Esperanza says Julie Andrews is pretty.

"More on young," Lucy says.

Why does she say that? An insult. I gave her something valuable and she is not grateful. I never told Bong Bong my offer. It was the largest decision I made alone, since I married him. I sink down next to Williamo.

Clarisse holds up one finger. "I am giving you a warning." All of a sudden, a hive forms over Williamo and Brando. Clarisse lifts Brando into the air, his legs churning. "We're leaving."

"I didn't hear you, I didn't know," he yells as she carries him to the door. "I won't again," into the silver rain. From living here, I wonder if you could change a boy like that with praise. In the Philippines, we would hit.

"What is *supercalifragilisticexpialidocious?*" Bing asks.

"It means: Always respect your Lola." Every weekend, I work for his parents; but they do not anymore pine for Lola. The cheese stands alone.

"But Mary looks like Jane and Michael," Lita says. "She could be the mom."

The room changes. Babysitters slump, like housekeepers on the Wilshire bus looking nowhere, still far from home. I glance at the small TV. We cannot snap our fingers to make their blocks march off. That is why we teach them to help. Even my pupil the doctor, she could not change the taste of medicine; we had to force the Motrin down his throat. When I sing, there is no orchestra. I am like Bert, a clown. Julie Andrews is a white that does not look like us.

"You know, the Castle?" Lita says. "They move in already. Three cars. Yesterday I see the wife. Filipina but American born. Graduate UCLA."

This makes a bad end to our fairytale. Not only drab babysitters blow into the sky, all Disney nannies vanish. Our children concentrate on the ending, hoping we will someday dissolve so that they can be raised by their parents. But their fathers work in Hollywood; that is harder to quit than a bank. When Lettie left, Simon and his sisters got Cheska. And Melissa, she does not even work.

The doorbell rings. Under porch light, my handsome weekend employer stands with his own halo of smoke. He follows me, his eyes counting over the crowd to find Bing. We stand together watching the full room—my accomplishment.

"In the great green room, there is a television," I say, but he does not know the *Goodnight Moon*. With my pupil, they have gone far. But my weekend employer has a secret. He prays Catholic. Once when I went to a 5:00 a.m. mass, it was only the two of us and some olds. He asked me not to tell, and I have not. They turned me into a better Lola because they believed I already was one. Drops of rain glint in his red curls.

"I had some good news today. We got our actor. I thought I'd take the family out to dinner."

"Congratulations," I say. "You can celebrate also the raise of Lucy." Already, I have lost more than eight thousand. I have sent ninety-four hundred this year so far. It could have been almost double.

"And Lola, you're about due for one too. Consider yourself raised."

He picks me up off the ground! "To one hundred a day also?"

"To the moon." He puts me to the ceiling. I touch.

"The moon, that would be one hundred ten."

"Okeydoke." His eyes slide to the small TV. "God. He looks so young there."

"Daddy!" Bing shoves up at the sound of his father. But my weekend employer was not meaning him.

Bing collapses back into an *h* against Lucy. My chance and I gave it away.

"So young," my employer says again.

Because his wife makes for me coffee, I make for him, the slow way.

"I wanted to be Dick Van Dyke. Grew up watching his show. And then I saw him in the elevator of a New York hotel and I told him, *I loved your show, you made me want to direct.* He looked at me and said, *Yeah, well, the show went off the air, I became an alcoholic, and it's been a struggle ever since.*"

I hand him the warm potion. "Did you get the autograph?"

"Huh? Nah. Was trying to act like a professional. I didn't think, *Dumbhead, this is the only time in your life you're going to see your idol.*"

My second eldest was national secretary of the Beach Boys Fan Club Asia. She will know how to get the autograph.

"Probably better if I never met him. Could've gone on thinking he had this great life."

"Do any have?"

"Comedians? Not Chaplin. Not Keaton for sure. Buddy Hackett maybe."

Buddy Hackett! I will tell Lita! Her employers live in a mansion once owned by Buddy Hackett. They bought from his daughter Ivy.

I have to warn my pupil: Mary Poppins, she will never have husband.

Claire

THE POX

"Yup, you got 'em, my friend," Paul said. "The Pox." He gathered his baseball cap and jacket and gave Will high five.

It had been a normal morning, threads of music bobbing in the air, and now I was out for the day. I stood on hold with the doctor's office as Paul walked backward, making a pratfall. Still, there was a certain relief, stepping into the bright winter morning, the clouds majestic, western above the sharp line of mountains. The air sparkled, and I became a citizen, with manageable duties. We walked to the doctor's office, past a florist setting out potted daffodils. This was easier than composing.

I listened to the doctor, steadied by orders. Anyone could see me in the pharmacy, prescription in one hand, Will in the other. But I was thinking of Jeff, in his baggy white shirt, his straight arms caging me against an outside brick wall.

Did an affair have a moment when it was still innocent? How would I know? I had to believe a guy like that would turn out to be a nightmare. But what was the difference? The decent guy left you alone with a sick kid anyway.

The pharmacy carried two brands of bath powder. Paul had just signed a contract; I threw both in the basket. I paid ten dollars for a clay pot of daffodils, innocent as nuns. After his oatmeal bath, Will ran a silver train car over his bedspread while I dabbed the dull ointment on each pox. Lola burst in with a package of cotton gloves and fought them onto his hands. "So he will not scratch, Claire. That will scar!"

We took out every toy in his room and played until its magic drained. A watery breeze lifted the curtains and time bent. I thought of old church music, the modal scales. Maybe while he slept, I'd work.

I remembered the way Jeff had looked at me. Was this odd sugarhouse I was building still okay?

That night, I woke on top of the covers, a rustling in the closet. Paul looked caught, with a stack of blankets. "I've got to sleep in the den. I just can't catch this. We have a table read tomorrow."

"I'm worried about work too. I didn't get anything done today."

He sighed. "At least you don't have a deadline."

I never did anymore. At 2:00 a.m., I ran another oatmeal bath to soothe Will's ragged itching. Buttoned into clean pajamas, he fell asleep again.

Days later, when we found ourselves dropped back into the regular world, my upstairs room looked dusty. There was my music. Just paper. I sat down at the piano and touched a sour A. I should have called the piano tuner while I was out. I'd have to call him now. But instead, I called Paul.

"Got to call you back," he said.

"When?"

"I don't know," he said, and hung up.

Paul liked classical music but he didn't listen to it. He said he needed concentration and he was so exhausted that it tended, as reading did, to put him to sleep. Most musicians I knew had married other musicians. I was beginning to see why.

I fumbled at the phone.

"Helen's at Pilates," Jeff said right away.

"Actually, I wanted to take you to my jewelers. Valentine's Day's this week."

"It is? God, that's bad news. Let me think about it. Can we keep this a secret?"

I repeated his little speech to Lil.

She laughed. "The keeping it secret part. Sounds like code to me." We were middle-aged women with small children. We needed to laugh.

But if Paul didn't require music, he still saw a slash of brilliance in me. That gave me a feeling of safety, going to sleep in the still house. He'd once memorized parts from my two CDs, and he could hum them the way he whistled Top 40 tunes, getting dressed in the morning. And when those two-musician couples had children, their kitchen walls thickened with grime.

I could still talk myself into our life.

On a Sunday evening in March, Jeff came over and lay on the floor of our small living room. "You can marry a wife or a housekeeper," he said, an arm stretching to grab a chair leg. Paul paced, tapping his pen on the legal pad. Since his show aired, Paul felt more his equal.

Wife or housekeeper: Which was I?

The doorbell rang. Helen, wearing cute glasses. "I need to talk to Lola a minute." She went out back, without explaining. Lola had just returned from their house. When Helen passed through again, Paul asked, "So what's up?"

"Oh, God." Helen rolled her eyes. "Lucy stood in front of me; I can always tell when she wants something, she lines her breasts up with mine and looks down at the ground. 'Helen, there is something I need to talk to you.' "

"The 'something' turned out to be a cleaning woman," Jeff said, from the floor.

" 'Now he is so actif, Helen. I really have to watch him every minute.' " She imitated Lucy's voice. "So I asked Lola. 'Bing has to come first,' she said. She had this little smile inside her smile."

"Bet she did," Paul said. What did he think? It was us against them?

I imagined the household I could run with Jeff's money.

"Thanks, bud," Paul said. "Wonder how long it'll be before Lola's asking us."

"Hey, man, Helen's the general. I'm just the foot soldier."

But the general of what?

I liked baking and dresses. One from the housekeeper column, one from the wife. Helen left, and the guys went back to work. Jeff came into the kitchen asking for something to eat just as I was taking a tray of Japanese purple yams out of the oven. (Housekeeper.) I fixed a plate for Will.

"Thank you for caring about my hunger," Jeff said when I gave him a bowl. "I didn't think I'd get any of this—the wife, the child, a home."

"Have the father of the autistic kid say that."

"That's good." Jeff called to Paul, "She's good."

I heard them laughing, late into the night. I fell asleep to that sound.

In the end, we hired Ofelia too, for a half day every week, to clean our house, even though Will would be starting preschool in the fall.

"Keeping up with the Filipinas," Paul said.

Every Friday, Ofelia came to our rental house, carrying her own vacuum cleaner, the corrugated trunk over her shoulders. At the end of the afternoon, Lola would leave for the other house, and Ofelia dandled Will on the floor with her odd words of English, waiting for her husband to pick her up. From upstairs, I'd hear a toot, run down, scoop Will in my arms, and stand barefoot waving goodbye to the family in the huffing, chugging car, remembering Jeff hold forth at the Ivy, "You know how they could really clean up the air in Los Angeles? Just get rid of all the cars more than ten years old. Make 'em illegal."

One of the large, unsolved riddles in my life was how I could love people I didn't respect more. "Drive safely," I called out, weakly, weekly.

My mother, a lifelong beauty, at seventy still wore high heels. She claimed flat shoes hurt her feet. In a white pantsuit, a white hat, and white four-inch-high espadrilles, she brought over a gosling. "When I was little we used to get baby chicks in different colors; they shot dye into the egg." She lifted the infant bird carefully out of its box. "With a long needle." It quivered, adorable, soft yellow.

We took pictures of the gosling in Will's cupped hands.

"Do you want to stay for dinner?" I asked.

They had to go, though. "Rhododendron Society meeting," Tom said.

But the gosling made noises in the night. So I moved it, in its box, from his room to ours. "Claire," Paul called, "could you please come here!" He stood, a towel wrapped around his waist, just out of the shower, wiping his heel with a Kleenex. "I stepped in bird excrement. In our bedroom. That thing has to go."

I waited until ten to call her. "Two incontinent beings in the house are too many."

"Well, he won't be that way forever. But I'll come get him. I can take him here."

"You're going to raise a goose in your apartment?"

"Sure. Why not? He can live in the upstairs bathroom."

After I hung up, Lola said, "Why you not put it outside? A goose is like a watchdog. In the Philippines, we always get a goose near Easter and the kids chase it around the yard until one day, *qweek*, into the pot."

Tom and my mother arrived that afternoon, my mother in olive green. Tom wore his usual khakis and the same striped shirt.

"I'm going to take her to Twin Dragons," Tom said, "but, geez, she drives me crazy. She orders the steamed snow peas with no sauce and then when they come she complains they're not hot enough. But the sauce is what keeps in the heat."

"He'll still be your goose," my mother called to Will, as she directed Tom to carry the box to the backseat of his car.

Jeff called at the beginning of April. "I guess it's past Valentine's, but you think we could go to that place?"

I showered. Blow-dried. I tore another pair of pants off the hanger. Had all my clothes gone out of style? Was this flutter necessary, for a thrill? I didn't know if I had the stomach for it.

The phone rang as I was trying to put on makeup I'd bought more than a year ago, and I knocked over the little bottle of foundation, which I'd already "feathered" on half my face.

"Haven't heard from you," Paul said. "You having a good day?"

I usually had a thousand things to tell him, but now all I could think about was dabbing enough spilled foundation to feather the other cheek. "Not really," I said. Then I looked in the mirror and decided to wash it all off.

Jeff and I peered at diamonds, our hair touching, over the velvet. I stilled my head, and he hooked a plank of just-washed hair behind my ear and screwed in the glittering chip. The ones I tried on cost three thousand dollars.

"Do you have any less expensive?" he asked.

"Sure." The jeweler shrugged, then smiled. "But these are very good quality. To keep the same you're going to have to go smaller."

The next pair didn't sparkle as much.

And we went smaller still.

"I'll take them," he finally said. "You can't really tell the difference."

The jeweler's eyebrows lifted involuntarily, then he controlled himself, set to cleaning the studs with a chamois cloth dabbed in alcohol, and installed them in a box fitted with slits. His gift in a light bag, Jeff walked me to my car.

"You watch Hitchcock?"

I nodded sure.

"I was thinking of *Rear Window,* how the waltz saves the wallflower's life. He had really amazing scores. Boogies, street noise. So what're you guys doing tonight?"

I shrugged. "Paul's working." I leaned against my Jeep, arms crossed, shuddering in the sun. "I'll throw Willie the ball. We have mitts."

"You love that boy, all right."

"Even though I work and everything, it's—" My hand landed on my chest.

"I get that. And I understand about your work too. But you know what, Claire?" He gripped my arm, below the shoulder; he liked me, this guy liked me. "You and Paul should have more sex." The puff of his breath warmed my cheek. "It softens everything."

I'd have more sex with you, I thought, lifting a hand to my face, which all of a sudden felt unstable. He wasn't handsome exactly. He just missed. His front teeth overlapped. He hadn't had braces. But his profile against the sky, in the parking lot, I thought I could love him.

"Try the sex. Really. It just loosens everything. We've found that."

I guess they still had it. That went into me, a splinter.

He knocked the tiny bag against my hip. "Thanks for this."

That afternoon, I ran a mile. Since New Year's Eve, I'd started running; that was the real gift from Jeff, I thought. I could grade my run by my stomach. And I'd managed some improvement. For the second week, the diapers remained on the shelf.

I ran past the big houses, west of Seventh, where I'd heard that a movie composer, who had four kids and a jet, lived in the dark shingled Craftsman with a red door.

It turned out, though, that running wasn't the only gift from Jeff. A week later, a package arrived. Bose noise-canceling headphones, with a computer-printed card. *To dull the leaf blower. x, j.*

My mother and Tom visited on a cold June afternoon, fog blowing in, lidding the sky. She stilted up the lawn on heels carrying a jar of applesauce. "Just heat it up a little, it's those good yellow apples and cinnamon. Boy, it's really what they call June gloom."

She instructed Tom to carry in the goose, now a waist-high, honking, plangent animal, erratic in its movements.

"That goose is making her sick," Tom muttered, hands in the pockets of his familiar pants. "She's up in the night. A goose is a very dirty animal."

It nipped me with its bill, which didn't feel as rounded as it looked.

"There, there," my mother said, petting the thing's small head, an inverted note. "He's still your goose," she called out to Will, who was sulking in the yard as they loaded it back into its box in the car.

When they left, I dialed Paul.

"Yes," he said, sotto voce. "What?" I'd already called twice that day. My quota. "My mom," I said. "When I go to Lil's, you can't leave Will alone with her."

"Claire, I'm *in the Room.*"

"She can't take care of him." She was a terrible, distracted driver. She'd scan the ribbon of stores outside her window, then say "Ooop," slamming on the brake.

"Fine," he said and hung up.

His sister in Boston—who had a law degree but now worked part-time—took home movies of her baby during her maternity leave, so her husband could watch them at midnight.

I did try to be a wife. How many dinner parties did I cook that summer for the guys Paul worked with and their wives? Jeff and Helen came too. Lola made a diary of our menus, and she took pictures of the food. Paul kept the conversations going. I didn't understand the references, the names of actors. I got up and down, taking in plates.

Late, the nights of the parties, Lola and I cleaned the kitchen, talking about which recipes succeeded, picking at leftovers. Finally, that August, she started eating with us, except on the rare nights when Paul came home.

The evening with Buck Price and Sky, my dessert, a latticed rhubarb tart, turned out exceptionally well. Buck said, "We'll have to have you guys over too."

"Or go out," said Sky, daughter of a ballerina, slipping her shoes off and taking one of her slim feet in her two hands. "I don't cook."

As if I'd been born with a measuring cup in my hand! As if I weren't meant for more. I just looked at her, but Buck quickly mumbled, "We'll take you guys out."

"So we'll go out," Paul said later, as if we'd both been unruly children. We never did go out with them. That didn't bother Paul. He didn't need friendships to catch.

Once, I delivered a script to the showrunner's house. His wife, a Chicana who'd grown up in Boyle Heights, gone to Harvard, and then dropped out, stood issuing instructions in fast Spanish to her maid, a small woman working furiously on hands and knees. Then she gave me a tour of their house, pointing out the new den where the enormous TV stood. "The decorator suggested an armoire, but I think we can't hide it. That's where it's all coming from." I felt her awareness that her husband was Paul's boss. She asked me to wait while she paid her maid, who was just then leaving with her daughter.

"Maybe she'll be like me," said the showrunner's wife, cupping the child's head. I suppose she meant Harvard and marrying the showrunner.

Maybe she doesn't want her daughter to be like you, I thought.

But of course she probably did.

I disobeyed the school director's advice and flew to Lil's fortieth. The school director was undegreed anyway. On the airplane, though, I missed Will's weight on my lap. It was the first flight I'd taken alone since he was born. *Go. We'll be fine,* Paul had promised. I expected Will to eat cereal for supper but it was only a weekend. I'd be back Sunday night. Wives in Santa Monica had fortieth birthday parties too. Helen was hosting one for Melissa, whose husband was putting together a slide show in the partners' conference room. The husbands didn't seem to have parties. They had work. Women, I guess, got lives instead.

Music was all or nothing. Art gave no B pluses, no credit for trying. If I couldn't make *that*, I'd be better off tending my son or working in a hospital. I still didn't know if I could make that. And I was almost forty.

I'd always wanted only this.

And now William too.

I had fragments of the first movement. I'd scored the main theme, giving it to the French horns. I gave an accompanying figure to the oboes, a melody of tender attentions I'd written the week Will was born. But I was stuck in the exposition. I couldn't imagine the whole structure.

On the layover, in Chicago, I called Harv and played what I had, holding the small tape recorder up to the pay-phone mouthpiece.

"You and your C-sharp minor," he said.

Cut the difficulty in four, Yo-Yo Ma's father had told him. That's what people do when they practice. Break it down into measures. I had a phrase in F-sharp major. One of the held notes was a G. The notes leading up to the arrival point implied other, short-lived harmonies. I pictured the symphony like a square cloth of fabric, moving, I could put my hands underneath. And it would stay together, woven. I sighed as the plane landed in Philadelphia. Composing was the most important thing, but it didn't make me happy. Lil had found art everywhere. Then her kids came along and they were art too, for her. As much as I loved Will, I wanted to make something longer than life.

My existence had caused too much pain. Having a child wobbled and undid my mother, forced her through strenuous marathons, at the edge of her capacity. She made it to the finish: she kept me till I was seventeen, then sent me out mostly intact, with an instrument to hold. My mother had wanted to do something artistic—she'd spent our scarce money on my lessons—but because she had to, she'd made a living teaching people to talk again. *I wanted to be somebody,* to justify all that work.

In the rental car, alone, I chattered out tunes with my teeth. "Tiny Dancer." "Billy Jean."

Lil had once collected braids people had made out of their dead loved ones' hair. I called her from the airport. "We're making scrap screens today," she said. "I'm gluing on wrens." The party was to be tango dancing in their barn.

If I made any money from this symphony, I wanted to buy one of her old pieces.

This is important too, she'd told me once, of her life with children. *Letter to a Young Mother #2.*

Will ran down the long corridor, legs greedy for motion, all knees, then swoop! Into my arms. Paul materialized from behind a pillar, bent to kiss my cheek. He'd driven to the airport, with Willie clean in clean clothes. Going home, we talked softly between Will's happy jabber, but when Paul pulled into our driveway, he lifted my suitcase to the porch and said, "I better get back."

"But it's Sunday. Almost seven."

"They're there breaking a story. I left a couple hours ago. I've got to get back."

Was he lacking because he wouldn't take off the extra hours, or was I for not appreciating what he did in fact give? The unanswerable riddle of our marriage. Still, the house felt like itself without him. Will tuckled with me in my bed until I lifted him, asleep, into his own. In the middle of that night, I rose to turn and found Paul sitting up. "Are you awake?" he asked.

I tried to be.

"I have to tell you something. He almost died, Claire." He was heaving. "It was that goose."

"What?" Will slept in the other room. I'd carried him—then slid him between clean cowboy sheets.

"Your mom and Tom took us to lunch." Paul talked in gulps. "Twin Dragons. We walked in that park with the pond. They had that goose along, and I saw a huge piece of glass. Like a windshield. So I asked her to watch Will while I moved it. I even made a joke. *Don't just watch the goose. Keep an eye on your grandson too.* I asked her because Tom was on the other side of the pond, picking up trash.

"And when I came back, I saw his jacket floating with the hood up. I literally thought, Claire, I thought, How could there be another jacket like his facedown in the pond, and then I began to look for Will and I didn't see him and it took me I don't know how long probably a minute to put together that I didn't see him and that that was him in the pond. So I jumped in with all my clothes on, my boots are ruined, and he was gulping water. I was so scared, Claire. How would I tell you?"

I felt dropped two stories. I'd asked him not to leave Will with her. Hadn't he heard that?

"I get it now," he cried. "I really get it."

So he'd heard. He just couldn't fathom the fact of an adult who couldn't be trusted: the central fact of my childhood.

We both stood over Will's little bed, watching him breathe, safe among his animals. He slept on his back, an arm thrown over his head.

In the bathroom, I noticed his gas station attendant's outfit, muddy, ruined, hanging over the lip of the tub.

"Can I ask you something, now that I'm back? I was thinking on the plane. I need some days, some days when you get home for dinner, when you kind of just take over. I'm not good at this alone."

"Okay."

"Any two days, whatever's best for you. Maybe we could start this week."

He shook his head. "I can't even think about it until after the network pitch."

"But I have work too. I need to finish this symphony."

He sat down on the bed. "Claire, you'll finish. This is a young man's career I'm in."

"And you're a young man."

"No I'm not. Not for here, I'm not." What was he saying? His voice turned soft. "If I get a show and it goes, it could be enough money for us not to worry. Life is long." He got up, walked to the bathroom, and turned the shower on. I heard him brushing his teeth.

You can have your turn, only later.

"What if I say no?" I said, in a normal voice.

He stepped out, still dry, a towel wrapped around his waist. "Claire. Just leave him with Lola." His voice had completely changed. "You can compose from nine until five."

All along, Paul had agreed that he wouldn't keep working like this. He was agreeing still. The *when* just got pushed further ahead. I kept asking for and receiving my future promise, which I carried around in my pocket. Now I felt like a bill collector.

My symphony could never earn the money a TV show might, if it sold for syndication. I understood Paul's logic, but that wasn't the hierarchy I wanted to live by. I'd known at fifteen that classical music didn't earn big money. I'd danced around the apartment kitchen in my socks when I'd opened my Guggenheim letter. We'd put that money in the bank and, eventually, used it to move here. I felt embarrassed now for how proud I'd been, for thirty-seven thousand dollars. Having a kid made the amount of money you needed grow a zero. I paid Lola every week; I understood how close her wages came to mine.

At one time, the question concerned who would *make it*. Now it seemed a matter of attrition. Musicians, excepting harpists, generally stayed. We packed the world full of piano teachers who'd once done something more than flashcards for children with half notes and quarter notes and pick-a-scale-out-of-a-hat parties.

I just wanted to be one of the ones who stayed.

The network had ordered two extra episodes this year that Paul would be paid for. The first thing he intended to do with that, he said, was replenish the thirty-seven thousand we'd taken out of savings to make the move. I suppose, then, my contribution would be settled. I was asking for something. He'd first politely said *No, not now,* and given me a wrapped box of earrings. Today, after I pushed it, he told me less politely. *Not now.* But now was when Will's life was.

"More than half my practice is with women who would give their right arm for a man like Paul," the couples' counselor said. She rocked in her Eames chair as she talked, her bare and not particularly lovely leg swinging. A huge toe was the engine rocking it all. She looked like a younger, less-dressed form of Paul's mother. *She* would have given her right arm to have a man like Paul. "Okay," I said, standing, "we're done."

Paul chuckled, still sitting, looking at her from under his long lashes. *You can't really blame her.* "This was your idea," he said, throwing up his hands.

I tried to do it Paul's way. I asked Lola to copy some program notes and fax in a contract from Kinko's. Pushing Lola seemed more promising than pushing Paul.

Then, one day when I came home from Colburn and had to dress to go out with Paul's mother, Lola gave notice. "Why, Lola?" I asked. "Are you unhappy?"

"I am working too hard. And Ruth, she is calling me, there are jobs for elderly they are paying a lot already."

"What if we pay you more?"

"At night here, too, I am working. We are always cooking! You have too many parties."

I paid her extra whenever we had a dinner. It wasn't as if *I* got *extra.* "Fine. No more parties. Please consider staying, Lola, we need you. Will loves you. And I hate to do this, but I have to go now, I'm already late for Paul's mother."

She sat in the restaurant booth, with a glass of white wine.

"Sorry I'm late. We had a calamity at home."

"Of course," she said. "Don't worry."

Her tempo jarred me. No *What calamity?* And didn't she mind sitting in a restaurant with only me after flying three thousand miles to see her son?

"How is your mother, Claire?"

"Well, she got a goose for Will, but we didn't want it so she's been raising it in her apartment. But now it's big and needs more room. So she's been going crazy trying to find it a home." She had three adoption possibilities. A petting zoo off the Pacific Coast Highway, a farmer Tom knew in Oxnard, and a normal Topanga family.

"Oh, honestly," Paul's mother said.

"It's taking a lot of her time." I nodded. "I'm a little distracted tonight because Lola gave notice."

"Claire, did you tell Paul?"

"Tried. Left a message." I shrugged.

"I wonder if it would help if I gave her a little present and said, *Just because we appreciate all you do for William.*"

"That might be nice but I think we'll have to pay her more."

"You know, Claire, every summer Marjorie would go home to Mississippi, and I never knew whether or not she was coming back."

"Really? Paul always told me Marjorie was so close to you."

"She loved the children and that's why I put up with it. But I never knew." She sighed. "If Lola becomes unreasonable, do you have agencies you can call?"

I couldn't even think about that. Whatever Lola wanted, I'd have to give her.

"But isn't it exciting, Claire, that Paul's pitch went so well?"

Paul had pitched his pilot to the head of comedy, who'd given him the go-ahead. He'd still have to be in the Room; he'd write the pilot weekends. We were supposed to be celebrating.

"Do you think two people who work like Paul should have kids? If both parents left at, say, eight-thirty, and that's the last the kid sees of them until the next morning?" Paul's mother hadn't worked hours anything like Paul's hours when she'd had children and neither did his lawyer sister in Boston now.

Just then, nine o'clock, Paul slid into the booth, hands up Pierrot style.

"Of course," his mother said, shooing away explanation.

"We were talking about whether two of you should be allowed to have kids." But would I have chosen to be Paul? I'd miss Will too much, the feel of his shins.

"I say yes," his mother said, "if they spent weekends with the children. They'd have to take their holidays with the family and sacrifice romantic vacations."

She and her romance! *Go. Work. The boy will be fine,* they both believed. As if all those women who stayed with children, for countless centuries, had been fool idiots.

"How's your teaching?" she asked, obviously pleased with this new tack.

"Teaching is a job for money," I said. "For not enough money. On my salary, it would be hard to afford a family vacation with clean bathrooms."

Later, I told Paul about Lola's threat.

"How much of a raise are you proposing? There's got to be some point at which we say no."

I balled a fist inside my pocket. "Easy for you to say."

We bickered three days. Finally he said, "So why don't we raise her twenty a week?"

I told Lola twenty-five. I'd make up the difference without him knowing.

"You ride limousine?" Lola asked four weeks later.

"No," I said instantly, but Paul smiled.

"Well, it's in Pasadena and who knows what parking'll be like. The studio'd probably pay." Even though Paul's episode wasn't nominated, we still had to go to the Emmys.

"Yes, Paul," Lola said. "Claire, you ride in limousine."

He sighed. "I'd be more excited if my show were nominated."

"It should be," I said, setting down Will's pancakes—a recipe using only eggs, one spoonful of flour, and cottage cheese.

"My employer will attend the Emmy Awards," I heard Lola say at the playclub. "They ride limousine." The nannies aspired to Helen's life, not mine. The servants' dream was to have servants, not to free all the servants and make everyone do their own wash. That was Mao's dream, but Mao had been born rich.

The words they used! The moms were right. Not only *limousine* but also *rich* and *sexy*. All the realms we didn't want our children to know about.

One night in August, Helen walked over to show me the red-room class list. Helen had been in the director's office in April and had to dig out our file from a mess. I was so grateful. She seemed invigorated by the beginning of school.

Will ran out of his room. I chased him back. "Popple in bed!" People told me Will had a big vocabulary but what they didn't mention was how small mine had become. At the beginning, it's only you talk-ing. He and I turned in gray twilights, waking to too many dawns. Pulling Will's sheet up, I told him he and Bing would be in the same class.

"Oh. Good."

Play a William, Bing used to say. When had he stopped saying that?

"I brought popcorn." Helen followed me to the black kitchen. We microwaved it, and then took the bowl and a shaker of salt outside to the front step. She showed me the choices of what you could volunteer for, when we heard the high fan of laughter. She leaned over the paper as if it were complex business.

"More piggy!" he shouted from the hall.

"Come on," I said, putting him in bed again. "You really have to sleep now."

"A hole is to dig," I said, marching out. "A house is to live in, fathers are to, what?" Lola had taught Will to say *working.* So whenever she said, *Where's Daddy?* even on the rare nights Paul came home, Will would say, *Dada working.*

"I'm going to be Class Mom," Helen said, biting down her lip.

Then came the pell-mell of steps again, and he landed in my lap. I took my sweatshirt off and blanketed it around him.

"It's a lot," she said, "but Mary thinks I should do it."

"Dada!" Will verged up, pointing. At three, he recognized BMWs.

I corrected, "Yes, that's *like* Dada's car." But he wasn't persuaded, even as the dark sedan swam past. "It's not only Dada," I told Helen, "I'm every Jeep."

We kept looking over the list trying to remember people from our parenting class, our hands reaching into the bowl for popcorn without our eyes.

"No fat," she said, underlining something with a pencil.

The moon traced sideways, behind gauzy clouds, in the end-of-summer sky. "Where did it go?" Helen asked, looking down into Will's face, because sometimes he and Bing had played hiding games. "Where's the moon?"

He shrugged. "Working."

173

I patted his knee, watching Helen, to see what she made of our boy. She didn't question herself as a mother, the way I did. "How's your poetry going?" I asked.

"Sort of back-burnered now. My mom always worked," she said, I suppose by way of explanation.

Your dad always worked too, I thought. But I hadn't liked my mom working either; I remembered the YWCA, the strange-smelling locker room, dread folded, a child on my lap. Helen was back to being a wife and mom. The poetry contest wouldn't be mentioned again.

I looked down at Will's hair, thinking, Someday you will come to me and ask, Did I do my best? "You warm enough?" It was odd company, being with someone who didn't always answer. His thumb fit tightly in his mouth. I asked Helen, "How's the sleep going?"

"Done. When Jeff went on location scout, I Ferberized."

"And it worked?"

"I knew it would. My sister did it."

My problem was the lack of a sister. Or mother. One tends not to emulate the mentally ill.

I did have Lola, though.

Helen pantomimed a quick goodbye, wearing jeans, a waffle T-shirt, and new sneakers.

"Hey," I called. "You got them." I touched an ear. The diamonds. They looked bigger than I remembered.

"Thanks," she said, oddly. Maybe he gave them to her on just an ordinary day. He obviously hadn't told her I'd helped.

"So he finally did it."

"Cubic zirconium," she said. "Ten dollars at Drugtown. I got 'em myself."

"You're kidding!" Had he taken the earrings back? Or was he saving them? Why didn't he give her those earrings? All the little refusals. I didn't understand marriage.

As she walked away, I hugged Willie, feeling stabs in my chest, pulling him closer. I was wired wrong. But even knowing that doesn't make you able to fall in love with the next good-sense man you meet or, for that matter, your own husband.

I had a son in school. It was time to put those hopes on a high shelf.

Lola

IS THIS THE PHILIPPINES?

This morning I fought again with Issa long-distance. "He is making me prime the wall," she said. "I tell him, Mom is paying for me to study. And you want me to paint."

"Get him on the phone," I said. But then I listened Bong Bong and he is right. She cannot place herself above her sisters and she should not talk to him this way. I told him, *Put her back on.*

"I am here cleaning toilets," I said. "Working seven days no off. You can paint one wall and pass a test."

Actually, since Claire hired Ofelia, I do not scrub bathrooms anymore or make the beds on Friday. But Issa can remember her mother on her knees.

Today, I have an off for the wedding of Ruth. I told Claire, she can write her music; I will take Williamo for my date. She drives us to the Wilshire bus, and he sits stiff, dressed in his Americano. Finally the 341 arrives, swaying side to side, slow, like a jeepney in Manila. At first, we pass places Williamo knows. Karate Kids. "See, that is where Helen picked the convertible." I show him the intersection where the father of Esperanza stood, his first day here, with a sign that said ORANGES $1.00, PISTACHIOS $3.00, and a bucket of roses by his feet. He did not understand English or the American system of money, but anyway he made fifty-nine dollars. There is a man there today with that same sign. This interests Williamo. "Can you get me that job, Lola?"

"You will have higher jobs. You will get a big education."

I point the Federal Building and distant towers of UCLA. Beverly Hills, he does not care; the head drops. I feel a wet on my thigh. I will wake him when we pass Dodger Stadium to see the tunnel, built during the American Depression.

But the head pops up. "Are we there yet?"

The sky outside looks poor, strings of plastic flags over a car lot, prices scrawled in soap on the windshields. People many different colors walk the cracked sidewalks.

"Lola," he whispers. "Is this the Philippines?"

"No," I have to tell him. "This is Hollywood."

Rain is the wedding present to Ruth from God. The Sapersteins had offered their garden for the wedding, and Ruth could not say no. But now, the reception will be at the place of Ruth in Eagle Rock, and then Danny will drive a carful of babysitters to Las Vegas.

Williamo has never seen the place of Ruth. A smell of adobo comes from the kitchen, where Cheska stands like a trumpeter, blowing up balloons. Ruth wears a white dress, nothing like the cream suit we wanted. Maybe she went to Las Vegas and lost. Or maybe she quit like her kids beg her to and did not even try. There is something sad of that too. Las Vegas was the place where Ruth could relax, among clicks and rings, under the indoors light. And after, walking home from the bus, she felt a hundred percent herself, tired as if coming from a day of real work, cleaning, not babysitting. Maybe we are not meant for nine-hundred-dollar suits. This neighborhood, it does not blame you for not being more. Outside her place, she would smell leaves, where the old men watered. In the kitchen, the girls left a plate of dinner out for her. She could get her clean ice.

"Sapersteins will be here," she says. Danny stands in pajama bottoms, buttoning his good shirt. Then, out of nowhere, the slave beeps. After almost one year, why today? "Ask, does she have the passport?"

The slave does not have the passport. But today, the lady left the house with the kids and forgot to lock her in. They will be gone, she thinks, three hours. Ruth tells her to walk out the house right now, she will keep walking to a food place. What is the closest? Ruth asks. Taco Bell. They will send Shirley to pick her.

Williamo tugs. "What are they talking about?"

"It is a getaway," I whisper.

"Motion sensor," Danny says, and Ruth holds the phone out so we hear the blare.

Just keep going anyway, Ruth says. Walk quietly but fast. Keep going forward.

Even with stray showers, there is a line to get married at city hall. Ruth is not the only one dressed up. Young brides tip in huge skirts.

"Cream puffs," I say.

"Where?" Williamo asks.

I point. They look frightened and excited. They should be. People marry on a dime. Like me. Now, look—everything from that.

The sons of Ruth step out from the wall, wearing suits they do not own. They had to arrange offs from their work. But Natalie, who has no job all day, she is absent. And her daughter, Aileen, she is supposed to be flower girl.

When it is their turn, the lights remain fluorescent, and Ruth looks tired. It is only as a bride that she appears without her stature, arms pinched at the sleeves. Would it be different if we could have bought that cream suit? Danny stands in his *barong* Tagalog, looking slight and foreign, saying *I do,* for the green card. In this civil administration building, that is plain. Maybe Ruth hoped for more. Just at the end, Natalie arrives, pulling her daughter. Wearing just jeans, she stops the breath. She is the one should be bride.

Cheska has decorated the apartment with white crepe paper.

At two, Sapersteins arrive, the Dr. Mrs., the guy, and Ginger, the one Ruth takes care. They have never been to Eagle Rock before. Ruth gives Ginger a basket with rice and she throws it everywhere. The Dr. Mrs. asks different babysitters, are they sure they don't mind? But what can we say when Ruth has their old vacuum cleaner?

Aileen, the real flower girl, runs to the bedroom. Ginger Saperstein looks up a way she will all her life, unhinging herself from the commotion she has caused. Mr. Saperstein just stands eating. "Very tasty," he says.

Ruth is proud of Aileen and of Natalie, who sits too far back on the couch; she does not want them like this. "Natalie is too shy with Sapersteins," she whispers. "They never see her personality." Natalie twirls the ring her father put on the finger of Ruth. Ruth gave that to her today. It was not a marriage to cherish; there was violence. "Sex, like in America, did not work for me," Ruth says. "But God married us to make them." In a way she is still saying thank you.

Natalie, too, she is divorce. But the guy, he built bookshelves in her apartment. He and the Korean together! This summer, Natalie found a tumor on the neck of her employer, while she was massaging him. He gave her a reward and now she only paints her pictures. Ruth says they are all still pictures of beds. Made and unmade beds.

I hear the nudge of tires. Through the gauzy screen, someone steps out a car into rain. The slave, wearing a yellow shift. Very thin. Danny comes to stand behind Ruth. The Sapersteins, they will not understand. For the slave, Ruth will cancel Las Vegas. Let the casinos keep their store flowers and champagne. She will stay home. "My real wedding, no one here would believe. The orchestra, the silver." Her voice hushes. She means this time, at the core, there is one particle sugar.

The slave weaves to one side; something is wrong her balance. She is tall for an Asian, fine boned, but the cheeks fall hollow, dark around the eyes. Danny puts a hand under her arm; Shirley, on the other side, says, "This is Ate Ruth, I told you."

The slave lowers to a genuflection.

"See." I take the hand of Williamo. This is what we did not witness at the city hall. Ruth and Danny held the wick all along, but this one Ruth pulls up, she makes the spark. That is always the way with marriage. I tell him, "The arrival of the third one, the small stranger, that is what brings it to life. A real life." I finally understand why Ruth favors Natalie over her better sons. Some people, they can love only the broken.

Mr. Saperstein returns his plate to the kitchen, saying, "Very very good. All very good." His wife flies out to the car, making her coat a roof for Ginger. Then it is only Filipinos and Williamo. Ruth covers the slave with a blanket. "You can keep that. It will be yours." Even with so much party food, the slave she will not eat. Shirley says she does not want that anybody will see.

Ruth tells us to call the slave Candace. She should never hear us say "the slave."

I press the hand of Williamo on a paper plate of paint, to put it on a page in *The Book of Ruth*. He writes his own name and I add *Age 3, 1994.* I hurry him to finish his second cake before we start home, when there is a honk outside. Lucy stands. "Bye-bye, Ate. Bye, Lola." The door slams. Ruth shakes her head. "Does he ask if you need a ride? And out she runs."

"I'll take you, Lola," Natalie says, finally getting up from the couch.

"But we are not on your way."

"I'm driving Shirl anyhow." Shirley has been cleaning two houses since the divorce of her employers. She takes care five kids, doing laundry, cooking dinners, making the lunches for the school. She likes her employers and Cindy and Bob, the new husband and the new wife, she says they are also nice. When they have a party, Shirley is the one to serve and do the dishes, but she never minds because Cindy makes one of everything for her; if they are having fillet of salmon, Cindy will buy eight, not seven, one for Shirley too.

"So what's the prob?" Natalie asks.

"I met a lady from my province and she is earning the same for five days, not seven," Shirley says. "And you know what she is doing? She is just walking the dog!"

Claire stands from her chair, a cup of tea and her open book under lamplight. "How was it, Lole? Get your pajamas on! Brush your teeth! And what do you say to Lola?" She yells again. "William!"

"Thanks," he calls. "Night."

Claire

ALL THE CHRISTMAS PARTIES

Will walked straight into school carrying his lunchbox, trying to do everything right. I lingered at drop-off, hoping for some warmth, maybe a new friend I didn't find, but enjoying the fringes anyway, child-made pictures on the wall. When the teacher closed the door, I walked home past a high school and slipped into the back of the auditorium while the orchestra tuned. They were practicing *Firebird* that fall. "Okay, let's take it from measure one thirty-six," their patient conductor said.

At home, I made black coffee, carried it with me to my hot room, and stayed five hours. Even though I'd had Lola, the time when Will was at school felt different. My symphony eked out, measure by measure.

Finally, in November, I was down to fingerings. I sat at the kitchen table with a metronome and a laptop, notating the score. Quarter note 132. There were hundreds of details. Making sure the dynamics were correct in all the parts. I found a crescendo without a mark at the end. Then I went over all of the balances. One of my teachers in school told me, a wind instrument is balanced in weight by twelve to sixteen strings. Then I had a glitch and had to get the computer guy. After all that I changed the instrumentation with Finale. Finally, I pressed PRINT PARTS. It was amazing. You used to have to copy the parts yourself by hand. I carried my stack of paper to Kinko's and faxed it in.

"You probably won't hear until after the holidays," Paul said as we strolled on our main street Saturday morning. We bought little treats—coffee for me, an ice blended for him, a chocolate spelt muffin for Will—and pushed the stroller in and out of shops.

"Stop doing that," Paul said. My fingers were going on my other arm. Bach unaccompanied cello, which the guy in Australia thinks was written by his second wife. Anna Magdalena. Paul didn't like Will to see. He thought it made me look crazy. I stopped when Paul was there, but I'd long ago given up on Will not knowing.

Marriage seemed a huge machine, plowing forward impervious to my flimsy bubbles of feeling. Every day, I woke up to Paul's familiar noises in the kitchen. I kept the crush like a pill at the bottom of my bag.

We ran into Jeff and Helen on the street, and they came along into a store where Paul had seen a dress he wanted me to try on. They added romance to the day, I suppose, as did the high winter clouds. The friendship between the four of us made being grown-up calm and exciting at the same time, like a drink. My crush, which had once been alive, causing agitation, had stilled.

A dress. A frill. I was making progress. For a year, I'd run each day. A month ago, I told Lola to stop buying the twelve-packs. "Why, you do not need anymore? Good," she said, with what felt like warmth, an oblong suspended in the air. I moved the last package to the upper part of the closet with the white breakfast-in-bed tray we'd gotten as a wedding present. Our son was three, in school already.

I slid on the dress, pulling my stomach in, rising a little on tiptoes. I saw Helen notice my feet, toenails just the color of toenails. Women here polished.

"What do you think?" I said. "Be honest."

"Oh, it's great," she said, frowning. "Just take it in a little here." She pinched the fabric with authority, then went to ask the salesgirl to pin it.

After she left, I asked Paul, "Are my feet okay?"

He looked at me. "Are you crazy?"

But I slipped on my clogs before stepping out.

"You can wear it to all the Christmas parties," Helen said.

"You sound like an old holiday card."

"That's a dress that'll make you feel like the prettiest girl in the room," Jeff said.

"Not a feeling I've had."

Helen had put on a watch. Jeff picked up her wrist and assessed it. What had ever happened to those earrings?

Paul extracted his credit card, taking the matter of payment seriously. I was better off with him. "See that woman," I whispered. "My grandmother had that hair. *I'm a silverette,* she used to say."

A happy afternoon in Los Angeles, 1994.

Tom brought me two bare-root roses, setting them on the porch. I asked my mother if she wanted to see the dress.

"Just great," she said, when I came out in it, over jeans. "Wear it while you've still got the good arms."

I asked her about the goose.

"He's gone," she said.

"Well, that's good."

"I suppose."

"And you can always visit."

"Not really," she mumbled, as if talking to herself. "Not yet."

Tom shook his head, hands in pockets, looking at the ground as he usually did. His feet shuffled, in the same shoes he always wore.

"Which place did you choose?"

She looked up, her mouth peculiar. "None, really."

"What do you mean?"

"Well, he's in heaven now!"

"She had him put down," Tom said. "She didn't tell me either."

"But you had those three places. Why not the farm?"

She shook her head, wincing. "They seemed nice at first. But then when I really saw the way they treated the animals, I wouldn't have left him there. I think they would have eaten him."

She'd once talked about giving me away. She'd described the families she was considering. They'd sounded great.

The goose had never acquired a name. It remained only The Goose.

"We've got to go now—Bromeliad Society meeting. And then we're going to eat at Twin Dragons. Do you want me to leave them here?" Tom had dragged the two roses up to the door. I was still wearing my new dress.

"Just don't plant them in front," my mother said. "People will steal the blooms." Tom and I looked at each other. She carried a scissors in her bag when we walked. She clipped roses and hid them in the bottom of Will's stroller.

I got up at five and baked blueberry corn muffins from a recipe I'd scribbled in my twenties on the flyleaf of the *Tassajara Bread Book*. I was taking Willie over to play at Helen's, and I had to be careful now; Bing was his only friend in the class. Holiday cards cluttered their table, photographs with scrolly *Season's Greetings, Merry Christmas,* or *Happy Hanukkah* printed at the bottom.

"This makes a hundred twenty-seven!" Helen said, opening an envelope. "Jeff says pretension is the cardinal sin in the TV world."

"And there's the difference," Jeff said himself, opening the refrigerator and grabbing a kefir, "between network television and the movies." He took a Hanukkah card out of my hand (three boys, in identical white turtlenecks), assessed, and discarded it. "Why bother," came his verdict, meaning not *Why bother at all?* but *Why bother if you can't do a better job than this?* Which pretty much summed up my feelings too. We didn't do holiday cards. But Jeff had Helen. And she'd bought a small masterpiece.

She probably would have trooped off to Sears too, if she'd married someone else. But she'd squatted, a hot day in October, on a Silverlake photographer's cement floor, shaking her keys, making faces, then begging and finally bribing Bing to sit still in his reindeer cap. In the black-and-white photo, embedded in construction paper, the photographer had captured Bing, hat aslant, in an expression of awe.

I ran my finger over the seam where construction paper met photo. "How'd they embed it like that?"

"Took me a long time."

She'd made them herself! I stared at the card. I wanted one like this of Will.

"First, I glued the photo on a piece of green paper. And then, with a straight edge . . ."

Jeff walked out while she was talking. Lucy stood at the sink, sticking eucalyptus branches, buttons still on, among red leaves and hydrangeas. Why didn't Lola make flowers? She had time now. Will was in school until two. Chest up, belly high, Lucy carried her vase into the living room. I complimented her and she giggled. "In our place, Claire, we learn that in school. Flower arrangement!"

Helen continued to open mail. She and Jeff did things in front of people that most of us do alone. Maybe that was a sign of success. A photograph fell out of an envelope, *Helen, age 5* penciled on the white border. Girls stood at a ballet barre, Helen, age 5 concentrating so hard her tongue stuck out. Tummies, flat feet, legs like isosceles triangles: none of those little girls would become ballerinas. The room eclipsed them; an old scarred floor, a tin ceiling, and huge windows. The kids' tuition probably helped real dancers pay the rent.

"I went every Saturday morning for like ten years." She'd had lessons and tutors. Now she crumpled the picture in a ball, after her mother saved it. She didn't want *him* to see those thighs. "Why ballet? Those Upper West Side moms couldn't have imagined us actually growing up to be dancers while they sat sipping their Zabar's to-go's."

We drank nonfat lattes, ice blendeds, a dozen small consolations. But for what, exactly, were mothers always being consoled?

Those women must have hoped that dance would teach their daughters poise.

"From the gypsies they learned grace and speed," Helen said.

"*Grace and Speed,* a love story," Jeff added, passing to the refrigerator.

"At the end of the hour, one by one, we had to *chaîné* across the room, spotting."

"What's that?" I'd never taken.

"You look at a spot until the very last moment, then you whip your head around to find it again, so you almost never lose it, or for just a blink. I was screaming at Bing and Simon when they ran ahead of me in two different directions at the Farmers Market, and I realized *that's what it was for.* Training. For never losing them."

Bing and Simon. Bing liked Simon better now. Better than our Will.

Helen wore a black dress with a scalloped neckline and Jeff had on jeans. When we'd first moved here, I'd made the mistake of assuming that if the guys wore jeans, I could too. I stepped onto the porch in my new dress. Will ran to me and hung on my knees. I lost my hands in his curls. That night, I wouldn't have traded anything.

"No, Mommy, no, please!" His voice arched over the still, bluish lawn when I handed him to Lola and headed for the car. She carried him overshoulder like a log—I watched them as we drove up the palm-lined street, to the mountains. The palms tilted toward the beach. Every time I drove up our street, I felt like straightening them as they ticked by.

"Who's going to be there?" I tried to forget Will's cry.

"I think it'll be big," Paul said.

"Not just the hamburger-and-hot-dog crowd?" That's what I called the TV people; their lack of pretension extended to party food.

"She's actually supposed to be a great cook," Helen said.

I sank down in the dark red leather of the convertible. "Let's keep driving. Antelope Valley." Grass Valley, Apple Valley. Such pretty California names.

Jeff pulled to a stop in front of what you'd have to call a mansion; it was too wide to be a house. He turned off the ignition. "You guys ever get scared right before you walk in?" I kind of fell in love with him all over again.

Paul had a raring-to-go look. "You believe people our age own this?" With his pilot scheduled to shoot, Paul would finally be somebody to these people.

Kids darted through a huge room. Oh, I thought, we could have brought Will.

Paul and I walked over to the fireplace, where three guys from his show stood, hands in their pockets, looking daunted under the oversized mantel. They wrote comedy, but you'd never know it now. They all *wanted* to write for TV; they hadn't failed as screenwriters or *New Yorker* cartoonists. They thought the funniest stuff written now aired on prime-time television and felt aggrieved that the *New York Times* and their parents still thought Art meant movies. Nonetheless, they peeked over at Jeff, standing with Buck Price and Andy North. The directors *did* seem cooler than the TV guys, whose pants looked too distinctly pressed. Buck Price had on a vintage bowling shirt; Andy North slouched in a Patagonia jacket and looked like his wife cut his hair. They were guys who'd had girlfriends in high school; as if to prove it, Andy had married his—Alison North, who was a foot shorter and tucked under his long arm. "You married her before you knew you were going to be Andrew North," I overheard Jeff say once, meaning *before you could get actresses.* But they had four kids and stood laughing together. Buck had married Sky Tucci, the fine-boned actress who'd found her ring in the sand and wouldn't cook, but I didn't see her here.

The TV guys felt the movie people snubbed them and maybe they did. The movie directors thought their work was more important but the big TV writers lived in mansions. "Wow," Andy said, about the built-in stereo, as if we were in somebody's parents' house. The TV guys worked together thirteen hours a day in a run-down trailer on the Lot that had stained carpeting and lavish quantities of Snackwells, but they looked awkward here. The homes, you got the feeling, were all the wives' doing.

Jack, the highest-paid joke writer in television, ambled over, bald and frowning. He had a wincing quality I liked. I tried to nudge Paul into a conversation with him.

Paul began a story about his grandmother. When Jack relented a smile, I looked around. I'd cooked one meal for quite a few people here. Across the room, Jeff's fingers absentmindedly riffled a fern. He plucked off a frond, stuck it in his mouth, and gulped. I laughed, making Paul and Jack look up. Jeff could still thrill me. That was kind of a relief.

The hostess stir-fried at an enormous stove. Not counting her maid, she was the only woman in the kitchen who had a job. She was president of Fox TV. Everyone knew, though, that she *had to work;* her husband made experimental films. Barefoot, her hair tied back, wearing what used to be called a muumuu, she seemed to have given up on looks. Could I?

"Can we just give up on looks?" I whispered to Helen.

"No," she said back. "We're too old."

"Like this, Esmeralda," the hostess said, in the particular tone of bosses, scooping the contents of a white yam into the bowl of a food processor. I was hungry.

Several wives leaned so close they ran the risk of getting splattered. TV *wives* weren't dorky. One wore turquoise loafers thin as a sock. Brownish calves, like two-by-fours, stuck out of cowboy boots next to red pumps on the kitchen floor. These women understood shopping. I suppose I was staring at the ground.

Two women compared architects. "Which stove?" one asked the other. "Do you care about convection?"

"I don't know, should I? I like those red knobs on the Wolf."

Copper pipes? Yes. Wool sisal for the kids' rooms or something synthetic? Synthetic cleaned better, but was it just too icky? They concurred on gas tankless water heaters. They'd learned these names, features, potentials for durability. They spoke in burdened tones of complaint but underneath ran straight lines of pride. These young women assumed so much: a house and kids. One-two-three.

A redhead we'd once had over to dinner said, "Hey, where're you guys now? Didn't I see you in that open house on Latimer?"

"Oh, we're still in the same place." I looked down at my pumps. I'd bought three pairs of them almost a decade ago with Lil. I'd thought they were classic, but here they looked dowdy, too dressed up. I'd loved that shingled house on Latimer. In a narrow room with a straw crucifix over the bed, a daughter had lived all her life until college, the Realtor had told me.

"Why doesn't he buy you a house?" the hostess asked, turning from her stove.

Then they were all looking at me. Every wife in that kitchen had a house. They nodded, defending my rights. But I felt exposed, as if Paul hadn't given me a ring.

"Your place is great," Helen said. "And you have an incredible deal."

"Too bad they won't sell you *that* house," the redhead said.

But we could never afford it. These were the women I'd expected to be impressed by Paul's pilot order. I had too little kick in me. "Excuse," I said, without the "me," a little homage to Lola.

I locked myself in the bathroom. I had a small yellow *Anna Karenina* in my purse. In long-ago Russia, Kitty dressed for a ball. I sat on the floor. According to Tolstoy, there was a time in a woman's life for parties. For me, that time had passed. I slowed down, not wanting

Kitty's happiness to turn. Once, my friends and I talked about people in books as much as we talked about our parents, more than we talked about ourselves. Startled by a knock, I shoved up. Kitty was giving away dresses—the brown, the violet—to her maid.

The redhead slipped in. "When we get settled, I want to have you guys over. I still remember that pudding you made. Was it warm?"

I found myself in a hall, hearing the cymbal shimmer of pans from the kitchen, then roamed into what I later learned was called the library. There were no books. Shelves displayed casted figures from *Star Wars* and a spotlit artifact labeled LUKE SKYWALKER'S LIGHT SABER. William would love this, I thought. So would Lola. There were big chairs, an Oriental rug, ottomans. I wanted to sit and read. But I made myself go back in, passing narcissus sprouting in crates. Next to the Tolstoy, a notebook rested in my purse; I penciled in *narcissus* below the number of a woman on Camden Drive who did movie stars' eyebrows. *I promise you,* Helen had told me, *there's nothing that makes that big a difference on a face.*

I stood in line for the bar. How did you talk to people at parties? I couldn't remember. I spoke to children more than grown-ups. And to Lola, whose first language was Tagalog.

I scanned the room. Paul coaxed a group into laughter like a conductor, bringing up the percussion.

"I'm their postmistress," the woman in front of me said.

"In my kid's school, they gossip about the *children,*" someone said. "This one cheats, that one bites. I'm more interested in the *parents'* cheating."

"The parents' biting."

These women had large glasses, large noses, and interesting jewelry: style, in other words. Working moms. The stay-at-home moms tended to be better looking; they did their tinkering internally, their bodies tight from workouts, their skin from God knows what. They maintained regimens strict as those of actresses.

I sat down next to Helen.

"The tennis coach, the band leader, the math tutor, the speech therapist," said a woman whose pants ended in fringe. "They all have to be birthdayed and Christmased."

Suddenly, invisible lashes from the fire touching me, I was happy. I had Lola's gift in my desk drawer. I'd found a beautiful pair of old diamond earrings at Jack's Jewelry, set in white gold from the fifties. A little bit, I wanted them myself.

"You can tell she'd be beautiful," a man behind us said, "if she wasn't pregnant."

Helen's hand went to her tummy. "Bing and I made wrapping paper this afternoon. Potato prints. And I sent off my out-of-state packages, so that's all done, and after, I asked the parking attendant if he'd like a cup of coffee. He's just cooped up in that little booth all day. I still had to pick up brandy and check Fred Segal for my mom, but I drove and got two fresh coffees. He was so surprised when I came back. I haven't gotten that much gratitude from anyone for years."

When I thought of Christmas, I thought of women alone in cars.

"For me, it was from nursing my dad before he died," someone behind me said.

The woman had freckles, which seemed to clash with her pumps and sheer stockings. Her face had a symmetry I caught glimpses of but then lost again. Freckles. Maybe she's only half black, I thought.

"Tuesday, Thursdays, I see patients without health insurance. I can do that without jeopardizing my kids' tuitions, because of my husband. I want to work more than I did ten years ago."

"I want to too," I said, "but I don't."

The front door opened and a man ushered in two girls in ballet costumes and a nanny wearing dirty running shoes and a parka. "Melissa's in Connecticut," he offered, by way of explanation.

Jeff walked toward us. Helen's spine straightened, breasts perking. I felt my hips unmold too.

"How'd you decide on ob-gyn?" I made myself ask the freckled doctor.

"One night I was in ER, and we lost every single person. I decided I wanted life."

Jeff could change a conversation; I'd seen it often enough to recognize the sudden lidding of fun. But the woman in the fringed pants stood with her back to the fire, recounting a series of disastrous presents from her mother-in-law. A sweater stretcher. An errant cotton-candy maker. "Her next gift was alive . . ."

Jeff assessed her, looking down her front with a flat glance, like a blade separating peel from a fruit. "Anyone know where I can get a Santa suit?"

"I do," she said, facing him. Then he touched her chest with the back of his hand. Helen looked down. In front of us, her husband was enjoying this woman's body.

Now I understood: *he just did this.* It wasn't me. It probably wasn't ever me.

Paul came up and started rubbing my shoulders. The fire still shifted, murmuring.

"Hey, what about you?" Jeff asked the freckled doctor. "You work Christmas?"

"A big day in maternity. Lot of little Jesuses."

Across the room, girls in tutus minced out, arms tuliped above their heads.

"A long long time ago, in a place where it snowed," a girl stood reading, "the Queen ran away. Her daughters went to find her."

Two Asian girls titied out on point, their legs so even they looked as if they'd been turned on lathes.

"We should have brought Will," I whispered.

"No, we shouldn't have," Paul said.

Jeff sat on the arm of Helen's chair. " 'In the room the women come and go talking of Michelangelo.' "

"You wish," I said.

"The King didn't have time to find his wife. But he gave his daughters money and their nanny packed lunch."

A man behind us said, "Eight o'clock was up sixteen percent in eighteen-to-thirty-four, but dipped at nine in eighteen-to-forty-nine."

"Lost how much of the demo lead-in?"

"The head of Sony," Paul whispered. "And my agent's boss."

One small girl strayed out into the audience to find her mother (who turned out to be the freckled doctor). Oh. *The Chinese Adopteds.* The hostess stood and clapped. "I'll feed the kids now in the kitchen.

They can take their plates to the library and we'll put on *The Sound of Music*."

Around the room, sharp whispered conversations ensued.

Alison North stood adamant, hands on hips. Soon, Andy carried the kids out to the car. "I'm a sleep Nazi," Alison said. "And we have a twice-a-week video policy." None of the directors' wives allowed their kids to watch TV.

"I'm easy," the freckled doctor said.

Before I lived here, if I'd heard the words *Hollywood party*, I'd have pictured ball gowns and men in tuxedos. If I'd imagined servants at all, they'd have been in black and white too. But the men here turned their baseball caps backward. The nannies wore everyday clothes. Aleph Sargent, the only movie star I recognized, had on jeans.

In the kitchen, nannies hovered around the table where the kids ate. I thought I recognized the one with the adopted Chinese girls.

"When they're done, serve yourselves," the hostess called over to the nannies. Mothers stood near the stove, too, excitedly discussing a cooking teacher for their help. This took place in front of Esmeralda, who removed dirty pans from under the hostess's ministrations and washed them, so that the elaborate dishes, being carried out on platters by college kids in white smocks, seemed to come from a clean, dry kitchen.

"Count me in," said the woman in turquoise loafers.

"My housekeeper just tears. I'd like things to be a little more seemly. Once she's done with a chicken—" The redhead stopped and shuddered.

"My nanny cuts great," Helen blurted. Lucy arranged their take-out food on platters, added lemon slices and parsley.

Just so it's a little pretty, I'd heard Lucy say.

Lights lowered in the dining room, and people found their seats.

A man to the right of the hostess had seen a civil war in Africa with real slaves. He had the footage—"Well, a third of it, anyway"—for a documentary.

The reigning comedy wife, Katie Jacobs, whose husband, Jack, created *Danny* ten years ago, listened with her head cocked in a way

191

that meant *We'd contribute.* Katie pointed her fork at Jeff. "Your movie's about Africa too, isn't it?"

"Well, it's kind of a personal story. About sex, mostly." He shrugged, shooting a nervous glance at the documentarian, who was talking about clitorectomies. "About a woman learning how to have sex without props."

"Learning how to *love*," Helen corrected.

College kids set down platters of salmon, tureens of mashed yams, and bowls of the greens we'd watched wither. The documentarian was going on about a slave encampment. Annoyance showed around Katie's mouth; I hoped he'd stop, for the sake of his budget. Two women to my left talked about getting their nannies to do more. Helen glanced over to Jeff as he leaned in to hear the freckled doctor. "When the women had kids, they quit." But Helen didn't seem to mind. Maybe she knew he wouldn't fall for a black woman. Or a doctor.

"I never put in gas anymore. I tell her, *Check it every night and take Brookie and Kate to the car wash.*"

"How many times a week does she change the sheets?"

Since Will started school, Lola had begun to watch *As the World Turns,* the whine filtering up through the pipes. Should I be getting her to do more? I felt sorry for the nannies showing up to work tomorrow, or waking up at work, more likely.

The documentarian was still describing his slaves. But by now everyone had had enough of Africa.

"You can't imagine how many manuscripts I get from the wives," the agent said to the studio guy.

Jeff's hands steepled. "How many babies you think you've delivered?"

"These yams are no fat," the hostess called out. "No butter."

Men on both sides of me marveled, forking the potatoes. Jeff took seconds.

"I wish I'd paid more attention in the kitchen," I said to Helen.

Then the hostess, beseeched by the persistent, thin agent, listed ingredients: "Thyme, garlic, salt, olive oil."

"Darling. Oil is not nonfat." His fork, bearing a lump, returned to the plate.

"I told my nine-year-old if he didn't make his bed, I'd dock his allowance," said the woman with the fringed pants. "So now I'm making beds for a nickel a day."

"I don't know when I stopped remembering their names," the doctor said.

Two men joined the conversation about housekeepers. They sounded satisfied, reporting audacities.

"And then she . . ."

"Well, ours . . ."

A thousand-dollar dress had been tossed in the dryer. "Brookie's American Girl doll's wearing it now." An Ansel Adams mural was Windexed.

"Oh, we get a detective," a bearded screenwriter said. "Have him tail her."

Lights went off and the hostess floated through the dark carrying a flaming baked Alaska. "Homemade ice cream," she called. "Pumpkin from a real pumpkin." She raised a champagne flute. "I want to thank Roger, who allows me to do all this."

Years after that night, Paul would mimic her, arms spread. "All *this*."

"None of them were lactating at their eight-week checkup. These women are garment workers; they can't afford formula. So I found out. They pay brokers to take their babies back to China. One asked me to make a scar on her preemie's foot so her mother in Xian could recognize him."

Helen listened to the woman with fringe talk about managing children with no help. I listened too, though I had only one child, a nanny, and not infrequently I cried in my closet.

"If you count the baby nurse," Katie said, from the other side of the table, "I have more nannies than I do kids, and I still can't get anything done." She spoke with the unapologetic air that came with money.

"How do you manage with Jack working so much?" I asked.

The thin agent had his hands on Paul's shoulders, saying, "Your mediocre rise."

Paul looked up. "I do hope you mean meteoric."

I went over to the table where Esmeralda was setting up a coffee urn.

Andy North asked me how work was going.

I was probably a curiosity to these guys.

I began to blunder. He and Buck listened solemnly, with no twinkle of play. Then Helen walked up, touching Buck's elbow, and their faces opened.

"Let's get out of here," she said to me. Jeff and the freckled doctor were the only ones left at the table. A small black-and-white picture rested on the cloth in front of them. Jeff noticed us coming. The doctor stood, saying, "Congratulations."

"Congratulations for what?" I asked, bright with the premonition of pain.

"We'd be greatly honored if you'd deliver us," Jeff said.

I stood numb. Helen looked annoyed. She hadn't even told *us* yet. And her husband was offering her womb to a stranger. I watched her privately rearrange. She could count on his forgetting. Doctors' appointments fell far beneath his radar.

Helen needed more children, I told myself, the way I needed work. I made myself move.

At last we stood in the drafty entrance hall, waiting to say goodnight. Husbands shouldered on wives' coats. The hostess stood by the open door, barefoot, chatting here and there, as if tasting her guests. "Happy house hunting!" she called to someone on the lawn. "We're house hunting too."

Alison North gasped. "But this house is so great!"

"I deserve a bigger kitchen," she said. "I read the multiple-listings book before bed. Better than any novel!"

"We're off to Hawaii!" someone called from the curb.

I fell into a late conversation with the redhead, who was telling me that Will tripping and scraping himself and not crying but just getting up and running was typical of autism. The way he spun the wheels of toy cars was another sign. "Sounds like he's somewhere on the spectrum," she said.

And I'd been thinking about Jeff Grant! She hadn't asked about the place on Latimer to humiliate me. She'd been looking for a way to bring up their new house, which she'd selected because she'd decided Canyon Elementary was the best school for their daughter. Most of her life was spent attending conferences, trying to understand Elissa's disease. She hoped to get Elissa into a school where next year, for first grade, she wouldn't need a shadow. They hoped Elissa could be mainstreamed by second or third grade. Later, they would hope that for middle school.

"I have to get your doctor's number," I said.

"Talked to Shields," Jeff told Helen as we walked outside. "So this weekend, we'll do more looking. We'll just up the price to what it takes." I happened to see the skid of victory, unmanaged on her face. Maybe there was an essential agreement at the bottom of every marriage. I supposed it was time I read the fine print of my own.

In the car, Helen said, "I'm going to get Lucy to do more."

"Wonder what they'd make of Lole," Paul said. "She's not a trophy nanny. But she loves them."

"I feel like rich people have a whole 'nother kind of nanny," Jeff said. "Hey, I'm hungry again. Want to go someplace?"

It was cold in the convertible, the stars sharp.

"Pasadena," I said, the way I'd said Antelope Valley earlier.

"That doctor I was talking to?" Jeff said. "She had her own kid who died the day he was born."

Wind touched my head in patches; I began to tell Paul.

"*He's not* on any *spec*trum. Too smart for his own good, that's all."

Helen turned around to tell us that three couples they knew had had their kids tested after the redhead thought they were autistic.

"Guess autism is just kind of like kids in general," Jeff said.

"This woman asked, 'What do you *do*?' I hadn't heard that for a few decades," Helen said. "I said I'm home with my son. I'm fortunate I don't have to work."

"*Nothing, I do nothing at all*, I used to say when people asked." When I was trying to be a composer, before I'd had anything performed.

"Hardest job I ever had," Helen said.

"Let's go to our place," Paul said. "So Lole can go to bed." Lucy had a room in their house; she was probably sleeping already.

"Can we just stop home a minute?" Helen said. "I've got to get out of these shoes."

We shuffled in, a party of revelers, and Lucy appeared at the top of the stairs in a high-necked nightgown, robe, and slippers.

"He asleep?" Helen whispered, taking off her shiny paper hat.

On their dining room table stood a severe rectangular structure that resembled a Quaker church. Helen had gone to a two-day gingerbread workshop. Her house alluded to children, but if a real child had worked on it, it couldn't have looked like this. It would have been smeared with frosting, lopsided, the roof laden with candy. No, this wasn't authentic or even useful. Only beautiful. What her life now allowed her to make.

"Bing keeps asking when we're going to eat it," she said.

"Helen, I told you I want to put it in the movie."

"Speaking of eating," Paul said.

"Promise me you'll put it away? I don't want to have to worry about it." Satisfied, Jeff opened the front door, offering us the night, an inverted bowl of stars. We walked.

At our house, Lola, who'd been on the couch, sprang up like a cat and collected the things around her (keys, her magazine) to carry back to her place.

"Pay you tomorrow," I called out after her.

I sent Paul to the garage for firewood, handed Helen a corkscrew and a bottle of wine, set water to boil, dressed arugula, and took eggs out of the refrigerator. In a few minutes, I carried nuts warmed with rosemary to where Paul knelt, trying to blow up a fire. "Want help?"

Jeff, as always, handed me a wineglass.

"I think the wood's wet. Decoupage," Paul said, standing, abandoning the logs. "I do *de*coupage." Paul's pronunciation made Jeff hoot and slap the front of his jeans, a fire growing behind him at the end of my hands. "Assemblage!" Paul said. "I require a studio to assemble my assemblage! He allows me to do"—he spread his arms, the fire caught and noisy—"*all this. All what?*"

UCLA kids and a dark-skinned woman had served and cleaned the kitchen. Still, even with help, I didn't think I could cook for that many people.

Hardest job I ever had, Helen had said, about being a mom.

Paul didn't think it was a job; he didn't think it was hard. Paul considered music on an altogether different plane than decoupage, assemblage, raising children, and *all this.*

I wasn't so sure.

"Guess the wood dried," Jeff said, elbowing Paul as flames popped and sassed.

"As I said this morning, when Lola was holding the ladder and Claire put the star on top, *Jews don't fix.*"

"Speaking of Lola, what are you doing, a bonus and a present?" Helen asked.

"Definitely a present," I said. "Lola's family."

"Homemade, you think?"

"Maybe." I hadn't told anyone about Lola's earrings yet. Not even Paul.

A few minutes later I served the wet pasta, the arugula just wilting, an egg on top, with tin tongs. I sent Paul in with the plates, his sweatshirt falling over his wrist. In profile, he was so handsome. I'd once rubbed my hands together, relishing. That made me feel wistful, as if something irrecoverable had been lost.

"So two, huh?" Paul said, when Jeff followed us into the kitchen. "You'll be in Africa, right, when the kid's born? She okay with that?"

"Who, Helen? Oh, I think Helen's having a ball."

I waited until they left, then lay on my side, and the pain, somehow liquid, flooded in. They were having a baby. He touched that other woman too.

Why had Jeff had to flirt with me? He could have left us, in our modest marriage, alone.

"Ofelia!" Paul fell down onto the bed, arms out to the sides. "Who's Ofelia?"

"Ofelia is the woman who irons your shirts."

"I overheard you and Helen talking about bonuses. So, what're you thinking?" In the minutes we had before sleep, he elected to talk about this. "What are *they* giving Lola?"

"Three hundred, I think." Helen had said two fifty.

"So let's do that."

"But she works for us five days! Lola's present should be more than the cost of one dinner out."

"I just gave her that VCR." In November, someone had had a VCR delivered to Paul as a thank-you present for punching up a pilot. We didn't need another, so he loaded it, still new in the box, into the trunk of an old green car. Lola had arranged for a friend named Danny to drive it to Ruth's place. I'd wanted to set it up in her room here.

"But that's not a present! She has it already. She thought of it as something you didn't want. The way we hand down our old clothes."

"This was a brand-new VCR. Sony!"

In front of our fire, Helen had told me she had a persistent day-dream: a shiny package, wrapped in pink, with long white ribbons, and inside a check that would astonish Lucy. She wanted to send Lucy back to school, to give her the calm peace of her own college days, albeit late, in another country, and though, according to Lola, Lucy already completed *ten years medicine.* Helen liked to picture Lucy walking through a campus, taking tests at long tables, filling in the little ovals, getting them all right. *We'll lose a nanny and gain a pediatrician,* I'd heard her say.

Paul shook his head. "Lola'll send it all home anyway, but do what you want. You're a forty-year-old woman."

"We have a lot of money, you know."

"I know how much money we have. And I also know what our expenses are."

Our arguments felt futile and engraved. Trembling, I wrote the check for one thousand, balancing the checkbook on my knee in bed. I didn't tell him about the earrings.

But Paul was right. Our gifts didn't astonish Lola.

"Claire and Paul, thank you," she said, the next day, with the same inflection she'd had last year, when it was three hundred. She shambled off, hands in her shorts pockets, and from behind doors, edging out of tree trunks, squatting behind bushes, more people rose, all foreign, looking like Lola but each with one thing wrong: a patch of hair missing, teeth broken, thick legged. Multiplying, they advanced toward us. Aunts, cousins, distant relatives, even dead parents stepped from inside trees and ghosted up with open hands. All the money we had was not enough, all the money we'd ever have.

I'd wanted to save her. But Lola refused to be one person.

Lola

THIS IS WHY MY LIFE

In the kitchen of her employer, Lucy listens to hearts. Babysitters who six months ago doubted her degree unbutton their blouses, all because she is now one hundred a day. She handles her stethoscope like a clarinet. "Very expensive, Lola. More than two thousand pesos." But I know the price of a stethoscope: we purchased one for Issa long ago.

"Heart murmur," she tells Mai-ling, "You know you have that? You go where they have EKG. Do you get Kaiser?"

"No. I work seven days."

The doorbell rings. Tarek, the bottom helper of my weekend employer, carries a pink box tied with string. The birthday cake. "I'll put it in the fridge." He is used to this house already. He follows me into a fight of hard whispers.

"Almost thirty-three already," Ruth says.

"It is Luisita," Mai-ling tells us. "She will not hear anyone but Tony."

"There was a dentist, Lola," Esperanza says. The boyfriend of Esperanza, he is not her boyfriend anymore. The divorce, he said, cost him too much. So he can stay rich, he went back to the ex-wife. "The dentist has condominium in Glendale. And hand-sum."

"Tony is handsome too," Lucy says.

Tarek looks to me.

"Yes, but Tony . . ." I cannot explain Tony to the bottom assistant of our employer. Tony honks his car outside and never comes in.

Ruth looks down. "The dentist, he is the brother of my cousin's wife."

"And before he saw Lucy and he likes!" Esperanza says.

"He has savings already."

200

"Tony has been here long time." I would finish *And he has nothing* if Lita was not here.

"Before he is immature, but the army really change him. Tarek," Lucy says, "they think because Tony is in the U.S. nine years he should have money. Like that."

Tarek studies her, up and down, the way a Filipino man would. She is dedicated, honest, brooding. Faithful to her private feeling, watching its value drop. He shakes his head. *How much could Tony possibly make at whatever he does? How much do I save?*

But Tony could. The U.S. government pays his rent and food. Like me, he works live-in! And I have saved a lot.

Tarek looks uneasy. He is only the bottom assistant, twenty-two years old. "China!" we hear from the living room, then a crash.

Tarek puts a hand on the shoulder of Lucy. "I'll marry you, Luce."

"You would marry me!" Her voice, it is often exclamation.

"But you are too young," I say. "You should not marry for immigration."

"Danny, he is saying too, 'After I receive my green card, I can divorce Ruth and marry you.' But I am waiting for a real, like that."

"And you'll get it too," Tarek says. Relieved, probably.

"We need to find for my pupil a guy in his forties. Thirty-five minimum."

Lucy taps the arm of Tarek. "You want I take your blood pressure?"

Esperanza and I get out our index cards. She paid for a lawyer and she was on the list to get a green card this year, but now the U.S. government added a test for English. She took that twice and did not pass. So today I brought a dictionary.

Lita says, "Remember my teddy bear?" From her purse, she lifts out a cassette. "I finally have our home movie."

It is strange to watch. You understand how much professional cameras add. We see people in a kitchen talking, but mixed in equal is the sound of running water. The camera does not follow faces, only torsos move in front of us, random dark fish passing. "Listen to here," Lita says.

The torsos say what their nannies do and do not do; they compare us.

A small voice says, "I never put gas in my car anymore. I bought a duplicate key and told her, just check it."

Lita presses PAUSE. "Next day, Alice gave me a list. Once a week car wash."

"I'm going to get Lucy to go." Helen!

"And how many times a week does she change the sheets?" another asks.

Then, a sigh I recognize. "Like she said, they all have to be birthdayed and Christmased."

I could save her trouble. Cash is Christmas enough for Lola. But I touch the earrings in my ear. I like them.

We see the dark hand of the helper chopping, taking the pan, returning the dirty to the always running water, while the women with their shaky small voices make plans for the improvement of their lives.

For us, this is cartoon comedy.

For the birthday of Bing, the dad auditioned pantomimers. If there is a person wearing a ragged Barney costume, kids will sit for an hour and watch. I saw it at the party of China. But here they run away from the silent white-painted man.

"He's an artist," Helen says.

But kids, they want to see someone they know already from TV. Grown-ups stand in the backyard holding blue drinks, but Helen forgot to tell the gardener to turn off the sprinklers, and high heels sink in the lawn. I stir a pot of milk with a foot-long bar of Switzerland white chocolate. Then Lucy and I pass the cups on trays, a cinnamon stick in each one.

"I hired her because she couldn't," Beth Martin says, behind me. "In the interview, I asked if she was planning to have her own. She told me, *No missus, I cannot. I am barren.* No problemo. I'm thinking, Great, she'll bond with Brookie and Kate. Not like the last one, who left in the middle of the night." She is talking about Esperanza. She is barren. When she was young, she had an infection, she told us, and her family did not have money for the medicine.

Brando squats near the deep end of the pool, pouring the hot chocolate in.

"Hey, stop it," Helen shouts. "I think Jeff envisioned it all being more magical. Lola, Beth's babysitter's going away for a month. Do you know anyone?"

"I will see." I amble, with the tray, over to the babysitters.

"Lola'll find someone," she promises. "She knows every nanny in Santa Monica. Filipinas are great." A nation of nannies, she is thinking.

Anyway, Esperanza will be gone more than one month. The guy, he spent his birthday with the ex-wife, but he did not save the rest of his life for her. So Esperanza, she will fly to Guatemala to take the baby of her sister. You do not have that here, adoption inside the family. Babysitters from Latin America and India say it is common. If a couple cannot conceive, one of the sisters will grow a baby for them. Americans, they are too selfish. They will not have a pregnancy if they do not get the baby at the end. Esperanza, she will have to cross borders, without a green card, a baby strapped on.

"You know somebody who will not steal that job?"

Ruth says Shirley can do three weeks while her divorced, remarried employers go to Europe together. All she has to do is feed their dogs and the cat. She can earn double.

"The rest of the time let them hire college girls. Then, when Esperanza returns, they will raise her."

While I walk with the tray, picking up empty cups, I hear a guy say, "She's fourteen, but not a fuckable fourteen." Maybe I heard wrong, but I keep hearing that again. My youngest, she is twenty-four. Virgin.

"I have one last try for the okay girl," I say to my former pupil. "Doctor, U.S. citizen. Working full-time Kaiser."

"Did he take his tests here?"

"He told Ruth, he is looking a Filipina."

She stares at her hands, no longer young, even always picking Dry, never Wash. "I think Tony, he really is the one for me."

"You have not met the doctor. Maybe he is also the one. Another one."

"With Tony, I feel different inside. Less selfish. So he will think well of me, like that. The way you are supposed to be for God."

"But a doctor. You would not have to work, you could study only."

"I will just wait and see with Tony."

She never asks me what kind of doctor. He is gastroenterology that looks all day with a tube inside the anus. As we come in the house of our mutual employer, the phone is ringing. "For you, Luce," Helen says.

Maybe a suitor.

"Cheska."

A year ago, Filipinos called here. Helen had to tell them *I am sorry.* There was the dentist, a man who owned a dry cleaner, and a widow Mai-ling met at the church. Now only Cheska. That is life. At one time, a small flurry. But flowers stop.

"So you will not meet the doctor?" I ask, after she puts down the phone.

She shakes her head. "When I was a baby, Lola, I had worms." It is an apology. *This is why my life. I am not like your daughter. Not doctor, that you wanted.*

Claire

THE PILOT SHOOT

"He'll be fine," Paul said. What I thought of now as his refrain.

Malcolm Lucas, a musician I admired, was conducting my symphony, but I didn't want to go. Had I always been so scared? I still wanted to work every day, but just at home.

"I guess you almost could do that now, with Paul making money." Lil sighed. "But you know, it's part of it. I think you have to go."

"Will doesn't have that many friends."

On a Sunday afternoon in February, Jeff sat flossing on our living room floor. He'd never directed for television before; we thought he might give Paul's pilot a little buzz. I offered coffee. All that was left of my crush was a faint bitterness.

"You know, you have to go." Jeff looked up at Paul. "I mean, she has to, doesn't she?"

"*I* think she should. I've told her."

"Isn't it a no-brainer?"

"Well, the show'll go on. But it'd be good to go."

They conducted this conversation about me as I stood there.

"Claire, when I have a movie, they send me to ten cities on what they call a tastemaker's tour. I talk to twenty or thirty people; it's not about box office, but they get critics and radio hosts and just people who they think'll talk. If you don't show up, it gives the whole thing an orphaned feeling. You wouldn't let William go out on his own."

"But I would be leaving him on his own."

"I beg your pardon," Paul said. "He'd be with his father."

"And Lola," I said.

"Okay, and Lola." Jeff's voice gentled. "He's close to Lola. Ten years from now, he'll want you to have gone."

205

I shrugged. "So I'll go."

"Good. Scared me there. You have something, you know." Jeff tapped my forehead, the way a nun had once rapped the front of my flat uniformed chest to say where my soul was. "You have to give it."

We'd had a whole affair he never knew about. Was it so different from any love, a state legendarily uneven?

Paul and I had Tuck and Head-on-Shoulder. He said, "Head on shoulder," patting; I fitted my head there and we could rest. I recognized his exhaustion. He understood when I found the noise of kids too much.

He didn't expect me to be more than I was.

Jeff would. Was there such a thing as too easy to please?

I flew alone; it was a little exhilarating to read the whole paper. *The New York Times* had changed since the last time I'd read it through. Now it was all about food.

At the rehearsal, ten o'clock Wednesday morning, Malcolm Lucas asked if I had notes. I stepped up to where he was. I wanted this part to sound like a country piano teacher humming to himself, with his hands in the pockets of an old sweater walking down a lane of trees. Dreaming up his little phrase. Rather liking it.

"It should be precise, but sort of lyrical underneath," I said.

He shrugged. I couldn't really communicate. A problem with music. The reason teachers play a piece first for their students. I tried to talk to the players.

"Off the string," I told the violins, and the sound came up bright. There was a passage where most of the strings had to turn their pages at the same time. I asked if they could practice doing that as quietly as possible, so as not to mess up the hush. Lucas looked at me as if I were crazy.

"Let's try it again," he said, and my heart flattened.

Malcolm Lucas didn't care for my piece. I had very much wanted him to like it.

There are different ways you can make a note, and he was getting all the sounds wrong. But maybe it was my piece.

My *Diary of a Country Piano Teacher.*
My year in C-sharp minor.

Lil's laughter reminded me of bells.

We sat in the hotel bar, two middle-aged women who no longer lived in New York, each wearing makeup inexpertly applied.

Since her third child, Lil had stopped trying to work. She sounded happier, though. She and her husband went for a long weekend, without the girls, to the Caribbean, and on the plane down, she'd asked him how many episodes he was expecting. "*I want a number,* I told him. I thought if I had a number, then, after that was done, I'd be in the clear."

"What was his number?"

"Six. When we landed, they gave us this coconut drink, and I think there was something in it, because we took care of the quota the first night, and then after that, I started to feel, I don't know, a little desire. A trickle."

Here we were, friends for twenty years, discussing married sex again. It felt harder to talk about their tender episodes than it had been to complain.

"We have cocktail hour every night now," Lil said.

That dissolved us in mirth.

Listening to her call home to say goodnights, I had a sense of the rigmarole it must have taken for her to leave. I called home too. Paul had seen Will this morning; Lola had picked him up from school, given him his dinner, and put him to bed.

"When I worry about Will," I said in the dark, "that he's not making friends, I don't know what to do but give him time. Time feels like all I have."

"I think that's right," she said.

For the fourth night in a row, I couldn't sleep. My fingers kept going. My second movement. Vinteuil's renunciation.

While we dressed in a zigzagging flurry, there was a knock. Flowers, I supposed. But Paul stood there. We'd decided he wouldn't, but he'd come anyway.

Arrange your mouth, I thought, he's meaning to give you something.

I had on the silver dress he'd bought me for Christmas. I turned around, held my hair up, and he zipped.

The three of us sat together in the round-backed burgundy seats. Paul smiled and Lil seemed to soften—he was handsome, I reminded myself.

When the violas started, it was thrilling to hear. I winced when the bassoon came in muddy. The cello surprised me.

The first movement eddied. Paul picked up my hand. He had a solemn look. He was always kind.

Brass floored in, strong and building, yet subdued under the force of something larger.

But in the second movement, a pause stumbled. I heard agitation, rustling. Those pages turning.

By intermission, there was a sense of weekday exhaustion. When we returned to our places, three seats in the row in front of us stayed empty. The woodwinds sounded chalky. It sounded as if they were working too hard; I wondered if I could have written their part more idiomatically. A high-pitched noise started in my ear, a shrill headache. I'd read about composers constantly hearing high As or A-flats. Dvorak had that.

I wanted it to be over, but then I'd have to stand up and talk to people. Lucas finally bowed, a quick nod, and motioned to me. After, we walked into the gilded hall, where hundreds of people moved in that giddy way of parties, black-and-white evening clothes, glasses tinkling, little bites of food. My ears hurt. People shook my hand.

My old pals came. Harv had put on a tie. The group I used to work with, who asked for a score. We huddled together. A guy I went to conservatory with walked in late because he was playing *Phantom of the Opera*.

After midnight, I whispered to Paul, "Can we go?"

"Just a minute," Paul said. "Be right back."

The crowd seemed to drift away and it was quieter.

I understood that pain had to do with the absence of sound. Someone had gone outside, downstairs into the wind, bought a newspaper, snapped it open in the cold, and read my future. He must have returned and whispered to someone who whispered to someone else next to him, who whispered . . . The texture of this silence held a crunch as if the air were frozen.

Paul returned, hard shoed, his footsteps audible. "I've got it." He tapped the rolled newspaper against his open palm. "But it's not good. Do you want to see?"

A matter of extreme difficulty to detect tangible musical themes in the second movement of loosely constructed, amorphous, atavisitic modalities.

Arid and gray music, devoid of grace, charm or smile.

I saw Lil across the room, which had emptied, laughing at something a man was saying, holding a champagne flute. *Flute,* I thought, stuck on the word.

I read the paper again, dumb. A large public failure, and I was only at the beginning. I'd failed not just myself but Little Will, I thought, who was right now alone in Los Angeles, disliked by the boys he wanted to play with.

Paul corralled Lil and managed us into a cab.

"Let's go home," I whispered. "Tonight if we can."

Paul looked worried, two lines above his nose.

"The worst of it," I said, back in the hotel room, jabbing things into my open suitcase, "are the moms in Will's class. They all subscribe to the *Times.*"

Paul talked on the phone, trying to change our flight. Jeff had sent a huge bouquet; it stood on the desk in the dark.

"But just to write a symphony and have it performed is a huge accomplishment," Lil said.

"They won't see it that way. *Trying* doesn't register. Almost the opposite. They consider it a vanity. If I'd made something they admired, they'd forgive me. And maybe make playdates with Will."

"Really? Is that true?" Lil looked to Paul.

He sighed. "They'd make playdates with Will if Will stopped hitting their kids."

"Aleph Sargent's kid's a bully but they all make playdates with him."

"And she's the biggest female box-office star in America," Paul said. "Why do you think *we* hear about everything he does wrong? They gossip about him plenty. They just want to say Aleph Sargent came to their house."

"But Will's not a bully," Lil said.

I sighed. "A little bit he is."

Paul huddled over the phone, scribbling numbers.

"They think I should spend all day with my kid. Like they do. And if all that time working ended up with this—if I couldn't do better, they'll think it serves me right. Yesterday, he pushed a girl off the swing."

"Really? How do you know?" Lil hadn't completely hidden her alarm.

"The school called Lola. She told me."

Paul had been wrong. Willie wasn't fine.

We packed the bouquet from Helen and Jeff into the back of Lil's station wagon.

It was raining when we arrived in LA and we rode home in an old taxi, jazz coming sketchily from the front seat. The driver smoked, his hand poised near his open window, and the rain smelled good.

Sunday morning, I woke in our bed, the room buffeted, trees outside blowing. I forgot where I'd been, until I was out the hall halfway to Will. Even when it slammed me, full body, it felt like a menace I could maybe outrun. The ocean in the distance looked dark and choppy; in overalls, Will clung to my knees, nothing wrong.

Paul pulled on sweats, and we ambled around our town. Sunday. Bits of leaves and eucalyptus riled the air, and I couldn't see. We did what we usually did together: bought coffee for me, an ice blended for Paul, Jamba Juice for Will, and roamed in and out of shops. The worst had happened, but we were still here.

I carried Will on my shoulders. Maybe I could do this. His shoes tapped my chest.

Paul nudged me into an antiques store, but for once I didn't want anything. No, I kept saying: No to the Miriam Haskell necklace, a handled glow on its old pearls. No to the wrought-iron porch furniture. I felt clear, a bow from an arrow. I would not dither anymore. The wind picked up invisible debris from the streets and barreled it in the air. I would work work work.

In one store, with shoulder-shaped chairs and a concrete floor, Paul plucked an evening dress from a rack. Chiffon, with an Indian-print jacket. Not on sale. When I came back from taking Will to the bathroom, he stood at the small desk, putting the receipt in his wallet.

How strange to walk in sweats, carrying this weightless treasure. For what? I'd failed and he bought me a dress. I was unhinged. *See,* he meant, *we're still standing.* He wanted to protect the person who protected his child, whose hand hovered before the dash. We ate an early supper and watched a movie. I'd be all right, I thought, if we could all be home and the wind didn't die. But, of course, tomorrow was Monday.

Paul took Will to school and the bravest of my old friends called.

"Fuck them!" Harv screamed. "What the fuck is an atavistic modality?"

"A bad performance can fool even a halfway decent critic." Said by someone who'd once received a rave from the same guy for his percussion concerto.

Others put in calls the way they would after a divorce. "You okay?" Lil asked.

"A little wobbly."

"Yes," I said to the next one. "I guess I'll learn from it."

"Well, you will," he said. "Like it or not, you will."

Harv sent me an e-mail:

> The reviewer in the *Allgmeine musikalische Zeitung* complained of "clumsy, harsh modulations" in Beethoven's early sets of variations and they found in his Violin Sonata, op. 12 "a forced attempt at strange modulations, and aversion to the conventional key relationships, a piling up of difficulty upon difficulty."

"How did your piece go in New York?" Lola asked.

"Not too well. They didn't like it."

"No? What do they know. Maybe other cities will like it."

She brought me lunch to my workroom on a tray.

The house stayed quiet. On slopes of the day, I'd feel a collapse and think, Maybe I can't do this anymore. But music was all I could ever do. I looked down the stairs, at the still living room, the empty chairs. I lay on the floor, listening to Wagner. Lola came in with a cool towel.

I still had so many streets to cross with William to deliver him to the other side.

Now I dreaded what I'd liked before, the drop-off. Lola picked him up from school that first week, and I met them in the park after to take Will for a walk. Before supper, I went out with shears and cut flowers for our table, arranging twigs and flowers that would last only a day. I'd studied Lucy. Maybe this was what I could do now.

"Flowers?" Lola said. "What for?"

She ate with us. I let her give the bath while I flipped through the glossy pages of cookbooks, glimpsing an alternate life. All the women here had turned themselves into grown-ups who could sit and chat and tend children. Could I? They believed a child should be attended by a mother most of the day. Paul didn't believe that.

I didn't know if I did. I hadn't grown up that way. But look at me! The high A-flat stayed.

On the weekend, we walked out again. The dense morning fog burned off; it was hazy and I still couldn't see.

Then I had to dress and go teach. The first day, my ears were ringing, but then it was done and over, the first day.

I winced a moment, thinking; maybe the mothers were right and it was arrogant to spend years making a gift no one had asked for. Still, I heard an implication of melody in some plane noise outside and put down the notes.

Lola knocked on my door with lunch. "I make egg, you want?"

When she returned later to take the tray, she sat at the piano.

"You teach me," she said.

I taught her the major scales. I took out the book I'd once bought for Will. She was more interested than he'd been. I wrote out the notes. Key signatures. Put her fingers over a few chords. Showed her the two places where there is no black key between.

When I went downstairs to start dinner, I complained for the hundreth time about the black kitchen.

"In our place, we know how to fix that," Lola said. "Not so hard. All we do is paint and put new tiles. I know how grouting, the problem is we have to get a guy to take these off."

Two days later, at breakfast, she said, "I talked to the old guy at the place of Ruth. He can take this off and bring it away. If you buy new tiles, I will teach you how."

"Really?" I'd lived in rented places my whole life. Even if we'd wanted to change things, they weren't ours. But this landlord lived far away. "Okay," I said.

Danny came one day with an old guy and they hacked off the tiles. "Demo," they called it and I paid them two hundred dollars. The kitchen was a dusty wreck, but before they left they put up a new surface, called a green board, and swept everything clean.

When he came home, Paul put a hand to his forehead. "Did we have to do this now?"

The next day, Lola and I started. She stirred a pot of something called mastic and we buttered it on the back of the tiles. She crouched on top of the counter and set on the tiles, with rubber spacers between them. I got good at the grouting with a small trowel and a sea sponge.

"See. You teach me music, I teach you this," she said.

"I owe you a bunch of lessons." I sat in the kitchen for a long time once we finished, in the clean watery light. Before she left to pick up Will, I brought the cello down and showed her dominant tonic, five one, five one, explained triads, and began to sketch out the sonata form.

The next week, I took Will to school. Now, with the pilot in preproduction, Paul left the house by seven. I saw Helen the first day. She didn't mention my being back or having been gone. In fact, she never made any reference to my symphony again.

"Thanks for the flowers," I said, standing by the cubbies.

"Sure." She held her tummy at the bottom. I thought of the dress I'd bought once, size 2, hanging in the back of Will's closet. For my girl. I couldn't afford another child now, though. Then there was the flimsy dress Paul had bought me, not on sale. Maybe what I could afford didn't matter anymore.

"How are you feeling?" I asked.

She looked at me strangely. "Paul didn't tell you? I had a miscarriage."

"Oh, I'm so sorry."

"Apparently it's very common." She shrugged. "We'll just do it again."

That seemed weird. Didn't miscarriages usually make people sad? I called Paul. When he said, *I'm in the parking lot, got to go now,* it felt like a cut.

Wednesday, I stood at the park, opening the stroller. For the first time, Will didn't want to come. So I followed him around equipment, the only mother there, the other adults immigrant nannies and guys playing pickup basketball. Lola crossed her arms. *If the mother is here, then why cannot I take an off?*

"I will be the one," she said, grabbing the stroller. "You can work."

But I didn't feel like working. I'd lost my way. At the top of the high twisty slide, I sat with my legs spread, Will between. Far below, my cell phone rang. This was March of 1995, when most of the moms had cell phones but none of the nannies did yet.

"Lucy," I shouted down. "Can you get that!" Lola would have hated doing it. She would have felt like a maid.

"Claire! It is *Paul!*" Lucy yelled. The romantic. She carried her front high, like a pigeon. She threw the phone underhand, and twenty feet up, I caught it, collapsing with that tiny victory, winded against the metal. "Hey! How're you?"

"Little stressed . . . Mary Catalanato, the one at the studio, production side . . ."

Though I waited for them, Paul's actual calls disappointed me. What did I expect, in the middle of the day? Willie climbed over my legs and whooshed down.

". . . on Friday. So you should probably make an appointment for your hair. And does *he* need a cut?" There: the coin dropped in its slot; he'd called to tell me to get Will's hair cut for the pilot shoot. There was a beep—his other line. "I won't be late. Eight, eight-thirty."

Ten, I thought. The phone sat, a bar on my leg. I leaned back against the metal wall of the room at the top of the slide. Somewhere, designers had decided to puncture red metal, so sky showed through, blue polka dots. Park designers! I wished I knew different people.

I'd wanted to tell him where I was.

Will climbed up to my room. He knocked.

"Hi."

He stood in the middle of the floor. "Hi," he said, looking down. "What are you doing?"

I picked up the cello, played a little of the phrase I was toying with. He pulled the collar of his shirt and started biting it. Many of his collars now were gnawed. I swooped him up and sat him at the piano, set his fingers to a C scale. "Should I teach you a song?"

"Not now," he said. "Later." Then he bumped down the stairs, face-first, the way he loved to that scared me. I didn't stop him. I wanted him to have thrilling pleasures. And so far, he hadn't hurt himself.

"He told you to get your *hair done?*" Lil sounded riled.

"It's not like it sounds."

"Really? Because it doesn't sound so good." Lil usually assumed a fond tone about Paul, as if he and her husband were good guys who just couldn't help not being, well, *us*. "I mean, he *should* find you beautiful all the time, shouldn't he?"

"That might be more realistic in your case than mine."

Her pause was the twinge between truth and kindness. We were awkward approaching this difference in our lots. "You're plenty beautiful."

"Speaking of beautiful, we have to have dinner with Jeff and Helen."

I was still hurt that they hadn't said anything about my concert.

That night, I thought of my conversation with Lil. All my life I'd made random stabs at beautification, usually alone. They'd been costly and they hadn't worked. "What do you do besides haircuts?" I asked Helen. "For female maintenance." She'd once told me about their sex life, but this felt more private. "I mainly do the dentist and the occasional haircut," I went on. "But I can tell there's more to it."

I watched her deciding whether or not to trust me.

"I do more than that," she said. "I'll take you, if you want."

"I've always been afraid of beauty shops. Meanwhile, Paul wears the same thing every day." I elbowed him.

"They all do." She shrugged. "But who'd want to?"

I would. There it was: my missing feather.

"Well, tell me when, and I'll book us." Then she got stiff again. A silence.

"She's upset," Jeff said. "She thinks you guys don't like the school."

"You know how many people begged us to help them get in? And you act like you'd rather be somewhere else."

"But we *do* like the school," Paul said. "We're just worried the school doesn't like us! Or him. Apparently, he's not big on circle time."

"Not big on circle time," I repeated.

"Go in and talk to them," Helen said. "They'll help you." Then she steered the conversation to her new concern: Was an immigrant nanny right for Bing *at this age*? "I mean, she's great with flowers and ironing T-shirts but—"

Paul and I looked at each other. Lola wouldn't touch an iron.

"Lucy's young, I guess," I said.

"Oh, it's Lola too. Bing tells her, *Lola, make me a grill cheese*. And she jumps."

"Willie does that." I sighed.

"I've seen Will hit Lola," Helen said.

I bit my lip. "Hope she did something about it."

Helen shook her head. "Bing is definitely outgrowing Lola."

Outgrowing Lola! "But she loves them."

"I think a college girl," Helen said, shaking her head as if she were far down a road of thought we couldn't hope to follow. "We'll see."

As soon as I began to feel settled, the terms changed. I was starting to understand why these women considered motherhood a full-time job.

When we got in the car, Paul said, "A UCLA girl isn't going to do the dishes."

"But I don't like it that he hit her! I'm sure she *didn't* do anything."

"We'll have to talk to him." Paul wanted to think about his pilot in a straight line, so the rest of us should stay in place—wife, child, nanny—until he had time to consider us all. If I pushed my work to the center the way Paul did, Will would grow up on the peripheries. I didn't work in a straight line, anyway. I had to sink into parts of myself I didn't know. That took the opposite of force.

And we needed Lola. Not only for Will but for us. Paul was never going to do the things she did that I didn't want to do by myself. She'd taken pruning shears to the Christmas tree, hacking off branches to make it shapely, before Will and I hung the delicate, shiny ornaments.

"I thought they still wanted Lola," I said. "Meanwhile, Helen's been dreaming about a Tri Delt."

"Sounds like they're canning Lucy, anyway."

Lucy made those flowers. And ironed, apparently. "Maybe we should hire *her*."

"Lola's better for Will," Paul said, reaching a hand over to rub my shoulder absentmindedly, impatient to get home. Probably every husband talked his wife into believing her nanny was best, the way we talked ourselves into believing that about our husbands.

Paul had been *on development* this year, which was what we'd been waiting for—it was supposed to be the time he'd be home. Once, he'd walked up the lawn while it was still light out with the manner of a man carrying a party in his arms. When he came through the door, Lola jumped up from the table with her plate and scooted out to her room. For months, he worked on the pilot in coffee shops, and then another long plan unfurled. When the pilot *went,* and the show got on the air, *if* it received good ratings—then we could live. I still believed that, sort of.

On Sunday, Paul took us to see the set. We fumbled fifteen minutes before finding light switches in the cavernous soundstage. Then Will climbed behind the three-walled house. This'll be part of his life, I thought, Hide-and-Seek on an empty soundstage.

Later, I stood by the fence at the ocean, with Will in his stroller, watching the sealed waves open. Long after we lived together, would he remember that his mother took him to see beauty?

Would it be different for him later, because he had Lola too?

Helen sighed as we walked into the loud square room, bored with beauty. Stylists gesticulated with blow-dryers at reflections of sphinx-faced women who gazed severely at themselves. A grandmother endured an intricate highlighting job next to a teenager sitting stiff in her chair. A dread filled me seeing them, so hopeful and so willing.

"Your color's a little washed out," the man said, lifting a piece of my hair to show me in the mirror. "You want to do some henna?"

"Sure." I worried what it would cost, but it seemed impolite to ask.

"Lean over, I'll layer it." He rummaged through my hair.

"Better, huh?"

My head looked strange, but I nodded.

Then Helen and I lay on parallel tables while a woman smoothed hot wax on our legs with a Popsicle stick. When she pulled the wax off, it hurt, it really hurt. She leaned to inspect the area between Helen's eyebrows. She took a tweezers to a few hairs, frowning. "Bikini today?"

"Brazilian." Helen continued to read *Newsweek.*

"No, thank you," I said. That seemed what starlets would do or women who hadn't gone to college. "Does it hurt?"

"A little, because you're not used to it. It's nice, though, if you put on pretty underwear." Pretty underwear! The woman pulled a curtain closed around Helen.

"Thanks, Marsha," Helen said, a few minutes later. "Feels clean."

"Maybe I'll try."

What a job: she took my knees, rocked them, put wax in spots that would normally be indecent. I felt like a baby being diapered, until the zip of pain.

"You get used to it," she said.

The waxer put on a pair of magnifying glasses like those I'd seen worn by Jack the jeweler. I lay on a crinkly sheet of white butcher paper while she examined, snipping, with a professional air. At the baby shower for Sky Tucci, two women at my table talked about when she'd sent Buck Price her panties, by messenger. That had shocked me too. "There. That's better," the woman said.

"He'll like it," Helen said, through the curtain. It took me a moment to remember who she meant. I'd slid off the globe of the familiar. I looked at myself. I didn't know if I looked better or only different. Did other people lose time like this? All afternoon I'd worried about the bill, and at the cash register, eyebrows restricted, hair blown to twice its normal size, legs waxed, toenails dark red, the total came to two hundred forty dollars, not counting tips. Helen wouldn't think of the money again after she'd signed the paper. She maintained herself like an asset that needed protection.

I was still thinking about the tiny triangular face like a fox. I felt nude in my underwear. The air glittered when we stepped outside. A breeze cut through my skirt.

I had a melody all of a sudden. For clarinets.

My grandmother had gone to the beauty shop Friday mornings. A woman tended her white curls, rolling each one, drying her under a steel helmet. Conversation about the hairdresser's truant daughter gave these ministrations a serious air, which ended with my grandmother counting out the tip in cash. This was the only ritual related to her appearance that my grandmother paid for. She did her own nails every week. She set up the whole business on the kitchen table using glass condiment dishes the filling station gave away that, later in the day, would be filled with mustard and pickle relish.

"You change your hair!" Lucy said, when I dropped off Helen. "It is too short!"

Home, I bounded upstairs to dress while Lola fluffed Will. She left in Danny's green Mercedes; she'd asked for five tickets to bring a group of nannies. I drove Will, suspendered in his car seat, to the Lot. We walked under huge painted signs—THE SIMPSONS. STAR WARS— to soundstage 6, where Paul stood in his billowing white shirt. The guard gave us wristbands, like the ones Will and I had worn in the hospital. Inside, lights caught us in the noise of a thousand people.

They sat in bleachers on our right. Why hadn't I known they'd all be here?

On the left, PAs milled, looking miniature in the sets, open on one side, like the rooms of an enormous dollhouse.

We had gifts for Paul. Willie had painted a mug at Color Me Mine, and I'd bought a silver fountain pen he'd probably return. Will handed him the decorated bag.

"Oh, thanks, can you keep it for me?" People circled him, waiting for us to get out of the way. He tapped a clipboard with a Bic.

"I'm going to assign Molly to you for tonight. You guys'll sit with the writers."

Molly installed us on director's chairs in front of eight TV screens. She fitted earphones on our heads. I felt privileged. Jeff and Paul wore them but the writers behind us didn't get any. I turned around. "Thank you for coming. It means so much to Paul." *First Lady manners,* my mother called them. She and Tom were somewhere in the audience too.

Jeff stood watching Molly walk off. "Helen wouldn't put up with that."

"We like Molly," I said, glancing at Will.

"Sorry."

"Mommy." Willie slid down his chair. "I know where Craft Catering is." Last week, Paul had given Molly his keys to drive Will to the set and then home again.

Bags of chips, cookies, and candy lay open on the counter, a child's treasure, all the things I kept him from. I let him fill a plate while I poured coffee, already bitter.

He walked back balancing his feast.

Among the throng—men moving lights, cinematographers pushing Panavision cameras on trolleys, a studio executive leaning against a pillar—I watched Paul, a nucleus, in his baggy white shirt. Actresses sat in chairs, getting made up in plain view. I would have thought that was private. A comedian walked to the center of the stands and began juggling. "Warm-up guy," Jeff said, walking past.

I heard a soft flurry of scribbling behind us. Paul *was* grateful. At breakfast, he'd tallied their fees. "The writers are essentially *giving* me a million dollars. When you figure their episode quotes."

"Wants us to work on the blow," Jack said. He came tonight as a favor to Paul. Within the comedy world, Jack was famous, though no one had ever heard him say anything funny outside the Room. I'd hardly heard him say anything at all. He drove a Civic with a bumper sticker that said KILL YOUR TV. I saw Paul in the distance, one hand on Jeff's shoulder. The younger guys here hoped he'd hire them when he got his pickup order. "Never seen so many writers at a pilot shoot," Jack said. "It's a testament to Paul. The perfunctory presents alone are going to bankrupt you."

He was right. Paul had spent more than a thousand dollars. Paul's mother had sent ten Ralph Lauren blankets she'd found in an outlet, but this time, he decided to buy retail. We bought those noise-canceling headphones Jeff had given me.

A young writer sighed. "Got to be an easier way to make six hundred thousand."

Molly handed Bing a napkin with two Hostess CupCakes, then sauntered off.

The eight TV screens blinked on and I gathered that the shoot had begun. I thought they'd have clackers.

The actress whined. I wanted to tell Paul, but I couldn't get his attention. This felt urgent. Her voice was ruining his lines. Paul had once missed a whole dinner party, pacing outside, begging her agent.

After every scene—which went like a volley—there was a mangled shout and applause. Paul moved, clipboard in hand, between milling camera people in the lit sets, where he looked more at home than he did in our house. All those nights I'd put down the phone, feeling socked, when he said it'd be another late one, this had always been here—PAs pressed around him offering food, Diet Coke—another fuller world. At home, it was just Will and me. And Lola, who right now sat somewhere in the bleachers.

Will pulled me over to see the warm-up guy hold a ladder in his teeth. Jeff bumped into me, his arm on my arm.

"Wonder what he's getting paid," I said.

"Maybe nothing. Probably sees this as his big chance." His hand arabesqued around my ear. "You do something to your hair?"

"Helen took me."

"I like your regular hair."

The clown's roommates probably knew about this showcase. Maybe they'd planned a party for him at home. But the studio guys stood, arms crossed, talking to one another. Paul wouldn't notice him either, though for his son, he made the whole show.

Between wonders, Will ran back to Craft Services, returning with a new flimsy paper plate. So far, by my count, he'd eaten:

> Two Hostess CupCakes
> One Twinkie
> Two cheesecakes
> A brownie
> Two Ho Hos
> Four Reese's Peanut Butter Cups
> Another candy bar I didn't know the name of

He now carefully balanced a 7UP can on the thin arm of the director's chair. I didn't allow sodas at home. Paul hid Diet Coke in Lola's square refrigerator. He'd go out at night, knock, and grab one.

Paul walked over, picked up Will, and guided me to another region behind a curtain. A guard sat at a wooden desk in the middle of the adjacent hangar, a ledger open. He let us in. In another room, walled with black curtains, there were overstuffed chairs, couches, a long table of food, and, on a high cart, one small TV monitor.

"The network people," Paul whispered. "*Their* caterer." The network would decide whether or not to buy Paul's show. All this time they'd been back here deliberating. Men in chef's hats served. "You're going to like this, bud." Paul handed Will a square of tiramisu.

We fell into a hard-whispered fight.

"Claire, we auditioned forty actresses, and she was far and away the best."

"Couldn't Jeff direct her to tone it down?"

"I can't be taking notes from my wife." Just then Molly came over with a clipboard. Paul lifted a piece of my hair, hooked it behind my ear. "Hair looks nice."

A tall camerawoman bent down. "Does he want to ride?"

So Will rode the Panavision, shaped like a huge whistle, scooting on tracks toward the underground cave of a false living room. Paul sprinted across stage. "Whoa. Hey, you bring a camera?" Before I mumbled no, he assumed my failure and began asking, "You have a camera? You have one?"

We had a picture of Will riding the Paramount golf cart. We should have had this too—Little Him on the Panavision, night of the pilot shoot.

When the camerawoman returned him, Will bit down on a Milky Way.

I grabbed Jeff's elbow. "The way Marly's playing Ellen, she sounds a little dumb."

"You say that as if it were a bad thing!" He walked off, shaking with little explosions.

.

People stamped on the metal bleachers. Then they walked out in bunches, laughing. The studio president stretched, in soft long sleeves. A hand on Will, I lingered near the executives coming out of their cave, hoping to overhear. But they were talking about an actor.

"Two years ago he was eating dog food from a can."

The camerawoman who'd given Will a ride squatted to lift cable, looping it around her elbow. *Pretty underwear.* She looked past forty, wearing work boots. I never would have guessed. Magenta.

She opened a hand spread with gum sticks and offered them to Will.

The warm-up guy heaved two duffels over his shoulder.

"Excuse," I said. "Could I have your name?"

"Sure!" He set the bags down and carefully printed his name and three phone numbers on a torn envelope corner; oh, no, he thought I was somebody. I was just Paul's wife. All I could do was send him a basket, next Christmas.

My mother and Tom came over, smiling, her arm on his arm. She wore all black with her good scarf, draped.

I reminded her about Grandmothers' Day at the school. Grandfathers' Day was a week later.

"I thought we could invite Tom," I said.

"Let's wait on that," she whispered, pulling me aside.

"Why? Will thinks of him as a grandfather."

"Well, he's not. He's just a friend. I don't really even like him."

Finally Paul tore open his presents. I could tell the way he turned the pen in his hand that he thought it was extravagant. But he clipped it to his pocket.

"We can discuss returning it in the morning," I said.

He laughed. "I *love* the mug." He twirled Will in the air.

I hoped Paul would drive. He could leave his car; I'd bring him back tomorrow. Will by now had gum plastered on his face and hung, a crooked star, over his father's chest. I'd taken him to the bathroom and tried to scrub the gum off, but little bumps lingered like a rash. When Paul set him down again, I saw the mess on his white shirt. "You go," Paul said. "I have to stay for pickup shots and retakes."

Will spread over me now, head on my shoulder. It was one-thirty, a spring night. Palms on the Lot, embedded not in dirt but cement, soared thirty feet. They looked like props too, but they were alive. I braced one hand on the smooth bark and held Will's forehead with the other when he bent over and threw up, again and again.

I carried him into the house and laid him on the bath mat while I ran water, with bubbles. I lifted him into the white mounds, holding him between my knees. Drying him, on a pile of towels, I saw his nails were too long, and as he slipped into the faint reassuring hum of a dream, I got out the clippers and, one by one, took his sleeping feet and hands to trim.

Paul walked in the door at four o'clock Monday, palms up. "Got the pickup order. Thirteen shows. They usually buy six or seven, this's the whole season." He never minded having to explain to me. Helen understood the business better than Jeff did. But Paul didn't even expect me to watch TV.

"Let's go out tonight. Celebrate," I added.

I waited on hold with our favorite restaurant; I believed in the rituals. Lil and I had had theories, but they didn't seem to be working on me. Some living fabric, slightly denser than air, held Lola, Willie, and me together. When Paul stepped into the house, something vibrated—a high string—with the twang of a stranger.

"I've got to scramble to hire. So far the only writer we have is Buddy G., and even he's telling his agent to play hardball." He sighed. "And we're late."

"Buddy? Really?" This kid, two years out of college, who rarely bathed, had a marketable skill. Thirty years of practice practice practice; why didn't I?

"Isn't that incredible? But I've got to make calls. So eight o'clock?"

I stepped outside, pulling the extension cord into the small courtyard I'd planted with Tom and my mother. The Boston ivy we'd staked was halfway up the wall now, the leaves red. The day Tom took me to the nursery to buy plants, he'd introduced me to the owner. I was curious as to what he'd call me. "This is Claire," he said. "I've been going with her mother for thirty-some years." When I told Paul, he said, "And that's exactly what he's been doing. He's been *going* with her." Fog blew in. My upper lip stung, and I fumbled in my pocket for a Kleenex. Will picked up colds from the other kids in school. "Two, please. Could we have a booth?" I'd stood here when I ripped open the envelope from the preschool, offering Will a place. *Yes!* I'd said then, making a fist. Now, passing through the kitchen, I grabbed a paper towel to blow my nose.

I needed my own triumph. But lately, I hadn't sent out any entries to the world.

I felt like the child I'd been, holding my knees, waiting. To be chosen.

In our room, after dinner, Paul said, "Oh, no. I feel that ball in my throat. I *can't* get sick now." He reached the spare comforter from the high shelf in the closet and took his pillow from the bed to sleep in his study.

"I'm getting it too," I said.

"At least you don't have a table read on Friday."

I was the one in the house with the insignificant cold.

Lola never caught any of our viruses at all.

I'd received a call from the Class Community Service and Events Mother asking if we would host the end-of-the year party. He had to be a little popular, I told myself, or they wouldn't want the party at our house. I held that all week like an unexpected check in my pocket: I went in for his teacher conference glad I had it.

The door swung open. "Shall we start?" Janet. The head teacher.

"Paul's coming too. He must be stuck in traffic."

Then, to my surprise, the school director entered, holding a folder. "Janet and Heidi have some concerns," she said. "That Will sometimes seems unhappy."

Unhappy? They appeared to be waiting for me to say something. Just then, Paul burst in. "Sorry I'm late, the 10 was jammed from Bundy on."

The director turned to him. "We called this conference because we want to help William."

Paul picked up three oranges from a bowl on the table and spun them in an arc. He tossed one to the director, who caught it. There. He had them smiling. "No, seriously," he said. "It strikes me as a matter of him having to grow into himself."

"Are you setting limits at home?" the director asked.

"I try," I mumbled.

"Maybe it's your housekeeper a little." Heidi, the assistant teacher, played with her fingers. "I don't think she can really control him. She has to tell him things a lot of times. He pretends he doesn't hear."

"She doesn't pick up the tones," Janet said. "He needs help knowing what's appropriate. Yesterday, she just grabbed Bing's arm and said, *Why you cry?*"

The director nodded. "We see this with a lot of the foreign housekeepers."

"Why *was* Bing crying?" *Crybaby.*

"Do you know?" Heidi looked to Janet. "I'm not sure either."

"But Bing doesn't usually fall apart for no reason," the director said. I slid a look at Paul. We weren't so sure.

"What do you recommend we do to help Lola?" Paul asked.

The director shook her head. "I don't know that you can."

"But the nannies' own kids are well behaved," I said. "They sit up straight at the table and take turns talking. I asked Lola how the moms get them to do that."

"She may not even know," the director said.

Janet said, "What works in their culture may not work in ours."

"Those children have been learning from their mother since they were babies. They're fluent in her cues. She may make a tiny facial adjustment and they understand she means business."

"So what can we do?" Paul said, hands on his knees. To the point.

The director said, "I'd think about replacing her."

"But she loves him!" I said. "And he loves her."

Paul put his hand on my arm. *Calm down.* He turned to the director. "Of course, we take what you're saying seriously. We'll have to think about all you've said."

"A number of our families have felt the way you do, and I can tell you that if there's been a goodbye ceremony, the parents are surprised. In a few days, the kids almost completely forget her."

"We're having the class party at our house." I wanted them to know that, even so, Will had friends.

Janet nodded. "Not all our kids can swim. And believe it or not, you're the only house this year without a pool."

Oh. "You think Helen complained?" I asked Paul as we walked out.

He shook his head, arms crossed. "Should've said something to us first."

It was a hard drive home. Lola helped us so many ways.

"Still, he's in school now," Paul said. "It's a big expense."

"Easy for you to say."

"Why, Claire? We're in this together."

But I was the one Lola helped. How had the food and the house become my job, though? Was it because Paul made more money now, or because Paul didn't care? He would have left the sheets on the beds indefinitely. Lola made *us* possible.

"She's not that much, compared to other nannies."

"We'd have to do it sooner or later, anyway."

I'd tried to talk to Lola about disciplining Will. Not spoiling him. When I was his age, I'd made my own breakfast. Of course, when I was his age, I'd coaxed my mother out of bed. I couldn't wish my life for him.

Lola had laughed. *Claire, when we are young, we have houseboys. We will not do anything. Then, when we had to, we learn.*

The teachers said she was indulgent. It was true: he'd hit her. And what did she do?

Maybe it would be nice to be by myself in the house sometimes.

But it wasn't only laundry Lola did. Every night, we ate together, the three of us. While I put him down, she cleaned the kitchen, then we sat again, the red teapot between us, my jar of flowers returned, and talked about Will's day.

She worried with me about Will. Without her, I'd be alone.

When I stood to wash the teapot Lola said, *Leave, I will be the one.*

As I opened the front door, I heard Lola upstairs at the piano practicing her song. "Clair de Lune."

Biting the inside of my cheek, I dialed my producer. In two weeks, the deadline set when I'd postponed would come for my songs.

"How do you spell that?" his new assistant asked after I said my name.

Lola

THE CHOP

Birthdays here, they are like weddings almost. Williamo and I attended a party inside a striped tent on the beach. My kids, they took turns. Each year, one got the party. But Williamo, he is the only, so for the first birthday, Claire set the alarm for six o'clock to bake a cake with a chocolate she special-ordered from New York. For the second, she made a yellow cake, very buttery, with white frosting. Last year, we toothpicked together three layers, with orange, lemon, and lime rinds grated in and also the broken petals of roses to look like confetti.

This year, for the fourth, Williamo and I cover balloons with newspaper dipped in paste to make a piñata. For the stuffing, we will use penny candy, and I am sewing little bags for coins. When I almost took the one-hundred-ten-dollar-a-day job, I thought I could buy presents Williamo would never forget. Huge robots already put together from the window of Puzzle Zoo. But I chose time over money. Lola over robots. Now, the day of the party, I wish I had the gift to open the eyes big.

Claire, she stands already baking. This year, she uses a book. Williamo tasted Boston cream pie at another house and he wanted. So she squints, her reading glasses on. I can tell she has lost confidence because flour dusts the counter and the floor.

Outside, cardboard castles wait. Lil gave Claire that idea, and I asked Sears for refrigerator boxes. But they looked not so good in the yard and yesterday Williamo and I painted a base coat yellow. The doors to all the castles flap open, the sky a California blue. I tie a bunch of balloons to the mailbox so everyone will know that this is the house of the party.

I hear shouting. Claire wants that Williamo will put on a new button shirt. She looks upset from this Boston pie. I hold my elbows. The mother, she pleads. Why will she not say, *I have for you a reward*? Just a candy.

I help. "Put it on, Williamo, and I will give you something."

Williamo sighs. It is what he does when he gives up.

Bing and my pupil arrive first. He runs in with wet hair. "I comb. Then just foof, with my fingers!"

"Where is your employer?" I say.

"I tell her, but she has Dr. Mars."

"But how many chances to see Aleph Sargent?" Helen, she attends Dr. Mars twice a week.

Then they all arrive, and I fold and stack strollers. Ruth brings Ginger Saperstein and her granddaughter Aileen; Danny drove them so they could all see the movie star. Babysitters arrange themselves around the long table with food, and the moms stay by the beverages, sipping different waters. Aleph Sargent stands, arms pretzeled. "Brando's mom," she says, introducing herself.

"A little on small," Cheska whispers.

"Not so much beautiful. Only just—nothing wrong," my pupil says.

"That is what is beautiful," I say.

"But she is not wearing a coat!" Cheska says.

Claire should greet the mothers, but she does not come out from the kitchen. Why this pie? I have seen her make two beautiful tarts in less than twenty minutes. Babysitters stare at the nanny of Aleph Sargent. Everyone wants to hear the life of a movie star. But Clarisse is talking about herself. "I've traveled many different places."

"You are live-in?" my pupil asks.

Clarisse snorts. "Oh, yeah, have to. Couldn't go a night without me."

"The boy, Brando?"

"The girl. Without me, she can't find anything. Sometimes we're out and I get beeped. *Oh, Clarisse, have you seen my hairbrush?*"

"Aleph Sargent cannot find a hairbrush?" Lucy says.

"Very dependent." When Clarisse shakes her head, loops of skin jiggle. Maybe she does not like Aleph. And Aleph, she is probably paying her a lot.

"Only babysit or clean up, too?" Mai-ling asks.

"I'm no housekeeper. I'm the nanny and she has me do her personal things. No one else *touches* her laundry." I think of lingerie, fragile as spiderwebs.

"Of all the mothers, your employer has the biggest wardrobe!" I mean that for a soft joke.

But the giantess eye-rolls. "Two full rooms." She nods, her head in a slant, the way of a horse, evenly chewing. "She converted a bedroom for her closet."

"She is movie star! To be beautiful, that is her job." I do not want to hear bad things about Aleph. She worked babysitter too.

"Li-ing!" Sue calls from the other table and Mai-ling springs up.

I follow because Claire may not even know there is a movie star in her backyard.

"Tissue, please," Sue says. Mai-ling always carries Kleenex, tucked in the elastic of her leggings. Sue is the one to squeeze the nose of China. Then she gives the wad back.

In the kitchen, I find my employer, flour in the hair, a champagne bottle open. "It's a disaster, Lole." In front of her stands the glass pedestal, with one thin layer, the height of a pancake. On top of this, my employer ladles yellow sauce. "Supposed to be custard."

"Where is the rest the cake?" I feel frightened; I do not want that she will fail.

"This is it, Lole, two layers. Hard as rock. We'll toss a coin who goes to Vons."

The layer should be more up. Custard should hold; this is a soup, spilling over the lip of glass. On top the mess, she sets a second layer. Then, she pours chocolate.

"Here goes nothing. Three and half hours. But he wanted it. And I tried."

"It'll taste great," Paul says, stomping through the kitchen, camera around his neck. He stops to snap the dripping cake. To him, there is no difference. But Claire, she could not live with someone who minded. She minds too much herself.

Outside, the kids paint egg crates to glue onto the boxes for shingles. That anyway turned out a good idea.

Claire carries the cake and I go to get Williamo. I find him inside the only box not yet decorated, sitting in the corner, holding his knees.

"Why you are not fixing your castle?"

"I don't know." If all the castles become decorated except his, for Claire the day will be sad. "Too much noise." We sit in the box together, hearing kids and mothers and babysitters; it is a lot of noise. I wonder if the things we do for kids are what they want anyway, because today he is not happy.

Then I lead him to the cake. Claire bends to light the candles and our boy blows. This is the only thing they still believe here. Wishes. Not prayers.

Claire cuts the cake and I pass around plates.

At the edge of the lawn, I hear a fight. But for once, I do not mind. Williamo sits here, looking at each bite cake. Aleph speedwalks to the hive. Clarisse stands and the whole bench shakes. Next to her Aleph is a stem. Clarisse pulls out Brando by the feet. China shrieks, climbing up and up on Mai-ling. Sue, ten feet away, says, "Oh, it's all right. They all do it." Sue, she is never the one to say, *They all do it.* Only when the mother of who did it is a movie star. Aileen runs to Ruth; she has a huge *bocal.* It seems Brando kicked her too.

"I'm sorry," Aleph tells Claire, "but Mary says when he does it I should take him home." Aleph leaves, carrying Brando, and it is like the air coming out a balloon. But now, we can talk.

"He does it to get at her," Clarisse mutters, following behind, a cream puff crammed into one side her mouth.

"Clarisse, I do not like!" my pupil says. "And Aleph, she is so sweet, Lola! She could have anybody!"

"But-ah, maybe she wants a white." I would like to see the inside of that house. My daughters, they will tell everyone that their mother in America visits movie stars.

Just then Helen and Jeff arrive, rolling in a red bike with training wheels, balloons tied on the handlebars.

Williamo hugs the thigh of Claire.

"Cake okay?" she asks. "Know it doesn't look so hot."

232

"Best cake I ever had."

I finally taste. True, the layers are hard, but they crunch, and the runny custard tastes like home and goes very good with the chocolate.

I give the little sack with my presents: a new ten dollars and a mustard seed in a crystal ball for around the neck. The gifts when he is opening them look flimsy. I wish I would be the one to roll in the bike with balloons.

I turn because I hear fighting. Ginger Saperstein pushes Aileen off the lap of Ruth and Aileen turns on the grass, making a noise.

"Shhh," Ruth whispers. "Shhh."

I have never before seen Aileen like this. I have never once seen her cry. She does not like Ginger Saperstein. She cannot stand to see her grandmother bossed. But Ruth she has to answer the wishes of her employer.

"Get up," Ruth says, down near Aileen.

Danny left already. Ruth will have to take three buses with Ginger back to Beverly Hills; Aileen will go home at the end of the day with Cheska.

Now the mother of Claire and Tom come up the lawn, her hand on his arm. She carries balloons and Tom hauls a small tree.

Ruth starts collecting paper plates to throw out. She always acts like this, too grateful.

"Why you leave before the piñata?" I ask.

Ginger Saperstein and Aileen only met at the wedding and once at Christmas when Aileen came dressed up to say thank you for her present. Even today, Aileen wears the old clothes of Ginger. Sue and another mother glance over. Ruth is right; Ginger becomes jealous. And today we have mothers who get jealous too. I will give Ruth cream puffs for the bus.

Standing with the bat, each child looks small, a little frightened. I am the one to tie the blindfold. Only one wins. And then just for a second. Williamo swings hard, but a little to the side. China, she slits the belly with her slug.

With paper plates, there is not so much to clean. Only bowls from the cake. Mai-ling sweeps, then starts wiping; she works like this. She will scrub every pan and then when that is done she will still be moving, clearing counters, drying the sink, polishing the spout of the faucet. I cover foods to save. The tablecloth, it is already spinning in the machine. It seems my body has more air inside, like angel food. I am wrapping cream puffs for Cheska and Aileen. We name the guests, remembering little bits of what they said. I feel proud we helped after the piñata that Williamo and China would not fight.

I walk with Cheska to the front, where wind tugs balloons from the mailbox. "That is her!" she says, pointing to a woman up the street. "From the Castle." The Castle. It takes me a moment to understand because the kids today have castles too.

"That lady! She is the one! But you do not expect a second wife to be fat."

Paul helps Melissa shove the castle of Simon into the back of her station wagon. The decorated refrigerator box of Aileen, they leave. She shrugs. They cannot carry on the bus. I pull a top off a lavender, for no reason. I am happy. Williamo said a nice goodbye to every one his guests. He kissed his grandmother and hugged a long time while Tom showed Claire where to plant the tree in the yard.

"I saw your boyfriend the other day at Sears," I say.

"Who, Tom? *He's* not my boyfriend."

I bask. Only a small bit more to do and the house will be back. Houses here most of the time only wait. The owners feel afraid to use their living rooms, as if they will break, but look, now it is the same again. Like our bodies; we feel happiest after we give all. Williamo sprawls across his bed. The pots are put away; I pick up rags to throw in the machine. Then my employers come into the kitchen and ask me to sit down.

So now I am sitting. This is the time every year they say my raise, the mint at the end of the meal. I am thinking, in a colored swirl, maybe this raise will be big. From my weekend employers, maybe they found out my offer.

But they chop me. With the air of the party still here.

She is talking in her voice with the teeth; I have seen it before when she is saying she is sorry, but really her teeth they are a gate, *Do not come at me.* He said already what he said. He talks loud over her; he is being the man. They appreciate all I have done for William, he shouts, what I have given him, but his show will not air until September and his contract it is not yet renewed. It will depend on ratings.

They cannot afford me.

She is still talking, talking, but it is already done.

They chop me and he is not yet five.

Claire

AND IS MY LOVE FOR SALE TOO?

We met Helen and Jeff because they wanted Lola. Once, they would have paid anything for her. I thought we could probably still talk them into it. We had a supper scheduled.

I told Lola while we were washing dishes at the sink. "Lole, we're having dinner with Jeff and Helen. Should I tell them they can have you? I'm sure they'll jump at the chance."

"Anyway, I will be there too." She shrugged. "So you will be the one to ask."

"I'm ovulating," Helen said, first thing, when we arrived.

"Really? How do you know?"

"Basal thermometer. The doctor said to keep my legs up twenty minutes after sex."

"The doctor with the freckles?" Paul asked.

"Isn't she cute?" Jeff looked at Paul. "I have a crush on her."

"We both have crushes on her," Helen said, and for once took the punch line herself. "But I have the more intimate relationship." Then she stood to take our plates to the kitchen.

"Sit *down*, I'll *do* it," Jeff said. "Or let them. That's why they're here."

Paul and I started stacking.

"Not you. Lucy and Lola."

In the lull, I lurched forward. "There's something we have that you may want," I began. They looked at each other and started talking.

"... your landlord would ever sell?"

"You think they would, you talk to them, I'll pay you, man." Jeff fisted Paul's shoulder. "Commissionorama."

They wanted to buy our little house! And Paul was listening! I stood up and ran to the bathroom. Then he was there, knocking. "Let me in."

I sat on the floor hugging my knees.

"Claire, it was a misunderstanding. They thought you were offering."

"You told them no?"

"Let me in. They'll be fine," he said, patting my back. "They'd just use it for his office. Course, if we did want to, we could probably make a pretty penny."

But what about the days I'd scrubbed the new grout with a toothbrush, or painted the inside back corners of drawers with that toxic enamel, work you do only for your own. "Is my love for sale too?"

"Claire, I was just saying. I thought you might like the cash for a down payment."

"I love our house."

" 'Kay. Done." He ushered me back outside. "Claire's put a lot of work into the house. She'll be burying me in the backyard. But what she meant, when she said we had something"—here he lowered his voice—"was Lola. We're going to have to let her go."

Helen lifted her fingers from the table, one at a time, keeping them straight. Jeff looked up into the jasmine as if he weren't following. They'd lost interest in what had once been so urgent to them. They were over Lola.

"And we thought, maybe with another baby," Paul continued.

But they had Lucy, who was fun and talented with flowers.

Helen shook her head. "I'll go a different way this time. We'll do a baby nurse and maybe a UCLA girl. We'll see. Bing has outgrown Lola." She rested a hand on her belly.

Time doesn't age you, Lil said. *Having kids does.*

As Helen served stone-fruit cobbler, Jeff grabbed her plate and lifted it. "You really want this?"

"Yes," she said.

"When do you go?" Paul asked Jeff.

"I told him, next movie's here or somewhere I can bring the

kids without vaccinations," she said. "I don't want to be away more than one or two nights. That's not being a mother. That's being a father."

I kicked Paul. "That was it," I said, finally outside. "That was my problem all along. I wanted to be a father."

"Maybe you should see somebody," Paul said.

Helen and Jeff passed on Lola. I hardly remembered the beginning anymore; I remembered it the way you remember someone else's life. There was a year he woke up at five. Paul changed his diaper and drove around until Will's neck wilted on the car seat. For months, I'd worried about whether I had enough milk. I didn't want Will to have a drop of anything else, even water. I pumped and Lola marked the date on each bottle. So many things that seemed crucial and excruciatingly hard ended and then didn't matter anymore, forever after. Little Him would never remember. All the closeness; looking up into your eyes as he sucked; you could have fed him unwarmed formula, for all he'd know by the age of memory.

At a year, Lola stopped boiling the bottles. At fourteen months, I weaned him. If I'd succeeded at this or failed, it was finished.

I tried to find what should have been my baby journal. The pages were blank, except one scribbled recipe for homemade Play-Doh we'd never used.

We fired Lola.

Lola

A WHITE THAT WANTS OUR LUCY

My weekend and five-day employers, my wand turned them into friends. The husbands, they close the door to laugh and get paid for it. My weekend employer is a famous. So why is not the contract of Paul renewed?

The door to the kitchen swings both ways, and Helen backs in, holding a platter. I am the one to take. Lucy is here too: for their dinner parties, they double.

"Lucy, you seem down," Helen says.

"I just do not know with Tony."

I have a much bigger problem, but Lola keeps her private life private. Maybe the advice of Ruth was wrong. "That is old news," I say, scissoring basil.

"Helen, there is something I want to ask," Lucy says. "Your friend Dale, once he said about a painter? Can I see that picture?"

Helen stirs the pasta, adding more salt to the water, even though we already put. This is the problem here. Women have helpers, but they do not let us make anything complete. Then they feel unnecessary. When I had helpers, I let them cook. I ate.

"Dale thinks you're gorgeous. We always tell him to bug off."

"This is a white? That wants our Lucy?"

The face of my pupil closes. She bites a noodle. "Done already."

Helen heaves up the copper and we both grab.

"He only dates Asians. The last American he went out with was in college."

"But Lucy is Filipina. She must marry a Filipino."

"What do you say, Luce? Think you'd ever date an American?"

"Blue-eyed babies," I say. "Coconuts. Brown bark, white inside."

Lucy mixes pasta into the sauce. "I will just see with Tony."

"She will not even meet Filipinos," I say. "Thirty-three already."

I sprinkle the confettied basil, hand the finished pasta to Helen.

"To be continued," she says, walking out backward.

We serve ourselves on the plates we use for the kids. Helen would let us eat on china, but these go in the machine. The cooking here, it really is too healthy.

"Me, I am eating salads, fish, like that. But my tummy, it is still big, Lola! And the girls here, they are so slim. Because they drink milk. They have long bones."

But some Filipinas are slim too. Lettie Elizande. Me even.

"The ones in magazines. Tony said, *I want your stomach to become like that.*"

"Those girls aren't doctors, Lucy. They're models," Helen says, here again. "They'd rather be doctors with a tummy."

But supermodels earn more than doctors. Anyway, Lucy is not doctor here.

"Let's put on the fish," Helen says, sharp in her voice. Before, she did not have that. I cannot tell if Claire has asked yet about me.

Lucy takes the pan from the refrigerator with salmon marinated in orange juice. There are too many vitamins in this food.

"I say to him, *Maybe you don't like me?* He says, *Yah, I like you.* But before he is saying we will be married. Now, no."

My heart speeds. My pupil, she will not be ready to give me her job. I should have found for her a husband first.

Helen looks to me. She wants to return to her guests. "What do you think, Lole?"

"Lucy knows I do not approve. She should be with someone who has savings."

"But she likes him." Helen sighs, backing out the swing door to her life.

I shrug. "Kids like candy."

I collect plates from outside; jasmine petals mix in the pasta. I eat one. It does not taste much different.

At the table, they are laughing. Are they laughing my chop?

My pupil gets ready the platter, ringing the fish with slices of lemon and orange, picking out the pits with the tip of a knife. We wash the pasta plates, so it will not be too much at the end. Lucy tastes the fish, frowns. "In our place, Lola, the fish is so sweet. The fisherman take right from the sea and you eat."

A shriek. I let Lucy go in even though it is my day. Bing sometimes he has nightmares. Williamo sleeps too, in his stroller, under a blanket, by the mother.

"Sleepysleep," my pupil says, closing the door.

I sit. The leftover pasta I put away already. But Lucy takes things off the counter to polish. "Why you do? You are making me look bad."

"I try to help them, like that."

"But it is not your house."

A long time under jasmine they talk. They will hand me from the one side of the table to the other, like a parcel.

"Lola, we are planning to rebuild our place in Iloilo. Last month I ask for a loan. An advance, like that."

An advance! That is why she is polishing. But they will want her to work that off.

"Next January, my father will go back for the two-year anniversary of our mother's death. It is our belief if you put on the roof yourself, that will be good luck."

This one, she has too many beliefs. First it was doors, that the doors should not line up so you can see through to the outside in their house in the province. I told her I would not pay to fix that. But she and Cheska sent home more than five hundred. Now it is the India trees in front of the house of Cheska. "They are saying that kind of tree, it is bad luck," my pupil said.

"But you have not had hard luck."

"No, Lola, it is. Butch, the son of Cheska, he got dengue. He almost die. And Mel, he is not sending much for the kids. Maybe he has another woman, like that. I told Cheska, cut the trees. We will just pay that."

I saw the pictures. They are beautiful old trees. They need those trees. For shade.

I am more plain. I pay for my children to get degrees. "You believe in ghosts. Me, I am a believer in money. How much did your employers contribute?"

"Two thousand."

Two thousand! Maybe that is why the talk outside is long.

"Jeff, he said, *I'd rather give you money for your tests. Who's going to live in that house?*"

"Here, they do not understand a double life."

"When I first came, I promised my mother we would fix the house."

For a promise. To a woman dead and buried. But my pupil, will she remember her promise to me?

I do not want that it will be a problem when I take back the job.

No, anyway, I want to go. Only one year, two years, like that.

"It seems in this house now, you are almost daughter."

"Yes, Lola. But I have lot of problem." She opens the oven door and a carpet of warm floats out; peaches bubble through a shell. "With Tony, I really do not know."

Normally, I would second the motion, but I have swallowed a question mark. I am wondering this white that says my pupil looks like a painting. The word *gorgeous,* that could work in her system like a drug. To Aleph Sargent, no. But for Lucy, this may be the first time anyone used that word. That is why it is important to have a mother. A mother can see behind flowers. Lucy is young, but she is not gorgeous. Me, I am suspicious. I was the same with my daughters and now the second eldest—she is married to a very nice Visayan, who owns a tilapia farm.

"You are always going with Tony to Chinatown. Maybe you need privacy."

"Because it is cheap, Lola. I tell him, it is okay; we don't have to spend."

Helen comes in carrying a book. "Time for Lola's coffee." She pours milk into a pot. "This goes out in the blue pitcher. Here." She opens the book. "Tahiti."

The seed of the areola. But the girl in the picture wears no shirt!

Flower behind the ear. I am thinking the white. For him, it will be like getting a slave.

Helen pours thick coffee into our mugs, and then she swings out again. Why does she keep going back and forth? They all know we are in the kitchen. Why cannot she sit?

I wash, my pupil dries, to keep the hands fresh. But her clock is past time.

"Maybe you can have your Tony," I say. "At last your teacher will allow. I will broker the marriage."

In her face, I see an opening. A fan of light from a door; it is hope, full of terror, wanting to grow. "Just wait, Lola." She blows on her coffee. "Just wait till I am more thin. One month, two months, like that. I have a video; it is Aleph Sargent and her mother exercising. A very nice tape."

But I cannot wait.

I keep expecting Claire to tell me, but when they leave she avoids my eyes.

Maybe they did not want Lola.

Monday night, at the sink, I ask.

"Oh, Lole, I don't know. When I said, *There's something we have you might want,* they assumed I meant something else. They think everything's for sale."

"But-ah, when you said, *No, it is Lola?*"

"I was so upset I didn't ask."

I am still taking care Williamo. How many more days? At five o'clock, I help prepare the supper, the sound of chop chopping the same. They still eat. There is really no one I can talk this. I do not want to tell Ruth. I hold it in my chest and breathe with this package hidden; up and down, it hurts. Others here have offered me jobs, but those spots, they filled already.

I can see they love me, Williamo does and Claire too, so the problem, it really must be money. Paul, what is the matter, all this time working, why he cannot earn? But every Wednesday I replace the underwear, washed and folded in his drawer, I see the card of the Hollywood agent. I see that rectangle with a spray of glitter. If Williamo starred in a commercial, maybe that would be the year salary for Lola. I call when he is at the camp. "I am the babysitter of the boy you met in Starbucks. We will try once."

"Well, it's more than a once commitment, if you know what I mean. We've got to get pictures and then there're auditions."

"Where?"

"You're in what, Santa Monica? I'm out there Tuesday, Thursdays. I've got my shrink if you want to know the truth. Why don't we meet Tuesday, and in the meantime, I'll see what's coming down the pike. He's what, three, four?"

"He is now four," I say.

Tuesday, I have ready a package of pictures duplicated.

"I meant head shots," she says. "We'll need eight-by-tens. Tell you what, there's an audition in Studio City tomorrow. Why don't you just bring him? It'll be a cattle call, but it's Volvo, so if he did win, the jackpot'd be big."

But he has camp tomorrow. To take without parent permission, that is a crime maybe. If they did not chop me already, they could chop me for this. Wednesday is the day that used to be our playclub. Nannies in Santa Monica know that at this house, there was a party. Almost every week, a few still arrive. All year, I had to tell them, the party is over; Williamo now attends school. I tape a sign on our door just in case. Today, after camp, there will be playclub at the place of Mai-ling. Her birthday, we will have to miss.

The bus ride it is almost two hours. On my lap he is becoming too big for, I tell him it is a contest and if we win we can surprise his parents.

"But what do we play?"

"You just smile. That is all we can do. Is smile."

In the big auditorium, I look around; I am the only nanny. Williamo becomes impatient. "I don't want to do this anymore."

I promise French fries after. We still wait and then when they call his name and he goes to the front, Williamo he does not smile.

The agent, still in silver, stands, jingling. "We'll have to work on stage presence," she says.

But I cannot take Williamo out again. I will have to tell Ruth. While we wait for our transfer to the Wilshire bus, we go in McDonald. I keep a Baggie of pennies in my purse, but today I just hand the girl five dollars.

The ocean, in the distance, has over it a net of gray. Like the iris of an eye, the color is never pure. Over the line of mountains comes a ribbon of smoke. Malibu fires. It is still hot, even now, after five.

By the time we reach the house of China, playclub will be near done, but we have never yet missed. We step over old toys in the side yard, pass neglected animals, mean birds in cages fed by Mai-ling; two rabbits that run wild almost trip me. In back, nobody but kids and babysitters. A small cake stands on the table; a knife jabbed into the fallen middle. Brookie and Kate stand up a huge girl between them. Esperanza returned from Guatemala with her baby.

The bigger kids cannonball in the water, holding their knees. Babysitters sit on the edges of the pool. Mai-ling, she does not have a suit. That is because she never had to take China to classes; a private swim instructor comes here. A hundred dollars every time. And China and her brother, they already know how. Stroke refinement, the instructor calls it. For the birthday, we all chipped in to buy Mai-ling a one-piece. We had to go a special store for large sizes. She is short, shorter than me, but wide. They waited for me to give her the box. Mai-ling opens, looking embarrassed. That was a different Lola who asked for the collection and got the card for everyone to sign. I have bigger problems now. To keep the world running, you need people like me before.

Esperanza stands in the pool. Brookie hands to her the baby. She holds the big girl, skimming her feet on the water so they dance. But a baby should not be so big. And Esperanza walked twenty-one days with that huge girl strapped to a basket on top her head. *"Rapidos!"* She shows me with one hand, up to here in water. "And now she no more cry." Esperanza arrived to the door of Beth Martin, carrying the baby and a sack of Pampers. The employers, they let her every day bring the baby. The USC girl they hired left wet towels on the floor and now they will have to refinish.

Stars of light pucker the surface of the pool. I just now realize, I love this, but I cannot stay. Still nobody here knows yet. If I could just get money, it would be as if it never happened.

"Everybody loves you," Esperanza says to Phoebe, the little sister of Simon.

"I know onebody that don' love me."

Esperanza stretches like a cat. Her body still has its own ideas. Water on her skin angles off into air. She shakes a bottle of glittery gold polish and flecks her toes. I tell her, for a baby, you have to watch, every minute, not for a second can you turn your head. But I really do not have to tell, I am surprise. Esperanza, with this baby that is too fat, you can see she already loves it. She reaches over to tickle it. Then she polishes the toes of the baby gold.

Lucy blurts, "I will lose weights. Because I am sweating!"

"The dryer beep," Mai-ling says.

"So leave the dryer." I look down my shirt. "I live with wrinkles."

Mai-ling nods, meaning, *You keep an eye, yes?* Then she goes to answer the dryer. My pupil is giving Bing up-downs, he shrieks, the way he does, and after a while they stop. I hear a difference. Too quiet. I look at the kids, count. "Where is China?"

We look. Nowhere. Then Lucy dives, hands prayered overhead. I see her body underwater, a dark shape in the blue. This was what she went to medical school for, to save life. *Jollibee. Be Happy. Feel Life.* That is a billboard in Manila. Jollibee, it is like our McDonald. While my pupil dives, I am thinking billboards.

She drags the small body out and we crowd around. For a whole minute, we do not know—maybe life stopped. But then, my pupil feels the pulse. "She is breathing," she says. "Unconscious."

"Call nine-one-one," I say.

Lita asks where is the number for the parents.

"They just go. All the time, they just go." Mai-ling, she is complaining them!

"Whenever the parents leave, you always get the number," I scold.

Lita wants that all but Filipinos get out.

"But when they leave, they will talk," I say. "Mai-ling should go. To the bus stop. Wilshire and ten. I will call Danny to pick her." I hear footsteps down the stairs. Maybe she will get her things.

"But nine-one-one is police. What about the ones without papers?"

Lita and I decide. "Only the legals stay." Lita is the one to call.

Not even a wall separates the room of Mai-ling from the laundry. Just the washer, dryer, ironing board, her small dresser and bed, China on top the white. Mai-ling tugs a lace dress over her shoulders, dry pink bougainvillea stuck in her hands. "Mai-ling, you should never move the patient!" Lucy shouts.

A pop and light: Mai-ling taking a picture. The employers, they gave her that Polaroid, for her Christmas once.

"Oh my God," Lucy says. "*Bu'ang.* She is really *sirang ulo.*"

"Mai-ling, she is a simple person, she believes things we do not even know what." Upstairs, we hear a commotion: the paramedics, thudding down in a stampede, doing what my pupil could not, taking Mai-ling off China and moving the girl to the stretcher.

"Which one's the housekeeper?"

Another says, "Whose of you speaks English?"

China breathes, only unconscious. And then they go, the siren, swinging like the incense in church at home, wailing into the late day.

Helen arrives just for a normal pickup.

I hear Mai-ling say, "Ma'am, I will get the electric chair."

Still here! She should be gone already. Helen is okay, but anyway not Filipina.

"I am the only one sending money," Mai-ling says.

"I've got to call Jeff." Whatever Helen says, he is the one to decide. She keeps dialing.

"I cannot leave," Mai-ling whispers. "They owe me."

"You worry that later. Now you go."

Mai ling looks up in a diagonal, like an animal.

"Well, Tarek, where is he?" Helen yells into the phone.

When Sue opens the door, it feels like a nightmare surprise party.

"Oh my God, my God, no." She bangs her head against the wall. Her thirteen-year-old son holds her shoulders. "Mom. Mom. Chill." The husband, he is dialing already.

When he hangs up, he tells us all to go. They lock the door and get into their car.

At the end of this day, I have a small tragedy my own. When I take the garbage from the bathroom of my employer, I see a shopping bag. I look the receipt. Barneys Mens: $1,275.00. So they are still spending. It is not true, what they said. I cannot believe anymore. And what will they do with Williamo while they work?

She said they will put him in Funcare at the school.

That night, I feel a hand on top my head. I was having a dream of white people giving Filipinas pedicures. Beth Martin stood polishing jewelries.

"I can't sleep," he says.

"Okay, then, we will look for stars."

It is cold on the step. But he feels warm, through the pajamas. I smell the skin smell in his hair. In the dream, we lounged around a pool, but Mai-ling fell in. I suppose it is an old LA fear. The fake blue sides. Careful mothers take their toddlers to swim class. Claire had me go with Williamo to the YM. And he is safe. That is enough. "Williamo, you are big now," I say. "Some-a-day I will be your buddy-buddy, not your babysitter anymore."

"Why?"

"Because-ah everybody has to grow up."

I must have mumbled, because Williamo asks, "Do you mean 'someday' or 'summer day'?"

Some-a-day. My word. Small kids and immigrants; we mix English.

In *The Book of Ruth* I read about Flora. She worked for a lady scientist who married the first time at age fifty-two. The scientist and her new husband sent Flora home to her province with a trunk of money, and Flora opened a confection store there. She sent a picture of the store for *The Book of Ruth*.

What is left of night, Williamo sleeps with me.

In my house, there was a corridor, leading out of our bedroom, the gray carpet with a large stain shaped like the continent of North America, from some long-ago spill of True Orange. They all came there with their shoes and beverages, because the television, we kept in our room. In and out, that was my family, the truest days of my life. I always wanted to replace the carpet and buy a TV set for the entry hall. Sometimes I would look at the old stain—many times I tried to remove it—alone in that room during the day.

Now that does not exist anymore.

I sent money a long time ago to fix.

Lola

THE PRINCE FROG

I am ready for our deal. But my pupil she will not like it, not yet. Not until her sailor turns to prince. He is still a frog. Monday, before seven, I walk the same walk I walk every day, but now I am remembering the raw taste of the food there. I will miss my own place. I have the key, but it is not my day, so I push the bell.

Helen opens the door in her bathrobe.

"I am asking if I will be needed, because-ah, Claire and Paul, they chop me."

"Oh, Lola, come in." My weekend employer hugs me, but she is not answering. "Come to the kitchen, I'll make coffee."

My handsome employer stands poking a knife into the toaster, the hair wet. "We have to think of Bing." He looks at his wife with a bar of warning. "He's attached to Lucy."

What do you know? I think. You are never home.

Helen hides behind her hair, measuring coffee. "Lola, sit down. Tell us what happened."

Lucy just sits, looking at the floor.

"They cannot afford me." I laugh. "Lola is too expensive. And I am cheaper than you." I stare at Lucy square, knee to knee. And what do they get for their money? A door opens. The pat of feet. I spread my arms and Bing runs to me. The smell of coffee today is thinner. Helen gives me my mug. I am the only one drinking. They all watch. But I will still take what is offered that is good.

"Let me talk to Lucy." Jeff stands. "If Lucy can stay, I'd have to think that'd be best for you-know-who. But if she might be moving on anyway, we should think about a change when Lola is available."

"But I will not take away the job from Lola, like that."

"No, no, you wouldn't be," Helen says.

But she does not know! Lucy and Jeff go out into the other room.

When they come back the verdict is wrong. There is no place for Lola. Lucy stares down at Bing: her excuse. But she does not love him. If Tony were the one asking, she would jump. But Tony will not propose her. He will only honk.

I walk back to my place. I will have to move.

But then my employer comes, with her teeth. "Lola, we have to talk about what to tell William."

"What do you want me to say?"

"In a way, the easiest thing is that you're going back to the Philippines."

What will I do in the Philippines? I need money. "But he will see me here. Then what?"

"Oh, okay. I thought if you were working in the Valley or something. Well, why don't we just wait."

The chop it is still secret. Before long, everyone will know.

By the end of the day, I have an idea. Maybe I should let her have her Tony. If I get for her her Tony, she will give to me my job. I hate my pupil now, but I cannot afford to. So I will broker the marriage. I call Tony myself; if he does not agree, I will tell Lita. But he right away said okay. We will meet. I borrow the car of Danny for the drive. On the freeway 405, I stay as far right as I can go, but then I have to cross, just to not get pushed out.

The naval base looks shabby, not like the U.S. government compound in Manila, where green lawns spread inside new-painted white fences and waves scallop the bay. Thirty feet above the beach, I saw a guy curled up asleep on the cupping branch of a chestnut, next to a fishtail palm. That is my Philippines.

In the café, Tony does not stand for me. Lita worked here in America when he was young; how could she teach the thousands of small ways? Manners, they are stitches sewn in the random hours. A frog into a prince, that is fairytale.

"You must be the one," I say, pulling out my own chair. I suppose he is handsome, but the strings in him should be pulled tighter.

He opens a small rattan suitcase, what we call native. He lifts out clothes, a yellow blouse, the shell buttons browned. A skirt of pale linen. A black-and-white picture preserved in the garments; a posed tableau of a family, the father wearing a tilted panama hat, two boys, and a girl with a ribbon in her hair. The mother wears the clothes that are now dry as pressed leaves, cracking at the folds. "When she got here, they made her wear a chicken uniform, with real feathers. Filipinas dressed as chickens, serving chicken."

I never knew that. Now Lita is proper, always a purse, not a pack. There is a restaurant I have passed in Glendale, built the shape of a chicken.

"*Lickin' Chicken.* I didn't see her for seventeen years."

"Oh, that is too long." But Lita did not have the green card then. "Lucy tells me that you are the one meant for her."

He shrugs inside his jacket. "Never felt that."

"I did not either. And I am married, thirty-four years."

He turns around his chair. "Lucy's a weekday—like air."

"Air is important. But-ah, she may be Wednesday to you, to somebody else a weekend. Holiday even. So you have been a ladies man."

He shrugs. "Girls like me, don't know why."

"According to Lucy, it is because you are handsome."

He smiles.

"That is no compliment. You did not make your face. Your bank account, that is your doing." I stand. "Show me a boat." I have noticed with kids, they talk more easily in motion.

He flashes his U.S. military ID and we walk onto the big pavement. The boat looks more a parking lot. On the first deck, there are all kinds of planes.

"She never says when she goes to see him, but I can tell."

Who does Lucy see? "The dentist?"

"I mean my mom. And the kid." A wall opens. Lita had a child here? But then, I know; he is talking the one she took care.

"That boy must be grown by now." We stand at the railing. Lita never told me she saw him; she only talks about the Chinese Adopteds. "My kids, too, they are jealous."

"Rainy day, she was tickling his back, I was alone the other side of the world."

I have missed things too. But I do not anymore mind.

"Strange power you get from a woman raising you who's your servant. You kick her a little."

"Williamo, he does not kick." But more than once, he hit. "My kids, they probably say the same. But now they have their degrees."

"I was too much of a fuck-up to stay in school."

"You were younger. Mine, before I left, they already started university."

"We shuffled through days. Then a package would land and we practically killed each other ripping it open. Now she's trying to make up time. First Christmas here she gave me a stuffed animal. *Lady—man, I'm twenty five,* I said. We can't have those years back."

"But you forget how poor you were."

"I know. All the little chants of America."

The ocean here looks different than the ocean in Santa Monica. Water churns brown bits of debris and chips of wood flicker. "These the years for Lucy," I say. "If you are not serious of her, you should leave her be."

"I like Lucy. Only thing with her, I never get that rush. Usually, there's something I want to find, some chase."

"Her friends, they are asking, *What was he doing here nine years that he has no savings?*"

"Did my digging for gold in the square of light on a bedroom floor."

"They are warning her against you." Lucy, she is thirty-four almost.

"Sometimes when I hear piano playing, I'm not getting it through my ears but my chest, you know? Sex was like that. For healing."

Nearby, we hear a foghorn. "Tony, this is a workday for me."

"My sad stories, I told to a married lady I was in love with. She made them into coins."

"Where is that lady now?"

"Still married."

"And what will those coins buy? But anyway, I am asking you to let Lucy alone. Because there is someone else, someone good for her."

His whole face becomes more up, the strings pulled. "Some other guy?"

"It is a friend the employer. Dale. A white." I bring out the book from my backpack. "He thinks she looks like the woman of this painter. Very famous." I nod. "Museums around the world."

Telling him the white—that is my trick. But the trick will not last.

Still, nothing lasts. And he is a sailor. Soon his ship will go again to sea.

For the second time, I have a gift for Lucy. I know from taking care kids, there are many kinds of gifts. Candy and arcade quarters buy a smile, but they do not add much to the pole strength inside. Tricks wrapped in shiny paper look like presents. I lent Lucy this job; she could use it, but not keep it. I wanted it for my insurance. Then she stole it from me. The gift I am carrying now, I really do not know. Like toys I sometimes buy Williamo, they may not be good for him, but anyway, maybe they will not harm. Some believe all sugar is bad; Claire wants that Williamo will have only music of orchestras, things that will teach him to do well in school, not songs from the Disney movie. But I want Williamo and my pupil, too, to hold the bubbles that look perfect to them, once upon a time in their hands.

Of course bubbles will break. But everything breaks.

The cars of my weekend employers are absent, so I let myself in. I find Lucy on the nursery floor, cutting out pictures from a magazine with child-rounded scissors. A table. A bed with four posts. Next to her a jar of paste. She is making a book.

"What are you doing?"

She jumps. "For our place." She and Cheska, they are fixing the family house. Maybe this is good enough a life.

I am tempted to get up and take my gift, unused.

"In our place, we have lots of woods. To pay a guy to build, it is so cheap, Lola. I will just show the picture." She has a look, part proud and part embarrassed. Even without children, Lucy has a purpose.

I look around the room. At the changing table, I remember my pupil, after the wipe patting on powder, chanting *Shoushou*. She pictures herself a young mother, everything pretty. *Sleepysleep,* she says when she closes the light.

I tumble ahead. Two and two onto the ark. I suppose it is best if everyone gets married. Do I still believe that? But my pupil is romantic; the dad Florencio, the mom Florencia, and they named their children all the same. "You better stop planning for your house in the Philippines," I say. "You will have your children here. I have talked to Tony."

Only a few times, I have seen on the face of Williamo what fleets across the features of Lucy now. The eyes open; the mouth falls. Hope, it is a temporary mirage.

It will break soon. But everything breaks.

"I will take back my job," I say to my pupil, at the park.

"Yes, Lola," she says.

So I can tell Williamo: I will still see him every day. Once a week, I can pick up Williamo and Bing together, so they become friends again. Claire, she worries that. But my pupil does not say when. Maybe Tony did not propose her yet. What is the lag? Almost two weeks already I am chop. Claire and him, they will give me one-month severance. I will use that for the first half August tuition. The rest and September, I can pay with savings. But October, there will be nothing.

Two weeks ago, I ask Claire, "It is okay I am still here?"

"Course, Lola," she said.

"For how long it is okay?"

"Forever," she said.

I still take care Williamo. Because he does not know. But Claire comes out to tell me she will write me a reference, and again she has the teeth. I hate her now.

"I will go," I say, "as soon I am needed."

Then I call to tell Ruth I am chop. It is not so hard, even when her voice hushes, because I hold a secret. She does not know it is a jungle swing, from one job to the next. The weekend will become the five-day, seven days even. One-ten a day, I will become rich.

Ruth says Sunday Danny will drive her here to move me to their place. Then I will have to tell Williamo.

As Ruth and Danny carry my boxes, Claire comes with an envelope of money. She hugs me, but I stiff; I do not like her touch. The guy, he is inside watching TV. I feel a grinding in my jaw. He is the one who harmed me.

Last is Williamo. He stands hands in his pockets.

"Give me high five," I say. "Buddy buddy, I will see you very soon, okay?"

But he will not look up the ground. He stands like that as we drive away.

"You have to become an agency now," I tell Ruth. "I cannot go the Valley or Hollywood. Because Williamo. He is not yet five." Right now I want day work, just to clean. She says she can find me live-out. Wednesdays, she thinks.

She cleared a bottom bunk for me already, below Mai-ling, next to the slave. She is not ready to work yet. Ruth took her to a doctor the priest knows. Because her body, it is marked with bruises that do not go away. From that guy throwing her down, she does not have hearing in one ear. And Ruth cannot send Mai-ling out for a new job either. Any employer will want references. She was in that house thirteen years.

"China is still sleeping," Ruth says. "Coma. I heard from Lita who knows from Alice." China is God's way to remind me a chop is a smaller thing, but his trick does not work; I still feel sad for myself. I worry for China but from far, the way we do for movie stars, when I read Julia Roberts, she is getting a divorce.

"Next job, I will do everything. I will work by night." Mai-ling stands on a chair, dusting each one the Venetian blinds, the way she used to in the house of Sue. The apartment does look very clean. "Maybe I am on television. Most wanted."

"No, Mai-ling," Ruth says. "In America, they have crimes with sex in them. Nobody wants you."

Mai-ling made a mistake I would never forgive my *yaya*. I lost my job too, and I did not let anybody drown.

"Remember," Ruth says, "your pupil went to New York with her employers and she met Filipinas in the park? She says they are earning big. Maybe we will drive Mai-ling to there." Danny has the 1975 Mercedes, pale green, that I drove to the naval base. He has owned it five years already, but this trip will be its first journey across the continent.

"I will wish upon a car," I say. "But what about your jobs?"

"I can get an off. But Danny will have to quit." She shrugs. "Not now. Not with Candace." It takes me a minute to remember Candace is the slave.

Mai-ling shuffles as we talk about her. She does not want that her son will be a drug addict. She thinks she did a wrong when he was small. Some strength she did not build, some might. But she hopes for his daughter. If she can get her in a good school, a Catholic. Inside her suitcase is the picture she made of China. She has confused China with the granddaughter she has never seen, so when she looks at the Polaroid she is praying for both girls. She believes she can hear the picture breathing.

I am sorry for her, but I have too many things to think.

She gives me a small sandwich bag. Without any of us knowing, Mai-ling took China to Echo Park and had her baptized. This is the baptismal certificate she wants me to give to Sue. "She will thank you, yes." She nods.

"When will I see Sue?" I say. "I am not even working now Williamo." But I take the certificate in wax paper in my pocket.

"Lita says her employer, she changed. Alice sits on the floor now and tries to play her kids. She is not anymore doctor full-time." Ruth raises her eyebrows. They think Alice is running around with my weekend employer. Because the day China drown, no one could find either one them. Maybe she will divorce. Ruth says before they divorce here, they start to spend more time with the kids.

That night, I cannot sleep. I look at another mattress through the bed slats. I miss my own place.

So it is over, no more Williamo and Lola. How can that be?

When I wake, there is already a crowd. Filipino bread on the table and boxes American cereal. Ruth has for me a cleaning job Wednesday, Fridays.

The second week August, I go to the park and ask my pupil, "So is there a date for the wedding?"

Because all the time I am thinking. Even when she quits, they may want her to stay two weeks. Three weeks. For transition. And starting now, I am sending savings.

"Not yet, Lola," she says, "I will talk to Tony."

September 1, I see my pupil again. Already it is five weeks since I talked to Tony. My savings are down to two hundred and ninety dollars. "I do not want to rush the honeymooners," I say. "But I need this job."

She shakes her head, kicking the playground sand with her foot. "Lola, Tony, he says, I have to keep working. He says we will need the money."

Once, long time ago, I told Ruth we should start an agency and call it Crooks and Nannies. When I could still joke. Now I sit in an agency I took a bus to. They photograph me, take my fingerprint, and Xerox my license and SS card for criminal search. I look like a criminal in the pictures. Front and profile. But the little folder they make says, *Introducing . . . Lola, a fifty-six-year-old, one-hundred-pound Filipina with a green card who drives and speaks English. She has a big smile (all her own teeth) and a big heart.*

I ask why the teeth, they are important.

The lady smiles. "Dentures scare kids."

The only nanny I know with false teeth is Ruth. She takes them out just at night, alone, in her bedroom; she floats them in a glass of water.

Now I have three weeks to make an extra thousand. A terror streaks in me; how? I am trying to be the old Lola. But they typed that I have all my own teeth. What if I lose one? I have not yet written home. They think I am still with Williamo. Because I have never once missed a payment. Far Eastern, they will not wait. My savings they are gone. I have only twenty days to earn more than I can earn in twenty days. And no job.

In the slow parts of the day, I touch my pocket, as if I am carrying the small soul of China, made of fog. I think of her in a coma, the climbing child finally still. Maybe when I tap the paper, China feels. I do not believe in heaven, but baptism it is still worth something; like a vaccination or a diploma, you join the club.

What you think about yourself really depends on your circumstances. The moms here, their number one concern is that their children, they will be confident. Nothing we do, nothing another kid does, should nick that confidence. But these kids, they will be confident because the world now, it is their way. Once, that was true in the Philippines. Then there was a day the stock market fell, and my father sat for hours in his study, lifting his glasses off and on. For us, it took years to go from being one kind of family to another. First we were a family that had what it needed—schooling, lessons, eyeglasses—and then, no longer. A bicycle stolen did not mean we could purchase another.

My pupil thinks of herself as a hundred-dollar-a-day nanny. She believes that is something inside her. But I am proof it is not. She gets a hundred dollars a day because now they will pay that. If they chop her, and they will if they want for some reason she may never even know the truth, it will not be so easy again. Most things do not transfer. When Lita finally got her kids here, only the daughter had good marks in school. Lita took the folder, with the transcripts and letters of recommendation, to Pepperdine and Loyola Marymount. But those papers were not worth anything here. The daughter had to start all over at community college.

I am interviewing again. I sit, listening to careful questions and two teams tackle each other: the confidence of Lola against the fear. If I cannot pay next month, Issa will suffer. Not Williamo. I should have put my own first. I could have been working two years already, for one hundred and ten a day.

Eleven interviews and still no offer. Ruth finds an opening for Second Nanny in Woodland Hills. I will have to drive freeways every day and be underneath the First Nanny. Danny takes me for the interview, but that night Claire calls to say they called her and asked about my breathing, if I am healthy enough to last. I must have breathed too loud. Ruth heard of other jobs from the priest, but those are low paying. Once, long ago, when I wanted to quit Claire, I told Ruth, *Find for me a good job.*

Really? she asked then.

Have you ever heard me say that before? I am not Lita.

Natalie telephoned that evening. *Dominique Garcia says her agency handles nannies in the range of a hundred twenty to two fifty a day!* But by then, Claire and I had made up.

Now I will go to that place. I take two buses. Because already, September is half done. As I leave to walk to the bus stop, Ruth puts an envelope in my pocket.

"What is this?" I can feel already it is thick. Money. "No. I cannot take." But still I am holding. Because I need to. "I will pay you back."

"It is not from me. The girls took up a collection."

A collection for me! I am the one to ask the collection. But now I must accept and say thank you. The collection they took, it is big, bigger than any I pooled, more than the plane fare to send Lettie Elizande home. It will be enough, with what I have, to send for tuition. I put it in my pocket, next to the soul of China. After the agency the Garcia girl recommended, I will go to the bank to wire.

Buckingham Nannies. But the office, it is no palace. The building has a traffic school and Persians taking passport photos; the agency is only one small room. Because the ones who see are out-of-work nannies; the moms just call. Unfair matchmaking.

Two guys sit, desks facing each other, eating egg-and-bagel sandwiches.

I hand them my résumé, including a picture Williamo made in school: I AM GRATEFUL FOR: MY LOLA.

They look at me up and down and start telling me jobs, eighty to one-twenty a day. "We'll schedule meetings day after tomorrow," the guy says, fingers on the phone.

"Wait a minute." I try to joke. "I have a friend who is employer. Dominique Garcia Weinstock. She told me some pay two-thirty."

Then I hear the clock. The guy resting fingers on the telephone glances at the other. "Well, there are American college girls. But let me tell you, those gals don't clean, they can't cook. I wouldn't get near one myself. They whine. Let's face it: What's a with-it college girl doing nannying?" He sighed. "But people worry about the accent. We see kids here who speak Spanish before they speak English."

Even one year ago, Williamo talked like me. But from the school, he learned professional English. So Filipinas, we are not even the highest. I did not know that.

"One way to make more. Would you be comfortable with twins?"

"I have five children," I say. "I can take care two."

They set up an interview for me in Studio City, for one hundred twenty. Danny drives me to the top a hill, with olive trees and small purple blossoms swaying, hot already, before nine in the morning. When I step out of the car there is low noise. Bees maybe. Closer to the house, a fountain runs. The two come out, each carrying one baby. We talk less than ten minutes, they look at each other, and the woman offers me the job, when I have not yet given them the numbers for Helen and Claire.

"Do you not want to check the reference first?"

"No," the mother says. "You're hired."

EMPLOYMENT AGREEMENT
Between Wanda Luwanza and Susie and Justin Gelfond

This is an Agreement between Susie and Justin Gelfond ("the Gelfonds") and Wanda Luwanza ("Lola"). The Gelfonds have elected to engage Wanda to perform the following duties in exchange for compensation stated in this Agreement. The purpose of this Agreement is to clearly state the agreed-upon services and compensation. This Agreement contains the entire understanding of the parties. It may not be changed orally but only by an agreement in writing signed by both parties. The parties agree as follows.

1. Wanda agrees to provide the following childcare and services:

Childcare for the Gelfonds' twins, Franny and Gardiner. This includes but is not limited to every-day care such as age appropriate activities (feeding, bathing, changing diapers, clipping nails, singing, playing, reading, cradling, exercising motor skills, going to the park, supervising their interaction with other children, etc.). We encourage you to speak your language to them and to read to them whenever possible. We hope you, Wanda, will come to treat the twins as you do your own family, who deserve love and affection, challenge and support, humor and discipline. We encourage you to help them grow into fun, thoughtful, responsible, intelligent children.

We will ask you to bring the twins to our places of work for visits of varying duration. Several days a week, you will be expected to care for the twins in and around Susie's office.

In time, Franny and Gardiner's care may include driving them and accompanying them to various school-related activities, birthday parties, and doctor's visits.

When the twins enter school, we will expect you to use the spare time their absence will provide you to volunteer at said school, on committees, lunchtime service, library room helping, etc.

2. Keeping the house clean and tidy. This includes cleaning up the kitchen after breakfast in the morning and after use throughout the day; keeping Franny and Gardiner's rooms and the playroom organized, doing their laundry, sterilizing the toys, folding and putting away clothes, picking up after them, putting away anything (such as books or toys) used during their daily activities. Caring for the twins must remain the primary responsibility, but during their naps there should be ample time for such chores. Responsibilities also include grocery shopping, post office visits, film drops, clothing returns, putting away groceries, making beds, organizing cupboards and closets. A housekeeper will be employed once a week for more strenuous cleaning such as floor washing, bathroom scrubbing, etc.

Dinner preparation for the Gelfonds. This will involve setting the dinner table, getting necessary foods and making a salad, marinating or putting food in the oven, etc. We encourage Wanda to cook occasionally, if she likes. She is welcome to use anything in the kitchen for herself—including food and equipment—unless expressly stated otherwise.

3. Wanda agrees to the following house rules:

- Safe supervision of the twins at all times
- No visitors unless approved by the Gelfonds
- No TV watching unless the twins are asleep. The children are not permitted to watch TV without first speaking to the Gelfonds
- No smoking, alcohol, or drugs
- No spanking, yelling, hitting, or physical discipline of any kind is to be used with Franny or Gardiner

4. Transportation: We will provide Wanda with a car, in excellent condition, for the errands and activities listed above. Franny and Gardiner will always be transported in their respective car seats (pink and blue), and never left unattended in the car.

5. Wanda's hours of employment shall be Monday through Friday, mostly 6:15 am until 9 pm, although two or three days a week later, allowing the Gelfonds evenings out. Also, most nights we expect the twins to sleep through the night, but if they should wake up, the night feedings and rocking back to sleep will be Wanda's responsibility, as she will be able to nap while they do, the next day, while the Gelfonds will each be working. There may be occasions when the Gelfonds are both traveling or working and Wanda will need to attend to the twins several nights in a row.

6. In exchange for her responsibilities, Wanda will be provided with a guesthouse, including a bedroom, galley kitchen, and bath. We will ask her to maintain it as she would her own home, keeping it clean and tidy. We require Wanda to consult with us before making any material changes to the house, such as painting, fixtures, window treatments, flooring, etc. The Gelfonds will pay all utilities. A private phone line will be installed and basic service paid by the Gelfonds, but additional

usage, above and beyond the basic services, will be Wanda's responsibility.

7. The Gelfonds shall pay Wanda a salary of $600 per week, which shall be paid weekly on Fridays. The Gelfonds will deduct FICA and SDI from her salary. Wanda is responsible for paying her own federal and state tax. On those occasions Wanda works additional days, over and beyond the agreed-upon five days per week, she will be compensated an additional $5 per day, $20 for each full weekend.

8. When Wanda's services are not necessary and she is given 1 or 2 days' advance notice, the Gelfonds may ask for equal hours of service at another time.

9. Wanda shall receive the following days as paid holidays if the following days fall on a regularly scheduled workday: New Year's Day, Memorial Day, Independence Day, Labor Day, Thanksgiving Day, Christmas Eve, and Christmas Day.

10. Wanda will be allowed 3 days of paid sick/personal leave every calendar year. One day of this time can be used after every 120 days of employment. If Wanda does not use these days, she will be paid on a prorated basis at the end of twelve months.

11. Wanda shall receive no less than 7 days of vacation every twelve months of employment. Vacation time will be required to match the Gelfonds' own scheduled vacation—in the event that Wanda does not join us on our vacation. The Gelfonds will give Wanda four weeks' notice for vacation scheduling.

12. Wanda will be responsible for all healthcare-related expenses, including but not limited to prescription charges, copayments, deductibles, hospital charges, etc.

13. Other benefits include travel opportunities, flight miles, etc.

14. A job performance evaluation shall be held every six months.

15. Wanda's employment under this Agreement may be terminated upon one or more of the following events:

    a. By the Gelfonds for justifiable cause with 24 hours' notice. In this case, Wanda will not receive any outstanding payment for sick or vacation days. The Gelfonds can justifiably terminate Wanda for the following reasons:
       • Wanda fails to comply with the rules and standards established by the Gelfonds.
       • Wanda engages in fraud, dishonesty, or any other act of misconduct in the performance of Wanda's duties on behalf of the Gelfonds.

    b. By the Gelfonds without cause upon two weeks' notice or, in lieu of two weeks' notice, two weeks' salary.

    c. By Wanda upon six weeks' notice.

    d. By Wanda's permanent disability, such that Wanda is unable, due to illness, accident, or other cause, to perform the majority of her usual duties for a period of one month or more despite reasonable accommodation by the Gelfonds.

16. The terms of this Agreement shall commence on the signing of this Agreement and continue, in full force and effect, until otherwise terminated or revised as herein provided. The first day of work shall be September 13, 1995. The terms and conditions set forth in this Agreement shall govern Wanda's employment unless changed in writing.

We look forward to you being a part of our family for many years to come.

I sign the contract, but I do not join the Gelfond family.

Actually, I stay at that rich job only one week. Every day, they want that I will take the babies to the mom at her lunch, and on the regular roads that is more than one hour each way. The first day Franny cries and I have to pull to the curb to change the diaper in the back. The second day, they both scream and I have to feed. Finally home, the twins sit in their bouncy chairs on the kitchen island, waving spatulas like wands. I stir biscuits from a mix. I have spread out a map, to find a better route for tomorrow.

My weekend employer calls me. "There's a woman at Paramount, single mom. I don't really know her, but she just went into the hospital to have the baby and she needs help." She lives in Santa Monica, he tells me. Ten minutes from Williamo. She will give me two thousand for a down payment on a car and a good salary, he says, whatever you're getting paid there.

It is better really with a single mother, Ruth says. She does her job and you do yours. The ex-husband of Natalie, he can find a good car for you.

By the time my employers turn the key in the lock that night I am packed. I tell them I am going home. Before anything, the father runs upstairs, two at a time. Yes, they are alive, asleep, tucked in their cribs. I did not kidnap the prince and princess.

"But what about when you come back," the mother pleads. He panicked that they were dead or stolen. She frets; how can she go to work tomorrow? "The twins *like* you. *We* know you. I'll ask the agency to get us a temp."

But they do not know me. "I am old," I say. "I will not return here." I wait outside for Danny to pick me. Really, what I told them, it is the truth.

"This is Lola," my weekend employer says at the hospital, his other hand cupping the elbow of the doctor. But the doctor is Alice, the employer of Lita. So it is true what the babysitters are gossiping. Here Alice seems different, in a white coat and scrubs.

"I know Lola," she says. "I'll take you to meet my patient. This baby needs someone. During the birth, there were problems."

The mother, she puts the baby in my hands that first day. She gives her to me. A girl this time. No father. And something wrong.

The first week I make the mother soup and eggs. I took care an elderly, so already I am used to foods of convalescence. My job now it is not only the baby but to take care the mother so she can soon return to Paramount Pictures. It does not feel to me the house of a new mother. But my employer *is* a new mother, too, even in her forties. The baby, she still has no name.

"I've been overwhelmed," Judith says. A quick smile up at me.

It is quiet here. In back, the middle of three duplex units, there is an old sycamore and many birds, but we are the only ones to watch. Americans, they do not like to share land. We have an easy time, this baby and I. A baby really is the beginning of the world. If you slow down, you too will grow. With my own, I was too tired from the births. In the Philippines, we have only what they call here natural childbirth.

The mother sleeps, the eyes still sunk. I keep water on low, so as soon as she sits I can bring her tea. Especially now, I appreciate the sharp taste of coffee. I will take the tray away, and then she is sleeping again. I keep the *dede* in a can of warm water. The baby girl listens to the birds. My life is managing two sleepers, holding kites so the strings do not tangle. A tent slopes over us, of tender air.

The tenth evening, I tell my employer, "The hospital telephoned. You must give a name. Otherwise, the birth certificate will come back from the county clerk *No name Wilson*." She stays up past midnight at the kitchen table making a list.

> Natasha
> Claire
> Grace
> Anna
> Sophia
> Caitlin

"So which will it be?" I ask in the morning, rinsing her glass from the night.

"I don't know yet," she says.

I strap Little One onto my chest in the Snugli. Now when I walk to the Pacific, she comes along. The head drops by the time we cross Seventh Street, the sky a deep blue.

I tap the soul of China in my pocket. When I turn onto her street, there is a light in the kitchen. Donald Howard must be home, because the convertible is here, parked like a carousel animal, ferocious but still, made with the mouth always open. Maybe China came home from the hospital. The other ending is there too, an egg on the bone between my breasts.

Sue opens the door, hair just down. "Hi, come on in. I'm pumping."

Little One sleeps, her head to one side, looking like the neck is broken. I follow Sue to the kitchen. Claire had a rented pump, blue and yellow, like a toy. This one covers half the counter. When Sue puts her breasts in and flips the switch, milk runs through the clear pipes that circle around like a racetrack and end in two waiting bottles. The nipples suck forward and back. I step away. After all this time, Sue still has milk. The kimono falls, so her shoulders show. I do not think of Sue as attractive, her hair she just lets, but under, the body looks young.

"Used to wake up with my breasts full of rocks."

Somewhere in this house, I hear television news; Donald must be listening or the Harvard-Westlake brother.

She lifts off the funnels and screws lids on the bottles, then puts them in the freezer, where there are rows already. But who is that milk for?

I look down at this baby, whose head still fits my hand. When I came to the States, I did not realize any difference between breast milk and formula, only that breast milk was free. For my babies, that was all I needed to know. But this girl has many problems. She could use the vitamins of milk from a mother.

I give the wax-paper bag with the certificate. Many times now, I will pat my pocket before I remember that it is not lost but returned. If she asks me, I will say Mai-ling went back to Ilocos Norte. A bakery. I will answer all that is true for Lettie Elizande. But Sue does not ask. Tears run on her face, falling on the soul of China, wetting so it will begin to dissolve.

"I know. I am a mother too," I say.

She lurches into a hug, and I feel her breasts behind the silk.

"I am asking milk. For this one."

She gets a bag from a dress shop with twine handles and fills it with bottles. "China hardly nurses anymore."

"So China?"

"China! C'mere!"

China and the brother stampede downstairs. "She's watching *Madeleine,* but it's time for the *Simpsons* and she won't let me!"

Sue fixes them each with a different TV, and then I hear. China was in the hospital three days. She would open her eyes but close them again. They checked her reflexes to determine if she could feel hot and cold. They were not sure she would survive, and the doctors said she could have brain damage if she did. Then, after nine hours, she woke up, looked at her parents, and said, *Cake.* And after that, she talked.

Cake. The birthday cake for Mai-ling! She wanted another piece. I will call everyone tonight. The story will go from babysitter to babysitter until the word shines.

"She already started First Pres."

One year behind Williamo. "How is Williamo?"

Sue shrugs. "I heard something about him and another boy sticking their heads in the toilet."

I walk home fast to get the bottles in the ref. Two men stand at our curb, waiting to deliver a large crib, compliments the doctor, they say. Lita told me Alice was glad I took the job. She told Lita, *That baby needs something.* The crib was for her own baby who died. They had a whole room. Very expensive, Lita said. All match. She gave away everything. I set the milk in the freezer—wealth. I heat one bottle, mix with formula, introduce a tiny bit at a time, only one drop. I remember Williamo. But this one she accepts the better milk. She is like me, in with the many who need. I think about the soul of this one. I do not even know the religion of Judith. When she comes home, I ask. "Will your daughter be baptized?"

"I don't really go to church, but I suppose it couldn't hurt. What do you think, Lola?"

"Join the club," I say.

She sits in the dark again, frowning. She narrows down to the top three.

Ida Louise
Natasha Sophia
Laura Anne

"Which do you like, Lola?"
I pick Laura.

Laurita and I go to see off Ruth and Danny when they drive Mai-ling to New York. Mai-ling asks me if I gave the certificate.

"China is fine," I tell her. "At First Pres."

Lucy flutters around the car, because her father will ride in back. To an American, he and Mai-ling can look married, even though they speak no common language. They will ride through cornfields under lifting arrows of birds. But if I knew Lucy would be here, I would have stayed home.

There is Cora and Benny, Lucy remembers. But she cannot find telephone numbers. "I only see them in the park! The Hippo Park!" So in all of New York City, Ruth will have to try to find three Filipinas in a park.

I have five children my own and Williamo to age four, but I never had a baby like this one. She cries so I see lines on the walls, air comes to a crack in my head where air should not be. She arches her back and screams, to ask God for what she does not have. And God does not answer this girl. I wait with her, through the night. I need this job. I really cannot quit. The door of the mother stays shut, on the other side the kitchen. It might as well be the other side the world. But Judith has to get up early for her work.

At first, when Laura woke in the night, my new employer shuffled in, but the shrieking became more.

I said, "I will be the one." And the baby sucked my third finger. Her weight dropped in my lap.

So now it is Lola she wants. My employer, she sleeps, but Lola cannot rest anymore. I count money in a circle. This time I will try to get ahead.

With my kids, I had my husband and our neighborhood association. The job of even a baby, it is really too big for one person only.

I pull the legs every day so they will grow straight. I did not do for my kids. I come from an educated family that does not believe those old things. But my pupil pulled the legs of Bing, and now, they are growing good. My boss, she goes before nine in the morning and comes back at seven. At first I scheduled the bath when she got home. But she felt frightened holding the baby; she thought Laura would slip out of her hands.

"Your mama thinks you are a piece of soap," I tell her.

Now, when my employer walks in the door I have Laurita in foot pajamas, a tiny duck on the collar. I used to keep the evening bottle in warm water for the mother to give. But now I start the *dede* and Judith will finish. Judith when she gets home wants to look at her mail, eat some dinner.

Laura is dark—dark skin, dark hair. She could be Asian. She looks up at me, eyes to eyes. "When I first got the job, your mother said, *We won the lottery*. Because-ah the moment I held you, you smiled. I said, *Och, look, there is chemistry*."

Finally, for me, Laurita sleeps. I tell her, *Otherwise, Lola will be too tired to take care you. Help me.* I said that also to my own babies. *Help.*

I clear the kitchen table, make a coffee, take out my notebook, and mark how many weeks are left of the year. Since I have been in America, I have sent home more than $180,000. That is ₱4,495,485. In pesos, we are millionaires.

From six years working here, I have paid more than half the medical training for Issa. That money, it is my shipyard pile. As a married woman, I worked, too, but Bong Bong was the breadwinner. Since I came here, they are dependent on me.

I do not feel married anymore, even though I talk to Bong Bong every other Sunday and still receive a card once a week. In our house, we have drawers of cards. *Christmas in the Philippines, Buko Pie for Assumption.* I remember when greeting cards came to the Philippines.

Bong Bong was working his first job, in the National Book Store, for Mrs. Socorro Ramos. People from Kansas came on Good Friday. That first year, Bong Bong drew on the kitchen table in the house of Mrs. Ramos. A year later, they had a warehouse with desks, at each one an illustrator. First you could only buy cards in Metro Manila. Now they employ four hundred people. We had times of softness too. But Lola did not get her grand passion. Alone here, at the kitchen table, I open my letter from home.

My daughters sent me a clipping from the *Manila Standard*, with a note. *Is this the lady you paid to send home?*

Oton, Iloilo—Faced with the challenge of raising four children, Lettie "Nang Palang" Elizande decided to bake and sell pies to augment the earnings of her husband Eduardo, then a public jeepney driver. In 1991 she went to America to work as a nanny. Two years later she returned home to Iloilo. "There I was having a nervous breakdown. My friends took up a collection to send me home." Once back, she started baking. She formulated her own recipes based on books that she read. She baked cassava puddings, banana cakes and buko pies using a gas oven that could only cook three plates at a time. After baking from her home in Barangay Trapiche, Oton town, she would sell the pies in offices and schools in Iloilo City, about eight kilometers away. On a good day, she sold ten plates at fourteen pesos each. She also received orders for weddings as well as baptismal parties. After just three years, Nang Palang's name has become synonymous with the tasty buko pie in the Oton town. Her earnings from the business were small but these helped send her children to school. In 1994, Nang Palang's husband quit driving public jeepneys and has since been helping in the business. The store now sells an average of three hundred plates daily aside from orders for special occasions. To cope with the rising demand, Lettie acquired two ovens that could bake seventy-six plates at a time.

Lettie! Good for her.

Maybe you are next, Bong Bong wrote in pencil at the bottom, from the other side the world. But I do not want to go back and bake pie.

Claire

THE WORST SUMMER OF THE MARRIAGE

Paul had grown up inside a family. He knew how to do this, even if he never came home. He didn't think it was so hard. I let Paul decide. I had no confidence for life. But as soon as we fired Lola, I knew it was wrong.

She deflated. Did a small bump stick out in her back? I realized she was a few inches shorter than me. I'd always thought we were the same height.

I knocked over a coffee the morning of the first day. She started wiping it.

"No, I'll do it," I said.

A light left her face I didn't see again, the rest of the time she lived in back of us.

Lola still lived in our garage and for first time in four years, she was there more than in the house. She took Will by the hand, pulled, and said, "We are going now." He looked back at me, a wish on his face. I didn't know what to do. She couldn't stand to be near me. She stayed ten more days and each one felt like an emergency.

Will gazed up at me when we told him. I said it would be all right. That was the worst thing. He trusted me and I lied.

That first week felt like a divorce, glittering with event. We'd fired Lola, but then we took her out to dinner, as the school director told us to. We had gifts to give. A card with money and a locket. But I didn't feel alive in my life.

We didn't know when she was leaving, so we couldn't interview other people. We'd told her we couldn't afford her.

Paul sighed. "We may have to say she has to move."

But I'd grown up with a terror of landlords. I couldn't kick her out.

His phone beeped. "I've got to get that," he said.

Then, the first Sunday in August, Ruth and her slight husband appeared. Ruth had gained weight. They carried boxes from Lola's room to the ancient green Mercedes, and they wouldn't let me help. Paul stayed in bed, watching television. He thought he was coming down with something. In a little more than an hour, they drove away, and Lola was gone, the door left hanging open.

An empty room and a globe.

Monday morning Paul came to the kitchen, carrying his briefcase as usual, showered, dressed, baseball cap on backward, ready to go.

I'd have William all day. How had we decided this?

I'd looked at my score before anyone else woke up, then I kept it on the table while I made breakfast. A teasing scale passage. I had ideas! But when would I work?

Paul had made the decision to fire her, but he still went to the Lot.

All of a sudden I understood with an awful clarity. He made more money than I did now, and for him that explained everything. Still, his show was in production. Right now, there really wasn't anything he could do.

He must have seen my face, because he scrawled out a number. "Here, call the agency and get somebody temporary. Just for a few hours. Go to work."

"You think he's going to *accept* somebody the agency sends!"

"He'll be fine," Paul said, and then the door slammed.

With school out, Will had nothing to do. I called each of the moms from the playgroup and left messages. No one called back. When the replies straggled in over the week, the moms apologized, with what seemed like excuses. Sorry they couldn't do Monday, they said, but didn't suggest other days. When I mentioned tomorrow, they said the next few days were crazy. In a week, it was evident; nannies had been calling for playdates with Lola, not Will.

And it became apparent how much Lola did. By Wednesday, the hampers in both bedrooms overflowed. By Friday, laundry spilled onto the floor. Then Ofelia called in sick.

"So we'll sign him up for another camp session." Paul looked over at the mound in the corner. "We still have towels?"

"Don't ask me."

But we did, thanks to his mother, the outlet shopper. Her boxes waited unopened by the door. I slit one, and bingo. Dark purple towels.

I did what Paul said. I signed Will up for another session of camp, but when I drove him into the state park, he didn't want to get out of the car. One of the teenage counselors helped with the extraction. Will looked at me through the window.

"All right, so he looked at you. It isn't the biggest deal in the world," Paul said. "Did I always want to go, when I could have stayed home with my mommy? Just say goodbye and leave."

I did. But camp only went until two.

During those hours, I called Lil to ask for advice.

Drop the ball, she said. See what happens.

That night we had takeout for dinner.

The ball dropped.

And dropped.

Paul won. I couldn't live like this. The next Tuesday morning while Will was at camp, I did four loads of laundry and went to the store to buy food. I did everything and felt exhausted by the time I put Will down. Everything but work.

I didn't see Paul at all that day. Or the next. I was asleep before he came home. Saturday morning, I said I wanted to talk.

"Can it wait until breakfast?"

In the kitchen, I told him I wanted a separation.

"Can we talk about this in three months?"

"I'm not joking."

He shook his head, clearing his plate over the garbage and leaving the unwashed dish in the sink. (For whom? He had odd cutoffs for decency.) "I can't even think about this until we finish these thirteen episodes."

"When will that be?"

"January."

January. I took that and held it like a promise. In the meantime, we'd go about our business. I'd try to figure out each day. Will's friendships. His meals and bath. The house. Huge boulders. Responsibility. Food. Shopping. Where was the music in this?

How had Lola done it? I tried to remember. For at least two hours, midday, she watched a soap opera in her room. She also took a walk every evening. But in the evening she'd had me.

The third Saturday, the parade began again. Molly had set up interviews through an agency. Paul had less time than he did the first round but more confidence. None of these women seemed possible to me. How could I live with another person? Paul favored a woman named Elizabeth who spoke accented English and drove her own car.

"But I thought their point was it should be an American."

"How long have you lived in the States, Elizabeth?"

"Twenty-two years," she said, her chin lifted. "I am American citizen."

Her first day at our house, she roasted a chicken with fresh garlic, olives, and lemongrass. "The people I work before, they *love* this."

But I'd promised Will fish tacos, so I left it for Paul.

I found him in the kitchen at midnight, chewing a bone. "There," he said. "You still want a separation?" He looked up from under his thick eyebrows. In profile, Paul was so handsome—wealth in a foreign currency. "A divorce?" he said, confidence building the joke. "Didn't you want to di*vorce* me?"

I liked this new form of play. The stakes were interesting, at last.

"I think so. Why?"

"Because we're invited out to dinner Friday night with the Grants. I thought it might be fun to try a new restaurant."

He'd come home once in August with flowers at eight o'clock, twirling on the porch, ending on one knee. Another night, he brought a wrapped box: earrings.

Why didn't I show up at the Lot and scream? Or take Willie on a plane?

I didn't want to blow Paul's chance. His show was a treasure. I couldn't live with the guilt of harming what he loved.

But I could live with my anger. I'd been living with that so long already.

Elizabeth picked up Will from camp, and all afternoon I heard her plead. When I came downstairs, they were locked in a fight, arms braced.

"He bite me," she said, looking up as if I were a monster.

He was a small child. A boy. Didn't they do that? Puppies did. "William," I said, "you can't bite. I'm going to take away a privilege. No cartoons tomorrow."

"I don't care."

"See," Elizabeth said.

I stayed up late to tell Paul.

"In a few weeks, school starts. Why don't we wait and watch how she does then."

That weekend, Paul felt sick and stayed in bed. Monday morning he roused himself, and Elizabeth arrived with a project.

"Pot holders," she announced, with satisfaction. The kids she'd taken care of before, she said, loved making pot holders.

"He's a pretty active boy," I said. "You might do better in the park, with a ball or some chase game."

"You will see." She issued a knowing smile.

She had a sour expression that night, but Tuesday brought another attempt: lanyards. A week later, when I told her it wasn't working out, she looked relieved.

I asked Paul once.

I asked him twice.

I asked him three times to leave.

This made the bookend to our courtship, when he'd pursued me until I said, *Well, maybe. Let's get married.*

Paul hired another woman. "Send her to the playclub. He can see his old pals."

I sent Vanji with Will and a tray of homemade oatmeal cookies. When they returned, I asked how it went. Vanji scrunched her nose. "They don' talk to us."

"Next time don't ask," Paul said.

When the big envelope from the school came, I studied the list. We invited the boys from Will's new class for a party. I wanted a good start for his year. The night before, I stayed up late making cupcakes. I was frosting them when Paul came home.

"When do they get here tomorrow?"

"Eleven to three."

"That's a long time. Well, she'll be here, too, won't she?"

"Who, Vanji? I didn't ask her. I don't think she'd be much help."

"Well, I'll try to get over at lunch."

Paul arrived like a movie star, late and dressed like the kids, in sneakers, jeans, and a T-shirt. Boys crowded around him. The way he wriggled his back when Will tagged him and then spurted forward, you could tell he really didn't want to get caught. Paul had a talent for fun. Forty minutes running with boys chasing him, and he was calling out to each one by name, smoothing over Will's bossiness, making it invisible. Then, out of breath, he leaned against the kitchen counter and ate a cupcake. He looked around the room in a way I knew meant he was about to go.

"You're good at this. I'm not. Can't you stay?"

But he had to leave.

I tried to take his place, carrying out the tray of cupcakes. I bit into one. Soft, with tangy frosting. I ate the purple pansy. It tasted like lettuce.

But by one-thirty, Will sat in his room, knees up, arms crossed over. "You can play with them. I don't want to."

I sat on the bed and stroked his damp hair, boys' voices coming through the gauzy screen. Did I have to make him go back out? What would the mothers say? But I let him look at his train book and quietly closed his door when I went to offer the guests sandwiches. I didn't want them here now either.

Was he like this because other mothers stayed through more? Crumbs on the counter, gibberish. Will and I had bright flashes of glory, but too many times I'd left him reaching for me, from a babysitter's arms. Am I still a mother if? I asked myself. If I went to the camp orientation, but had Vanji take my place at the picnic? What parts of the day could I cut out and still give him enough?

Paul never asked himself that. He thought he was a great dad. He did twice as much as his own father had. And he still got the day, whole as an uncut sail.

At the dinnertime call, I told Paul what happened. I could hear the alarm in his voice. "Who picked them up?" he asked. "Moms or babysitters?"

"Moms."

"Well, next time, make it shorter."

I sighed. "You're better at this, but you're hardly ever here."

"Like a drop of rare perfume." There was a pause. "Claire, it was *a joke.*"

I knew. Everything was a joke.

In September, two days after school started, I got a midnight call from the police, telling me they had my mother at St. John's. They'd found her outside and she didn't know where she was. "Is she normally okay?" the man asked.

"More or less," I said. "Why? What was she doing?"

"Well, you'll see."

I ran outside to Lola's room and banged on the door before I remembered. Her room had been empty forty days. Only the bare cot and a globe. I stood a moment and spun the orb. When we'd been planning our wedding, in that hopeful swath of time, I'd said I wanted to live in Europe for a year when we were raising our children. He'd agreed, though reluctantly, even then. Who was that young woman? Even my dream seemed average to me now. Probably most of the mothers here had told their young husbands-to-be similar wishes. They'd probably known long before I did that few of those acquiescences counted. They understood—a great open secret—the bargain: together they would make a family. The women would raise children; the men would go out into the world and provide money. Why did that contract do so little for me?

I called Paul, left a message, and then had to wait. What was I supposed to do? I had no way to reach him. I called Tom and the phone rang and rang. Tom still had no machine.

I found a bar of dark chocolate in the refrigerator and tore off the layers of paper and foil. She'd had two breakdowns, but she'd always gotten better. I tiptoed in to peek at Will, fast asleep, one arm flung over his head. I bent down to hear his breathing.

I was really absolutely stuck here until Paul called.

Had he ever, in the years since Will was born, been marooned? I thought of lifting Will into his car seat. Maybe if I was steady enough, he'd stay asleep. But they'd never let me bring him into the hospital. And I didn't want him there, in the psych ward. I stood, gnawing chocolate—when Paul called.

"I have to go! She doesn't have anybody else." This is the wild of life, I thought, walking with the phone, to my jacket on a peg by the door.

"Who can we call?"

"What do you mean? Paul, you have to come home. I have to go!"

"Claire, ten people are sitting here waiting for me. No thank you," he said to someone else. "What about that older lady next door?"

"It's after midnight!"

"Still, it's an emergency. I'd do it, for a neighbor. What about Tom?"

"No one answers. The guy still doesn't have a machine."

"Well, calm down. She's in a hospital. Nothing's going to happen. Hold on a minute." He punched the phone off before I could say anything. "Okay, I'm sending Molly over. She's on her way." He exhaled.

I waited on the stoop, the door open. When Molly pulled her car in, I had my keys out and ran down. I glided through stop signs, over dips and bumps. Then, when I stepped out of the elevator to the third floor, time slowed.

She sat in a gown, shaking her head. Her hair was flat and down, a way I'd never seen it. Tom stood, a hand on her shoulder, urging her to drink from a straw. Everything about the scene seemed normal.

"What happened?"

"My heart was racing."

"She just got a little overexcited, that was all," Tom said. "I wonder if something we had at Twin Dragons didn't set her off."

"The beans weren't the same," she said with bitter fury. "I told you so."

"They asked us never to come back," Tom mumbled.

I went out to find a doctor. Tom looked husbandly, fussing with the pillows, the planes of her face hard.

"She was hitting him," the doctor said. "She didn't recognize her friend. We had to restrain her."

Once, I'd seen a nurse's arms make a cage around her.

"Is she taking medication?"

"Just vitamins."

"She needs it. I've prescribed two milligrams of Haldol."

"What does that do?"

"It should calm her down. Does she see a psychiatrist?"

"She won't."

"She should."

I wandered through the halls past the maternity ward and thought of the night Will was born. A great night in my life. He lay on my chest, on a gurney, then, at last, on a bed inside a citadel of pillows. We'd lucked out; a slow week, they gave us a single room for no extra.

At the beginning, I still believed in our luck. I thought my wishes would come true, some of them.

I just have to go home, Paul said then.

He left and Will and I began. So many times Will cried that night, little fists shaking, and I didn't know why. I stumbled in my paper gown to the bright nurses' cube.

I called Paul in the middle of that long curved night. *Sorry for waking you.* The rind of hardness that grew later was for that *I'm sorry* that I said. But by then, I'd begun to collect stones.

I returned to my mother's room and sat, siding with Tom in a long repetitive argument about whether she had to eat.

"Last week I brought her half a turkey breast," Tom said, "and every day I'd check her refrigerator. She hadn't touched it! I had to throw it out. I think she lives on bananas.

"Why don't you try," he said, handing me the spoon.

I took a little of the pudding in the small plastic dish.

"You like sweets," I said.

She bit down. I had to tug the spoon out. Then the pudding came out, too, down her chin.

"That's what she does. She spits it out," he said.

In another hour, I walked to the glass wall where the field of babies slept. A young doctor came in and knelt before a clear plastic basinet. He took his mask down, lifted a baby's hand to his lips. I formed crushes everywhere now. But when he stood and pushed his glasses up, I saw that he was younger, probably a decade or more.

Back in the room, Tom was on his knees, trying to work my mother's left sock back on.

"She wants to take off her socks and shoes," he said. "It's the medicine they gave her. It's making her crazy."

Her feet had dark veins, the toenails yellow. Dark patches were visible under her eyes, her hair too long this way and lank, and I gleaned for the first time how much work it must have taken her to be beautiful still.

I ran to the bathroom for water and gagged.

When I came back, they were looking into each other's faces. While he stared at her, she made a new smile, then another. Now, here, finally. So, he had been right after all. They had something.

At last my mother fell asleep and Tom sat solidly in the chair, arms crossed, eyes closed. I rushed outside before anyone woke. A slap of wind hit my face. It felt like cheating. She was my responsibility, and there was no good end. I ran fast to my car in the gelling light. On our small main street, people in sweats and slippers followed the taut leads of dogs.

I remembered the room of babies, the doctor kneeling. I want another child, I thought. We had no marriage. But that morning, I didn't see what the two things had to do with each other.

Paul and I drove up to the house at the same time. Almost four. He would have lived like this. We could both make a snack, softly complain about our jobs. Peek in at our sleeping boy, wonder together about his day. Share a word the nanny had told one of us.

We had to shake Molly to wake her up.

When we were alone, I said, "I feel bad Will doesn't have a sibling."

"He's a pretty confirmed only child. Remember what he dictated on the card to Simon when his sister was born?"

Happy Survival.

"Well, when would you have this second child?" Lil asked in a tone not entirely kind. She had her three.

"Pretty soon, I guess I'd have to."

She didn't say anything. She must have thought we couldn't manage as it was.

The Emmys fell on the second week of September, and Paul had arranged for Ofelia to come over. Will hated her. He'd liked her fine before, but since Lola left he hated everyone but me.

For wives, the Emmys meant a chance to don a ball gown, though this ball was in Pasadena, in the afternoon. But I felt foolish in my long dress, giving last-minute instructions to Ofelia at the kitchen table. "He can watch *The Wrong Trousers*. Twice."

"Thrice," he said.

Paul stepped out in his new tuxedo, his handsomeness a form of rebuke. I could hear Will crying even after the driver shut the heavy door. Fog blew past. I wanted to run back and get a sweater, but it wasn't worth another goodbye. Paul got a call from the executive producer, who wasn't coming. "He figures we never win." But on the off chance they did, Paul had to write a speech, so he hunched over, scribbling.

I rubbed my bare arms. "Can we stop for coffee?" I had staff paper in my purse, but I couldn't think. I should have brought along a book.

He looked at his watch. "We better not."

Pasadena looked bronzed, from sun on the old concrete steps of the auditorium, glittering. When we stepped out, it was stingingly hot, even now, at four-thirty—and only forty miles away from Santa Monica, where I'd been holding my elbows. I saw the Indian woman who'd once told me never to leave without saying goodbye, her long hair pinned, her sari fluttering in a breeze I didn't feel. I imagined her daughters at home, playing fairly. Two by two, we filed in. This was the lesser ceremony, where they also gave out awards for lighting and makeup and that wasn't televised. Last year, Helen had gone to the Oscars. Her dress, her hair, the jewelry, had made a drama among her chorus, as importantly thrilling as her husband's nomination for best short. I had on a new dress tonight, the one we'd bought just after New York, but it didn't make my torso shiver the way I imagined a new dress could. We sat next to one of the nerdier guys Paul worked with, who had a beautiful date—a Chinese woman with slim calves. Paul told me they said in the Room that an Asian girlfriend was the last stop on the train before coming out. One step away from gay.

After an hour, I whispered in Paul's ear. "Can I go get a coffee?"

"Sure, take the car. Here's the driver's number." He extracted a card from his pocket. "Be back by eight-thirty, so if we win, you can see me." He sighed. "I could use a coffee too."

"Want a to-go?"

"No. Wish I could." This was Paul; he understood I'd be happier elsewhere, and he let me go.

I found our car at the curb and asked the driver to take me to a restaurant in old Pasadena that Helen and Jeff had mentioned once. My heel caught between cobblestones; I had to bend over to yank it free. In the restaurant, people looked at me, alone in my formal. But I spread out staff paper on a table. The ambient music—the Gypsy Kings—made me crazy. Okay. May as well look crazy. I got out my noise-canceling headphones. The waiter brought a cup of harsh espresso. The bitter sips felt bracing; what I needed. I worked and ordered another. And a water. I cherished this recovered time, looking out the window at the still street. A mother hurried along a young girl, in the late afternoon light.

"Can I get you anything else?" the waiter asked.

"One more," I said, scanning the square room. At the bar in back, I saw Jeff and Alice, the doctor I'd met once at a party, his long pale arm on top of hers. Their heads were close, the way they'd been at that party, in intent conversation. I sat watching, ghoulishly fascinated. He took a piece of her hair from in front of her face and slowly hooked it behind her ear. Then he covered her face with his. I left a twenty on the table and stepped outside, into the wavery heat. I had an answer now to my long yearning—the wrong one. He'd picked her. Not me. I had what I'd always had for consolation. I knocked on the pages in my bag. Beethoven was five foot four and had short thick fingers. He enlisted friends to help him look for a wife. But despite his dancing lessons and horseback riding and self-education, he never found luck in love. He kept getting deafer and he kept writing. When he was composing, his affliction hampered him least.

When I arrived back at the auditorium, the sun spread on the rim of the mountains, and guys with headphones unfurled a red carpet over the ramp where people would walk from the theater to the dining room. I slipped back in.

"Did I miss much?"

"Not a thing."

Forty-five minutes later, they announced half-hour comedy, and the show Paul had worked for won. Paul jumped up, bounding down the aisle. He looked small in his tuxedo holding the trophy. "I'd thank my parents but"—he paused and the audience rustled with tame, happy-hour laughter—"they also made me short."

When he returned, I tugged his sleeve.

"It can't hurt with the show airing next month." He gave me his program and notes. "We have to go in back for photographs. You go and find our table, 'kay?"

I wished, all of a sudden, I'd brought the camera. I should have taken pictures. *Paul with his Emmy.* I felt glad for him, from far away.

When we returned home, Will bolted up from the couch, where he'd been watching television.

"He no go to bed," said Ofelia.

He whispered up into my ear, "I waited for you."

"You be needing me *más?*"

"That's all for tonight," Paul said. "Thank you, Ofelia."

I wanted to tell Paul what I'd seen in the restaurant, but he'd quiz me: Could they have been talking about something else? Maybe Helen lost another baby? I'd have to describe the way they touched. And I couldn't. Not to Paul. I'd told him I wanted to separate. But I still couldn't talk about *this.* Sometimes, we sat together, sad and embarrassed, and watched people on a screen fall onto each other with hunger.

Jeff and the doctor had looked pensive. Old lovers.

So he did pick someone else.

After that night, I couldn't sleep and I had a hard time concentrating. I found a psychologist named Dr. Lark. She looked the way I'd always wanted to—skinny with dark curls—the age of my mother.

"It sounds like you'd like to hire Lola back," she said, near the end of the hour.

"I didn't want to fire her. But Paul did."

"I'd put my bets on you," she said.

Relief tumbled over me. When I unlocked the door, I asked to talk to Vanji in the kitchen. I paid her three weeks' salary and told her now that Will was in school, we wouldn't need her regular hours. I gave her the rest of the day off.

Will started telling me an interminable story about a flag. The phone rang; I picked up the receiver; it was a single mom named Judith who'd just hired Lola and wanted a reference.

"I'm jealous," I told her, and I was. All the while she spoke, I wondered if I could still talk Lola into coming back. But the woman said her baby had problems. There'd been too little oxygen at the birth.

I took Will to the next playclub myself. Helen still reigned, legs crossed on Beth Martin's butterfly chair, no sign of being wronged. Kids played outside with nannies, skidding in to grab chips. "That's enough, Bing!" Helen barked, her voice bottomed with satisfied authority. Her smugness had shifted: from having the marriage to envy to being the expert mother.

"*Sib*ling rivalry," the Indian woman said. "In India, we don't have *sib*ling rivalry. When Kasha is mean to her sister, I punish her for not being nice, not for *sib*ling *ri*valry."

Siblings. Soon, Will would be the only only child. Three seemed to be the common number here.

Helen was having an avid conversation with a young mom I didn't know, who held a typical fat, charmless baby.

I wasn't really listening but I picked out the words "still Lola on weekends." A string inside me yanked. They still had Lola on week-ends! But they hadn't wanted her! I almost cried. Nothing was fair. So Lola still went there Saturday and Sunday.

"How is Lola?" I asked Helen.

I'd called Lola twice but she hadn't called me back. Now I'd have to get my news from Helen. I felt an urge to tell Helen I'd seen her husband kiss the doctor whose Chinese adopted children were here, too, with their nanny.

Helen shook her head. "I think there's something wrong with that baby she's taking care of. She doesn't lift her head yet." Helen raised her eyebrows. "Single mom. No dad. Lola said nobody comes around."

"I think it's somebody really high up and married," Beth Martin said. Then she turned to me. "How's the show coming?"

Show? For a moment, that stumped me. They were all looking. "Oh, good, I think." I hadn't been to the set since the pilot shoot. Paul didn't seem to mind. Beth had once introduced me, *Claire's a baker.*

"He got an Emmy for his old show," Helen said.

Just then a nanny from outside came and whispered something to Sue. "Claire, Will's having a problem," Sue said in front of everyone.

Here it came. Out on the concrete, Willie sat cross-legged, frown-ing down with a particular expression I knew, shaking his head. "I don't want to be his friend."

Simon stood there, fists balled.

"Melissa?" Sue called back into the room.

I knelt facing Willie, but I couldn't get him to look at me. "Willie, you don't want to hurt Simon's feelings."

"I don't care," he mumbled. "I don't like him."

Please don't say that. Simon ran up against his mom's calves. "He said he didn't like me!" Melissa picked him up. Her hair, which had once fallen out, was a beautiful dark brown.

Sue looked at me as if Will were a criminal. "You want to just try another day?"

I said hurried goodbyes. "Don't worry," Melissa said, a hand on my arm, her eyelids half closing.

Helen sat, stilly regal. "Call you later. I have to talk to you about Lucy's wedding. I told her I'd do the cake and I need help. We can all go together. Lola'll be there too."

"Well, I hope you're happy," I said, in the car. But back in our yard, I felt glad to be home too. "We can still have a good day," I said as he sluffed in. "But, Will, you have to get along with the other boys. You're going to want friends."

"He's mean, though. He just doesn't do it when you're there."

I sat on our little stoop, arms around my knees. "That happens. That happens even with grown-ups. But sometimes when people are mean, it's good to just ignore them and play with the other people. That's what I do."

"Why can he be mean and I can't?"

A profound question. "Well. It's just a way I manage."

"It's all right, Mom. Let's not talk about this anymore."

He knelt on the floor, running a truck over my knee. I sat with a book. We were finding things to do together for longer.

"Do you like the playclub?" I asked after a while.

"Not really."

"Did you before, with Lola?"

"Not that much. I just liked being here with her."

"Well, we don't have to go again."

We stayed there for another hour. Maybe we could live without Lola.

The Saturday before the pilot aired, Paul took Will to buy a new TV. Molly drove over that night to set it up. On the day, I made a fish stew, rouille, and molten chocolate cakes for twenty, which I planned to serve with a sprinkle of powdered sugar through a sieve. Without Lola, this took me all day. I felt happy, though, handing out plates to the writers and their wives. They laughed through the show, hooting and footstamping at the actress's jokes, so I suppose I was wrong about her. They left right after. A school night. Paul kept answering the phone. I had a sense of accomplishment, washing dishes. Everything had turned out.

But I heard Paul in the night, as if the dark had metal parts. He woke me, banging into the dresser, and seemed annoyed.

"I don't know what we're gonna do." He sat in a chair, in his boxers, letting me stare at him. "The ratings are awful." He shook his head.

I needed to adjust. I should've taken this in hours ago. Mechanically, I remembered handing two guys second helpings of the warm cakes. They'd been laughing. "I can't believe it."

He'd written numbers on an envelope, what he'd prepared for all these years.

"Doesn't it take a while for a new show to catch?"

"Usually the first week's higher and then it falls. If they'd advertise or something. But with ratings like this they won't. All that work." He let the envelope drop. "They're probably not going to renew my contract. I thought it was funny."

"It *is* funny."

"I guess people just didn't think so." He sighed, flopping on the bed.

What he'd said about his contract terrified me. What could I do? The Da Capo had commissioned Annabel Grass. I didn't earn enough from Colburn for us to live on. But I heard William waking. I'd have to make breakfast. Still, it didn't feel right to leave Paul. "What can I do?" Noises lifted outside.

Just then Willie appeared, a truck dangling from his hand. I got him washed, dressed, breakfasted, and then stopped in the doorway. "I'll take him and be right back."

It was a glorious day, clear, the ocean dark blue and choppy. But we'd be broke. I didn't know if I could recover as a breadwinner. I gave Will a quick kiss and signed him up for Funcare. Then I ran home, fixed eggs and toast, and carried in a tray. "Why don't we stay in today? I'll go to Vidiots. We'll get your favorite comedies and watch."

He frowned. "That won't help."

"Well, I mean, when I have a defeat I guess I end up going back to what I love." I thought of deep chords pounding. A kind of warning. A kind of command.

"I don't work that way. I get things from magazines, or just from life."

"Well, you tell me, then. What would help?"

The phone rang. He lurched. "Not going to be anything good." He walked around, buttoning his shirt, talking. "You think there's a chance they'll advertise?"

I sat on the bed, pulling up a corner of the comforter.

"Okeydoke. Thanks, Rich." The other line was ringing. "Let me get that."

"Should I turn it off?" Jeff had once ripped a phone plug out of the wall.

"No," he said, slapping a magazine in his palm. "I better get going." He sighed. "We've still got a table read Friday."

I felt his disappointment more sharply than my own. He'd tried so hard! This wasn't fair. But Paul seemed to want to go it alone, so I tried to stay out of his way.

The second week's ratings fell, as he'd predicted. Five shows aired in all, and the network pulled it, as by then we knew they would.

A familiar stone tied us down. I couldn't leave him now.

Lola

A PAY CHAPEL

Too many mothers of the bride.

The first time I see Claire again, she looks up, nervous of me. Both my Santa Monica employers bend into the Jeep trunk. They have a Mixmaster there in a box.

"We didn't make the buttercream yet, Lole," Claire says. "We'll frost on site."

"But-ah, the dairy will go bad." It is hot, dull, typical Los Angeles weather. A sapling grows beside each parking meter. On Wilshire Boulevard long ago, large elms gave shade, Lita told me. In Los Angeles, you hear many rumors about trees. "Where are the naughty boys?"

Helen points. They snore, asleep, seatbelted. They are big now, long.

My date wears her gray-blue party dress with the matching ruffled bonnet. Her arms wave out in front, like feelers. But the place of the wedding is a pay chapel. Why do they not marry in a church? "When you get married," I whisper down to the Snugli, "we will have a high mass. Organ music." I remember then, this one she is not yet baptized.

The groom stands filling out forms for a lady behind an iron cage. My pupil, she has been dieting to fit her dress. *Tony said, You just spend for that*, she told me. She shows the bouquet: waxy orange blossoms with dark leaves, the wood stems wrapped in white ribbon. "I made myself." She must have polished; orange leaves fur with dust.

"Well, that's good," Tony says, not looking at her flowers.

Maybe it is already broken.

Compared the wedding of Ruth, this one, it feels small. On foldout chairs, Natalie sits with her Korean. Her mother not here to see, she is the way Ruth would want her, the hair clean, wearing a dress. I know from Ruth that this Korean, he wants to be writer.

"Maybe some-a-day you will write the story of Lola," I say.

He manages the tree nursery of his parents in Bonsall. One night a week, he drives to Orange County for a novel class he has to pay to attend. But I can see that Natalie loves this Korean. She sits knees together. Feet straight. She unfolds from her purse a clipping from the *Los Angeles Times* about another escaped slave. *The California Court ordered the former employer to pay 1.5 million dollars damages.* But most of the people Ruth helps, they are illegals. She feels afraid of lawyers. "We will save this," I say. "For the book." In the place of Ruth, there will always be a next person. "Where is Aileen?"

"Playdate." Natalie, her mouth loves the word.

The bride and the groom stand facing each other, her breast lifted, his hands behind his back. Cheska tears open a box of Minute Rice. I want a handful for Laurita. "Here is your throwing rice," I say, but she pushes her head into me.

Filipino weddings, you pin money to the bride and groom. I have a one-hundred bill, but I do not want to tear her dress with the tail. That one-hundred bill makes me think all the money my pupil the bride stole from me. But I only say, "Can I borrow from you your husband?" I pin the cash to his sleeve.

Lita stands, clapping along.

"Congratulations," I say. "Filipino grandchildren. Guaranteed. You will be the only Lola."

Lita stays close to us. She has elected me for the wedding. I do not want to be near Lucy. I do not want to be next Claire. I am the ball on a pool table avoiding too many holes. Then I see Williamo wake up. Williamo! I open my arms.

But he does not come to me. He stays with the mother.

We drive to Barrio Fiesta, the Chasens of Filipino food, located here in a mall. The bakers of the cake ask at every small store if they can use electricity to fluff their butter, and a beauty salon says yes, so I have to kneel on old hair to plug the cord while they unwrap cakes.

I do not like to help, but Helen paid me two hundred forty for this weekend.

"The Cake Bible?" I know all the recipe books of Claire.

"Don't tell anyone, but we ordered these. After that Boston cream disaster, I lost confidence. I can't do it without you, Lole." She has a strange laugh now.

"You bought? Then why did not the bakery frost?" If I pay, I want the expensive bakery roses. For the wedding of Laurita, we will have those.

I should have known they did not bake this cake. To bake, they need me to grease their pans. And Helen gave me an off. Anyway, I want to quit that job. Last week, she told me to fix his study. The Academy movies, I asked, can I get those? I found, stuck in a book on the floor, a note: *You always felt to me, in every way, exactly right.* The problem was the envelope, addressed not for Helen but to Alice, the mother of the Chinese Adopteds. The employer of Lita. So all they are gossiping, it is really true. I did not want to give the envelope to Alice, but I did not want to leave it either. So the cardboard box or the black garbage bag? Where once I carried the soul of China, it now waits in my pocket. Not even licked shut.

This room is arranged the style of a Filipino wedding, the bride and groom at one table facing the rest, so we can watch them eat.

"All that time I was taking care Max, I loved my own kids," Lita says. "I thought God would see and reward them."

"God did see," I say. "He gave you Lucy." But she is not such a gift.

Under tablecloths, boys run together, Filipino and white. A look from the daughter of Lita stops hers. That daughter, she is now RN here. I follow Williamo, everywhere he bounces, like a woman in a room with her husband and her lover. But I wanted you, I cannot explain to him.

"I loved them but I did not know the details," Lita says.

"You were working." Lita missed too much, it is true, but that is over now.

"Hello, Mother, thank you for everything." Lucy kisses the cheek and Lita winces, but this is what she wants!

"Lucy, if you have children," Lita says, "do not do what I did. Fine to nanny now, but when you have your own you quit. And I will help you."

Lucy's head holds still, like a bird. Now Claire and Helen carry in the cake. Before, I was always proud for Claire. Glad to be a part of her achievement. But I heard they have other helpers. Everyone claps the cake. Five layers and little candied violets at the edges. Some take flash pictures. In Tagalog, people say the employer esteems Lucy that she is the one to bake the cake. But Helen, she cannot bake. Who knows what else they lie?

Waiters circulate heads of pigs in pots, partnered with plates of fried skin.

"She'll take her tests for here," Helen says.

But Lucy will not be passing doctor tests. Bride at thirty-four.

"I married him," Lita says. "The day after, he asked what was wrong. I told him, *My kids*. I thought God would stop their favors because their mother was not clean. After that he never bothered me again. We were animals from different parts of the world that only in this modern time would be in the same cage. Still, everything of his, I wash and iron. I missed thousands of days. But if I went back, we would have had to take them out of the school."

Now comes seafood, with bitter melon, very expensive. Who is paying this?

Then like the heel of a footstep, I know: Lita.

"Every month when I sent home my pay, he added. Finally I told him, *I still love my husband in the Philippines.* I called my husband and he said, *You stay with that guy.* I thought it was because I was used. But later on I found out he had another girl."

A man hunches in the front snapping pictures. Lucy calls Lita to be in.

"That's Tony's mother?" Claire moves her chair, to see. She chop me. She hires others. Williamo, he is busy with new things. Baseball, Lita told me. "She's very elegant."

Lita wears a yellow dress, the shoes and purse match. Just then, while the flash sputters, her employer arrives. Alice. I look through the crowd to find Helen. Helen is squatting, wiping the face of Bing. Alice looks away. She does not act guilty. She stands like an Africa queen. I touch the pocket of my backpack, where I keep the letter. She does not know I stole a piece of her life.

I will really quit that job. My weekend.

Why you need me? I said last Sunday, the parents both at home. *I will go.*

"So you think Judith sneaks out to see her lover these weekends?" Helen asked.

"I do not know. You are the one with a husband working Paramount." But my employer, she is lower down. Judith told me she never sees Jeff Grant.

The wives, they are all looking for a romance story. And they have their own—a bad one we do not yet know the ending. I remember the first time Helen, she cried for him. Maybe there is really something to cry for. In our country, a woman with a guy like that, she will take the kids and go back with her parents.

Judith works weekends the reason I do. The majority of mysteries, they are not glamorous. At the bottom of most lives is the need for money. Judith gets a lady from the agency, a new one each week. The one last Sunday, I caught watching TV: loud shouting in Spanish! And this baby, she easily scares. The women sleep in my bed and do not change the sheets. I line up the bottles and write everything down, but they still forget to give the medicine. It is Laura too. She will not eat from anyone but me. When I go back Sunday night, I see her bones. She reaches for me from the sitter. Only when I hold her, the shaking stops. Ah, Laurita.

I take her outside now, to change the diaper. I kneel down; spread the mat on hot pavement. Middle of the day Sunday. The few cars in this mall look old. In the distance, pink and beige apartment buildings crowd under bent palms. The air is still, hazy. Some-a-day I will leave this place. But what will become, then, of Laura? She burrows her head into me. Her right hand, it is a little crumpled. She wants to hold it to her chest.

We give the bride a present from the Philippines, sent by Lettie Elizande. She remembered my pupil chipping in one hundred to her ticket home.

For the wedding of Lucy and Tony—

Buko Pie

SANGKAP

3 cups flour
2½ tbsp. sugar
¾ tsp. salt
¾ cup vegetable shortening
3 egg yolks
½ cup ice water

Filling:
2 cups young coconut, shredded
½ cup young coconut juice
½ cup condensed milk
⅔ cup 1% milk
4 tbsp. sugar
½ tsp. pure vanilla extract
½ cup cornstarch
½ cup cold milk

PAGLUTO

To make the pastry, combine flour, sugar, and salt in a bowl. Cut in shortening with a pastry blender until mixture is crumbly. Combine egg yolks and ice water and blend into flour mixture until it turns into dough. Add a little more water if dough is still crumbly. Refrigerate for 30 minutes. With a rolling pin, roll dough thinly, about ¼ inch thick, on a lightly floured board. Bake the piecrust, set aside, and cool. Combine pie filling ingredients except cornstarch in a deep saucepan. Cook over medium heat, stirring constantly. When boiling gently, add cornstarch, stirring fast, until combined mixture has thickened. Pour mixture evenly into prepared piecrust. Let cool, then refrigerate until firm.

For Lettie, this was the recipe for wealth at home.

Claire and Helen walk over as I give to the bride. Now I am with all I do not want. "I am the one to arrange this marriage." I tell how I said, *Show me a boat.*

"Didn't Tony want to propose?" Claire asks.

"It is fine. The way we do." Lucy puts down her glass, a period.

"I will not anymore come weekends," I say to Helen. "Your Monday-to-Friday, she will need extra money."

I watch Claire: she has to down her mouth from smiling. She wants me out from everywhere. I reach my pack and feel the letter from Jeff. I almost think it is written to me. Williamo comes, out of breath, to stand by his mother. Maybe we were only a boy and a babysitter. But then he falls onto me and for a dark moment, it comes back.

Claire grabs my elbow. "Your new employer called for a reference. So is it a good match?" She has the teeth again, waiting my answer.

"Yes," I say. "There is chemistry."

I am the one to plan the baptism. The priest gave me a form; my employer signed. Then when the day comes, she cannot get an off. Only Laurita and I and some elderly at the back of the church. "There," I say to her after. "We have insurance."

At the park, all over, they are asking, Is that your daughter? Because she is dark.

"No," I say, "I am just babysitter." But a smile opens in my back.

This job it is not only Laura but also the house, the grocery, the dry cleaner, the videos, even the gas-meter reading. I say to Judith what I said to Claire. "Soon this one will be crawling. And if it is a choice between the house or the baby, I will have to chose Laura." Every Westside babysitter I know has said this, to get a once-a-week cleaning woman. But here the trick does not work.

"Well, Lola, there's only two of us. I'm working hard too, and I can't pay you more."

That is plain. She comes home tired, the short skirts and blouses wilted by the end of the day. I wonder if, at one time, flowers arrived here. The mother of Judith lives far away in Minnesota. Judith eats leftovers holding a paper towel under for a plate. Even with the silver VW, more calls come for Lola than the mother.

So tough luck. "Now again, I am scrubbing toilets for your allowance," I tell Issa. Laura cries and I cannot always satisfy her, because I am the one to buy the food and take out the garbage. My new employer, she works a long time every day, so I work long time too.

All through November we receive postcards: a restaurant built in the shape of a hamburger, an enormous turnip. The second day in December, Ruth telephones from the YW in New York. "I will not tell anything. Only that Mai-ling is old, so better just to clean, not for kids."

Just then I realize she is asking me advice! "Yes," is all I think to say.

A week later, Ruth calls again. She found for Mai-ling a job full-time laundress. Five hundred a week.

"They ask I iron the lady shirt. And they like it," Mai-ling says.

She will stay in the apartment of Cora and Benny from the Hippo Park. The landlord pays the heat. Mai-ling will have a bed against the wall and a dresser where she can keep her altar of China. Outside the window a faded horse is painted on a brick building with the Marlboro Man. They can see him now, Ruth says, through a blizzard of snow.

Claire

JOHNNY CARSON WAS AN
ARISTOPHANIC SCHOLAR

I sat writing at the kitchen table. I'd managed to make Will's lunch and wipe down the counter before I took him to school. Since we'd let go of the last nanny, I wiped down the kitchen twenty times a day. I liked the empty house, the clean hours. I should have called the agency, but I just marked the scraps I could conjure on staff paper.

Hitchcock's career, I'd read in a book Jeff had given me, was an unending search for the right song. So was mine.

At eleven, I banged a pot of water on the stove for soba noodles, measured out sesame oil and red pepper flakes, ate, and had the bowl rinsed in under ten minutes. Then I fell asleep on the sofa. Twenty minutes later I returned. At two, mad at myself for not calling the agency, I ran to the school. My run for the day.

I heard the sound of jump ropes hitting pavement. Double Dutch. That rhythm. Yes. Ropes, I could put that sound at the beginning.

We came home for our snack, and then I offered the park.

"It's okay, Mommy. You can work," he said.

I found two jump ropes, different sizes, and taught Will to spin them with me. Then I brought my papers down on the floor while he stacked LEGOs.

I hummed as I scribbled, and Will said, "That's beautiful, Mommy." What would happen when he became aware of other hummers, hierarchies in the world, not subject to his love? Would he, in the course of my diminishment, feel smaller?

These hazy hours (sponsored, it seemed, by Starbucks) while Paul was gone, I entered childhood from a different door.

Maybe we were building something, too, that would last.

Paul called at five to say that a friend of Jeff's owned a no-longer-hot restaurant, and Aleph Sargent had made a reservation. The owner wanted to fill the room.

"Tonight?" I reminded him we had no babysitter.

He sighed. "Maybe it'd be good for us to get out." He'd started back on his old show, working for Allen, the showrunner, again. He'd write another pilot for a midseason replacement.

"I could ask Molly."

"I don't know if he'll go to sleep with her."

Then Tom and my mother stopped by and we ended up with all three, my mother unstable on heels, holding another Mason jar of persimmon sauce. "It's so good if you heat it up and put it on ice cream."

She and Will stood on my bed, in a pillow fight, while I debriefed Molly. Tom moved in the yard, inspecting shrubs. I showed him where we planted the orange tree they'd given Will for his birthday.

"We need to aerate it, okay?" he said. "Do you have a hoe?"

I brought him a trowel.

"What have you been doing?" I asked.

"I've been getting my garden tours together for the class. That was a real nosebleed."

It was actually easy to leave. "Good one!" I heard my mom call, through the open window.

Happiness. What almost could have been.

"Where's Paul?" Jeff asked, when I slid into the booth.

"On his way from work."

"So same old same old."

But now that Paul had had a disappointment with his show, I didn't want to complain. The large restaurant room waited mostly empty.

"We invited Lucy and she said, *But, Helen, we are only wearing our regular,* so I told them—her sister's there, too—they could raid my closet. Now I'm thinking Cheska's pretty big."

Then Lucy and her sister walked in wearing Helen's clothes. They had the best skin. I'd never seen any of the Filipinas in makeup.

The last time I saw her, at Lucy's wedding, Lola had had fewer wrinkles than I did.

"Clothes okay?" I whispered. "Not stretched?"

"Looks like she found stuff from the back of the closet I never wear."

"You should, though." The black skirt looked great on Lucy.

I should have dressed up more. I was just wearing a black blouse and jeans.

Even offered the whole closet, Lucy understood what Helen wouldn't want her to take. We scooched over in the booth. "Hey, married lady." Jeff handed them menus. "Everybody order *lots*."

They each ordered steaks, giggling, looking down at their plates. I asked how Lucy's studies were going.

"It is slow, Claire. I am too tired."

Like well-behaved children in my generation, they didn't speak unless spoken to.

Jeff asked for flounder, no oil no butter, some chopped cilantro on top if they had it. Helen ordered lamb.

The redheaded woman who'd once thought Will sounded autistic stopped at our booth. "Just got back from Europe," she said. "Elissa and I. Great trip." Pleasure, she meant. So much of what we did for our boys was for their future. Did I even know how to just play? This year, he'd started T-ball. I loved watching him run with the other boys, the clumsy mitts on their hands almost tipping them.

Helen shook her head. "She's at that school *every day*. Just fighting to keep Elissa *in*. They might have to sue the LAUSD. We're lucky, you know?"

Jeff nodded obediently.

"You hear they're divorcing?" She shrugged. "That's what happens to people who hang up their love letters in the guest bathroom."

I didn't know if I should order for Paul. Why couldn't he ever just be here?

"In the Greeks"—Jeff flipped open a small green book—" 'tragedy was always set in the past.' Comedy"—he socked his other hand—"is right now."

"Only you could read out loud at table and seem just a little obnoxious," I said.

"You been served," Helen said. "Hey, knock on wood. We're pregnant again."

This time it didn't floor me. Would the freckled doctor deliver this baby?

"Three thousand dollars of couple's therapy later," Helen grumbled.

He put his arm around her and whispered in her ear in an obligatory way. She looked up at him. A show.

Lucy stared at the plate the waiter set in front of her. "So big, Helen!"

Jeff got up. He pushed open the swinging doors to the kitchen. I assumed there was a problem with his fish. "Yoo-hoo! Anybody home?"

Cheska whispered. "Helen? Aleph Sargent, she will be here?"

"There's her table." An empty booth with one rose, a branch of pine, and a RESERVED card. Helen frankly worked at her chop with a fork and knife.

I glanced at the door. "I guess movie stars eat late." As did comedy writers, apparently.

When we stood to go, the table with the reserved sign remained empty, and Paul was still at large. Nourished by flounder, Jeff regained charm, snapping the small book closed. "Johnny Carson considered himself to be an Aristophanic scholar." While I waited for my car, Annabel Grass walked in. An oboist, she'd never married, never had children. She must have been forty-five, but she still wore her hair long and straight, *Alice in Wonderland* style. She strolled into the restaurant at ten-fifteen, carrying a backpack, full of wildflowers. "I just drove in from the desert," she explained.

When I unlocked the front door, Molly sat up. "Paul's not home yet?" I should pay her, I thought, but I wasn't sure what. When I tried, though, she refused.

"Really, it's no problem. Your mom put him to bed. I had to read this script anyway. Oh, that persimmon thing your mom made? It was awesome."

I liked Molly for what might have been the first time, feeling inordinately grateful. She appreciated my mother's confection. I wished Paul had heard her say so. Too few kind things had ever been said about my mother.

Just as Molly's car pulled out of the driveway, Paul burst in. "Oh, man, you can't believe the inanity. The human comedy. What'd I miss?"

"They're pregnant again," I said. "The movie star didn't show. Lucy and Cheska came. Seeing them made me think I should call Lola to see Will."

"Yeah. We probably should."

This was what I liked: talking about Will. Agreeing. Paul sat on the other side of the couch and our jeaned legs entwined. I wanted to talk—I always wanted to talk—but I didn't know where to start. He asked how the songs were going. I said I wasn't finished yet. He bit his bottom lip. "Takes a long time." I'd gone on the field trip to the zoo and another day to a playdate with a new boy who could maybe become a friend for Will. I'd worked almost every night for a few hours after I put him down and I was near the end of the seventh song. I talked with Harv and Lil about these daily shifts and calibrations. Paul knew my general trajectories, but he didn't have the details.

I made a mewing sound he understood meant backrub.

"Okay," he said, from behind a magazine. "C'mere." He rubbed with one hand. I closed my eyes to feel the sparks shower down my neck. I wanted two hands, but he'd have to put the magazine down, and that carried the risk of hands roaming. I looked around the room. "Rake," I said. That was the term we used for scratching, with spread fingers, through each other's hair. I thought of the afternoon I'd seen Jeff at the bar in Pasadena. Paul would never be at a bar with another woman. He was so much better than Jeff. But better as he was, when his fingers strayed toward my breasts, I felt I had to stop him, the way I had in high school, when a guy tried to get something *off of me.* An aversion. When had this started? In the other house right now, clothes were probably flinging, and Helen, in those tiny strings I'd seen hanging on the rod, knelt on the bed, tense and eager. But what about the doctor? Was their sex the same?

"You know my mom's persimmon sauce?"

"Mm-hmm." Paul was deep in an article. "New magazinage." He tapped the cover.

"Molly loved it. Want some?"

I stirred the thick sauce in its jar rattling in a pan of boiling water. The sweet carmelly confection hardened on the ice cream.

"Molly's right," he said. "It's great."

Then we began. I turned my head to the side when he kissed, so his mouth reached my ear, making it tingle.

I stood up naked, after. "We should do this more often. I feel better now. It's just before."

"You always say that."

That night, I fell asleep on his chest.

December 1995.

After winter break, the news at school was Melissa. Her cancer was back, stage four, in her liver. The moms galvanized; Helen was already planning a blood drive. "It's bad. Really bad. Harry wants to take a leave of absence, even though the case he's been working on for three years is finally going to trial. But she wants him to try the case. She says, *If I live, I don't want to have to move out of the house.* She's stopped doing the photo albums, that was her big project she wanted to finish, and now she's writing letters for each kid to open on their eighteenth birthday." A tear formed at the corner of her eye. Odd to see someone so determined cry. I couldn't donate to the blood drive, though, because I'd contracted hep A once on a USIA concert tour in Turkey.

If I got sick, Paul would hire someone. He'd find the best person he could, from a day of interviews. And here was the thing: I'd want that person. Paul could never sit still at home with me. One day in the kitchen, Lola and I had talked about getting old; I'd asked her what she would do when she retired.

"Me, I will go back to my place. Here, it is hard. If you do not have money, no one will take care you. If I am strong, I will take care you, but I don't think so, I will be too old. We are too close the same." That may have been the first time I ever heard her use a contraction.

"Maybe I'll come with you to Tagaytay."

"Yes, Claire. You can still write your music. You come there."

I'm sure she hadn't meant that, exactly. But I still held it, like a promise.

Lola

IT IS GOOD TO OWN A HOUSE

For a long time, Judith tried to hide her purchases. She would leave the bags in her car and sneak them in while I slept. So the first I would see was when she wore the blouse or put it on my chair to take to the dry cleaner. But I am the one who empties the trash, where she snipped the tags. Anyway, the price of clothes, I approve. If it will work to find a man who can be father for Laura. My daughters, I would never allow. Soft hair, it is okay. A fine gold chain. But Judith is not the natural age for pairing. And she does not have many advantages. If there is a help she can buy, then we have to pay that. My employer, she watches the weight. The face she cannot change. The thing that bothers me is not her wardrobe. But more than she is paying me, she gives the landlord. At the end, it is not even her house. One day in winter, when Judith comes home, dropping her scripts on the table, a flyer from a real estate agency flutters down, with small dim pictures.

"Good to buy, Judith. The rent here, it is too expensive."

"To buy, we'd have to move. To Mar Vista maybe. Or Beverlywood." She sighs.

I have heard these places. "But it is good to own a house." I am thinking for Laura. That someday she will be owner of a house.

Saturday morning we drive, the three of us. In Manila, too, we have graded neighborhoods. Cheska has a house not far from mine in a new development. You see factory chimneys and in the empty lots, just dirt and goats. Still, the way Cheska spreads her shoulders, I detect a flutter—that somewhere, across the world, she owns land.

But walking through the insides of American houses, there is an air of loss.

"It is okay," I say to the best one.

"Let's go for breakfast." When Judith becomes depressed, she will take us to a restaurant. It is how we pretend to have more. Really, that is what restaurants are for. The people who can afford them do not need their spell.

Laurita sees a pancake with little cubes of canned peach and a swirl of sprayed whipped cream and she reaches for it. Today, we want to match her desire.

"You know, we don't have to move. We can just keep doing what we're doing."

"We can move," I say. This job, it is really different.

"But what about your friends?"

"Make new friends." I shrug.

Every month we will pay into something, money dropped in a jar. Better to someday own a house in a lower neighborhood than someday own nothing here.

There is a FOR SALE sign in front of the Castle.

"Divorce," Lita says.

"Your house we will never sell," I whisper Laura. But every month now I put the postage stamp on the payment to the mortgage company. What if something happened Judith? Tonight, I will have dinner ready when she comes home. We will treat her like a Filipino husband.

The pager of Lita beeps. My former pupil. From the Christmas leave of Tony, Lucy became pregnant, and now she is pregnant like a queen. Bing is the one to answer the door. Lucy stays on the couch, holding her stomach. "I am worried the baby."

In emergency, Lucy goes to the front of the line, because Lita called Alice. She hears the heart, and Alice tells her the pregnancy, it is normal, but still my former pupil rides home in the front facing forward, a hand on her belly. She goes right away to the couch. Bing sits alone on the floor, TV on. And he is old enough now to tell.

We move into the new house the first week of June. One by one, Laura and I fix the rooms, her in the Snugli with a dry brush, pretending to paint. "We are the ladies of the house," I tell her. "Later on, we will give party." Judith buys an electric sander, and I strip every window frame. All July I rush through errands to come home to sand. In August, I put primer and stay up late painting. All the time, I think of a party. We will invite everybody, I tell myself while I work. My weekend employer, it is hard to remember I cried once for that house. At night, I stood outside in the dark. They were more than employers then. Without that, work looks a little dirty. Rain feels cold, not silver. Out of the ground, the sun lifts a smell of rot. Some people experience a great love. When Esperanza was rocking like a cup in a saucer on a table that had been banged, we said, *It will not always stay so bad. This is the worst. And the worst cannot last.* But Esperanza, until now, she never got over that guy. Not really. She attends night school, to be a teacher, Tuesdays and Thursdays. Those evenings, Beth Martin keeps her daughter.

But mine turned out to be only ordinary love. I still think about the years I lost forty-seven fifty a day; that is all. In the end, I quit them.

Williamo, I saw every day, but they always love the parents more. I never wanted to admit that when I was taking care him, and the first year, you really cannot tell. Then at ten, eleven months he cried and cried, and it was only the mother he wanted. You do everything and then, they love someone more. No fair. Just true life.

But I am the one Laurita wants. With the mom she cries. It is something, to be loved like this.

I was the one to pick the name, to baptize, to take Laura to the doctor appointments. I told Judith to buy this place.

In the new neighborhood, it is not easy to make friends. The babysitters, they are not nannies. They are not even full-time. They are what the people here can afford. I had to tell one girl, *You can never shake a baby.* A yo-yo, it is not safe either.

Ruth calls me on the telephone. I am here seven days, my only off Sunday mornings. Ruth returned from New York, and now, two years after her escape, the slave is talking about her master. He drove her around South Central. *We will let you out,* he said. *They'll find use for you. Like a dog.* She told Ruth, *Because he did not use me in a sex way.* They beat her. Ruth says she remembers the bruises. "And whenever we give her anything, she asks if she can keep it."

I hear this in our faraway kitchen, that Laura and I painted teal. We came home at five, we had bath time, and got on jammies. Now Laura has her music hour. I moved the playpen, so she can see me make our dinner. While Ruth tells the problems of the slave, I am thinking we need bay leaf; I will buy a plant. Tomorrow chicken adobo. The slave started a job in Malibu. A three-year-old said, *I'd like a Pepsi. Please bring it to me half filled with ice and my cherry floating on the top. Otherwise I can't drink it.*

I laugh along; Ruth always jokes about how they spoil kids in America, but then, she says, the Malibu brothers pushed the slave into the pool. She tried to paddle to the side and they poked at her with the stick of the net. She swallowed water, but finally, the assistant, who sat typing recipes into a computer, ran out and put a broom into the pool for her to grab.

The slave choked. The assistant dialed the mother to tell what happened, to see if the boys should be punished. But the mother said, *Oh, it's a hot day, she probably enjoyed getting cooled off.*

Ruth asks if I have seen Williamo because, long time ago, I said Jean, the one next-door Claire, would hire the slave. "That baby must be born by now," Ruth says.

"I do not know," I say. "We are too busy."

Lucy finally quits. She wants that I will take care Bing, but I cannot.

I am needed here.

"Double up," she says. "They just have to buy a double stroller, like that. Maybe if you tell Judith she can pay less, she will say okay."

"But, Laura, she will not say okay." The employers of Lucy pay a lot. They will not have problems. "Call Ruth," I tell my former pupil, as Cheska studies the review book for her nursing exam.

"The guy, he is going so many doctors, now, Lola. Sometimes two in one day. He cannot sleep. He is depress. They are giving Prozac."

Cheska pops up from the review book, puts a feather to mark her place. "Prozac! Many things contraindicated for that. Dairy!" She is studying again for the exam. She failed four times already. "Anything ferment, like that."

"Lita says until now, the doctor comes home in the afternoon and kneels on the floor with her daughters. But Alice, she does not know how to play." I would have said that about Lita. But I have noticed, mothers and nannies, they sometimes match, the way of dogs and their owners.

I do not ask Judith to buy a double stroller, but I ask if I can give away the crib. For the one-year birthday, I want to buy for Laura a low bed I can put on the floor next to mine. And when Lucy quits, my old employers, they do not even ask me. They hire a white.

"I just do not know this one," Lucy says, when she and Cheska come to get the crib. "We can tell from the face. Lola, Jeff, he is disappeared all night. Helen called police and they found his car on Pacific Coast Highway. She is afraid suicide."

Suicide? I really do not know. "You told me he is taking Prozac."

Cheska lifts her head. "Maybe he ate cheese."

Today, it is supposed to rain, so I have pots on the floor, places marked with small *X*'s of masking tape to remember leaks. In one cupboard I keep old pots for this.

"Why you are not using the dishwasher?" my pupil asks, when I rinse her cup. She opens the dishwasher that does not work, sniffs. We are saving to fix that too.

"It is okay," I say, holding Laura. "We are cowboys here."

I touch the letter of my former employer in my pocket. Later, I dial the number. He answers. What can I say? *Good, you are not dead!* So I hang up.

For the one-year party, I invite both my former employers, Bing, Williamo, Lita, the Chinese Adopteds, and kids Laura knows from here.

I have my girl dressed in silver with a bow.

What I promised some-a-day for Williamo, I make now: the ice candy. My kids finally sent me the plastic cases to freeze. We found a recipe Laura loves: avocado, milk, and maple syrup. My former week-end employers drive up in the convertible, like you would see in a movie. The guy, he used to look at Bing and say, *And this is still all before he'll remember.* That was his refrain.

He bounds up the stairs to our small house, taking them two at a time, holding the hand of Bing, a merry glint in his eyes. I keep looking, once and then again, because in his other hand raised up he is carrying a live bird in a light green cage. The cage swings a little with each jounce step and the bird stays perched to a branch inside, yellow feet curled around.

Why do they bring with them to a party their bird?

I inventory the rooms of their house, my mind going down hallways. They do not have a pet bird! I understand even as it is happening—this bird is a present.

No! Who would give a live animal without first asking the grown-up?

They are saying if we do not want, they will take him back, even as Bing holds open the cage door and Jeff coaxes the yellow stick legs onto the finger of Laura. They are explaining the habits, showing the little trough hooked onto the bars where goes the water. They have, with her name on it, a book about this kind of bird—the cockatiel.

Claire

THE TWO BOXES

"You don't seem pregnant to me," Helen said.

"I don't *feel* pregnant. I just haven't had a period for a while." But I didn't keep good track. "With Will, I threw up."

"So you're not, then," she said with authority. Up close, there was something plain about her face. "Do you even *want* a second child?" Once in a while I remembered: people found me odd. "It's a lot of work," she said, holding her belly.

She sighed. They all thought we couldn't manage Will as it was. *I* couldn't.

I bought the little thing you pee on.

Two lines came. Bright pink.

I'd wanted a divorce. Now I'd have a baby instead. I tipped, leaned my forehead on the cool bathroom wall. That size 2 dress in the closet.

When I told him, late that night, Paul started shaking his head. "I love children. I would have liked more, if I'd married a different kind of woman. But given both of our work . . ." He sat and rubbed the arch of a foot. "Claire, I don't think our marriage can withstand another child."

He stared at me as if I were new. "That was the one time we've had sex all year."

"What does *that* have to do with it?"

He started pacing. "He's already in school. Next year, he'll start kindergarten. It'll be easier from here on out." His voice calmed, telling me we were near the end. If I could hold up, steady my nerves, we'd pay people a little longer, and then we'd be out of the woods. But I'd waited, was waiting still, for us to enter together, one on either side of Will, and come out, a long time later, somewhere else.

"Why is it so hard for us to manage?" I said. "Other people manage."

"I don't see that many people who both have major careers."

"I don't have a major career."

"You're one symphony away. And having another child won't help."

"I told you before we got married that I couldn't have an abortion."

"I know you said that, Claire. We had a fight about that then, too, if you recall."

We'd never settled that fight, as we didn't settle most of our fights. We left them on the floor and turned back to daily cares. When I'd had the amnio, he'd said, "You'd abort before you'd chose to carry to term a baby with a terrible disability, wouldn't you?"

I'd been softer then, bridelike. I put a hand on his arm. When I think of our young marriage, that's what I see: his dark arm and my wrist, a musician's hand, with clipped nails. "Just wait," I'd said. "We'll get the results in a week."

Now he stood with the same strange smile Will got when he was going to be stubborn. "I'd choose the marriage over a child we don't have."

Would I? I didn't think I'd choose the marriage over anything, though I no longer seemed to have a choice.

But it turned out to be a false positive.

It started in the smallest way. One day in April, Paul came to the kitchen as he did every morning, baseball cap backward, carrying his briefcase, but this time holding his tuxedo. He looked around, then hung it on the door. Before, he'd always given his dry cleaning to Lola. Now there was only me. Still, he hesitated. I suppose dry cleaning fell into the housekeeper column. His mother had raised him to know the difference.

But Will had dressed himself in a T-shirt I liked; his long hair curled up in the back. I'd made barley bread for the first time and Will was eating it, with honey. "Do you want me to take that in?"

"Could you? Thanks." Paul sighed. "I should get a new shirt. I let the salesman talk me into that one. Mistake."

"We can go look," I said. "The Emmys aren't till the end of the summer, right?"

"I have to have it to take to Alfie's wedding. Didn't I tell you? It's black tie. That's so like him. The human comedy."

"Who's Alfie?" Will asked.

"Alfie's daddy's cousin, who lives in Baltimore." In the nine years we'd been married, I'd spoken to Alfie exactly twice, when he'd called after each of Paul's episodes aired. Apparently, he was now marrying. Paul said he'd leave on a Thursday, getting off early to go to the airport. He'd return Monday morning and drive straight to work.

"You've never taken four days off to spend with us," I whispered.

"They're not inviting kids. Otherwise, I'd bring him and you could come if you wanted or stay home and work."

A race started in me. "No," I said. "This isn't fair."

"It's done. Molly already booked my flight."

"You don't even *know* this guy."

"His mother would be very hurt and offended if I didn't go."

"I'm hurt and offended." All for a cousin we hadn't seen since our wedding. A cousin Will had never even met. My outrage spun a web.

"I'd like to talk to him," Lil's husband said, when I called that afternoon. "She's got me trained. I mean, if you want to work the kind of hours he works, with that focus and that commitment, then your free time isn't yours. That belongs to your wife, and she can do what she wants with it."

Lil said, "It just sounds like he doesn't listen to you."

This was what his mother earned, I thought, those times she waited with her glass of wine and just got me. Absolute obedience. But there wasn't enough of him to share.

"I don't want you to go," I said, as he stood packing, the suitcase open on the bed.

"Claire, I have to."

"If you go," I said—but what? I had nothing he wanted that I could deny. I kept asking, it came to me in a rush, for time. And the answer was no.

But the days he was gone felt like vacation.

We took a long walk with my mother and Tom, who'd come from lunch at Twin Dragons. They brought their fortune cookies for Will.

As we strolled, my mother looked down. She told us the plumber had stolen her rings.

"Maybe you misplaced them," I said. "Remember the time we found your money order."

"No, he took them, I'm sure. I know it."

"How do you know?"

"They're gone. We looked everywhere."

"We looked everywhere," Tom echoed. "I called him and said, I have your name and your insurance number. I said in twenty-four hours we're going to file a police report. He said he didn't do it, but I don't believe him."

I turned to Tom, sharp. Didn't he remember, she'd once accused *him* of stealing from her.

I didn't like William hearing this. Wind gusted eucalyptus buttons, and Will kicked them with the round fronts of his sneakers. Leaves rattled above.

"The eucalyptus smell good," I said.

"There are six hundred different kinds of eucalyptus in Santa Monica," Tom said. "All from Australia."

He took the bag from Twin Dragons away from my mother. "No, don't do that, don't. People don't like that. They don't like it."

"Well, some*one* does."

"She thinks she's feeding the animals," he told us. He bent down to pick up a wet lump of mu shu pork from a lawn.

Friday night we went to a Buster Keaton festival, with pizza and good ice cream. Will stood up on his seat and the men behind didn't mind. After Will fell asleep, Paul called. "This rehearsal dinner. Everyone made a toast. And the bride's father . . ." As he talked, I moved around my office. There was a box in my closet. I'd brought my things in it to California years ago. I put in a bent pinecone and a picture of Will.

The next day I stood at the bank depositing a check from an orchestra in Arkansas. There was another one from the radio station affiliate that aired *Saint Paul Sunday*. I filled out the deposit slip to put the money in our joint checking account. The total was twenty-three hundred dollars. I deposited those checks, and then took out cash. We had a four-hundred-a-day limit. I did it Sunday, too, dropping the envelope of money in my box. On a whim I called my mother. "We found the rings," she said.

Paul returned Monday night after I was asleep. For once, the next morning, I woke first. On the table, right inside the door, was a hexagonal box, made of dark pebbled red leather. A gift. I thought of my two boxes. I tried to imagine this one inside the other. Even though the hexagon was so much smaller, it didn't seem to fit.

My friends had stood at our wedding by the chuppah; they'd promised the rabbi to help keep us together.

"Well, you know what Beethoven's mother said about marriage," Harv told me. " 'A little joy and then a chain of sorrows.' He overheard this—no wonder the guy never found love."

"Even if he does just a tiny bit you like," Lil said, "you may miss that tiny bit."

She suggested a vacation.

"With *him*?" I couldn't really imagine it.

For a long time, I'd had a separation alone. I'd had a whole love affair with Jeff, without his complicity. It was about time I started having relationships with people who knew about them.

Still, I'd married late, and I had a schoolboy.

Nothing could turn out anymore.

Paul didn't attend the end-of-the-year conference. The teachers told me Will had trouble with impulse control. He talked too much. We'd let our nanny go, as they'd said to, I told them. And he was improving, they said, but when I pressed them, they couldn't tell me what had actually improved. And we'd lost Lola. Or I had.

I went to Dr. Lark.

"What is it you're afraid of?"

"Worst case? Worst case might be that he can't make friends. That he has to go to a special school."

"He has a sweet connection to you. He'll find friends."

"He just doesn't behave well enough."

"I'd put my bets on you," she said.

"Well, I can't leave Paul now," I said. "When Will's having trouble."

"It's hard to know how these things play out," she said.

When I was leaving, I turned back. "Do you have children?"

I expected her to have two or three. Her research concerned mothers with infants.

"No, I don't." She paused. "I married late."

I began to imagine being alone.

Money was going to be a problem.

I always knew the name of the place. The redhead had once tried to get Elissa in. I didn't call her, though. I just looked up the number and then got flustered when the woman at the switchboard asked my name. Michelle Berend, I said. Paul's sister in Boston. I didn't want my name on their books. I'd had a so-so conference with Will's teachers. That was all. I just wanted to see.

Special needs.

Maybe we all have special needs.

On the tour, the classrooms looked normal enough. Papers hanging on bulletin boards. Lockers in the hall. Rows of new white Apples in the computer room. A small library lined with posters of Einstein, Tommy Hilfiger, Whoopi Goldberg, Tom Cruz. Jay Leno. Richard Ford. John Irving. Hans Christian Andersen. Walt Disney. Then, in the music room, a guy with long hair, wearing jeans and a dark T-shirt, lifted the needle of a portable record player onto an old Piatagorski recording of Saint-Saëns's First Cello Concerto. Kids sat in a circle on the floor, each holding a baton. He walked around behind them, moving an arm, in rhythm.

When the piece ended, he stopped in back of one kid and touched her head. He went to the piano, banged out a chord, and asked for identification. She got it right, and then she tapped another head. He trilled a shivery high E.

I noticed men's arms. Paul had a yeshiva boy's arms, the kind I'd always liked. This guy had muscles, but they weren't ugly. Then the bell rang, and the kids' shoulders bumped one another.

"Okay, five minutes of Duck Duck Goose," he said.

The tour guide herded the six other parents and me toward the new gym. But I lagged back. A boy now skidded around, tapping heads. I'd never noticed before how hard it was to run in a circle. His sneakers squeaked. I sat on the floor with them and closed my eyes. I wanted the teacher's hand to hover over my head; I wanted to be Goose.

Then a second bell rang and the kids shouldered their backpacks and thudded out. I was the only one left on the floor.

"Was that a conducting class?"

"I'm just a dad. My kid's in fourth grade."

"Oh," I said. "You're a musician."

"A chemist, actually, in real life. But I play with the Glendale Chamber Orchestra."

I looked at his hands. No rings. But hadn't I read that married men went bare-fingered and married women didn't? *I* was married, I remembered, but I'd spun my ring on the floor one night, and it fell down a heating grate.

Still, musicians look at hands.

"You're not a Park Century parent?" he asked.

I shoved myself up. "No." Willie didn't go to school here and I hoped he never would, Tom Cruz notwithstanding. And Hewlett of Hewlett-Packard.

The guy gave me his e-mail address to get the orchestra's schedule. Just then, another group entered, its guide pointing out violins in the cupboards. "Lola!" I hadn't wanted anyone to know I was here. And seeing her now made me trill.

"I am looking for the grandson of Lita. He is an autistic."

I kept the slip of paper with the guy's e-mail in my case, in the compartment with the rosin. That smell came up to my face every time I opened it. But I never e-mailed for the schedule of the Glendale Chamber Orchestra.

Call lawyer, I kept putting on my list.

I asked him again to move out. He said he wouldn't, not now. He'd sleep in the den. We could talk about it after the pilot season.

When was that? I asked.

Summer, he said.

He left the room then, the bedroom that was now mine. The bed made, a lawn mower going somewhere outdoors.

Jeff had introduced a motif, a fugitive melody, nothing real. I understood he'd never felt what I had, but he'd made me hope for something. Slowly, I thought, I'd become the person I'd been before, fragile and eager.

We finally agreed he'd move out August 1.

Now what I talked to Harv about was money.

"You think they'd go back to me? I was late. And they've commissioned Annabel Grass twice."

"Yeah, and she writes music as tight-assed as she is."

One afternoon in July Will was at camp, and I heard Paul thud in. We both roamed through our paths in the house. He'd been sleeping in the den since March.

For some reason I remembered his saying, "That's the only time we've had sex all year."

When it had been the last time, we hadn't even known.

We ran into each other in the hall, passed, and then he turned back. "Are you sure you want this? Because once we tell that little boy, there's no going back."

Was I sure? No. I glimpsed a side of our familiar living room, stable and quiet. But I didn't know how to make it better.

"Our sex life has been pretty terrible for a long time. You've been unhappy with that."

"But how big a deal is sex, really? People say it is, but we don't really know what goes on in other people's houses. We don't really know."

Paul could always soothe my envy, my ever-long sense of being outside a better life. Here was a good man I'd known for years offering a raw vista: *This is who I am. We can take it easy. We can stay.* A long soft part of me, which curled up against my right rib cage, wanted to follow him to our bedroom and pull the shades down.

"I don't really think of you that way anymore either." Sex, he meant.

"Do you think of other people?" I asked this idly.

By now we'd flopped on our made bed, fully clothed. He folded his arms behind his head.

"I never did, but just in the last year or so there are women who've expressed interest in me."

Let him go, I thought. He can find life. Maybe you can't, but he can. Let him go.

Lola

A PORPOISE

I ask Lita if she can get an off.

"No," she says, "my employer, she is back working. Alice is not moping anymore."

Lucy moved to the naval base in San Diego. In October, Lita told me that she had the baby: a nine-pounds boy. Then, in January, I received the announcement.

Mrs. Lucila Pasqual gave birth to
Asher Pasqual
9 lb 2 oz
October 20, 1996

A Sunday near the end of February, I pick up Ruth and Aileen to drive down.

Ruth brings snacks, so there is the air of a party in the backseat. Aileen half stands, dancing to a song on the radio, and Laurita tries to copy, punching the arms at air.

My former pupil greets us in an apartment bare but tidy. Tony is gone, on a boat. "I am with Asher all the time, Lola. It is so much work." Before, she took care Bing but she had Ofelia too.

He is a cute baby, though, the hair long, and she keeps him very clean. I recognize the outfit with suspenders from Bing. Lucy stands barefoot, her toes polished black. Judith subscribes to *Vogue*, so I know that is the style. A curve settles in me: my pupil, she has found happiness. Not doctor, but this is something too. Before I did not believe in it, but from Laura I learned that life is not only diplomas. Lola too found luck—a correct fit in the bedroom—and maybe my Laura, she will find a private happiness, just a small one. She will never be the prettiest. I feel a pang for Issa, twenty-seven years old, working in the hospital forty hours at a time. Maybe I have been too strong with my own. Not allowing even a crush.

I look around the living room. My pupil, she used to decorate the house of Bing with flowers. Here I see no frills. The crib of my Laura that came from Alice makes the center, with a new denim bumper tied on.

"Target," she says. "Twenty-four dollars. Cheska bought."

I finger the round wooden table, the best thing here. "Helen gave," she says. "Have you seen them, Lola? The baby?"

"No, with Laura I am now seven days." I, too, have found my life.

"A girl. Jessica. Maybe they will be happy. I really do not know with them." This table has a jar of baby food, a spoon in, a bib, and a half-open book. "The review course," Lucy says.

"For doctor?"

"Just nurse, Lola. To try for nurse." Ten years medicine, then when she should have started, they came here. But Lucy did not go to Far Eastern. Her hair, it is chop short, not the hair of my daughters. She was always poor.

Before we leave, I go to the lavatory, and when I return, Lucy makes the center again, the way she used to at our playclub. "Because I do like this." She bends her knees, barelegged, a way that would be indecent if we were not grandmothers and children. My pupil, she gained weight again. She will have to diet before her sailor returns. "I push." Her feet spread wide, pelvis moving, eyes squinting to demonstrate. "I try hard. I do my best."

Once again, my pupil, she is telling her success story, even here in this plain apartment. Ruth and I sit, hands on our laps, each of us a mother also. We try our best too and we know—life, it can turn out a different way.

"So she will not be doctor after all," Ruth says, in the car again. Every time my former pupil got another raise or her taxes paid or when they hired the immigration lawyer, Ruth used to call me. *What will be next? She will be doctor! You watch.*

It seemed my pupil, she could go so high. We always understood she would leave us behind, but now that she was not going to be anything, we wanted her to. Our poster Filipina. But Lucy ended up like the rest of us, not doctor, just a mother. Maybe she was not as much as we always thought, or our own lives were more.

Then I notice Aileen, too quiet in the back. "What happened you?" I turn. "No more dance dance?"

"I lost my dancing powers," she says, her head resting on the car seat of Laura. Laura's face makes a wavery smile. Aileen has grown up used to people watching her as a favor. Is that why she is kind?

One day Laura falls at the park and gets a huge *bocal.* I push her in the stroller to Burger King to ask ice. As soon as I pick her up to apply the cold pack, she purrs. That is the thing with this girl. She loves me a way the boys, they never did.

Someone taps my elbow. "Hey, Lola. Remember me?" China. She is holding a mitt, wearing a team uniform. She must now be almost six, like Williamo. "Lola, d'you ever see Mai-ling?"

I tell her Mai-ling lives on Park Avenue. "In New York everyone wants Filipinas. A Filipina there is worth three times a Filipina here. But me, I do not like. It is too cold."

Four months later, Mai-ling is back. Every August, the Sapersteins take a two-week vacation. During that time, they pay Ruth to stay there, feed the pets, collect the mail, and keep the machines running. Monday, the pool man comes, Tuesday and Friday gardeners, Wednesday Salvadoran sisters who clean, Thursday the water delivery and a different Salvadoran just for laundry. And while the Sapersteins swim in Massachusetts ponds, the friends of Ruth drive to Beverly Hills to flutter their legs in the turquoise water of the pool. Danny grills *lechon.* I attend with Laura and she follows Aileen, trying to dance along her dances. Mai-ling stands by the grill, hands in her pockets.

"Manhattan, it is too big," she says. "Taller than Manila. More on glass."

Ruth shakes her head. "Nobody here will pay you six hundred a week to iron." She wants Mai-ling out, far away.

"I saw China," I tell her. "She is asking you."

Cheska holds the stick with the marshmallow for Phoebe, the younger sister of Simon. Since Melissa died, Cheska volunteers at the school. This year she will be Class Mother.

"How is Williamo?" I ask Simon. "Are you still same class?"

"Guess so," he says. Cheska nudges him.

"He's fine, Lola," she tells me.

Natalie and Aileen sleep in the yellow gingham room of Ginger Saperstein. When Natalie goes to teach her class at CalArts, Ruth watches Aileen. In two days, the Sapersteins will return; Ruth has to get groceries, she says, so they have fresh milk and strawberries when they wake up their first morning back. Should she leave Aileen with Candace, or should she have the babysitters babysitter ride the bus up? Eight years old, Aileen can almost take care herself. Watch TV. The babysitters babysitter, they usually just give her a few dollars or a pie or a cake from the store.

I ask, What day? Maybe we can help.

But Tuesday we have the occupational therapist.

Ruth did not leave Aileen with Candace. She called the babysitters babysitter to take the bus up from Eagle Rock. Ruth bought her a Whole Foods cinnamon coffee cake. And while that lady was supposed to be watching, Aileen drowned. But Aileen could swim. She took classes in the big pool at Pasadena City College. I saw her once dive in a crescent off the high board there. The babysitters babysitter said Aileen was in and out, pulling herself up, on the metal poles. But the babysitters babysitter had to go to the bathroom. When she came back, there was a shadow in a corner. Aileen must have hit her head.

I could not attend the church funeral because Laurita, she had chicken pox. Lita and Cheska went, and they decided that the Korean, he is good. The Korean quit his writing class, cut his hours at the family nursery. Now he just takes care Natalie.

Ruth paid for the high mass, the flowers, the stone, but she did not quit Sapersteins. Natalie says she will sue, she wants to call the lawyer from the *Times* to imprison the babysitters babysitter, but then she slides under again and needs to sleep. The Korean drives her to the apartment and they give her another pill. He sits on the bed, puts a towel on the forehead, and pulls her T-shirt over her head. I never thought before but all the problems we pitied Ruth, Natalie must have been a good mother. Because Aileen, she was a very nice girl.

Ruth did not talk about the accident. But the coroner sent a report; paperwork arrived from police also. The Sapersteins called Ruth into the downstairs den, the Mother and Father both, his knees spread, hands on the creases of his pants.

They asked her did she want to stay there working.

"If I am needed," she said.

They wanted to know, probably, if she would sue. Ruth, she did not say anything. It was not a yes-or-no question. They gave her a check for ten thousand to help with the funeral expenses and to send *the mother of the child* back to school. Ruth did not tell them she already paid the funeral or that Natalie would not take any more school. She accepted the money and said thank you. The whole thing it was not even a half hour.

That room, I have seen it; painted dark red, it has no windows, with an L-shaped velvet sofa built onto two walls. *The drinks room,* they called it.

I heard all this by telephone. Laura, she had chicken pox eight days, and we were in and out the oatmeal bath. I put cotton gloves on her, but she pulled them off in her sleep. I sat next to the bed so she will not scratch. It is the face and she is a girl.

Then, in the morning, the mother asks, "Why are there no more paper towels?" The grandmother had scheduled a visit from Minnesota, and Judith canceled. "Too dangerous for an old person," she told me.

She either thinks I am not old or does not care I die.

Laura, she is not like my kids or Williamo. She is behind.

I am the one to take her to the speech therapist. We every night blow bubbles in the bath. When she learns a word, I write it down and put on the refrigerator. *Lola,* she said. Her first word. I waited for the second. *Go.* Then I let her pick out the Winnie-the-Pooh magnet.

From no words age two, by the time she starts school a year later, we have more than a thousand. We cut Joan, the speech therapist, to

Tuesdays only. My third daughter wants to get married at Christmas. I price the ticket and make the reservation, but when I tell Laurita, she screams, "You will never leave this house!" She knocks the sugar bowl off the table. "I breakeded it." She takes out her money, crumpled dollars and neat birthday bills in an envelope from the Minnesota grandmother, coins from her princess safe. "I will pay you one hundred dollars to stay." One hundred is the total, all she has.

I taught her the days of the week, but she will never say Sunday, because that is when I take my off. Okay, I decide. My daughter can have her wedding. I will stay until Laura is five. I will write that for *The Book of Ruth*. But as we put the money back in her safe, I tell her, "Some-a-day your Lola will be old. She will have to go home."

This job, it is a big responsibility. I try to teach her, also, not to use money with people. Because the teacher called to say Laura is giving money to a girl she likes. One dollar every day. The teacher made that girl return the bills, but the girl got mad, saying *Indian giver*. Some things they can come only as gifts, I explain. When you try to buy things that should never be sold, they turn into something else, like the princess who became a bird. Money cannot buy love, I say, but maybe it can. Not to the one paying, but for somebody else. Judith pays me and I love Laura.

"I am lonesome," I say, on the phone to Ruth. We talk now, at night after I put Laura down. "But I have purpose."

I hear the door creak, then Laura runs to my lap. "You have a porpoise? In the Philippines?" She pretends to be a baby, the finger in the mouth.

"Yes, there we have many porpoise. What you do up?"

"Za ert!" That is how she says "dessert."

My third daughter gets married in an office; she will save the church wedding for me. And exactly the month I would be mother of the bride, the teacher at the school tells me in learning, Laura is a little slow. What Laura loves, I tell the teacher, is hula. She can hula-hoop for long time. It is her special talent.

"But she will have to learn her alphabet too." The teacher writes a note for my employer. So we have to go to Dr. Hallian again. He has a room of toys, but he will not let Laura play them. She should sit at a little table and take his test. Well, she does not want to sit! Many of the pictures he shows, I tell him, *But she knows that, she just wants to play the truck. She does not have a truck like that at home.*

So to Joan and the occupational therapist, we will now add a learning specialist and a social-skills group. The week does not give enough days. I am no longer on the team with the ones who win. But you can love them, this way, just the same.

Claire

THE HUMAN CONDITION

Then it was the day to tell. William. Of our failure.

We'd planned for months with a tall, grave child therapist Dr. Lark recommended, who met us in his backyard cabin, with a fire always burning.

Then it was the day. We did it in the kitchen that had once been black. Sitting around our old table, in the morning, we began a scene we knew we'd never forget, not one of the three of us. Paul took William on his lap, and I didn't want time to move.

I wonder how many people stop then. And turn the day into a regular one. What a relief and reclamation.

"We . . . have something to tell you," Paul said.

"What?" Terror recumbent in his voice, or did I just imagine it?

Paul gave the little speech and Will gasped. Once. The sound unmade everything. He fell into his father's arms, collapsed. There seemed to be no air in him. I touched the soft flannel of his sleeve. Paul, the man he was and would always be, kept talking in a good voice, a high child-explaining voice, making it simple. *Now Mommy and Daddy will have two houses. Daddy has a new house and you'll have a room there and your room here and some nights you'll sleep in Daddy's house and some night's in Mommy's.*

"I never thought you two—" Will said.

He looked straight at me for a moment. "We're going to be all right," I said, remembering in that instant that I'd said this same thing when Lola left. When we'd fired Lola, Paul had made the decision. The school director told us to and we followed along.

"I promise." I'd make it be true.

Will cried himself out, Paul stood up, and it was still the morning

327

of the first day. We got into Paul's car and drove to the new house. We parked and stood outside on the damp lawn. Paul had rented a good, family-looking house on a wide street. "Should we go in?" I whispered, but Paul motioned that he thought it would be better if we had lunch first. We had to be at the field an hour before Will's game. We went to a place that had been our favorite for a few years then and that, after that day, I never stepped inside again. They made a pasta we liked and their own ice cream, a different flavor every day. That day was mint, white, not green. It was hard to think of things to say. I felt grateful for the luxury of Paul's car.

I had Will's baseball uniform in my purse. I helped him into the long socks, one leg at a time in the backseat while Paul walked over to talk to the coach.

Then Will ran out onto the field. Simon stood in the cage already, skinny in his catcher's gear, and Bing leaned listless against the fence. Another hot Los Angeles day, the sky a dull white. The assistant coach organized drills. I saw from his posture that Paul was having words with the coach.

"They've got him pitching." Paul shook his head, landing next to me on the bleachers. "It's too much stress. But the coach already told him at practice. He's afraid it'd be worse if now he tells him he can't. If he can't concentrate, he'll pull him out."

We sat in the stands together. As the game started, we cheered along with the others. Across the field, Jeff and Helen came carrying coffees, both wearing white shirts. For a while, I thought I could have loved him. I bit the inside of my lip. What do I do with that? He looked over at us, raised an arm. Did he know he'd lifted my hopes? Did he care?

He was reckless and she was impervious, cleaning up the street before their own house, as best she could.

"Hey, I want to ask you about pianos," he said. "I want to buy a really good one."

"What for?"

"I want Bing to take lessons eventually; who knows, maybe Helen'll learn."

Next to me sat Paul, whom I couldn't quite love. I had once. Where had that gone?

We watched the slow tense game. The sky had turned an opaque blue. In the last inning, Will struck out two batters. The next kid hit a line drive and skidded into second. Then Will pitched balls. The coach slowly pushed out the pitching machine to the mound and conferred. The next batter smacked the ball hard and high and Will ran backward and caught it.

Paul looked at me standing, his face his face, then suddenly moving. The waves a rope makes when you swing it up and down. He held me. "He's going to be all right."

The other boys ran out and lifted Will on their shoulders. We hovered around the kids. Pizza and Cokes with the team made dinner. We stayed until the end. Then we drove to what would now be Mommy's house to get my car. We'd asked Will if he wanted a sleepover with Daddy the first night. Paul's mother had flown in two weeks ago; his sister had sent housewarming gifts. An aunt, the mother of the newly-wed cousin, gave an Oriental rug. Here it all waited: towels in the guest bathroom, pajamas already in the Pottery Barn Kids dresser, the rooms better decorated than our places had ever been. He'd proven that even at the few small things I'd tried, he excelled. He'd taken one of my ratty treasures for Will's room. A map of the fifty states marked with their native birds I'd once salvaged from a Dumpster.

Paul had rented a movie for them to watch.

I left while it was still light. I couldn't exactly breathe when I stepped outside. Everything turned unreal in the flat California light. Had I made this?

I stood outside, looking at his solid, complete house.

When Lola left, no one had asked anything. The difference had been profound but private, like the end of an affair that turned out to be the love of your life. Separation turned out to be extremely public.

For a day, I made myself sit by the phone and call the moms.

"Wow, gosh, I really wasn't expecting this. From you guys, I mean. D'you guys ever think of seeing a therapist?"

I heard the cranky melody *all around the mulberry bush* under the voices, *POP* when I got to hang up.

The kindest mother turned out to be Cheska, Simon's babysitter. "Do you want we do something?" she said. "We will help. Sure."

I called everyone on my list. That was the evening of the second day.

I bought a mitt and tossed the ball to the boys during practice, learned the arcane hieroglyphs of scorekeeping. I loved watching from the bleachers; you could see our boys improve, week to week, from barely being able to hold the ball to moments of offhand grace. That's the way I'd felt once upon a time with Paul, the way family life should be, I supposed—effort, applause, small improvement, a feeling of inevitable advance. One day, Simon's father came at the end of practice, still in his suit and tie. Cheska shouldered Simon's backpack to go home and start dinner, and he took her place on the bleachers.

"How you doing?" he asked.

"M'kay," I said. "How are you?"

He told me he was working to finish the albums Melissa had started, on a table in the partners' conference room. He was trying to do them the way she would have. "But there's a real break. You can see the difference." He shook his head.

Eventually, I saw those albums. Cheska showed them to me. Melissa had done them by year, and at the bottom of each page, she'd written a sentence in a beautiful slanted hand.

Will was in three pictures. Bing was in many. I wanted Will to be in more.

Just then, practice ended, and the boys all pressed around Will. He'd just gotten a cell phone, the first. The moms looked at me: the woman who'd said no to soda, no to Game Boy, no to Nintendo had bought her son a cell phone.

I whispered, "When you divorce, the first thing the kid shrink says is *Get him a cell phone*."

Beth Martin grumbled, hauling Brookie's heavy bag to the parking lot.

"You can have a cell phone," her voice carried, "if I can get a divorce."

"Are you still in the same house?" Sue asked me, collecting China's mitt, visor, and knee guards in the slow-gathering dusk.

I nodded. Was that something you'd ask a married woman?

That was Five Pitch in 1996.

At Little League, a year later, she asked me the same question.

By the time Will started All Stars, I thought of it as her refrain.

The human condition, Paul said.

He could still make me laugh.

Lola

DATE. AN AMERICAN WORD

The month Laurita will turn four, my employer comes home carrying bags: clothes, makeup, everything wrapped in tissue. She plunks down these riches on the kitchen table, looking defeated. "I have a date," she says.

Laurita and I glance at each other. I had given up on that.

Date. An American word. There is no such thing in our language. It would not happen the same in Asia. We have romance, of course, but even that, in our place, it is more serious. Still, good if my employer can give Laura a mother-father home.

Then some-a-day Lola can leave.

"When do we see this prince?"

"Friday night."

We will have to help her use the purchased magic. Judith jokes that I am her how-to manual. I put on my glasses to read the instruction booklets for the paints and glitter. But we will need demonstration.

I take Laura to the cosmetics counter of a department store.

"We would like to enroll," I tell the lady. We sit on high chairs and watch her work the tiny pots of improvement. See how beauty hides in money. Like everything American, it seems unnatural, but it makes the race more fair. The lady paints with little brushes. I do it there at the counter twice to get used to the powder for the caves around the eyes. At the end, I offer her five dollars. She taught us almost an hour. "For tip," I say.

She pushes it away. "My job. It's a slow afternoon."

I am grateful when someone is kind to me in front of Laura.

Friday, we make a party. Every item Judith owns is out on her bed, over the chair, or hanging on a doorknob. We pick a skirt. The blouse, I am the one to open buttons. We brush on eyeliner, puff the powder. We have become experts.

But the Prince does not come to the door. In our country, a suitor will arrive to meet the family. After Judith leaves, in her own car, we turn on music and hang up everything, so it will be her room again, the same. Then I seat Laura before the mirror and paint her face, dab perfume. When I put her to bed she is laughing.

I wait up. After eleven, I hear the door creak, then water in the pipes. I go to the kitchen and open the refrigerator to make a noise. But her light stays off. The next morning, she talks on the phone until we leave for ballet.

Back home, I say, "It is twelve hours and you have not yet told us the date."

"It was okay," she says. "I don't know. I guess I'm out of practice."

The birthdays of Laura, they are my doing. There is no Claire to bake the cake. But we invite the ones Laura likes from her class, two neighbors, and the Chinese Adopteds. We have ice-cream cake, princess favors, and games; we experience the air of a party. If you work for someone who makes from-scratch cupcakes, with ruffled frosting, and on top each one a pansy, it is different. Here we huff, blowing up balloons. (At my weekend employer, the balloons came delivered, the long satin ribbons tied to make a bouquet.)

"The mother of these, she is not the one going to playdates either," Lita says. "She works in the hospital long days."

"But, anyway, your two. They are easy."

"You know where she is today? I have to laugh. Till eight, nine o'clock at night in Chinatown, and here she lets her own, Chinese also."

But this no longer sounds to me a joke. All the time I planned for Parent Association parties in Tagaytay, I am doing more now. More than when I had Williamo too.

Lita shakes her head. "Did you hear about your former employers? Lot of trouble. Divorce maybe."

"He is depress again?" Maybe Alice left him. If she is not moping anymore. Lita says she is older now, sadder, but in a straight line.

"No, I am talking Claire, the mommy of Williamo."

They are divorce now too! That is what they all do here. In the Philippines we cannot; we are Catholic. But I do not want to hear this from Lita.

I shrug. "He work so much anyway. Why they have to divorce?"

I think of the table where Claire and I sat, after the day was over, to say, *Well, we did our best,* one more time, Paul gone, Williamo asleep in his bed that I every morning made.

The girls stand, doing fast claps with their hands.

I went downtown
To see Charlie Brown
He gave me a nickel
To buy me a pickle
But the pickle was sour
So he gave me a flower
But the flower was dead
And this is what he said.
Icky icky bubble gum
Icky icky ewwww
Icky icky bubble gum
A boy loves you.

At the "icky" part, they jumping jack.

Alice arrives for the pickup, dressed like an older woman, the style of my mother, with clear nylons. Lita tells me that the grandmother is Altadena head librarian. Every spring, she sends Alice and each the Chinese Adopteds one hundred dollars to buy a new dress. Until now, she still sends. Alice, she has no idea that I am the one who stole the letter that saved her marriage and talked Lita out of quitting all these years.

I ask Judith, "So will we be needing again the magic powders?"

"That's a good question," she says.

"More than one week already," I say. "He did not call?"

"Oh, he called."

"Imagine," I say, sweeping the kitchen. "Eight years already, I am working seven days, with no off." For a moment I forget Judith is my employer.

But she looks down at my broom as if she sees a rodent scuttling across the floor, thinking, Lola, does she want more from me?

No, I do not want more. I understand she has done her job too. She is the one to worry the mortgage and tuition. On holidays, she gives me one and a half times pay. Two different occasions, she pressed a roll of cash in my hands, damp hundred-dollar bills and twenties mixed, I could not tell for any reason. Some surge of gratitude, maybe. A person from the school of Laura or at her work said something kind. My employer is a person who, every once in a while, needs her cry. My youngest is like that; certain animals, they are weaker. With Judith you can watch it build. Nothing is good enough anymore. She begins to move in circles, fast steps; *things have to change around here.* After, the world sparkles, rinsed for her; that is when she will give me a handful of money.

"Lola, I need to talk," she says. "After Laura's asleep."

During the bath, I worry, is my job still safe?

I find Judith at the kitchen table with a stack of papers. "Lola, I'm making my will. I have it now so if anything happened, Laura would go to my mother, but she hardly knows her. I'd need you to stay."

"You want that I will go to Minnesota?"

"I'm taking out a life insurance policy that would pay your salary. With a three point five percent raise every year."

I never tell Bong Bong that on a legal document, I have given away our future.

Here I am working for things I did not think about with my kids. My kids, they had too many friends. Friends I had to limit, like sweets. *You are preventing me!* my eldest screamed a night I dragged her out the neighbor house for homework.

I ask Laura what girl she likes best. "Raime, I guess," she says, "and Georgia." I have observed Raime. She is not a good choice for us. So I call the mother of Georgia, and she says yes. She will bring Georgia to our place.

Saturday morning, I feel nervous. Like my employer, I am out of practice. What will I do with the mother? I need Judith to meet and greet—the two could sit, talk about the school, and I can take the girls. I hint for Judith to stay.

"Oh, Lole, I need my yoga today. Can you just handle the play-date?"

What will I say? She is paying me. "I'll be back," Judith calls, carrying her rolled-up purple mat. We take out LEGOs. The dress-up box. A small trampoline I got for the birthday waits clean-hosed on the front lawn. I have ready peeled carrots and yogurt, for a healthy snack. I dig out the recipe for homemade Play-Doh Claire wanted me to prepare. This girl and her mother, they will come to a far neighborhood, and no parent home, just a babysitter. How does that look? All the handmade touches I refused Claire (at that time I thought I was too busy) I do here by myself.

The doorbell rings. There they stand: the two. The mom pushes the back of Georgia. As if by signal, the girls run into the room of Laura. The mom looks around. Roses I cut from the yard open in a jar. Her arms pretzel as she examines bookshelves. She glances inside the empty bedrooms where I already made the beds. Then she walks into the room of my employer! She would not do that if Judith were the one here.

The bedroom of my employer, I only go in to sweep or when I carry a stack of new-washed clothes to put in drawers. Sun makes rectangles on the floor. The unused room in the house, holy from quiet, in the day no one, at night only Judith sleeping.

"Would you like coffee?" I say, to herd her back where she belongs.

"She's not working is she, on a Saturday?"

Is it better if Judith is working? I really do not know. When this woman picks up, Judith could return, wearing yoga clothes, with her rolled-up purple mat. I copy something I have seen babysitters do before; I just do not answer. She will think either I did not hear or do not understand. I pour her coffee; offer milk and sugar. Then I make an excuse of bringing beverages to the kids.

Georgia sits with her legs open, building; she is all on that. Laura keeps hauling out other things from the closet to show. But I must return to the mother.

"They okay in there?"

"Yes, they are playing good."

Maybe she usually talks with the other mother. Or maybe we live too far to go and then come back. I wait a few minutes, then, when it is too quiet, I say, "I will shape the Play-Doh with them. We can bring Georgia home later on or she can stay for dinner if she wants."

"I'll just read my book here if that's cool," she says.

"Oh yes, of course." I refill her coffee. She takes from her bag a thick paperback.

I am not used to being observed. I nudge the door shut with my rubber shoe. Georgia sits intent upon the built world between her legs. She deliberates, then adds another piece. Laura might as well not be in the room. She looks at me full of longing, so happy to have captured Georgia, here touching the things she uses herself alone, but she does not know how to make it be more. And she wants. That is the thing about this girl.

"Okay, you two, I have Play-Doh. We can form statues, jewelries."

Georgia does not move. "Oh, Georgia, look at what you built. I do not think we ever made towers that high."

Pretty soon I have them taking turns rolling. They compare ice-cream flavors, which they like, with which topping. Three girls in the class have the same kind of shoes but different colors. Hours of my life pass this way: the voices of children saying what they like, comparing. I forget the woman in the kitchen. Laura is a happy bird. The girls cut Play-Doh hearts. I have to wire money home; there are extra expenses for Issa. I will ask Judith for an advance. My youngest a doctor. On the floor all of a sudden it hits me.

"You're poop," the playmate says to my Laura.

I shove up to stand. I want to throw her out, but I remember the mother in the other room. These women, they will talk. Laurita, she is laughing. *Stop,* I want to tell her.

"And you're pee-pee!"

"No, I'm poop and you're pee-pee." This makes them both giggle, high chains of noise. So it is back and forth. Okay.

When we return to the kitchen to bake the Play-Doh, the mother puts away her book. While I make grill-cheese sandwiches, she starts them sifting flour for a brownie she knows how. Judith still does not return. I never thought before, but she has me so she can just go— a way no one with kids can. It is dark already when she walks in with her mat. Our dinner plates cleared, we are eating brownies.

"Here's one for you, Mommy." I want to knock down the plate. What has she done to deserve! But my employer sits in her throne— the mother—and talks about the assistant teacher the way I wanted her to hours ago.

After Laura goes to bed, I will ask my advance.

That Wednesday, I receive a call from Deb, the mother of Georgia. So Laurita will now have a friend.

Georgia invites Laura for a sleepover at the end of the school year. Deb will pick them from school on Friday and she will stay whole night.

"Oh-oh, Lole, I've got plans Friday," Judith says. "And sometimes they don't make it through the first time. You may have to go get her."

So Friday afternoon I stay home. The house, it is clean already. I arrange the toys, the hair bands, and things small small. I subtract my checkbook. Then I am done that. I fix drawers. I think of calling home, but too many parts of my life Bong Bong, he does not know. I feel tired to explain. His letters have changed; I read a twang of complaint in them. In one year, Issa will graduate. We already paid the first installment tuition. The house, it will be painted this summer. The second time. Usually, in our lives, I supply for him the answer to the question he cannot ask. But this time I keep quiet.

I take the colander to the sink and rinse a lettuce. I am eating already like an American. I watch TV news, switching channels. I read *California Examiner,* and then already, it is ten o'clock. She must be sleeping. The phone, it will not ring anymore. But I remember from my own children, sometimes middle of the night, one staying over would wake up crying. In our place, I could walk to the other house, open the door, and lift out mine.

I measure hot chocolate. I have never made just for me. Exactly when I do not want, Judith walks in, to see me stirring in milk the expensive powder. She will think I use for myself every day. But she is happy tonight—I can tell from her shoulders.

"What has happened? You met a prince at Fox Studios?"

"No, but I saw a good movie, for once," she says, taking off her jacket. She peeks into the lit room of Laura. "She still out?"

"The phone did not ring."

"Good for her." Judith takes a banana and peels. "She's really made a friend."

"Now Lola has to make a friend too." I say it to get a laugh, but it has been a long time only working. "Did you eat?" I take from the refrigerator leftovers, give her a plate, a fork, and napkin.

Claire

THE COMET OF 1999

"You still in the same place?" Sue asked me, in the parking lot. Small planes zoomed overhead. The baseball diamond was in a park that had once been a McDonnell Douglas plant, just south of the tiny Santa Monica Airport.

Bing had invited Will to his house for supper, so they climbed into the back of Helen's van and I shouldered his bag to take home. I called to Helen that I'd pick him up in a couple of hours.

It was a warm night, still light out. Soup waited on the stove. I'd already set the table, but I wasn't so hungry. I stood outside a moment, to shake off the sadness that overtook me whenever Will was away. The ocean, in the distance, was a clear deep blue, the waves breaking evenly. Japanese pines, planted on the cliff, seemed not to move at all. Then I ladled a mug of soup and carried it upstairs and sat down at the piano barefoot. Even though I was teaching more now and worried about money, it felt easier to work.

After an hour, the doorbell rang. Paul. We still talked every day; you do if you have a kid together. My old self had come back—the downs but the highs, too, sometimes over nothing but the sound of a human voice, its stops and implicit melody. Paul had been my Prozac.

There he stood at my door, the beginnings of gray in his hair.

"Got out early for once and thought I'd stop by and see him."

"He's at Bing's. You want to go there?"

"No, I'll leave him. How that going? With Bing?"

I shrugged. "Okay, I think. Baseball helps."

"He's staying for supper? Well, you want to have dinner?"

"Sure. I have soup. I can make a salad." Most often when we ate together now, it was in my kitchen, when he came to drop off Will.

340

I still fed him. He still got up right away when he was done. But I didn't mind anymore.

"Let's go out, in an an hour or so. I'll run home and take a shower."

"Like a date," I said.

"Yes, Claire, like a date."

In the restaurant, we gossiped about Helen and Jeff. Talking about them, we remained loyal to each other. When we'd first separated, Helen had arranged herself lavishly in Jeff's arms, laughing up at him, in deliberate tableaux of intimacy. I supposed since she'd confided in me, she'd wanted to be clear: there was nothing deeply wrong with *their* marriage. Maybe divorce seemed contagious. But I'd heard the rumors about Jeff and Alice. Beth Martin said that it had gone on for years. *Years,* she'd repeated.

Paul shook his head. "He told me he couldn't leave the marriage, he'd tried. But he said Alice was his great love." He put his glass down. "So. Are you dating?"

"Not really. How about you?"

"I tell people not to fix me up, and every time I go to a dinner, there's a single woman in her thirties seated next to me."

"Well, that sounds good, I guess."

"It does *sound* good, doesn't it?"

On the way home, he said, "I should have done more with Will while we were married."

Fluids moved under the skin of my face. Was he apologizing? I didn't know.

"We were something," he said.

"I'm still trying to figure out what."

When Paul left he did a little twirl, then waved, his hand behind his back.

Paul runs now. He reads. His house felt like a certain kind of hotel, sunny, stylish, but where I knew all the smells. The last time we'd run together, I took a shower in his bathroom. After, I dressed in his closet and put on a pair of his boxers under my skirt.

After he left I called Helen. The boys were fine. They were talking about a sleepover, but it was a school night. She said she'd call when their movie was over.

I turned to my table in the dining room, where I had the photos spread out.

We hadn't taken that many pictures. All of ours filled up just one album and that included quixotic pages, like the ones Lola had snapped of our party meals.

I finally started putting together our wedding album, for William. I wanted him to know that he was started in love.

The phone rang at ten.

I went to get Will from Helen's and we walked home in the dark. When we looked up from our street, we saw the comet of 1999. Will didn't want to go in and so I brought him a blanket. I made hot chocolate, and when I carried the mugs out, it was still there, brighter than the Los Angeles lights and the surrounding stars, its tail a bright white blur.

Lola

THE PHILIPPINES, MY PHILIPPINES

I read in a magazine Aleph Sargent said girls should buy jewelries for themselves, so I turn into a car dealership to take a tour. For my birthday, last day August, my kids each sent cards. Bong Bong made an ink drawing of our house. But this year I want a bigger gift. Silver Toyota RAV. Very cute. I set up the paperwork while Laurita plays with Georgia, and then I drive in it to pick her. Until now, I had the same used Honda the ex of Natalie found when I started with Laura. When Natalie first married that guy Ruth cried because he was only a mechanic, but that car he picked, it still runs. I can sell it to the slave. Ruth says she still does not want that anyone will see her eat; for her it is the same as people watching in the bathroom. Maybe I will just give it. I can afford.

Laura and I drive to Starbucks to celebrate, and there I see my old employer.

"You got a new car!" Claire says.

Filling out the paperwork for my loan, I did not think of my old employer seeing. "My kids in jobs, all but one married, my youngest doctor next year. Their school is paid. So"—I shrug—"enjoy your life."

"Will you go home, then?"

She still wants me out! If I am not working her, I should be off-shore. I used to tell Williamo I would return to the Philippines. *I will sit in my hammock.* But Laura, she looks up for my answer. "I will have to stay here. Who will make the payments for my car?"

"It's sad. All of you here without your husbands."

Maybe she does not want to tell me the divorce. I make a joke so she will understand I know. "People ask how we stay married so long.

It is because he is in the Philippines and I am here. To live with a husband, that is very difficult."

In the kitchen we tiled white, chopping, the window open over the sink, cricket noises lifting in—that was the two of us. I have questions about Williamo, but then she might ask for Laura and I do not want people gossiping. So I ask about her music. That was always an important topic that she could only talk with a hush. But today it is seems she had been waiting for me to ask.

"Oh. Well, I'm collaborating with a chamber group in Glendale. They're performing a new piece of mine next month. I'm here working." She lifts her paper with the notes, one-flag notes, two-flag notes. She taught me once, how to read the key signature. I still know that. Some-a-day I will teach to Laura. I am saving already to buy her piano.

That same day, on the way home, I lose a tooth. Just sixty, first new car, silver. An adult tooth. That will never come back.

"You need the tooth fairy," Laura says. "Too bad you are her."

A Friday night in October, Judith calls to say goodnight to Laura. "It'll be a late one, Lole," she says and she is still not home at ten. I check the girls—I have Georgia too for sleepover—and close the lights. I try to sleep, but my employer sometimes lets the door unlocked. After she is in bed, I always check. In a dream, I ride waves, a deep, pleasurable sleep, but then I push up, cover myself with a robe. I want to go back, but the worst is true. At the room of Judith, the door is open, the bed still tight. The window I leave for her to close hangs at a slant, the screen black, noises point in from outside.

Should I call police? It is after one in the morning. I have two girls asleep in the other room. But what if something happened Judith? The grandmother is old. Maybe she will get sick, and I will have to take care her too.

Judith said she would be late. But what if she had accident? Her car, it is too small. I think of Judith broken, by the side of the road, in the black skirt and purple blouse she wore this morning. At this hour, it seems unfair that she should have to be the breadwinner, Judith in those flimsy clothes. I make a deal. I will not call police, only hospitals. I am on hold with Cedars-Sinai—they ask the type of car—when I hear tires. I run to my room and shut the door. But I have seen the picture of the tight-made bed, a breeze running loose in the empty room.

At seven, I am up making pancakes when I hear her shower. But she does not come out. Laura runs there to say goodbye before ballet, and after, we come home to an empty house. That night, Judith walks in with her mat and I understand I will never learn what happened. We eat and then she takes Laura on Rollerblades while I clean.

Two weeks later, I am waiting again. After midnight, I hear the lock, then footsteps. The refrigerator sighs open. A pop and then voices. His and hers.

What is this? I feel like a mother hearing what I should not hear—the romance of my children. Glasses ring, I pick out words, never a whole sentence, and I fall asleep, but only lightly. A thin blanket over me. Too soon in the cold, I wake up to check the door. When he left, maybe she forgot to lock. I walk through the kitchen—yes, this is the back of romance, crumbs over the counter, eggs left on a plate; ants will come. Two-thirty. I check the door. See! It is unlocked! How many hours already! Somebody could have come in. And Laura sleeping.

Even my children, when they had parties, they knew to put away food. Olives spoil on the table. I pour wine down the drain, scrape eggs into the garbage. Laura and Judith will sleep straight; noises do not wake them. As I wash, I tick off the areas: to the right the sink, the counter, wipe the table down. I will have to sweep. There are crumbs and a lump of cheese on the floor, and then my eyes hit something. Shoes. One next to the other, facing forward. He left his shoes! Then I hear a slow run of water in the loop of pipes. He is still inside! Do I go in my room and pretend sleep? Then her door opens, and it is a man stooping down to pick up shoes.

He walks like that across the floor, diagonal, bent over. Out the front.

I keep doing what I am doing, because I know how. A little more, a little more, until done. Is this their romance? What of courtship? Did not the mother tell her?

There will be no courtship now.

But it is backward here. After Christmas, Judith calls from the car to say, have Laura with the hair in the black headband, for the three of them to go out. That Sunday, he brings Chinese food, so many bags they gave eight pair chopsticks. No florist deliveries. Only him.

With each daughter, I hoped for a doctor or lawyer. Instead I got a tilapia farmer, a manager, and an engineer. This one, he is never married. Maybe he is okay.

The night of the first sleepover, when Judith came in loose armed, that was the start of Allen. Now, he stays. In the morning, he goes jogging and then returns to shower. The house, after him, it has a different smell. I drive Laura to school and do my shopping, so when I come home he will be gone and I can open windows. Her room, it is not holy anymore.

Today the principal from the school of my children will eat at my table. Here on a tour of America, the old nun had to skip Disneyland to see me.

"Now your president is scrubbing toilets," I say. She knew me when I was more. President of the Parents Association, five terms.

"You are still the president to me," she says. "Anyway, we are all servants." She means servants of God, but to be a mother, that is service also. Then she tells me news of my officers: my treasurer died of kidney, my secretary has gone fat, and my vice president is now living in Saudi. Mothers she names wish me well; the one who washed the blankets pesters her, Will Lola ever come home? She tells me about the fund-raising drive, then asks, "What has your life been here?"

I tell her the children I took care. Williamo, my first, who juggles. Bing, the whistling baby. And now Laura. She can hula for almost half an hour and not only the waist; she can do also the neck and the arms. I tell her about Aileen. We talk until it is time for me to get Laura; then I drive her to the hotel. At her age, almost ninety, we may never meet again. She will not return to American soil. "Once in a lifetime," she says.

"I will go back in oh-six for my class reunion," I say. "The fiftieth. I am the only one working domestic." But six years. That is a long time for her.

She blesses me on the forehead, the chest, left, right.

That night, on our knees, I explain to Laura: *Lola, Inday, Nanay,* and *Ate.* Williamo, he never asked that. To this day, he does not know my given name.

When I was living in my own language, in my house in the Philippines, I did not have to think where I was, but I never knew how to pray. That is something I gained here. It started around the time I began to hear Spanish. Esperanza taught me words one by one, and then we hooked them together. She invited me to her swearing in. I would like to attend, but it is too far. A city courthouse in Arcadia. But she will now become U.S. citizen. One day long ago, falling in line at Whole Foods behind two housekeepers, I understood what they were saying. A minute later, I remembered they were talking in Spanish. The same thing happened praying. I tried to teach Williamo words Tagalog. With Laura, we kneel down next to her bed.

Lola is grandma.

Yaya for nanny.

Ate, older sister, she can say for the Chinese Adopteds.

Tita for auntie, she will use with Lucy. Lita.

Inday, little sister—she can call the younger girls at school.

They are names but they are not exactly names. They are positions. I do not teach her *kuya* or *tatay.* Then we say together the rosary. *Aba Ginoong Maria, napupuno ka ng grasiya.* Sometimes we pray for *bago. Bago* means new. *Bagong* car, *bagong* life.

Something restless roams in the mind of Bong Bong. I feel him rambling around our house. We made the final payment to Far Eastern. Now it is different than the other times; he has been waiting too long. We were fine before. We had to be. My working here was necessary, for more important things than our lives. Now we have the American problem of choice. He wonders if the answer I am not telling is *forever.* I always said to the other babysitters, *I hope my Bong Bong is faithful.* Because I knew he was. But this time I think, Go. Use your life. I am not there. I cannot be.

While we move in the boxes of Allen, I remember the night of the date. Then I thought almost any decent guy would be better for Laura. But at seven o'clock, he says, *Isn't it her bath time, Lola? Shouldn't she be getting ready for bed?*

And Laurita and I angeled over Judith, sitting cross-legged before the door mirror, putting on her fairy powders and glitter.

After six weeks, Judith stomps into my room and says they would like me to iron his shirts.

"I cannot iron," I say.

"Lola, Laura's in school all day now. From eight until two."

Laurita has been in school three years already! I do not answer. The next day I take Laura without saying goodbye.

But that night Judith returns. "Lola, the budget is tight, and we hope you can do your part. We really need you to do a little ironing."

Well, why is the budget tight? Before, Judith paid all. Now there are two. I have not received a raise. They stay long time at the table, and I clean twice, first from Laura and my dinner and then theirs. But I cannot ask my employer why her boyfriend will not help. In our place, even a cousin boarding, she will chip in. Buy an equipment. I have not seen any new machine here.

"I never iron," I say. "My own clothes, they have wrinkles. See. Like Lola."

Wednesday, we have an appointment with the developmental pediatrician. Once every year we come to this office. The tests they have changed, from stacking blocks, simple puzzles, and raising the left arm, to a paper portion, and then the doctor checks her reflexes, her strength. The first time here, in the waiting room, a boy banged his head against the wall again and again; I thought we were embarking on a train, Laura and I, taking us far from what we knew.

When the door opens today, though, Dr. Hallian smiles. "A-plus report card, Lola. We'll see her again in two years."

"So we have graduated?"

The doctor looks at me. "She's a success story, Lola. You've done an amazing thing."

I feel glad with this in my pocket. But when we arrive home, Judith calls from the bedroom, "Where've you guys been? You're late." She has forgotten again the appointment, even though it is written on the calendar I put every month on the refrigerator door. After Allen moved in, the Winnie-the-Pooh magnet we had used since Laurita was a tiny girl was replaced one day with a plain steel one that looks like a bolt, no picture of anything. Winnie-the-Pooh, he must have taken and thrown far away, because I could not find him anywhere. (After a party once, at the house of Claire, I recovered a missing fork in the alley garbage can, but I never found this magnet again.)

I wait to tell my employer alone what Dr. Hallian said. Allen, he will not understand.

But in my bedroom a large Mexican pushes an iron not ours back and forth over the board. "This is Marta." Judith explains, she works housekeeper for a guy at her job, she does not speak much English, but she can give me a lesson. "Just watch her. She can go over it as many times as you need." After this, Judith turns and clacks out, leaving me with this woman in my room that smells metal. Steam puffs out of the iron. She keeps smiling at me and then nods down at the board. I sit on the bed, in this house where I painted with Laura every wall and every ceiling and every trim, and decide, as she goes back and forth her whole arm pumping over the sleeve of his shirt, then shaking it out, careful, with the peak of the iron to dainty his collar, No, I cannot, I will go.

Late the next night, a piece of paper comes sliding under my door. A poem.

Ode to Ironing

Poetry is white:
it comes from the water covered with drops,
it wrinkles and piles up,
the skin of this planet must be stretched,
the sea of its whiteness must be ironed,
and the hands move and move,
the holy surfaces are smoothed out,
and that is how things are made:
hands make the world each day,

fire becomes one with steel,
linen canvas, and cotton arrive
from the combat of the laundries,
and out of light a dove is born:
chastity returns from the foam.

—Pablo Neruda

I keep this folded in my pocket, with the letter from my former employer, where I once carried the soul of China. I was going back and forth. The poem tears me.

I love Laurita.

But I love myself too.

In *The Book of Ruth*, I promised I would not leave until Laura became five. Last September, when she turned five, I change that to eight. It made my hourglass. But there are other clocks. Before, when I came from the Philippines, I had a number in pesos: nine million. Later on, my dreams unfurled in English. But I always planned that after I hit that number, first in pesos, then in dollars, *ding,* right away, I would return. I came when my youngest was just starting, and medicine in our country it is ten years. Even at the beginning, my goal was a success; to have a daughter accepted by Far Eastern. Every year, the tuition increased, one year there was a big jump, but before Laura enters kinder in fall, I will achieve my ambition. Issa, my baby, graduates FEU. Dr. Issa. They want me to attend for the taking of the oath. *You have to come because you are a part of that,* Issa says. *The money you sent.*

I did not think I could go, but now I will. "I cannot say no to my last," I will tell Judith. But I am afraid Laura. They Xerox that poem from a book, though. He probably stood at the copy machine, telling the other lawyers, laughing at me. I go forward trudging against what I want. I love Laurita, it is true. I worry her.

"Your Lola is going away," I finally admit. "But only for two weeks."

"If my Lola is going then I will go too."

"No, I cannot take you. You have school. That is the law. Besides, you belong to your mother."

My third daughter and her husband waited to have the church wedding. Bong Bong and I, we will celebrate our fortieth, the ruby, renewing our vows. I describe to Laura the party, the dress, the attendants (the same ones we had the first time, another couple we hardly know anymore). For our colors, we select silver and ice blue. My daughters will buy the dress, hire the photographer, and order the cake. From Hallmark, Bong Bong gets invitations free. "My sister, she will pay," I tell Judith. "*Because I will never experience that,* she said, *I want that you will have.*"

"That's sad," Judith says, "for her, I mean."

"No, she has her divorce club. They are now in Alaska on a singles' cruise."

"You are leaving me," Laura says.

"I will return. See. I will give to you the keys for my car."

She throws them against the wall we painted yellow.

I call Lucy to fill in for me, but she cannot. At the end of our talk, she cries. "Lola, it is really hard. I am so tired." Ruth gives me Candace. Candace has had jobs, but something always goes wrong; now Ruth keeps her home for a pet.

So I have everything prepared. When I am gone, they will see— like the employers of Esperanza. After I return, maybe they will not say anymore about ironing. But Friday night, after Laura is asleep, Judith says, "Now that we're alone, Lola, we can talk. I'm kind of assuming once you get back home, you'll want to stay there."

"I return the twenty-first," I tell her. "Four in the afternoon, my flight lands."

She looks at him.

"Well, maybe it's time for a change," he says.

"With Laura in school all day, maybe this job's not enough challenge," Judith says. "You always liked having a baby."

"You've helped her," he says. "And now I think the job's done."

"What you mean? You will not be needing me anymore?" The job done! Laura, she is five years old. Issa, my youngest, she is thirty, graduate medical school, and my job is not yet over.

They sit there. But this is too fast.

"We thought with your daughter finishing school and everything, you might be happier there. Laura's settled now. We'll move into someone more a housekeeper. And I'm thinking of cutting down my hours at work."

Now I am stuck. More than five years, almost six I have taken care this girl. Every day did the exercises. Worried over what girls she plays with, steered her to the better ones, and helped her see the good in them. I just now realize that I love this. And tomorrow I will be packing again. I thought this was my last home. He is the one who ruined us.

The hardest minute of my life is when I have to tell Laura.

"Your mother and I talk and I will be going. But-ah, you and me, we will still be buddy buddy." It is like she is made of dough: I stuck my finger in and she just falls. Her arms around me hold. I did it. And now cannot take it back. Over the years, she has had many ways to tell me no. For a long time, she screamed, she made baby sounds, she thrashed, she kicked, she threw. When she was first mine she would only look at me and now she is back to that. This time she stays quiet. Too quiet. She does not even question. She accepts that she will be unfortunate again.

I tell Judith about the slave. "Laurita says she is okay for her. Ruth will train. Because I gave her my old car, she will work two weeks free. And she is cheaper than Lola. She can even iron."

"We'll see," Judith says. "Marta knows some people too."

Laura keeps at my side, helping me wrap my treasures in newspaper. They have left us alone in the house. She says, "Remember the poison?"

When Judith worries for money, she asks me to pack her lunch. I make like for Laura, with a plastic fork and knife wrapped in napkin. One day, when Laura and I washed the car of Judith, I found one of those old lunches in the trunk, the food grown fluorescent in Tupperware. I put on gloves to sterilize the containers, using tongs I had for bottles when Laura was small small. I made her sit away. I did not want her near bacteria.

"We can poison him," she says.

She opens the closet, where once hung only the clothes of Judith. In a row hang his shirts: gray, blue, white, the colors separate, like a picture in a catalog. I once counted seventy-three. He has me take five or six every week to the Chinese laundry. When they come back, I have to transfer to wooden hangers.

I have a small craft scissors I keep apart from the regular ones, because cutting our chickens dulls the blades. I could use these scissors to snip off one triangle of each collar, the side near the wall. I picture him taking out one shirt, not noticing until he looks in the mirror. Then another. That is the ending to a fairytale.

But I cannot do in real life. I am that much Catholic.

I pay the penalty to change my ticket to give us one week more. My things, I sent already. From my old employer, I have a box of books— the plays of William Shakespeare, abridged for children. I read *Julius Caesar* in high school, but in real life, envy is a not such a problem. Before I used to make Laura push through a chapter book. But now, I want to enjoy our life. In the bottom of the box, I find *Nancy Drew and the Secret of the Clock.* I make hot chocolate, then I am the one to read and she listens. Even after Laura falls asleep, I cannot stop.

I finally understand Lettie Elizande. Because, now, I am depress. I will ask Alice for Prozac. On a scarred pole, under power lines, I saw a thumbtacked sign. ACCENT ELIMINATION. I wrote down the number. I remember Laura, when she was small small, saying, *I losted it.* Maybe I need speech therapy too.

Ruth wants me to partner for an agency. She says there are good jobs, high paying, newborns even, but I do not want to start again. I had my baby. It is time to go, I tell her. But for what? My kids, they are already grown.

My car I sell to Lita, for Tony and Lucy. I touch the oval of my locket and think of Laura, next year in kinder, carrying her backpack. I know all her clothes. I iron on labels with her name. For that, I will iron. I leave open my Wells Fargo account. Once, it was going to be my surprise money home. But my kids, they do not need anything. I purchase an international cell phone plan, so Laura can call me. I let her pick out a tiny orange phone. I will pay from that account. I have more than fourteen thousand. So this is not my good-bye to California.

Judith is the one to take me to the airport. They decided it would be too hard for Laura. Almost six years, Judith and I have lived together; we cooperated, but we are not close. Many times she said things that hurt me. Like in a marriage, those do not go away. They stay stones inside. We made a so-so marriage, like many others, bound for the love of a child. When I first came here I was already a Lola and I was a better Lola than a mom. With mine, I had too much pride in them. I wanted them to be more than I was. I was never a student, only the clown. And when I had my kids, I had to earn money too. I got to be, for this girl, what they call here stay-at-home mom.

At the airport, I tell Judith, she does not have to park.

"You sure? I'm not going back to the office." Now her job, it is more like ordinary work. She says she is thinking of quitting. She has time finally when she no longer needs it. Laura already in school, this fall kinder.

"I am okay," I say, like the kids talk. "My bags, they are not heavy." I wear around my neck the locket from Claire, with a picture of Laura.

"All right, Lole," she says. "Good luck. Thank you for everything."

And that is the end. She thinks this is the last she will see me, saying to herself, *There goes Lola.* I turned her broken baby into a real girl, and now I should go back where I came from, an island of dark millions, all good with kids. But Disney did not draw me. And I refuse to dissolve into sky.

Before, America looked bright, as if our cars and machines in the Philippines were hand-me-downs from here. But now LAX looks like Ninoy Aquino. Birds peck at soiled carpets. I think of Snip; I have been the one to keep him alive. Afraid her mother would forget to buy feed, Laura asked me to take him. But once he left, he could never come back. Bird without green card, I explained. So I bought ten bags bird suet and I taught her to replenish the seeds.

On the plane, I try to remember the video they sent of my house. They fix the upstairs and the garden. The house should be my accomplishment. They will have it that way, like a present. But I wish I were going back to the old.

The Philippines, my Philippines. I imagined this return too many times. The sheds at the airport seem low and old colored. My daughters stand, wearing dresses, their long hair, square at the ends, lifting in breeze. Bong Bong shrugs, a kind man, shy, the same, with lines of worry between the eyes. My son hands me our itinerary he made with the computer. Tomorrow already comes the taking of the Hippocratic oath. I will have to be awake and I cannot complain jet lag. I was supposed to arrive last week.

In our house, I stand in the entrance like a guest. My daughters run upstairs to get the dress. They say they worried, maybe I had become fat. But everything fits. The suit for the reception, the dress for the church. They brush on makeup, comb my hair, fondle. I remember these touches, but faint, like music in an ice-cream truck, far away. It is only afternoon, but I feel tired. Before I left, Lita asked Alice to give pills for me. I take two now with water. And it is a good feeling, going down in this house.

Our daughter, still small, stands with a white coat over her dress, her hair combed out on her back. Her face a little Lola. No holes in the ears, a fine gold chain with a cross, tiny diamond in the center. Virgin. She lifts her slender wrist to say the oath. A very great event. We stand in a courtyard of the hospital, with leafy trees, then high buildings, on all sides. She talks afterward with the other young doctors; they look up at the thousand windows where will be their lives. All the time she was studying, I did not think of her entering the world of the sick. The others come from good families also. Too many wear glasses. They sip punch with the people who paid for them, but they want to go in. Go, I think.

I roam to the hospital gift store to buy an international phone card. Tomorrow, it will be the teacher conference. I have never left this girl— not like my kids. Something I cannot describe—there is no word— I get from her that I cannot live without. I do not want to anymore.

"Do not worry, I still love you," my eldest says, leaving to the law office.

"Still love me. You should love me. What is the 'still'?"

All of them, they have made new habits that are not anymore to them new. In less than one week, I think, this was mistake. There is nothing for me to do here. My kids, they are busy. And I cannot sit still.

My daughter-in-law gives to me her sons. But babies do not talk. My older grandson when I pick him from the school, he does not talk either. They only want what I buy for them. And here, I am spending too much money. I need a coffee in the morning and a chocolate latte in the afternoon. Easy come. A dollar, it is so much here.

I try to join up with my old friends, but the clubs I started, they do not exist anymore. So I make friends the branch librarian. I finish *The Clue of the Whistling Bagpipes*. She gives me more Nancy Drews.

Then it is our anniversary celebration. Five o'clock, in the church, me in my dress, Bong Bong in his Americano, my third daughter, pregnant with her second, says her vows and it is our turn.

"Do you take this man to be?"

"I do," I say, but we did not live together. That is why I do.

The other couple, our witnesses, they have both grown fat. I stay slim because at my age, I am still chasing kids.

Then we go in a limousine to the hotel, full with people I know only the faces. My daughters took trouble to arrange the same center-pieces as at our wedding, but I never liked those. Gladiolas. My mother had picked, without asking me. I was too young—younger than my daughters now. *It is the thought that counts, the intention.* How many times have I said that to Laura? Still, this intention does not seem enough: I am their mother; they should know me. Tents roof the courtyard. Men in white jackets serve grilled squid on banana leaves, but my stomach feels tight.

Our friends, they look the same, but they talk about Manila restaurants, festivals at the church, and the schools of their grandchildren. I answer along, but I do not care. Each family, though, has someone in America—a sister or a cousin or the wife of a brother—and that lifts my attention. Where? I ask. For how long?

They ask me if I am glad to be back as if I have been on a vacation. They ask about Hollywood movie stars. No one asks my job. Maybe they think I am ashamed to work domestic. But they do not know Laura. How can I live here?

Then waiters circulate translucent slices of *buko* pie and a spotlight on the dance floor lockets Lettie Elizande. She traveled from Ilocos Norte to surprise me, she says into the microphone, and brought with her a truck of pies. She toasts us for happiness and long life. That baby she came home for is now grade 3.

All night I only picked at food, I could not touch the tilapia from the farm of my son-in-law, but I eat the *buko* pie. Two pieces. It has a taste I need.

On the way home, I notice, the old trees full and open.

I am reading *The Mystery at Lilac Inn*.

That night, my eyes open in the dark and Bong Bong sits. "Can I talk to you?"

I am surprised. Before he was never the one who wants to talk. But his chest bubbles, sobbing. He has a large basket to give. Rotten fruit.

She is a lady I know from our neighborhood organization, a helper when I was president second term. She took in laundry; she was the one to wash the blankets of the school. This is why she is asking the principal if I will ever come home! Her husband gambled cockfights. She had too hard a life. Actually, she admired me, the way I raised my children. I am almost glad she has for once something good.

"Never until two years ago." His voice catches in the throat. "But the tuition was finished, all but Issa married. I stopped believing you would ever come back."

"Maybe I should not have." I look around at the new walls. "So now what do you want?"

"Everything is over. She knows. I just don't want you to blame her. Blame me."

"Okay, I blame you." But I am joking really. We have been apart too long.

On the phone, Laura says Lola and Bong Bong are like the end of a story the teacher read from Junior Great Books. *The Odyssey Abridged.* I request from our library. It had to be transferred from another branch, but when I finally obtain, I call to tell her, we did not mean to have our lives apart. We had our youth together and those are important years for love. Until now, Bong Bong and I, we talk every other week.

I had to go to America. Once upon a time, the Trojan War maybe, the men went out. But in our life, I was the one who could earn. When I signed up to be a mother, it was already decided. And I was success!

357

In all, I sent home almost a million. Imagine. From taking care kids. Sometimes Bong Bong talked about coming too. But what could a Filipino man do there? "In America you will not be anymore executive Hallmark," I told him. "Here you will be an immigrant. Jobless." And Bong Bong has a good position. Now more than two hundred Filipino greeting cards, drawn by him.

The cousin of Lita told me about her job in California, then I saw the flyer, and we bought the ticket. If someone looks inside, that is the contents of Lola; that I went to America and took care kids. By loving them, I was able to pay the tuitions of my own, so they are now professional class. My children, they will not have to go anywhere. They can stay home. That is what I did for my life. "And I made some women laugh along the way," I say. "America was my adventure. With the other babysitters."

Also, I tell Laura, I am not like the one in her book. I stopped trying to keep everything inside the same. I did not every night unravel. "By the time I came to you, I wanted to move forward, I was no longer waiting."

"I'm glad you're there now," Laura says, "in your hammock."

I do not tell her, but I cannot anymore rest.

The librarian suggests for me other series; I try Sherlock Holmes, but why should I read a drug addict?

On the new arrivals rack, I see a picture of Aleph Sargent, Clarisse on the back, a tree, lipstick painted over bark. *Star Mom: Aleph's Nanny Tells All.* In the first pages I read, *She lies about her age.* The next chapter says that she is always shopping. But it is her money! Why should she not spend? I check out the book to read on the phone to Lita and Ruth.

She said she never slept with him, Clarisse wrote about the first director. *She told me her stepbrother molested her. "I was trying to grow my virginity back at that time."*

But we know Aleph is good, from Jean, next-door Claire. Two years ago, after her husband left, Jean drove her kids to see the snow. It was their first time staying in a hotel. "I just did it," she said, "and we ordered room service if we wanted hot chocolate and cookies. We took cross-country ski class." She held her breath when she went to the counter to pay, but the man said the bill was already taken care of. Aleph had called and put it on her card. Clarisse will never write that in her book.

Coming back from the library, I stop to get the mail and there is a letter. My hands shake. I put the brake on the double stroller of my grandsons. I mumble our little prayer, and then tear it open.

Dear Lola,

I had to take the cell phone away from Laura. After your calls, she can't calm down. She loves you, but she has to adjust to her life, accept Willa and treat Allen with respect. We're working on having another child.

I'm sure you'll understand.

Love,

Judith

I stand in the sun holding that. Every night, before bed, I write Laurita a card, but now I bet he just throws them, like the Winnie-the-Pooh magnet.

So I will stay away. But the voice of Laura, it was so much!

My older grandson looks up at me. There is nothing I can tell.

I want to send her a present, but it has to be small small. I shop for a week, then buy a charm. For the fifth birthday, I bought a bracelet with the state of California. Before I left, we added on an ice-cream cone. Now a tiny Philippines. Fourteen karat.

I send to Claire, ask, will she give it to Laura while Judith is at work? Claire, she still owes me for the chop.

I know Laura will not show to them.

One month I do not hear anything. Then a Wednesday, the phone in the hall rings, an old ring.

"Lola, is it you?" Claire, the world away, with static. "I visited while they were at work. The new babysitter arranged it. Willa. On the phone, she told me, *Laura said, 'I love Judith, but Lola is my mother.'* I went a little after three and the babysitter opened the door. *The mother and him, they are witches, rata,* she said, right away. *I don't love that girl, I don't even like her.* Then I saw Laura. We sat at your kitchen table. Laura wanted ice cream and she went herself and got the box from the freezer. There was a squirt bottle of chocolate. *No, Laura, that's enough,* I said, when the babysitter didn't do anything. The babysitter grinned. *She wants it, she will get it,* she said. *The mother is trying to diet her. Rata,* she said again.

"And, Lola, the mom's right. Laura's put on weight. Her belly and her arms strained the blouse. *She wants it she will get it,* that woman said. Laura put on more and more chocolate, lines like a spiderweb, then just a smeary mess. And she ate it all."

My Laurita.

"She slipped your box in her pocket. I don't know, Lole. You bring her with you to the Philippines, that's the happy ending."

"That I would raise her in my house? The mother would never let me."

"But the mother works all the time."

"I work all the time too. That does not mean I will give to you my children."

"I have to call Judith and tell her that babysitter is no good."

"But the Spanish they are like that. When you chop me, Esperanza said, *See. I told you. It is only a job.*"

"Esperanza works in Funcare now at Will's school."

"Did she every marry?"

"I don't think so. She has a daughter, though. A big girl."

I stand shelving books at our branch library—my friend gave me a fill-in job. Even libraries, they do not keep books forever. I arrange according to a list. Alphabetize on the shelf or take down and put on the cart with wheels for the fund-raising sale.

Someone taps my shoulder, I turn and it is her—Claire, in Tagaytay!

Claire

TAGAYTAY

"So, what you do here?" Lola said.

I told her right away, both of us standing in that branch library. "Judith wants you back. She called me three days ago. I guess she'd quit her job; they'd been trying to have a baby. Then the boyfriend moved out. She has to find work again, but nobody wants D-girls over thirty, she says. The bad babysitter left too. Abandoned ship. *I want to keep the house,* Judith told me. She looked terrible. And actually, before she called, I'd already started writing you a letter, to ask you to come back and help me take care of my mom."

We both still stood there, our legs cooled by a rotary fan. She didn't answer.

"Judith says you can let the house go, forget everything, just take care of Laura. She said to tell you absolutely no ironing. She can't pay you that much, but she says at the end of the year, whatever she's made, you get fifty percent."

"Half-half," Lola said.

"And I was thinking, since Laura's in school till three, you could help my mom in the mornings. You'd make two salaries."

She looked at me. "You come here for something music?"

"No, just to see you." This embarrassed her so I fumbled in my bag. "I have stuff from Cheska to deliver to her kids. I wanted you to know things were dire."

"Come," she said. "I will take you to the house of Cheska. You want a tour?"

"I'm only here two days. Paul took William for the weekend to Las Vegas with guys from the show."

"A long flight for a short stay," Lola said.

361

The stewardess had said the same thing, reading my ticket. *Business or pleasure?*

Neither really. Or, both, I hope.

Next to me on the plane had been two guys, young, a little heavy-set, easy around the jaw. I got a glimpse of one's iBook. Square postage-stamp-sized pictures, one of a tiny brown hand around a large penis. They were taking off on a sex junket.

In an open field, goats and a sign saying GOATS 4 SALE.

"We like to eat goats," Lola said. Chickens roamed the dirt street, dogs chained to slim-trunked trees in front of cinder-block houses barked, and an animal I didn't recognize dreamily grazed. "Caribou." She pointed.

Cheska's house looked hand built, cement, with plywood patches. "Here," Lola tells me, "there used to be trees. India trees." Inside, two teenage boys slouched in a living room with a giant TV, wearing new basketball clothes their mother must have sent. Both studied at University Santo Thomas, Lola said. The eldest boy was handsome, big mouthed. "He plays street basketball under the bridge," she said. "He is a Manila boy."

"Are there Manila girls?"

Their *yaya*, Charita, said something and Lola translated. "No, there cannot be. Cheska tells him, he cannot get married. He has to think of his studies." Charita was small and solid; both still and busy at once. She set down plates to serve us lunch.

"Charita is a mommy to them," Lola said. "Since Butch is one year old. She is from their place. Her mother was the one in the house. Only thing she cannot do is homework. So they always have a cousin boarding. Noli is college graduate."

The college graduate came downstairs just to eat. "She wants to be policewoman, but she is too short. So she is studying criminology."

Then I noticed: *They are wearing my shoes.* Lola always had a box in the corner she was sending home. Charita was wearing moccasins I bought on Melrose one breezy afternoon with my mother, in a store with a brown-and-white-striped awning. "Get 'em," my mother had said, still young. Noli had on my old running shoes. A trainer once told me, *Throw out your shoes the minute the first layer of rubber wears off.* Noli took her plate to the counter and returned upstairs to her books.

Charita said something. "She is telling Butch he will be late for the game."

"I am the star." He grinned, "They will wait for me."

"Where you sleep?" Lola asked. "You will sleep in my house?"

I dug out the slip of paper from my bag, with my reservation.

"Makati, that is where the rich people live," Lola said. "Maybe you invite them to see." She talked to Charita, who giggled, a very high light sound. "She says slippers are not allowed in Makati."

Slippers? The boys wore rubber flip-flops. How can a whole neighborhood ban flip-flops?

"What will Charita do if the boys go to LA?"

"She will just stay in the house."

The jet lag slammed me like another body. I said I could take a taxi to the hotel. Lola talked to Charita in fast Tagalog. "Charita, she is yelling at me, for taking you on the jeepney. You are American. This is a poor country. Too many snatchers."

We rode in a semiprivate cab. In the car with us, two young people bent over their laps, each studying a thick paperback TOEFL. This whole country was studying to get out.

Asia. Here it was. Tall towers. Swarming traffic on narrow roads without lanes. A flashing giant TV-screen billboard: Samsung. A cigarette pack, called USA.

I pulled out a device I'd bought in a stationery store. You could record a fifteen-second message and show a picture. Years ago, Paul had given one to William to carry around. I opened the clamshell to Laura's picture and her voice singing *From a distance . . .*

"Ah, did Judith pay for your ticket here?" Lola said.

"She would have. But she has no money. And I need you too."

"You are rich now?"

"I don't have money either, I just have airline points. Frequent-flier miles."

Three girls strolled by drinking something from rubber-banded Baggies through straws, their arms swinging like girls anywhere.

"Coke," Lola said. "Cheaper, Claire. You do not have to pay the bottle."

In the bed, I fell down into sleep. When I woke, Lola stood waiting to take me to dinner with her family.

We went to a restaurant that could have been in San Francisco. At the table next to us, a beautiful girl in spaghetti straps sat with a nun in full habit.

"I live in the house during the week," Lola's eldest said, in perfect English.

"Who stays with your children while you're being a vice president?"

"The *yayas*," she said. No American woman I knew could say that so simply.

I loved the dessert, called *quinumis*, served in a coconut half. There was a milky coffee drink, sweet, with little flakes and gummy tapioca balls you ate with a spoon.

By the end of the evening, I began to think class here had something to do with hair. Lola's daughters had long, smooth hair, straight, combed out on their backs.

The next day Lola took me to Antipolo, the church they go to, to pray for a good voyage. There, I heard what sounded like a eunuch choir. "Who's singing?"

She pointed to a tiny room, far up on the wall. The old modal scales.

"Paul called," I told Lola. "You know who they saw in Las Vegas? Lucy. She's working in the M&M store."

Alone, I told Lola about my mother, her memory loss.

"It's bad," I said. "She can't find anything. She thinks people are stealing from her."

"Does she still have Tom?" Lola asked.

"Yes. She wants Tom to live with her now. But he says she'd drive him crazy and she would. Every time she uses the sink she wipes the faucet so there are no water drips. He lives with stacks of old newspapers. The guy keeps a pet crow in his dining room."

"Your mother, she is very difficult," Lola said. "I sold my car. I could have a bed at the place of Ruth."

"We have room, Lola. Your old place."

"There with Judith, she will want me live-in."

"So you'll have two salaries. Two rooms. For your weekends. Your offs. You can bring Laura too. I want it to be your American home."

She doesn't answer me.

"So will you come?"

"I will go for Laura if I am needed."

Outside I bought red candles shaped like men and women, made with cookie cutters, thinking like a tourist already. I wrote down the addresses; I'd send American jeans and computer programs for Lola's grandsons, money at Christmas.

FEEL LIFE, it said on a billboard, out the taxi window on my way to the airport. JOLLIBEE. BE HAPPY.

A day later, I picked up William from Paul.

"So Lola's coming back. She'll live with us again," I said. "Sound good?"

He shrugged. "I don't remember Lola."

Lola

MY HOLLYWOOD

I visit each my children. I meet the radiologist asking Issa to the movies. But she says no, she is studying; she wants to pass the test for residency at UCLA. My second youngest, the lawyer, she earns more than her papa, already associate in the firm. She tries to give me her card. I say, *I do not need that. I know your name. I gave it to you.*

"Magmahalan kayong magkapatid, dahil kung wala na kami, walang ibang magtutulungan kundi kayo din." I delegate in advance.

My kids, they are asking me to stay. I say, "Only if you will pay me a salary."

"Okay," my son says. "We will pay you, but your salary it will be in pesos, not dollars. We are five here. Why you are going back for one?"

But Laura is young. Maybe she will still need her Lola.

Because I have been gone a long time.

Really, I don't know why.

I will give Bong Bong to the lady who loves him. He is different than he was to me, unlocked. I could not do that for him. I did not know how. It is okay; because I had my love, too, mine not the shape of romance. But I am old enough to understand it is the same as big, the same as true. And now I love people in two places.

Then, the week before I am scheduled to leave, we watch the plane going into the tower on the television, again and again. "Now you really cannot go," Bong Bong says.

"It is not there I am flying. I live in California," I say. "No one will bomb Hollywood. Even Muslims, they like to watch movies."

"Wanda, look at Mindanao. They do not even want electricity," Dante says.

"But I have nonrefundable ticket." They all stare at me.

America, it is like a drug addiction.

My last day Bong Bong and I amble through our house. Issa lives here also, but she is at the hospital. My son, his wife, and their boys have the second floor, but they are out too. The downstairs, it is worn from years of children. Cracks, fingermarks, leaks—the kitchen, it really needs fixing. But even broken, it is a good house, in a neighborhood with old trees, better than the houses of Claire and Laurita where I am returning. My daughters wear soft sweaters, slender gold chains with each one a tiny diamond. They are what I wanted them to be: polite, modest, educated women. My son, like me he is the clown. It is easier to do the job I am going back to if you see everything for class. But I cannot anymore—it will not fit. I remember Claire, the way she sat on the floor by her heating vent and ate alone.

"Why you want?" my husband asks. "You have achieved your goal."

I look around, cracks web the ceiling. "I will just go until we have money to fix the kitchen."

"I think you are done, Lola. You have worked hard enough."

"Only a little more."

He does not answer. All my children and grandchildren stand in the airport as I climb back up the ladder onto the plane.

"Lola is still big in the Philippines," Dante says. The clown.

It is strange arriving back, past my mark. LAX, it is not Ninoy Aquino—you stand under concrete, cars zoom on top your head. Fine soot floats in the air; the sky has a dirty sparkle. My hands rub together, beginning again—here, where the world is.

Danny drives me through the marina. On Washington, we pass banners for the Venice Art Walk and the picture they use is a rusted bed frame with grass growing up from a wooden sandbox. UNMADE BEDS: NEW WORK BY NATALIE BERSOLA. So she is the artist she always talked about being. Danny frowns. "But she look old." LA seems bright, scrubbed. Everywhere flags. We pass a flower shop with a huge banner: WE WON'T LET TERRORISM HAPPEN HERE!

Ruth does not work for the Sapersteins anymore, Danny says. She finally opened an agency. Danny goes there sometimes; when they want the bikes and toys clean, he washes them, and they give him one hundred dollars, just to wash with water.

China now is on all-star soccer. He knows from Mai-ling. All those years Sue and Howard fell behind with her pay, but Mai-ling returned to them. She lives there still. I am thinking, The same false blue water. But while we were getting one hundred a day, one hundred ten, we left our own with someone we gave only a grocery store cake.

Ruth gets Candace day jobs now—she is at the place of Judith until I arrive. She likes my old car. "I thought the world would be worse," she told Danny.

I will have to buy another. You cannot live LA without a car.

I have Danny let me out in front. I want my reunion with Laura to be private. But when I come in, no answer. The refrigerator hums. Candace sits at the table, her face like a hook. She is still a slave, I think.

I open my purse to give her money. She just looks at it.

"It is okay for me," she says. "I need experience. And you gave me the car."

"Here. You take. You need experience and a little money. Go now," I say.

I am happy to be back, but the air in the house feels wrong.

Candace pushes up when I tell her to leave. She moves slowly behind me. She is a person used to being yelled at.

The sound Laura makes when she sees me! We clamp around her wrist the charm bracelet. It is tight; she is too big now.

"Next time you go to the Philippines," Laura whispers, as if she has finally won a long game, after too many times losing, "I come."

When the slave is out, Danny honks, and we are alone. Okay okay okay okay okay. So we will build back. It is not only Laura who needs our easy hours. That first night, after I give Laura her bath, she will not sleep. So we watch a movie. *The Parent Trap.* I make popcorn with butter. "Open your legs," she says and I hold her.

When she is finally sleeping I sit at the kitchen table. The bird looks at me. The fish, he pushes his mouth against the glass. I sprinkle a little food on top the water. I am the one to keep alive the pets. The day of my interview for the job here, I wanted that my car would be clean, so I took it to a car wash and they gave me the fish in the bag free. He was the gift I carried in to her. The bird, they did not take out enough and now he has become a little mean. The attention he wants, he is also afraid of. When I get him he squawks, he tries to fly. I need to give him more. More on love, my pupil would say.

Because this bird, he is my old employer, his movements, his jittery humor. He crawls up my arm, walks on my back, bites under my hair. The earrings I wear with small diamonds, he pecks.

Once I unpack again, I see my room became shabby. The whole house, it needs repainting, dirty from lack of care. I go to the small closet where is the washer-dryer and begin to separate laundry. I start a load of coloreds. Judith walks in while I am spraying stains. She looks at my coffee I am drinking now with a straw. Tony, the dental hygienist, he told me to do that. My pupil makes him clean my teeth once a year free.

"See," Judith says, "no one else will accept you, all the coffee you drink." It is not a joke, really. She is trying to be light for her pride. "I want you to watch the sweets," she says. "For her own good. The kids tease her. Two girls in her class are really evil." Because the bad babysitter, Laurita has become chubby.

"You do not have to worry that," I say. "We will exercise."

Before, we attended specialists; Laura has been many times tested. Sugar, that is not so large a problem. Tomorrow while she is at school I will buy for us two bicycles. All my life I have saved. Now I will spend.

I am returned to die on American soil or maybe, who knows, some-a-day I will die in the sky, between. Where will the bones of Lola go? To the Philippines. Majority rules. There is only Laura to vote the American continent.

My Lola died here in America, she will say, *in the year two thousand what?*

ACKNOWLEDGMENTS

I worked on this book over too many years and days to thank properly all the people who helped me. But I'd especially like to thank Jennifer Gully and Cecily Hillsdale, who assisted with my research on immigration and domestic work in its many forms over the past century, and Magdalena Edwards and Caroline Zancan, who shepherded the book to publication. Elma Dayrit and Denise Cruz vetted and tweaked the Tagalog idioms and Filipina-American phrasings until they rang true in both vernaculars. I'm grateful to my editor, Ann Close, whose subtle advice coaxed me to think through the deepest questions of the book. Binky Urban has been my counselor for many years and every book. My friends read the novel many times, especially Beth Henley, Craig Bolotin, William Whitworth, Allan Gurganus, Richard Appel, John D. Gray, Laurel Leff, and Jill Kearney. Leon Botstein and Michael Druzinsky made sure my musical lexicon didn't sound like music for the movies. Finally, I'd like to thank Richard, my lifelong friend; my brother, Steve, who has taught me a great deal of what I know about love and family; and most of all Gabriel and Grace, my kind, patient, quixotic, and ever-beguiling children.

A NOTE ABOUT THE AUTHOR

Mona Simpson is the author of *Anywhere But Here, The Lost Father, A Regular Guy,* and *Off Keck Road,* which was a finalist for the PEN/Faulkner Award and won the Heartland Prize of the *Chicago Tribune.* She has received a Whiting Writers' Award, a Guggenheim grant, a Lila Wallace–Reader's Digest Writers' Award, and, recently, an Academy Award from the American Academy of Arts and Letters. She lives in Santa Monica, California.

A NOTE ON THE TYPE

This book was set in a modern adaptation of a type designed by the first William Caslon (1692–1766). The Caslon face, an artistic, easily read type, has enjoyed over two centuries of popularity in our own country. It is of interest to note that the first copies of the Declaration of Independence and the first paper currency distributed to the citizens of the newborn nation were printed in this typeface.

Composed by Creative Graphics, Allentown, Pennsylvania
Printed and bound by Berryville Graphics, Berryville, Virginia
Book design by Robert C. Olsson